ANCIENT
lights

the watchman diaries

September, 2007

Hamid —

May the Lord bless your
ministry. Enjoy the book!

Kingdom Blessings

[signature]

ANCIENT

lights

the watchman diaries

RALPH D. CURTIN

Destiny Image Fiction

An Imprint of

Destiny Image® Publishers, Inc.

P.O. Box 310

Shippensburg, PA 17257-0310

ISBN 0-7684-2167-5

For Worldwide Distribution
Printed in the U.S.A.

This book and all other Destiny Image, Revival Press, MercyPlace, Fresh Bread, Destiny Image Fiction, and Treasure House books are available at Christian bookstores and distributors worldwide.

For a U.S. bookstore nearest you, call **1-800-722-6774**.
For more information on foreign distributors, call **717-532-3040**.
Or reach us on the Internet:

www.destinyimage.com

DEDICATION

To Kathy, my helpmate and companion in the faith, who has been a continuous source of edification and encouragement in both the good and difficult years. May the God whom we serve pour out His blessings on her life and our marriage.

To the student of prophecy, I along with Paul, salute you. For your longing and study of Christ's soon coming, an imperishable crown of rejoicing awaits you: "For what is our hope, or joy, or crown of rejoicing? Are not even you in the presence of our Lord Jesus Christ at his coming?" (1 Thess. 2:19)

ENDORSEMENT

The newest novel that portrays the biblical prophecies of the endtimes is *Ancient Lights* by Ralph Curtin, and it may be the best of them all! Ralph Curtin's book presents an exciting fast-paced picture of the events and scenes that lead up to the end and to the revelation of the antichrist and Armageddon. Its plot combines startling archaeological discoveries with intrigue in the Israeli government and international organizations. The action involves the U.S. White House and nefarious characters in the Middle East, as well as believable personalities struggling spiritually in the last days to find the truth of the events happening around them in the Holy land. I could not put down the book!

At first some might wonder about the meaning of the title, *Ancient Lights*, but soon they will agree that it is astoundingly appropriate! Christians and truth-seekers alike will find *Ancient Lights* both exciting and edifying; it suggests how prophesied events might come to pass and how those alive at the time might react to them. Read it and give it to a friend!

Gary G. Cohen
Author, Bible translator
Professor, Trinity International University
South Florida campus

PROLOGUE

These are the descendants of Aaron, the first high priest: Nadab, Abihu, Eleazar, and Ithamar. From Eleazar to Jehozadak, 20 generations. Then Jehozadak was deported when the Lord sent Judah and Jerusalem into exile by the hand of Nebuchadnezzar, king of Babylon (see 1 Chron. 6:3-15). There could have been no place for the functions of the high priest during the captivity, but the family line was divinely preserved. Jeshua the son of Jehozadak was among those who first returned to the land of Israel.

The family line of Aaron continued through his son Eleazar down the ages after Jeshua to Simon, the priest at the time of Alexander the Great in 332 B.C. The high-priesthood passed to the priestly family of Joiarib during the reign of the Maccabees, then to the Hasmonean line during the reign of Herod the Great, tetrarch (ruler of one-quarter of the empire) of Judea from 41–4 B.C. During this period until the destruction of the Temple in A.D. 70, five priestly families held power.

Herod the Great, the eldest son of Antipater, was an Idumean descendant of Esau and a Jew by religion. Regarded as a "half-Jew," he lived perpetually under the suspicion and prejudice of the leaders of Israel. Living up to his monstrous reputation, Herod exterminated the Hasmonean line and bestowed upon his brother-in-law, Aristobulus, the position of high priest. He continued to arbitrarily depose and appoint high priests as he pleased and did away with anointing them. Herod proved himself to be exceedingly crafty, jealous, cruel, and vengeful. Continuous defiance of his Jewish subjects, including the introduction of Roman sports and heathen temples, outraged the nation even further.

In time, Herod attempted to conciliate the Jews by rebuilding, at no cost to them, Solomon's Temple, which had been destroyed by the Babylonians in 586 B.C. The religious leaders viewed this as a sinister move to destroy the genealogical records of the expected Messiah, lest the Messiah usurp Herod's throne.

Qumran, 32 B.C.

A man named Amariah, of the priestly line of Aaron and appointed by the Most High God, determined to flee Jerusalem....

Having traveled 13 miles southeast of Jerusalem through the Judean desert, Amariah arrived at dusk at the fortified settlement at Qumran, named the City of Salt by Joshua. The trip across the arid landscape had been extremely arduous for a frail 68-year-old widowed priest who felt alone and abandoned by his people.

Amariah sat down to rest at the base of a waterfall adjacent to the city. Copious amounts of water from flash floods across the wadi cascaded down the limestone cliffs into a catch basin. The water was then blocked by a dam that channeled the rainfall into stone troughs leading into deep cisterns to form an elaborate water system within the community. Amariah's donkey, laden with his priestly garments and meager belongings, drank of the fresh water while Amariah surveyed the land.

Perched on the edge of a marl terrace at the base of high limestone cliffs on the northwest shore of the Dead Sea, the nearly inaccessible City of Salt stood out as a lone sentinel among hundreds of caves carved in the cliffs and provided a secure fortress for the lowly Jewish people known as the Essenes. It was here that Amariah hoped to live in truth, away from the corruption that had overtaken his nation. It was here that he hoped to be healed of the hatred for the Romans who had brought compromise to his faith.

At 1,300 feet below sea level, the surface of the Salt Sea was the lowest point on the earth. Fed by the Jordan River down from Lake Galilee in the north, the Sea had no natural outlet. The water evaporated quickly, making the Sea nearly six times as salty as the ocean. The rapid evaporation left vast mineral deposits of potash, bromine, gypsum and salt. The Salt Sea was 47 miles long and had a maximum width of about 10 miles. Amariah recalled the belief that the cities of Sodom and Gomorrah had been nearby. He envisioned what it must have been like to see the cities destroyed by a holy conflagration and wondered at which end the remains were buried.

"It is time to go, my friend," Amariah sighed while rubbing his donkey's mane. He led the beast up the earthen ramp that stretched from the valley floor to the Essene city on a rock terrace where he believed his life would be born anew. The whole concepts of pious communal living and isolation promised Amariah anonymity, as well as protection of what he considered to be the last vestige of his nation's treasury.

At the summit, he was met by a stone wall that enclosed the city, being interrupted only by a narrow archway over a path that led into the colony. The entranceway was guarded by a simple wooden gate, the only obstacle separating him from the lonely desert and the community he hoped would welcome him. Once inside, Amariah noticed that the community was a well-planned metropolis featuring two distinct compounds. One appeared to be an administrative center; the other looked like a communal center for eating and sleeping. He realized at once that rumors of the city being a military outpost of sorts were untrue.

Amariah looked toward the sun to fix the time of day, for the absence of visible inhabitants puzzled him. He paused to listen to what sounded like thousands of muffled voices off in the distance. Then he recognized the clinking sound of many utensils and plates coming from the communal center. "Aha, it is dinner time," he realized aloud.

"Stranger!" a voice from behind yelled.

Quickly turning toward the voice, Amariah reflexively replied, "I come in peace!" while gesturing with his hands that he carried no weapons.

A man, dressed in what looked like a well-worn monk's robe, approached Amariah, then stopped to look him up and down. He noticed Amariah's dark shaded outer cloak over a tunic or robe, held in place by a wide linen girdle. "You are from Jerusalem?" the man ventured.

Amariah nodded. "I am Amariah, a believer in the God of Israel. I seek refuge among your people—if you will allow it."

The man smiled warmly. "All who desire to serve God are welcome here." He reached for the rope bridle around the donkey's head and added, "I shall tend to your animal while you speak to Manahem, our chief elder."

Amariah slowly backed off, still holding the rope. He could not allow his belongings to fall into curious hands. "My *friend* is weary from the journey, as I am, and will be comfortable only in my presence."

"As you wish," the man cordially allowed as he motioned for Amariah to follow him.

The setting sun cast long shadows that obscured the fruit and vegetable gardens lining the paths leading to the building complex. The man led Amariah through a courtyard, past a pottery workshop, to an impressively big stable. "You must tie your donkey here," the man said as he touched a hitching post outside the stable in which hordes of horses, mules, and donkeys were housed. Nodding, Amariah tied the donkey, then unloaded a large cloth bag and flung it over his shoulder. He followed the man into the communal building and through a hallway that connected to another courtyard. They passed the dining hall, pantry, an extensive culinary department, and a laundry. Amariah noticed that there were no doors to the communal rooms.

At the end of the hallway they passed through a portico into an atrium-like structure connected to several buildings. "This is our administration area," the man informed Amariah as they walked by two storerooms and an enormous room he called the scriptorium. Amariah stopped to peek into the writing room. Wooden benches and chairs were placed at variously sized wooden tables that resembled desks. Manuscripts made of parchments, carefully ruled to guide the scribes, lay flat on the tables. Scores of inkwells made of pottery were scattered around the room. Numerous copper scrolls and papyri documents were meticulously arranged on an extended stone table that spread along one wall. One parchment, comprised of many sheets sewn together end-to-end, stretched over 20 feet in length. Several rolls of leather where stuffed into a large pigeonholed cabinet that lined another wall. "I spend a great deal of my time in this room," the man affirmed.

Amariah had heard reports that the Essenes were writing and preserving, in massive libraries and cave vaults, scriptural texts from Genesis to Malachi, the Tanach, as well as apocryphal and pseudepigraphal books. He hoped to be able to observe the exacting practice, once he was settled in.

The man stopped in front of a large archway leading to a great room. "Wait here," he said, just above a whisper, and walked into the room.

About five minutes later the man returned. "I have explained your arrival to Manahem. He will see you now."

"God's blessing on you," Amariah pronounced as the man walked away. Amariah approached the entrance to the great room, then paused momentarily when he realized he had never asked the guide his name.

"Come in, Amariah," the chief elder beckoned in a mellow voice that seemed to reverberate off the rock walls, yet was somewhat muffled by several tapestries hanging next to the windows and many massive stone tables lined in rows along the walls. Amairah recognized the room as a formal meeting place.

Once inside the doorway Amariah bowed before Manahem, then straightened up and said humbly, "I am honored to meet with you."

"Josiah, one of our overseers and your guide, tells me you are from Jerusalem," Manahem began as he walked and stood in front of him, "and that you are seeking asylum from the tyranny of Rome. Is that so, Amariah?"

The appearance of the man before him took Amariah totally by surprise. Reports about the Essenes' simple lifestyles and diets engendering good health and longevity were undoubtedly true. Manahem had a short cropped beard and a full head of hair accentuated by streaks of gray at the temples. His robe labored to mask his well-built physique. Amariah took him for about 43 years old, but in reality he was 62. "It is so," Amariah replied, "and that is not all. My heart breaks for the Temple priests who choose Rome over our God."

Manahem nodded in assent as he extended his arm, resting it on Amariah's shoulder. "We will welcome you, Amariah, and offer you sanctuary, but first you must take a vow before God and pledge to obey our rules. To begin with, we require that you surrender all your possessions to the community and undergo a trial period of one year. During that first year, you must take up the three symbols of purity and wear a white robe. Naturally, you will perform certain menial duties." He paused and peered into Amariah's eyes in an attempt to probe the motives of his soul. "Are you prepared?" he asked.

While opening his sack, Amariah replied, "I am prepared." He pulled out several articles of clothing, stacking them on one of the stone tables next to him. Manahem watched closely as Amariah placed on the table his breeches, two robes—one white, one blue—his ephod and its girdle, and a pair of onyx shoulder pieces. Then he pulled out the mitre and placed it on top of the pile. There were other items in the bag, but wisdom dictated to stop when he did.

"*Mashallah!* (What God has wrought!) You are the high priest?!" Manahem exclaimed with sudden realization.

"I am," Amariah breathed. "The *ha-kohen ha-gadhol*, of the line of Aaron on my father's side, and Zadok on my mother's."

Awestruck, Manahem took a step backward. "Adonai!" he proclaimed in reverence. "Are the Romans chasing you?"

"Not that I am aware of," Amariah asserted. "I have told no one."

"This is good," Manahem replied with a nod. "I am curious," he queried. "Our people frequent the city, but do not have direct access to the Temple. What really is going on down there?"

"Since the time of Herod the Great the high-priesthood has become totally corrupt—especially the Levites, the chief priests. The Romans set up and depose the chief priests at their pleasure—to the degree that it has become an annual event. Many of them are not really from a family line of priests, but mere imposters, to whom the Romans simply give a uniform. What's more, Herod has this notion in his head to 'help' the nation by refurbishing the Temple. I am persuaded that his ulterior motive is to have access to the genealogical records so as to thwart the recognition of the Messiah when He comes." He shook his head in disgust and began to weep. "I fear for my people," he lamented as he pointed heavenward. "God is very displeased."

"The priesthood has succumbed to the world of politics," Manahem observed glumly. "They have become bedfellows with their oppressors." He walked around the table and sat down on a padded bench. Gazing out the window, he said, as if quoting prophecy, "The day will come when our oppressors will desecrate the Holy Place once again, leaving the Temple desolate."

"May it never be," Amariah groaned as if his ears had just heard a blasphemous remark. Just then his stomach growled.

"Aahhh! You are hungry and weary, my friend," Manahem consoled. "Normally you would have to provide your own food as a novitiate; but because of your service to God as the high priest, we are compelled to make an exception. Let us go and eat." Amariah smiled and turned to leave with Manahem. He reached for his priestly articles, only to be restrained. "Please, Amariah, leave them with me. I must make a report to our tribunal tomorrow."

Amariah acquiesced graciously, then Manahem extended him another courtesy (ordinarily granted to newcomers for purification after one year)—a bath.

Shortly before sunrise, Amariah heard a gentle tap-tap-tap on the door to his cell. His eyes fluttered, then focused on the rectangular window opposite the wooden door to his cubicle. Outside his door he heard the shuffling of many feet walking by. He donned his white robe, then walked to the window just in time to see the sun rise above the Judean mountains. Splashes and bright streaks of light reflected across the surface of the Salt Sea. "How manifold are your works, oh Lord," he whispered to himself.

After a brief period of praise and thanksgiving to God, Amariah stooped down beside the small wooden table under the window and pulled out his sack. He checked the contents and nodded his head. *The nation's treasure is safe*, he reminded himself.

Tap-tap-tap-tap.

Amariah opened his door to see Josiah smiling at him. "Amariah, my brother, we must join the others in prayer before we begin our work." Amariah closed the door behind him, but not before he shot a prayer to God to protect his belongings.

Multitudes of men dressed in both white and brown robes walked quietly through the corridors into the assembly hall. "Tell me something, Josiah," Amariah began just above a whisper. "Manahem said something about three symbols of purity. What was he referring to?"

Josiah paused, took Amariah's hand, and said, "Every newcomer must begin his novitiate on the same level. The purity symbols are reminders of our common heritage—we are all of the seed of Adam, mere mortals with bodily functions, human desires, and weaknesses that must be restrained under the divine guidance of God. They are designed to purify the soul while promoting avoidance. The first, the spade, is used to cover your excrement out in the fields—a reminder of the common necessities and urges of life. Second, the apron, or girdle, to cover the loins for modesty, and the third..." he pointed to his white linen robe, "is your white dress. It is a reminder of the reason for our celibacy and chastity vows—to remain undistracted and dedicated toward God." Josiah prompted Amariah to move on and added, "By the way, you will have to take your oaths after your initial 40 days." Amariah nodded in assent as they entered the assembly room in time for the invocation.

Josiah escorted Amariah to the communal dining room where priests of the order ritually prepared food according to the law of Moses. Once they had their portion, Josiah diverted the newcomer to a small table in the corner of the room. "I met with Manahem before calling on you," Josiah began. "He has appointed me as your guide and companion."

"My heart rejoices," Amariah replied happily.

Josiah grasped Amariah's hand and said softly, "He confided to me about your circumstances. I admire your courage and uncompromising spirit."

Since the time of his wife's death, nearly a decade ago, Amariah had noticed a great longing for comradeship and the need to build relationships with people of like faith. He perceived that Josiah was heavensent during his transition period in the community. "Thank you for your encouragement. Tell me, Josiah, how long have you been here, and what is your assignment?"

"I left Jerusalem over fifteen years ago, when the Romans expanded the Greek practices—Hellenization, if you will—of forcibly parading our youth in the nude through their gymnasiums and into their track races. My stomach turned when their *puppet* priests would come and cheer them on.

"During these years I have been a scribe in the scriptorium and a teacher of righteousness. I have just finished transcribing the Book of Isaiah." He turned and with a sweep of his hand continued, "Every man here has important work to do." He pointed to a distant table and added, "The men at that table are the librarians. They record the nature and location of all the manuscripts. They also make sure that all the documents are safely stored in the cave vaults in the event of a natural disaster such as an earthquake, or…" he paused and looked up to invoke God's protection, "...a foreign power such as the Romans threatening us with an attack." Turning around he went on, "That group of men over there maintain the buildings and water system. They are the 'engineers' if you will. As you have observed, there is a large network of aqueducts throughout the community that bring water in from the mountain catch-basins and funnel it into our cisterns, bath pools, and irrigation trenches. Over here we have the dedicated caretakers who tend to the cemeteries. We have over two thousand men living here, so death is with us constantly. And of course there are the priests who direct the worship and food services, and others who are assigned to administration." He smiled and concluded, "And we all work together in harmony because we have a unified purpose—to honor God and protect His Word." Josiah stopped to take several bites of his meal while Amariah looked around the busy room, then looked him in the eyes and asked, "As your friend and companion, I want to know the *real* reason why you left the priesthood."

Several moments of silence passed.

"Before I tell you," Amariah leaned forward and whispered, "you must promise not to divulge the nature of our conversation."

Josiah reached over and discreetly placed his hand on Amariah's thigh, to cover the femoral artery and seal the promise. "You have my word, my brother."

"One day, early in the loneliness of my widowhood, I began to seriously study messianic prophecy. My labors brought me to the realization that the ancient rabbis have the wrong view toward Messiah. My study took me through the Psalms, namely those of David, particularly numbers sixteen and twenty-two, and into Isaiah, the very book you worked on, where I came to understand that when Messiah comes, he will be born as a man of a virgin and have to—"

"Die as the sacrifice lamb, like in chapter fifty-three," Josiah interrupted.

"That's right! You believe that too?" Amariah asked incredulously.

"Do not misunderstand me, Amariah," Josiah intoned. "I believe in our leader and the teachings of the Essenes for the most part, but many questions arise in my mind when I transcribe the Scriptures. Many questions remain unanswered."

"Such as?"

"The theology of the Essenes dates back to the reign of Aristobulus I—over one hundred and twenty years ago—and is similar to yours in many ways, yet profoundly different in others. We believe in the laws of Moses, angels, prophecy, bodily healing, and the imminent coming of the Kingdom of God at Judgment Day."

"I too believe in that," Amariah explained, "but what about Messiah?"

"That is where the theology divides and my questions emerge." Josiah squirmed slightly in his chair and continued, "The order believes that God's salvation, the Messiah, will come as king—hopefully to destroy our oppressors—and set up His throne very soon. They do not believe in Isaiah's portrayal of the suffering servant who will die as the atonement and rise from the dead as the prophets allege."

"But your heart tells you that this is the proper interpretation of the Scriptures, does it not, Josiah?" Amariah asked.

Slightly bewildered, Josiah shook his head and gazed off into the room. "I am not sure; perhaps yes, perhaps no. Then there is the matter of the resurrection; like the Sadducees, the order does not believe there will be one."

Amariah patted his hand and affirmed, "My friend, I will prove to you what Messiah's real mission is and that there will be a resurrection."

Suddenly a messenger arrived at their table.

"Manahem has summoned you both," the man announced.

Josiah traded a distressed look with Amariah then replied to the man, "Advise Manahem we are on our way." The man hastily departed.

When Josiah opened the chief elder's door he was surprised to see the tribunal still in session. The room was filled with more than 75 elders who represented the administrative branch of the community. "Come in, Josiah and Amariah," Manahem said with a wave of his hand. The eyes of the elders were riveted on them both as they walked toward the head table and stood before Manahem. "A short while ago, during our planning and discussion period, a runner from Jerusalem arrived with an important message," he began tersely while pacing before the members, "and that message concerns us." He turned to Amariah and put his hand on his shoulder. "Our sources within the priesthood advise us that the chief priests have branded you a traitor and an infidel. They have asked the Roman authorities to arrest you for capital crimes, claiming that you engaged in subversive discussions and have stolen important documents along with vital *articles* necessary for the operation of the Temple. The word is that they have launched a search to bring back the contraband and you—dead or alive."

"This cannot be done!" Amariah announced emphatically to the audience. "God has called me as the lone survivor of the Aaronic priesthood to guard those things entrusted to my forefathers from the time of Solomon." He turned to Manahem with vigor and added, "I cannot betray that trust."

"What is the nature of the alleged subversive teachings?" one of the elders grumped.

"My view of messianic prophecy differs from that of the chief priests," Amariah replied calmly with a slight rise in tone. Apparently the tribunal did not consider that terribly offensive; they let his explanation pass unchallenged.

"What about these so-called *articles*?" one member said aloud. "What are they talking about?"

Amariah temporized. "They are documents confirming my family's line back to Joiarib and then to Aaron."

"You must take them back!" a voice from the rear of the room shouted out. "Our community is endangered as long as you are here!"

"Never!" Amariah retorted. Then with pleading eyes he looked to Manahem for help.

"Let us not forget that we are people of peace," Manahem reminded the tribunal.

Obadiah, a man who recently had become a full member, stood up and argued, "Amariah, if you really are the high priest…" he turned to Manahem and added, "…and we really have no proof of that except those" (pointing to the priestly uniform left with Manahem) "pieces of clothing—which you could have taken illegally—then the responsibility that we should take the risk of hiding you is yours to undertake."

A great uproar ensued. The tribunal agreed.

Josiah nudged Amariah and whispered, "You must win their confidence! You must do something to convince them." Amariah nodded, then excused himself and ran out of the room. He returned with his sack, then stood in front of Manahem for several minutes.

Lord, I need your help, Amariah thought. *I had no idea something like this would occur. I do not want to use Temple fixtures for my own purposes, but I must give them some proof of who I am.*

"Let us get on with this!" The man seated next to Obadiah yelled out.

Amariah abruptly walked to the table to gather his uniform, then darted behind a room petition. The tribunal immediately broke out into a heated discussion.

Several minutes passed, then the voices died down to whispers. Manahem cleared his throat several times to stall for time, then finally said aloud, "Amariah, the tribunal awaits."

Another few minutes passed in absolute silence before the high priest turned the corner, dressed in full regalia.

"Look at his face!" a voice called out.

Amariah's visage had totally changed. His expression and countenance told of his relationship with the Supreme Being: He was able to communicate and mediate directly with Jehovah, the Lord of Hosts.

The white linen inner robe, a symbol of righteousness, was overlaid with a blue robe, woven in one piece to symbolize the eternal nature of God. The sleeveless linen ephod and girdle—embroidered with purple, scarlet, and blue and intertwined with gold—represented the royalty, atoning blood, and purity of God. On each shoulder was clasped an onyx piece of stone encased in a filigree setting of gold with the inscribed names of six tribes of Israel. Sewn into the bottom edge of the blue robe were pomegranates, pointing to the divine law as sweet and delicious spiritual food. Alternating with the pomegranates were bells. Each year, as the high priest walked into the Holy of Holies, the bells announced God's gracious salvation—for He had accepted the people in the person of their advocate, the high priest. The mitre or head covering, made of white linen fastened to a golden crown, was engraved with the words, *Holiness to the Lord.*

The tribunal was silenced by Amariah's presence.

Suddenly Manahem realized what was hanging around Amariah's neck. "Adonai!" he cried out. "The breastplate!"

At least 20 of the elders fell prostrate on the floor in consternation, chanting prayers up to God, while others jumped to their feet and wept.

"This cannot be!" Manahem said aloud. "The breastplate was lost centuries ago!" With that he walked to Amariah and fixed his eyes on the linen pouch with twelve precious stones attached, set in four rows. Fine gold chains suspended the pouch around Amariah's neck. Each stone was inscribed with the name of a tribe of Israel. The stones reflected dazzling light into the room.

"Stand back!" Amariah commanded Manahem. Stunned, Manahem fell backward against a table. Amariah reached into the pouch, withdrew three smaller stones, and held them in his palms. Then turning toward the direction of the Temple, he raised his head and prayed, "Lord God of Abraham, Isaac, and Jacob, let it be known this day that You are the God of Israel, and that I am Your servant, and that I have done all these things at Your word. Hear me, O Lord, hear me, that this people may know that You are the Lord God, and that You have turned their hearts to You." Then he stared at the stones for several moments before saying, "Behold, the Urim and Thummim—the *lights of God!*"

The stones began to vibrate in Amariah's hands.

Several members of the tribunal began cowering, while Manahem covered his eyes in fear. "*Ask God a question!*" Amariah demanded of Manahem.

Manahem stood speechless. "*ASK GOD A QUESTION!*" Amariah screamed.

"Is Amariah really Your high priest?" Manahem choked out. Then a sudden realization came over him. He remembered recorded history regarding the Urim and Thummim—that questions about God's will, a national crisis, the selection of a king or even political decisions, and at times, foretelling the future, were asked and answered.

Amariah reverently looked up and said aloud, "If this is true, O Lord, God of Israel, give Urim; but if this is not true, give Thummim."

With piercing eyes the tribunal members looked on as the stones began to illuminate. First the red jasper stone gave off a glimmer of light, then faded. The purple amethyst gave off a glimmer of light, then faded. Finally the blue sapphire glowed brightly. Not knowing the nature of the Urim and the Thummim, the entire body looked to Amariah for a correct response.

A twinkle appeared in Amariah's eye, then he bowed before the Lord and mouthed a prayer. In unison, a multitude of voices yelled out, "The answer is yes! God has answered YES!" Amariah nodded in assent as Manahem returned to his side.

"Brothers," Manahem announced as tears welled up in his eyes, "we have heard from God regarding our brother Amariah. We now put it to vote as to whether we will shelter him or cast him out into the wilderness to rely upon God's providence and mercy. I cannot bring myself as your leader to surrender him over to the Roman or temple authorities."

All but Obadiah and Joiada raised their hands to affirm hiding Amariah amongst the community.

Conversations between the tribunal members dominated their departure. They were puzzled over the apparent divine preservation of the breastplate and Urim and Thummim for centuries. Would not God have revealed to His people before now that such treasures were not lost? Why would God deprive His people of the ancient device used by Israel's kings to communicate with Him? Yes, they had the prophets, but it was not the same thing as having God's answers in the palm of your hands. Yes, they were confident the correct decision had been made; they would ultimately leave the judgment with God and Manahem.

As the last of the members embraced Amariah to welcome him, Manahem constrained Amariah and Josiah to remain behind. "We must speak," he implored.

Amariah nodded, then proceeded to undress and meticulously place his priestly attire and the sacred objects into his bag. "You are perplexed, my brother Manahem," Amariah soothed. He nodded to

Josiah and added, "This will be a hard thing for you both to hear, but you must know that I speak God's word."

"From the time of Moses and Joshua to Abiathar the priest in the Book of Samuel, the Urim and Thummim had been revealing God's answers to hard questions," Josiah rattled on impulsively. "It is only a theory that the sacred apparatus for worship was used after the return from exile, but it has not been seen since the time of David—we believed the breastplate and Urim and Thummim were destroyed when King Nebuchadnezzer destroyed the Temple. This apparently is not so?"

Amariah looked up to Manahem after a moment of contemplation and with an uncanny memory began to unfold the truth of the Urim and Thummim. "The Lord gave Solomon an immeasurable amount of wisdom when he ascended the throne after the death of his father, David. Adding to that wisdom, God gave him supernatural revelation that enabled him to plan out the construction of the Temple. In fact, it was to be built after a pattern, the original being in Heaven. You see, the Temple was to be the dwelling place of the God of Israel—the God of the universe—to which all the world could come to revere and worship God here on earth! This was not to be a small thing!

"God superintended the construction of His Temple. It was made to last, but our people saw the Temple as a good luck charm and considered themselves inviolable, hiding their sins of idolatry and wickedness behind the protective shield of the Temple. They thought that as long as the Temple was standing, they were impervious to enemy attack and could go on doing shameful things to offend God. So when Jeremiah warned them to repent or face the Babylonian threat, the people scoffed at God's word. They continued in their ways, thinking, *Solomon's Temple has lasted four hundred years! We need not fear.* But history tells us that God demands obedience to His laws, and that He *will* bring judgment to punish offenders. So, after thirty years of wailing against Israel's forsaking God, Jeremiah witnessed the fulfillment of his prophecy when the Babylonians invaded and took Israel captive. The complete destruction of the Temple followed.

"But to preserve His sacred objects from falling into heathen hands, God had instructed Solomon to build an underground labyrinth as a vault to protect His treasures entrusted to the priesthood. That secret labyrinth is where the treasures of the nation have been kept."

Manahem leaned in closer to Amariah. "Where is this place?"

The aged priest looked Manahem in the eye. "In a secret vault underneath the Temple Mount. There is a main underground tunnel that runs for over one thousand feet along the west wall, and off that tunnel are several passageways that branch out. One leads to the entranceway into the Holy of Holies. Another passageway leads to a great room with numerous secret chambers that hide the national treasures. This is where I kept the breastplate and Urim and Thummim. The location of these objects has been a guarded secret since the time of David. Only the high priest knows."

"And when it came to revealing God's will?" Manahem asked.

"The high priest would clandestinely inquire of the Urim and Thummim, and in the form of a prayer request or recommendation, pass the answer up to the Sanhedrin, the supreme tribunal. The Sanhedrin would weigh the consequences of any political or national issues and make the decisions."

"Most of which were not in God's will. That's why we are under Roman domination," Manahem observed glumly.

Josiah blinked in dismay, then traded a look with Manahem. "The ark of the covenant?"

"Safe, for now," Amariah replied with a thin smile on his face, "in a sealed secret chamber. But that will all change if Herod's plan to refurbish the Temple in Roman architecture comes to pass. His engineers will find it. That is why I had to smuggle out what I could. Naturally I could not carry out the Ark without creating mass hysteria and risk bringing the Roman government, along with Herod's *puppet* priesthood, down on my head. The ark will remain in God's custody until He decides to reveal it."

"And that is where we will leave this discussion," Manahem said wearily. "Rest up today, Amariah, take a bath; tomorrow you can begin your duties."

Amariah's fascination with the community water supply system brought him to the compound engineer who explained the system to him before he bathed. Rainfall from flash floods was channeled into an aqueduct that emptied the water into two huge cisterns or underground reservoirs within the commune. Branching off the cistern were underground channels that brought the water to the ritual baths or *mikva'ot*. The members walked down steps into the *fresh* waters and completely immersed themselves for purification purposes according to Jewish religious law.

"You have been assigned by Manahem to be a spiritual monitor that we call a *correct expositor* of *teacher* or *righteousness*," Josiah advised Amariah while escorting him back to his cell after his bath. "This position of honor is because you are the high priest," he added humbly.

"I am pleased," Amariah replied.

"In addition, you will conduct our Shabbat and Yom Kippur services," Josiah added joyfully.

"And you?" Amariah queried. "Now that you have finished Isaiah."

"A new assignment," Josiah explained gleefully, "in a different scriptural texts area. My particular assignment does not deal with the Tanach, but with the apocryphal and pseudepigraphal books, namely the history of the Maccabees and the Book of Jubilees. I shall find it somewhat appealing and relaxing since..." he poked Amariah in the side, "...my work on Isaiah raised many questions." Josiah touched his head. "My mind was always working so hard when I was copying the texts—I found myself trying to interpret them."

"What about your heart?" Amariah ventured, reaching over and patting Josiah's chest. "Did not your heart burn within when you read the passages on Messiah?"

"Now, now, Brother Amariah," Josiah chided, "let us not chase after that rabbit again."

They arrived at Amariah's cubicle.

"Come in, Josiah, I should like to show you something that will settle the conflict that started in your mind and ended up in your heart." With that Amariah closed the cell door and brought out his holy garments and equipment.

"Uh-oh," Josiah exclaimed when he saw Amariah dressed with the Urim and Thummim on. "What are you doing; why the private audience?"

"So that you may believe," Amariah asserted. He turned and pulled a voluminous scroll out of his sack, unrolled it and began reading excerpts from it. "Yet You are enthroned as the Holy One, You are the praise of Israel, in You our fathers put their trust, they cried to You and were saved...I am poured out like water, and all My bones are out of joint...they pierced my hands and my feet...all the families of the nations will bow down before Him...all who go down to the dust will kneel before Him..."

"Stop!" Josiah shouted. "Who is the prophet talking about, himself or some other man?"

"This is King David speaking under the influence of God's Spirit in the Psalms," Amariah explained compassionately, "and he wrote this over one thousand years ago. You will notice that he is using language that could not possible apply to himself. This can only be a messianic Psalm that points to the possibility that the Messiah will have to die in some form of execution when He comes."

"Go on, brother," Josiah begged. "I am very interested in your view."

Amariah unrolled the scroll further then stopped. "The Lord said to my Lord: 'Sit at my right hand until I make your enemies a footstool for your feet...'" This is another prophecy penned by David. He envisioned a heavenly scene where God invites Messiah to sit at His right hand, which means equality in kingdom vocabulary, after performing the atonement. To rephrase it, 'God said unto God, sit at My right hand...' You see, David knew that the Messiah must die as the Passover Lamb Isaiah described before returning to Heaven to ascend His throne.

"When we combine these passages with other prophecies in Deuteronomy, Daniel, Micah, and Zechariah, we have a more complete picture of Messiah's ministry that tells us clearly that He will come the first time to die for sin, the second time to set up His kingdom. Regarding His resurrection, both David and Hosea prophesied about it."

"My heart is heavy," Josiah admitted as he looked Amariah in the eye. "I believe in you, but I am not sure I believe your interpretation of those Scriptures."

Amariah nodded in understanding, then carefully placed the scroll back in his bag. Then he abruptly fell to his knees and prayed aloud, "Great Adonai, I come before You now and petition You to show Josiah that I am Your servant and that this understanding I have of Your Word is correct." He paused to stand up and reach into the breastplate to remove the three small stones. Then he raised his head and said, "If this is true, O Lord, God of Israel, give Urim; but is this is not true, give Thummim."

Josiah stared at the gems in Amariah's hands and recognized the *yes* answer immediately.

The taking of vows was celebration for the entire community. Forty days after novitiates entered the settlement, the written law required, they swore oaths of allegiance: To protect the secrecy of their doctrine and to live by the rules of the religious brotherhood. Amariah and 25 other probationers were officially ushered into the membership after making their public profession of faith. Josiah took note that missing from the gala event were Obadiah and his close ally, Joiada.

In the months that followed, Manahem reflected on Obadiah and Joiada's walk with God and concluded that they were pseudo-believers. They pretended to have a relationship with God, but had never experienced salvation where they knew their sins were forgiven under God's atoning blood. This regeneration would have brought them enabling grace to resist the temptation of the lust of the eyes, the lust of the flesh, and the pride of life. It would have altered their actions.

Joida kept watch outside Amariah's cubicle while Obadiah quickly rummaged through the room looking for the sack. As an ascetic in pursuit of self-denial, Amariah had few belongings. Obadiah soon spotted the bag and swiftly rifled through it, seizing the breastplate along with the Urim and Thummim. "There you are, my beloved," he whispered as he tumbled the small stones in his hand. Carefully Obadiah replaced the sack, stuffed the prize under his sash belt, tagged Joida, and the two surreptitiously slipped away.

The tranquility of the evening, together with the memory of the day he took his vows, brought a smile of repose to Amariah as he lay on his bed. He turned to the window to see the golden light of sunset and drifted off to sleep. Suddenly...he saw the brethren running from the compound in terror. The earth beneath them shook and opened to begin swallowing up the community. Geothermal gases spewed out of giant fissures that ran laterally along the ground, sparing nothing in their path. Amariah saw the central tower tumbling onto the glacis before it, trapping dozens of men. The giant cisterns bellowed with steam then ruptured, sending torrents of scalding water on the fleeing community. The staircases to the ritual baths separated, draining the waters to some underground cavity brought on by the shift in the earth's mantle. Everywhere he looked, destruction prevailed.

He gazed off into the distance and saw the cave vaults resting secure under the protective umbrella of the huge mountains that surrounded the community, then he turned and found himself looking at the documents in the scriptorium...

"Wake up, Brother Amariah!" a voice cried out. "Wake up!"

Amariah rubbed his eyes and saw Josiah leaning over him. "I had a dream..."

"I know, I know," Josiah soothed. "I heard you yelling as I passed by your cell."

Amariah sat up and rubbed his head as he looked over to his closet. "I, eh, I must ask God by Urim and Thummim about the dream," he said incoherently. "I...had a terrible dream about a..."

"Lie down," Josiah snapped. "You must rest! I will get it for you." Josiah opened the door to the closet.

"My spirit is deeply troubled," Amariah fretted frantically. "Something is wrong!" Josiah handed Amariah the sack. Even before opening it, Amariah cried out, "They are gone! They have been stolen!" He looked inside and cried in affirmation, "There are thieves in our midst!"

For over ten minutes Manahem silently paced back and forth in his room, considering the dilemma thrust upon him. Amariah stood gazing out the window at the caves while Josiah fidgeted in a chair. "You say that no one knows apart from you two?" Manahem finally asked.

"No one," Josiah replied emphatically.

"I fear for the thief or thieves," Amariah breathed in prophetic tones. "They know not what they do."

"We will call for a general assembly immediately," Manahem decided, "then we shall deal with the culprit! Punishment will be swift so that we as a people are not punished or cursed by the Lord. I feel like Joshua when he had to deal with Achan after the Israelites were defeated at Ai—all because Achan had hidden the booty in his tent."

Tears welled up in Josiah's eyes as he listened to his leader's verdict. It would have serious repercussions throughout the community. He then turned to Amariah and tugged on his robe. "Tell him about your dream," he whispered.

Not now! Amariah mouthed.

"What is it, Amariah?" Manahem asked after catching a glimpse of their motions.

"It is hardly the time, Manahem. I do not want to add more distress to the situation."

"Speak!" Manahem commanded angrily. "Let me be the judge of that!"

Amariah shot a prayer up to God for Manahem's sake and then threw his arms up in the air. "God has shown me in a dream that there will be a severe earthquake here before the year is out. You must prepare for it. The dream is certain."

Seeing Manahem begin to falter, Josiah ran to his father's side. "God will sustain us," he said wearily. "He will enable…"

"The settlement?" Manahem sighed. "Will the settlement survive?"

"You will have to abandon it, but the scrolls, when safely stored in the cave vaults, will survive. After many days your people will be allowed to return and rebuild," Amariah prophesied.

"Bless God," Manahem prayed aloud, "bless God. Shall we receive good from His hand and not calamity?"

Amariah nodded consolingly.

"Josiah," Manahem directed, "on my authority, give the order to have all library manuscripts placed in sealed containers and stored in the designated eleven cave vaults. Within six months, I want all the canonical books absolutely secure. This way after the earthquake and Roman threat subside, we can return." Josiah nodded in agreement. "As for the immediate problem, I will have all the members meet in one hour in the assembly hall to conduct a hearing and adjudicate this matter swiftly."

"Spiritual corruption has led to the sins of both greed and theft among us," Manahem began in his address to the entire membership, "and these sins will not go unpunished; the Lord is very angry with us as a people. I do not have to describe what was stolen, for the thieves know the nature of their wicked deed." Wisdom dictated that he should keep Amariah in relative obscurity from the masses. Only members of the tribunal were privy to the knowledge that the community possessed the Jewish nation's treasury. "I have discussed this grave matter with my advisors and our appointed counselors. We all agree that if the perpetrators come forward before sunset tomorrow, we will act in mercy. But—and hear me carefully," he paused to dramatize the penalty phase, "if not, we shall act in judgment." The crowd erupted in turmoil and with suspicious eyes looked each other up and down.

"Listen to me, my people!" Manahem shouted over their heads. "I have called a day of prayer and fasting to commence immediately, so go to your cells and petition the Lord to bring repentance on the person who committed this fiendish act."

The community filed out of the assembly hall into their respective living quarters.

"I have never seen this kind of growth before," Brother Eli, the physician, said to Obadiah as he examined his groin and rectal area. "It appears to be some form of tumor or boil or even an acute case of hemorrhoids." The affliction was so severe, Obadiah could barely walk or perform his duties. "When did you first notice them?"

"Last night," Obadiah groaned.

"Have you eaten anything outside of the compound?" Brother Eli probed.

"No," Obadiah replied with a worried look.

"What about water?"

Obadiah shook his head.

"Have you been bathing regularly?"

Obadiah nodded sluggishly.

"You will have to stop bathing for now," Brother Eli advised. "We cannot risk contaminating the community. This may have been brought on by some infectious blood disorder or possibly an insect bite," he surmised with the limited medical knowledge available to him. "Naturally you must remain in your cell under quarantine until the condition improves."

"The pain is worsening, Brother Eli," Obadiah rasped. "I feel lumps in my throat as well." Brother Eli examined his throat and neck area.

"I am concerned about this," he observed bleakly. Walking to a foot locker the physician pulled out one vial and one small jar. He held up the vial and said, "Mix a small portion of this liquid with water and drink it immediately. Repeat the dosage once every day for five days." Then he held up the jar, which contained a yellowish powder, and added, "Both of these are from deposits in the Salt Sea basin area. We know that they have healing powers. Stir a tiny amount of this powder in water and apply it to the infected area. Gargle the same mixture for your throat and return tomorrow."

Obadiah agreed and hobbled out of the dispensary. He went directly to Joiada's cell to report Brother Eli's diagnosis and share the medicine, since Joiada had also contracted the bizarre disease at the same time.

Three days later, Obadiah's condition was upgraded to serious, and he was restricted to the infirmary area.

"This is a curious coincidence," Amariah said to Josiah after the latter returned from Manahem's quarters. "Manahem told you that Brother Eli has reported two cases of tumors in the compound?"

"Yes. Obadiah is in the infirmary. The other one, Joiada, is in his cell for now. Our medicines are having no effect on them. Manahem's concern is that this may escalate and spread."

Amariah turned aside, walked to the corner of his cell, and stood there for several moments. *Lord, reveal to me what is happening*, he prayed. Memories of the Philistines' being smitten with tumors after they captured the ark of the covenant from the Israelites and took it to Ashdod floated through his mind. Moments later, after carefully choosing his words, he said, "There is no chance of this spreading."

"What do you mean?" Josiah asked.

"God has shown me His plan, and you need not worry about it. The disease will be limited to Obadiah and Joiada."

"Praise God!" Josiah rejoiced. "Now we just have to find the Urim and Thummim," he added in somber tones.

"I already have," Amariah replied and walked out.

The settlement's infirmary consisted of 22 wooden cots covered with straw mattresses overlaid with linen sheets. A woolen blanket was neatly folded at the foot of each bed. Several large medicine and herb cabinets lined one wall, while a long wooden workbench with numerous mortars and pestles lined another. Clay jars, vials, and bundles of linen cloth for bandages were strewn throughout the room. Small wooden tables, each with an oil lamp and washbasin, were strategically placed to minister to the needs of the patient.

Amariah walked in and spotted Brother Eli changing the dressing on Obadiah's neck. He stood still until Brother Eli finished, then motioned for the physician to accompany him to a distant corner. "Brother Eli," Amariah began, "how is Obadiah feeling today?"

Brother Eli shook his head gravely. "He is not responding to our medicine. And that is not all. I just completed a physical examination on his belly and I can feel the tumors inside his body. I am afraid that his condition is critical." He gestured toward the cells and added, "And his companion, Joiada, strangely enough, has exactly the same symptoms."

Amariah sighed deeply after hearing the report. "I should like to speak to Obadiah, if you do not mind." Brother Eli bowed before the high priest and retreated to his workbench.

Obadiah's tumors were now as large as hard-boiled eggs. His top bed sheet was stained with bodily discharges. The goiter-like growths exuded pus that saturated both the sheet and the newly-applied bandages surrounding his neck. He was unable to move his head. His buttocks were elevated with a pillow to alleviate the excruciating pain. Obadiah's eyes were tightly closed, and his body wambled in response to the presence of the alien growths within him.

"Obadiah, I am Amariah, the high priest," the good man whispered. Obadiah's eyes opened a slit, then closed again.

Amariah repeated the salutation, then added, "I know what you have done."

Obadiah's eyes blazed open as he began twisting in the bed.

"God has shown me that you have stolen the Urim and Thummim, and He has stricken you with this disease because of it. If you want to be healed, you must tell me where it is. I know that Joiada is your accomplice, but God is holding you responsible. If you do not divulge the truth, you and your companion will die."

Obadiah tightened his jaw in silence.

Amariah lowered his head, then put his hand on Obadiah's chest and prayed aloud for the man's heartfelt confession and repentance. After several moments Obadiah raised his eyelids in complete defiance. Amariah read his heart through his eyes. "Very well, then, my son. May God have mercy on your soul," Amariah pronounced.

Joiada's condition was far worse than Obadiah's; he was unconscious when Amariah and Brother Eli arrived at his bedside. Brother Eli held his nose while he lifted Joiada's eyelids, felt his pulse, and concluded that he was in a coma. "Joiada will not last much longer," he prognosticated. He unwound the soiled bandages off Joiada's left leg to reveal several ulcerated mounds that oozed a putrefying liquid. An obnoxious odor began to permeate the room. "Whew!" he breathed as he turned his head to avoid vomiting.

"Joiada, *WAKE UP!*" Amariah yelled at his face.

No response.

Amariah covered his hand with a cloth to avoid defilement, then grabbed hold of Joiada's arm and repeated his appeal. Again, no response. "Today is the day of salvation," Amariah whispered softly to himself as a reminder that any decision to follow God cannot be put off.

A cool breeze drifted in through Amariah's window as he lay sleeping. In times like this he looked forward to sleep as a place of refuge; a sanctuary to escape the grief of the past two days; a place where pain did not exist; a solitary place where he could dream about his God and how he would serve Him in glory—the ultimate ministry.

Deep in his dream Amariah saw himself—on the day he had arrived at the settlement; on the occasion of announcing and demonstrating to the tribunal his office of high priest; on his discovery of the horrible theft of the Urim and Thummim.

Suddenly Amariah's eyes flew open. He saw Obadiah standing over him, his raised hand holding a pharmacist's pestle.

A hand slipped into Amariah's hand and began to lift him off his bed. He looked into the face of a figure that he didn't recognize at first. Then his spirit testified that it was the One he had been reading about in the Scriptures—the Shepherd of David's psalm, who had promised to walk him through the valley that led to the place of peace and glory where he could serve God forever. A broad smile spread across Amariah's face as he realized that everything he had come to believe about the Messiah was true—He was Wonderful, the Mighty God and Everlasting Father, the Prince of Peace.

When he looked back at the body on the bed, he saw a battered shell that he had once occupied.

"Amariah has been murdered!" Josiah screamed through the hallways as he ran to Manahem's cell. "Amariah has been killed!" His voice echoed through the settlement nestled in the Judean wilderness, waking the community hours before morning prayer.

Josiah burst into Manahem's cubicle, panting. "What is this, my brother?!" Manahem gasped. "What has happened?"

"I heard terrible noises coming from Amariah's room so I went to investigate…" he trailed off, gulping for air, "and when I opened his door, blood was pouring out of his head…" He sighed deeply then held up a piece of cloth and rasped, "I found this strip of bandage on the floor."

Manahem grabbed the poultice strip from Josiah's hand and examined it for a moment. "Let us go to the infirmary at once," he said in reflexive alarm.

The infirmary smelled of death. Aromas from emollient balms were unable to overpower the stench of decaying flesh that hung suspended in the air. "Where is he?" Manahem demanded of Brother Eli. "Where is Obadiah?" Brother Eli turned and pointed. Manahem and Brother Eli went directly to his bed, only to find it empty. Manahem and Eli searched the room as the rising sun began to illuminate it, but Obadiah could not be located.

"We found him!" a frantic voice from outside the room shouted. "He is in his workplace, at the wood shop—he is dead."

"Joiada is dead too!" another brother yelled at Manahem.

A large contingency of members followed Manahem and Josiah to Obadiah's workplace, where they found him sprawled on the floor with one arm outstretched in the direction of a storage cabinet.

Manahem quickly surveyed the scene, then stepped over Obadiah's body and opened the door to the cabinet. He spotted a sack hidden under several tools and scraps of wood. He pulled the sack out and looked inside. *Looks like God's justice won out once again,* he thought as he spotted the breastplate. *And the Urim and Thummim are safe,* he added to himself as he counted the three gems. Manahem turned to Josiah and said tearfully, "Call for the mourners." He then went to the window and let out a sharp, shrill, ear-piercing shriek to announce the death of God's servant.

Mourners carried the body of Amariah, dressed in his high priestly clothes, and placed it on a stone table in front of the assembly in the center of the tribunal counsel room. Manahem walked to Amariah's body and began beating his breast to pronounce Kaddish. "Alas, my brother!" he cried out in grief. "Your selfless duty to God has been rewarded, for you now stand in His presence."

Manahem then chanted a psalm for several moments as the assembly joined in to pay homage to their fallen brother and priest.

"With heartfelt sorrow we cry out to God," Manahem continued, "and speak to your lingering spirit, oh Amariah, that you forgive the trespass of Obadiah and Joiada." He turned and looked at a table in the corner where their bodies, wrapped in linen, were awaiting burial. "For God, our Judge, has meted out punishment to the apostates, for now and all eternity." Lifting his arms up he petitioned the Lord, "*Baruch haShem Adonai*! You, Amariah, were ordained by God to a holy calling, engraved on your heart, that you faithfully discharged. Therefore, you shall be placed in the hall of the faithful in the heavenly place where God dwells." He sobbed for several moments, then motioned to Josiah to lead the procession for the brethren to view their friend one last time.

The setting sun indicated that it was time to lay Amariah and the criminals to rest.

"To protect our community from the Romans," Manahem ventured wearily to Josiah, "we must bury Amariah far away from the compound. I have studied our mountainous surroundings and decided to use an isolated cave near Ein Feshkha for his final resting place. Bury Amariah in his priestly uniform. I want a special headstone prepared for him as the high priest, with the unpronounceable Name engraved in it above the menorah."

"The breastplate and the Urim and Thummim?"

Manahem closed his eyes momentarily to think on the question. "Place them in a sealed earthen jar and bury it with him. Without a righteous high priest, they are no good to anyone here or in the Temple. Our God will look after them."

"Obadiah and Joiada?"

Manahem shook his head. "The wickedness of their unregenerate hearts brought them to ruin. We must rid the commune totally of this disgrace—the criminals shall be wiped from our records. Bury them in unmarked graves with Amariah."

In the spring of 31 B.C. an earthquake along the Jordan Rift Valley brought enormous destruction to the community of Qumran, as well as sealing several nearby cave vaults. The settlement remained uninhabited for 30 years.

CHAPTER

1

Central Israel, A.D. 2002

The bells in the tower of the Greek Orthodox church in Jericho swayed slightly as the ground below began trembling. Several citizens meandering in the vicinity turned toward the aging place of worship and looked up, thinking they heard the bells tingling. They stopped to listen, then went on their way when the sound did not return. No one noticed the sudden drop in water level in the church's irrigation lake that indicated an impending cataclysm.

Sixty-five miles underground, geodynamic frictional stress continued to build until the rock strata fractured, causing one of the many floating tectonic plates that form the Afro-Syrian fault line to shift, overlapping the fault plane. Without warning, from the villages in northern Syria to the shopping malls in southern Jordan, great vibrations that turned to violent shaking began, sending seismic jolts through the entire Middle East.

Forming one of the longest and deepest fissures in the earth's surface, the Jordan Rift Valley or Afro-Syrian Rift Valley is probably the most vital continental rift system known to geologists. The fault line covers a distance of four thousand miles, starting in the Amanus Mountains of southeastern Turkey, continuing south into western Syria, and running parallel with the Red Sea in Israel down into Ethiopia where it branches off. Spreading out of this major crack in the earth's mantle are scores of secondary fractures that make a geologic mosaic of Israel.

With multiple epicenters, the strike-slip generated seismic waves that spanned the earth's crust in a matter of moments. At the Israeli seismographic station in Nablus, the Richter scale vacillated between 6.5 and 7.3 for more than 67 seconds. Instruments using a form of advanced triangulation put the central epicenter eight miles east of Jericho, just north of the Dead Sea. Seventeen hours later, major aftershocks were still reported as far south as the Gulf of Aqaba.

Casualty reports included 207 killed by collapsing hotels in Bethany as well as 1,100 killed when a giant fissure in the earth swallowed up most of the town of Kafr Kanna, just northeast of Nazareth. At the fortified settlement of Khirbet Qumran, on the northwestern rim of the Dead Sea, many of the standing buildings and caves were once again reconfigured by the hand of nature. At the southern rim, at the ancient fortress of Masada, Herod's one-time palace dislodged from the giant mound and fell over the precipice 1,300 feet down to the sea bed. More than 40 tourists were trapped in the debris and were presumed dead. The upheaval in the earth radically changed the topography of this barren region where God had seen fit to bury great treasures.

Ishmael ben Azin, a precocious, modern-thinking 18-year-old Bedouin from the ancient tribe of Ta'amireh, believed that the earthquake could turn out to be a blessing from his god, Allah. In the early morning before the elders awoke, he slipped into his Levi dungarees and T-shirt, yanked on his Nike sneakers, then saddled his camel and secretly departed from the family campsite. Ishmael, a nomadic Arab with aquiline features, a swarthy complexion, and a very lean body, traveled over four miles to the caves located halfway between Qumran and Ein Feshkha, an oasis near the northern edge of the Dead Sea. Three years earlier, his older brother had escorted him to Wadi Murabba'at to explore the four dominant caves that had been excavated by archaeologists in the 1950s. These finds had yielded considerable written material on the Bible, dating to the seventh century B.C. Since that discovery, folklore had emerged that became the conversation of every weekly tent meeting in the Bedouin village. When the wandering tribe migrated from the desert plains into the rocky terrain near the Dead Sea, excitement prevailed in the minds of the young tribal boys until it was appeased by days of mountain climbing and cavern exploration. Over the years, the dream of uncovering *antikas* that would bring recognition to a tribal family became an obsession with Ishmael. *Perhaps, like my fellow Arab shepherd who in 1947 discovered the Dead Sea Scrolls, I too will become famous,* he dreamed.

Dismounting at the base of the high limestone cliffs in the general vicinity where he knew the caverns to be, Ishmael stroked the few bristling hairs on his chin that would someday emerge as a beard, then looked at the north face of the mountainside as it glistened in the early morning sunlight. His stomach growled in indifference to its surroundings. He reached into one of his saddlebags and pulled out a piece of dried meat and a goatskin pouch filled with goat milk. Pulling a pocketknife out of his dungarees, he cut off a hunk of the meat, then took a swig of milk as he scanned the mountain scape. "It is different from what I remember," he whispered to himself. *This is good*, he thought, *because earthquakes can bring changes to the terrain that can benefit man.* "But where did the caves go?" he muttered in dismay while continuing to survey the mountainous slope.

After pushing the meat into his mouth, he stowed the foodstuff in his saddlebag, secured the camel's rein with a large rock, then scurried up the precipitous slope. *This is steeper than I remember*, he thought. After climbing approximately 225 feet he stopped to catch his breath, turned and waved to his camel, then looked searchingly for the ancient caves. His eyes stopped at a vaguely familiar point 75 feet ahead of him, a place resembling the contour of a ledge that he remembered led to the caves.

His pulse quickened with anticipation as he frantically clambered upwards toward the ledge. The mantle rock flew out from under his feet, tumbling down the mountainside to the valley floor, reminding him of the treacherous land he lived in—a land of radical geographic variables and divergent people. Twenty minutes more of vigorous climbing brought him to a newly-formed summit where he immediately saw that the mouths of the caves were barely visible, having been blocked by tons of rock debris from what looked like a recent avalanche. "This was a powerful earthquake," he whispered aloud as he looked back down below into the stony valley. Through Ishmael's mind flashed a fragmented scene from the past—of an elder advising the boy's father that God often brings earthquakes as a sign of His displeasure. He fell to the ground to rest. It struck him as odd that Allah would suddenly decide to change the shape of this sanctuary in stone after two millennia. *Ah!* he rationalized, *perhaps Allah is not displeased with his creation, but he is about to make a great announcement to the world.* Maybe.

It was in this Judean wilderness area, archeologists attested, that David and his guerilla forces camped while fleeing from the wrath of Saul. It was in similar caves that some Bible books were written in Hebrew on papyrus or copper by ancient scribes fleeing persecution, determined to perpetuate the words of God. Other important Bible passages were written on leather scrolls in lampblack ink made from carbon and gum. The scribes wrapped the documents in linen, then squirreled them away in sealed pottery jars to preserve them.

Reveling in the thought that he himself might be the very instrument of such an announcement, Ishmael renewed his climb with determination. He fumbled to his feet, then looked for familiar landmarks, then back to the north face of the mountainside. He sensed that he was in the right place. His heart beat faster. He looked at the east side of the known caves and saw what appeared to be a recent opening in the mountain. "A new cave!" he yelled heavenward in thanksgiving. Forfeiting regard to injury, he scrambled around the debris and ran to the mouth of the cave entrance. There he stopped abruptly and held onto the wall as stale scorched air invaded his nostrils. He held his breath, then covered his nose with the tailpiece of his kaffiyeh. The foul odor that signaled a fresh upheaval in the arid terrain drifted out and slithered down the side of the mountain to mix with the hot desert air ever present in the barren wasteland.

Several boulders partially obstructed the cavern's entrance, but the inquiring sunlight penetrated and illuminated a peculiar path nearly 30 feet into the cave. Ishmael peered into the earthen cavity for several moments, surveying the ceiling, walls, and floor. He had a hunch that the cave ran much deeper than the light revealed. A stone that he picked up and threw with Herculean strength well beyond his view made no impact. The cave *did* run deep. He took another step, then stopped. A thick layer of dust covered the floor. To him, dry meant preservation. The desert climate was good for *antikas*. Ishmael reached into his dungaree pocket and pulled out a Mini Maglite, praising his god for Western technology. He took a deep breath and warned himself, "Okay, nice and slow."

With mounting curiosity and undaunted courage, he stealthily advanced into the unknown. His flashlight overpowered the darkness that apparently had filled the interior of the cave for centuries. The cave was void of any bat droppings or signs of animal foraging. This was also good. The absence of these elements indicated that the cavern must have been sealed shut by catastrophic forces some time in the distant past. *Could Allah have opened up this subterranean hollow in the earth at this special time to reveal some ancient secret to me?* he thought.

At about 120 feet, his light suddenly fell on markings on the cave wall. At first he thought they were some primordial inscriptions etched in the rock by prehistoric cave dwellers, but close up, he quickly recognized them as ancient Hebrew writings. His heart fluttered at the prospect of finding something of value from the distant past. Running his fingers over the engraved letters, he attempted to mouth out some of the unfamiliar words. Although it was an ancient dialect, Ishmael was able to decipher some of the key words—they spoke a curse upon anybody disturbing the bones of those buried there. He nervously ran his thumb over his badly stained angular teeth, gulped, then looked around carefully in the nearby vicinity. There were four mounds of dried sand and pebbles, each one about the size of a grave. His blood ran icy cold and his heart froze at the paralyzing realization of his intrusive presence in a hidden cemetery. As he began to circle the graves, his foot kicked a hard object upon which he immediately shined his light. It was a stone head marker about nine inches high and six inches wide. His eyes widened when he saw chiseled into the thick stone a seven-branched menorah. The other graves were unmarked. He blinked in bewilderment, but knew instantly that his dream of finding something of value may have come true. Testing the firmness of the mound, he made the decision to dig despite the warning, then quickly left the cave to fetch a shovel from his saddlebag. Within an hour, he was back at the site.

Setting his flashlight on a rock shelf to illuminate the area, Ishmael began at the foot of the marked grave to excavate with utmost caution and deliberate purpose. Initially, the shovel met with resistance as it penetrated the thick crust of the conglomerate sand mound that was consistent with the surrounding terrain. Suspecting a shallow grave, he set aside the shovel after the first incursion to ward off any potential damage to the hoped-for treasure. With his pocketknife and fingers he began to penetrate the ground of the ancient resting place. The underlying ground stubbornly yielded to his inquisitive, nimble fingers; apparently the dry environment had prevented complete compression of the earthen cave floor. Within 15 minutes Ishmael had penetrated the hardened outer strata and discovered a softer, silt-like layer that resembled coarse desert sand. With keen sensitivity, his adroit hands sifted through the gritty eolian matter for several minutes. Reaching into the grave with both hands, at a depth of about 21 inches, he hit upon a large thing that was nothing like what he expected to find in a tomb. His mind reeled in confusion at what happened next.

Instead of finding skeletal remains or bone fragments, his hands grasped what felt like pottery. Bracing himself to acquire the needed leverage, he slowly lifted the artifact to allow the sand to filter through his fingers. It was an earthenware jar of some sort. Stunned at the prospect of his find, he delicately placed the jar on a clear portion of the cave floor. A broad smile came over his face as he marveled at Allah's goodness. In his spirit Ishmael sensed that a blessing was about to unfold.

He scurried for his flashlight to closely examine the *antika*. He estimated the jar to be about 25 to 27 inches high and about 10 inches wide, with a mouth of nearly 5 inches across. The stopper appeared to have been made from wood, covered over with a hardened pitch-like substance, common to the Dead Sea area, that ensured an airtight seal. Hebrew handwriting encircled the jar. Ishmael wiped the side of the vessel to reveal the words, but the abrasion of time had eroded most of the letters; they were marred and faded. He could only make out the words, the *lights of....* Squeezing his eyes shut momentarily in concentration, he whispered to himself what he thought they said, "the *lights of...*" Perplexed, he set the jar and his flashlight aside, then frantically grappled in the grave for more relics.

His fingers sifted through the sand mixture for nearly ten minutes to no avail. Obviously, if there had been a skeleton buried here at one time, the coffin, coffin pegs, and bones had completely disintegrated over the eons. Tired yet exhilarated, he moved toward the other graves to complete his exploratory process. For the next 35 minutes, he carefully performed on the remaining burial sites a crude exhumation that yielded nothing. Disappointed but not discouraged, he turned to the jar with great expectations. He carefully embraced the jar and grave marker as tears welled up in his eyes, then retreated from the cave into the light of day.

Squinting from the blazing sun, Ishmael sat on a newly-formed rock ledge to examine what he believed to be Allah's divinely appointed prizes. First, he studied the memorial tablet with the engraved menorah for several moments, shrugged his shoulders, then stuffed it into his shirt for safekeeping and further analysis. Next, he stood up, wiped his hands as if preparing to perform a surgical operation, then approached the jar with a holy reverence. *This is it*, he said to himself, *this is going to be the very thing that brings recognition to tribe Ta'amireh—this will be our great hour of triumph!* He slowly walked around the jar, studying its shape and lettering, then picked it up to hold it to the light. When he rotated it he heard objects rattling inside. It sounded like rocks and cloth hitting against the sides of the jar. *Could there be stuffing colliding against a broken inside layer?* he wondered. "Allah, don't let this be just filled with potsherds or be a worthless storage vessel of some kind," he said aloud. Sitting down he looked over the seal, which was apparently watertight. He did not want to damage the corking device, yet he had to see what was inside the jar. After a quick petition to Mohammed to intercede to Allah, Ishmael carefully slipped his pocketknife blade between the mouth of the jar and the stopper and ran it full circle. Remarkably, he heard a faint hissing sound as if he had broken a vacuum seal. He closely examined the stopper and jar, rejoicing that his forced entry had left no visible damage.

A parched mouth triggered by a surge of adrenaline accompanied his electrified emotional state. *Think*, Ishmael demanded of himself. *What next? Should I proceed or wait?* After another moment of contemplation he decided to take the risk. Meticulously his hands maneuvered the stopper a fraction of an inch at a time until it dislodged. Finally after ten minutes of field precision he lifted the age-old plug from the jar and carefully placed it on the ground out of the sun.

The smell of linen exposed to constant dry heat arose from the jar and penetrated his nostrils. He snorted to expel the odor, then reached inside and pulled out three of the hard objects along with a piece of the cloth, which shredded in the process. The objects were brightly colored stones entangled in faded threads. Resplendent rays of sunlight refracted off the stones, flashing his face and causing him to shield his eyes. He moved to the shade and glared at the gems, which possessed a vitreous luster. One was smaller than the other two. Excitedly he removed his headdress and placed it on the ground, then turned the jar upside down and emptied it onto the makeshift drop cloth. Out tumbled ten more large rectangular stones and two small circular stones along with several pieces of linen. He held one of the bigger stones next to his thumb for scale, noting it to be slightly under three inches, and about half an inch thick. The smaller rounded stones were about the size of a large coin. The linen fragments were browned and curled from age, with what looked like gold embroidery forming a border.

The gems were various colors, including deep orange-red, a light yellow, a dark green, a transparent blue, purple, white, black, and opaque crystalline that he recognized to be some form of quartz. One was colorless like a diamond.

Ishmael was not learned in mineralogy, but his intuition dictated that Allah had answered his prayer most graciously.

CHAPTER

2

Jerusalem

Security around the Israel Antiquities Authority building in Jerusalem was extremely tight this morning. The Hamas, a Palestinian militant resistance organization claiming responsibility for the previous week's suicide bombing on a bus in West Jerusalem that killed 25 people, was on the move once again. The IAA, instructed by law to salvage excavations at construction sites wherever ancient bones had been found, had met with continued resistance and progressive violence by the radical group, which was opposed to digs in Palestinian-held territories. The General Security Services in Tel Aviv, responsible for Israel's internal security, alerted the bureau chief of IAA that an attack by Hamas at his central headquarters in Jerusalem was likely. Rehavam Krasnoff, a resident antiquities investigator with IAA, looked down at Sderot Ben Zvi street from his second floor office to survey the concrete barricades protecting the front entrance of the building. He shook his head in disgust and slowly walked back to his desk. *It is bad enough to make war with the Arabs in their countries, but must we also battle with them in ours?* he asked himself. Glancing upward he whispered somberly, "God, when does it end?"

He leaned back in his desk chair and scanned the array of family photographs strategically placed as a constant reminder of the ongoing Islamic war. His eyes stopped on the picture, taken five years earlier at their Passover dinner, of his beloved wife, Naomi, sitting at their dinner table alongside his younger brother, Gershom. Reflecting on the good times, he moved aside several site files containing maps, sketches, and notes from various expedition directors to view the photograph more clearly. "I miss you guys," he sighed. Both had been killed while shopping at a seacoast mall in Ashkelon by a Palestinian who detonated himself together with several sticks of dynamite. Tears welled up in Rehavam's eyes, as a surge of emptiness invaded the consoling memories of Naomi that had sustained him through the years.

Tear-filled eyes turned piercing as he turned to look at the glamour shot of his daughter, Leah, now 21, whom he saw as his heart. He put on his wire-rimmed glasses to examine the photo more closely. She represented the hope of everything that Naomi had never had the chance to be. He was determined to see her succeed in life. At 45, Rehavam did not run with a fast crowd but embraced a conservative lifestyle that seemed to come with his profession. With an analytical and, out of necessity, calculating temperament, his demeanor was somewhat subdued. During moments of reflection he realized how much he had changed since Naomi's death. Melancholy had replaced gaiety; discouragement had replaced ambition; compromise had replaced conviction, and aggression had replaced passivity. In his innermost thoughts, those he refused to acknowledge, he consoled himself with the notion that someday he would avenge his wife and brother's murders.

"Revi, a call for you on 01," the receptionist said over the telecom.

Snapping out of his pensive state, he picked up the phone. "Rehavam Krasnoff," he said in an official tone as he leaned back in his chair.

"Mr. Krasnoff, this is Ishmael ben Azin," the voice on the phone announced in strained Hebrew. "I should like to meet with you to discuss an important matter."

Krasnoff recognized the accent as Bedouin, then remembered as an agency employee he was required to be congenial and pleasant to all who inhabited and contaminated his land. His disdain for the Arab reflexively surfaced so he consciously pushed the bile reflux back down into his stomach.

"About what?" he asked intolerantly. He sensed the voice of a young adult, and experience had taught him to be suspicious of any claims from Arabs, particularly adolescents looking to make some quick money.

"I have read about your work on the dig out at the desert fortress at Machaerus, east of the Dead Sea, in Jordan, and would like to meet with you concerning a discovery of my own," Ishmael boasted.

Krasnoff bit his lip impatiently then said, "Discovery?"

Ishmael carefully chose his words. "Yes, I have discovered *antikas* and would like to discuss business with you."

"Where did you find them?" Krasnoff asked as a matter of fact. Identifying the location was an important part of qualification.

"I prefer to keep that information to myself for the present," Ishmael replied.

He sounds bright and informed; perhaps he has received training from his elders. "And the nature of the *antikas*?" Krasnoff queried with an edge to his voice. *Hopefully,* he thought, *this is not one of those arrogant punk Arabs who thinks his archeological discovery will somehow substantiate their incessant claims to Jewish land.*

"I found an earthenware jar that contained a number of stones and some linen..."

"Oh, really?" Krasnoff interrupted halfheartedly through a yawn.

"...along with a headstone that has a seven-branched menorah engraved in it. I think these *antikas* may be from the first century B.C.E.," Ishmael continued tersely.

Krasnoff's feet hit the floor. He blinked several times, then coughed to stall for time. "Interesting..." he paused again. "What makes you say that?"

"My people know the caves in the desert and besides..." he made his voice sound adult-like, "I read books."

Krasnoff quickly capitulated. "Where would you like to meet?"

"At the Burger Depot on George Street, tomorrow at noontime."

"Done," Krasnoff replied, then quickly added, "Ishmael, bring *all* of your discovery."

"Mr. Krasnoff," Ishmael returned defensively, "I am not a fool. I will be carrying a small leather saddlebag into Burger Depot tomorrow."

The phone line went dead.

Krasnoff stared at the phone for nearly half a minute as he reflected on the call. Could it be possible that a find of this magnitude would suddenly fall into his lap? "Yes!" he yelled triumphantly, then immediately changed his expression when his secretary spun around at his exclamation. With arms crossed over his chest he carefully contemplated his next move.

Authentication would be imperative. He mentally checked his knowledge and experience on the subject, and believed himself qualified to determine the genuineness of the discovery. He would not be able to bring in any experts to examine the find at this time. He recalled the problems surrounding the excavation at the rabbis' tunnel at the Temple Mount, and how the Arab zealots threatened war unless the dig was terminated. They forced the IAA to board up the unearthing and abandon it altogether. No—publicity would be the death knell that would bury the discovery in a political and religious quagmire for decades. *There is no way I'm dealing with the Haredim, the Jewish radical group opposed to archeology in Jewish land, or the Arabs opposed to digs in land they claim is theirs—not with an opportunity like this*, Krasnoff resolved within himself. Then there was the issue of money. He would bring agency documentation, then advance the deposit from his discretionary account, then settle up with agency funds after the transaction was complete. No problem. Promise of recognition would be officially finalized when the deal was complete. With the plan firmly etched in his mind, he sighed in relief and returned to his work.

As a Zionist, Krasnoff had little tolerance for Arabs, and to be in a restaurant owned and operated by them made him uncomfortable; he simply ordered a cup of coffee and waited for his appointment. At 30 minutes after the noon hour his patience began to wear thin. He clutched his briefcase as a reminder of the importance of the meeting, then purposed to extend his wait indefinitely. Fifteen minutes later a youthful looking European-dressed Arab sitting diagonally across from him stood up from the table. Immediately Krasnoff noticed the leather saddlebag under his arm.

"Mr. Krasnoff?" the youth asked while studying his face.

Krasnoff was the only Jewish man in the building. "Yes," Krasnoff replied.

"Ishmael ben Azin," he announced. "I have been observing you for the past hour—I enjoy watching people as they wait." Pointing toward the parking lot he added, "Can we talk in your car?"

"Ah, okay—of course," Krasnoff assented and stood up, surprised at Azin's appearance.

Quick to read his expression, Azin cordially remarked, "You expected to see me in a kaffiyeh headdress and sandals, right? Well, this is the 2000s!"

Krasnoff nodded in admiration at the aspiring businessman as they exited the building.

Annoyed at first, Krasnoff asked himself, *Could it be that this Bedouin doesn't want to be seen with a Jew? How absurd! Then again, maybe it is better this way.* He escorted him to his late model Ford Bronco and said with a chuckle, "Step into my office, friend." It was a matter of necessity that he win his confidence. The young man suspiciously scanned the vehicle's interior, then stepped inside.

Azin placed his hands securely on the saddlebag resting in his lap then looked into Krasnoff's eyes and said, "We Bedouins mature rapidly out in the desert, so don't let my youth deceive you. I purpose to do this thing right." With that he reached into the saddlebag and pulled out a large jewelry pouch. Unfolding it on top of the saddlebag, he handed Krasnoff two stones: one transparent blue, which he reasoned was a sapphire; the other colorless, resembling a diamond. He watched Krasnoff's eyes as they fell on the precious gems. Capitalizing on the Jewish man's facial expression Ishmael said, "Unbelievable, aren't they? Magnificent, really."

Krasnoff slowly examined the gems as he cradled them in his hands. Calculating quickly he asked curiously, "How many?"

"Altogether fifteen; twelve large, three small."

Krasnoff weighed the response in his mind for nearly a minute, then probed, "Can I see the others?"

"In time, in time," Azin soothed. He had spent enough time haggling in the marketplace over merchandise to recognize Krasnoff's mounting interest.

"The headstone and jar?"

Azin reached back into the saddlebag, pulled out the grave marker enclosed in clear bubble wrap, and exchanged it for the gems. "The jar is safe."

Krasnoff examined the memorial stone carefully. "We would need to test these for their authenticity."

Azin nodded as he retrieved the headstone and gems. "I'm prepared to accommodate you." From the saddlebag he pulled a legal size manila envelope, which he handed to Krasnoff. "Inside you will find fragments of the linen that was with the stones. Traces of the gold embroidery are still visible. This should be enough to convince your superiors for now."

Krasnoff bit his lip while considering his predicament. He looked inside the envelope and removed one fragment to view before negotiating. He held it up in the sunlight, then reached over for the clear gem and did the same. Dazzling light ricocheted throughout the Bronco. "How much are we talking about?"

The young Arab smiled. These were the moments that made his efforts worthwhile, especially when he knew he had the upper hand over a Jew. "Three million American for the stones; one-half million American for the grave marker. I will throw in the jar and linen free of charge."

Krasnoff looked at him in disbelief and shook his head. "Never happen. The IAA does not have that kind of funding."

Azin reached for the envelope. "That is unfortunate. I guess I will have to deal with the Jordanians or the British or the Americans—they all have plenty of money for *antikas*." His voice now dripped with sarcasm.

"My, my, such a hard line," Krasnoff said in mock contrition as he began to pat Ishmael on the back. "I'm sure we can meet your demand, just relax."

Ishmael moved away from him. "There is another condition as well."

Krasnoff retreated to his corner of the front seat. "And that is—?"

"We Bedouins want all the credit for this discovery. In particular, I want our tribe to get the recognition. Maybe even a film documenting my exploration that will bring attention to my people." He turned to stare out the window and added, "When these conditions are met, I can go to my people and rejoice with them."

Krasnoff found the hole he was looking for. "Does anybody else know about your discovery?"

Mesmerized by his expectations, Azin said, "My dream has always been to help my people. When the plan is secure, I will inform them."

"I see," Krasnoff replied sympathetically. "I hope we can help you fulfill your destiny." He opened his briefcase and handed Ishmael a clear zip-lock bag with two stacks of cash bound with rubber bands. "Here is twenty-thousand dollars American as a deposit. I will have the fragment tested today and call you to arrange our final meeting."

Azin returned the envelope and said as he opened the door to leave, "I will call *you* tomorrow."

At 4 p.m. the IAA courier arrived at the high security Yeroham Atomic Research Station, situated between Dimona and Yeroham, nearly 25 miles southwest of the Dead Sea. The armed courier handed Krasnoff's sample in a sealed envelope to a resident engineer who agreed to give it special priority. The instructions were to return the fragment and to deliver the results as soon as possible via an encrypted fax to Krasnoff's eyes only.

The laboratory facility was capable of performing any age-dating techniques. Krasnoff specifically directed them to use the radiometric age-dating Carbon-14 method, used to date materials such as wood, seeds, and bones; the Rb-Sr method (Rubidium-87-Strontium-87) that measured the rate of decay of the radioactive rubidium-87 present in rubidium-bearing minerals such as micas, feldspars, and glauconite; and the Neutron Activation analysis, a potent technique for multi-element analysis that involves neutron bombardment of a target to convert stable isotopes in a sample to radioactive isotopes. The organic composition of the linen together with the mineral content of the remaining gold embroidery would provide sufficient elements to assay.

Shortly before 10 p.m., as Krasnoff sat at his desk in anticipation, the fax machine whirred to life. He jumped to his feet and dashed to the machine across the room to key in his password. Three seconds later the machine printed out the report. His hand began to shake as he leafed through the pages while walking backwards toward his desk. Frantically his eyes ran over the pages to the summary that read: TENTATIVELY DATED BETWEEN 60 and 25 B.C.E. He fell back into his chair. After a moment of contemplation he said aloud, "Revi, you can't let this one get away—you owe it to your people."

Krasnoff's anxiety level soared as he sat at his desk waiting for Ishmael's call. The ubiquitous early-morning rain outside his window only heightened the tension building in his body. He rubbed his temples in a vain attempt to relieve the escalating pain. *I feel a cluster headache coming on*, he groaned. For over ten years, migraine headaches had plagued him, coming on without warning. He checked his wristwatch, then surreptitiously reviewed his oversized attaché case to reensure his readiness to complete the transaction. Inside the attaché case were precious gems ownership transfer forms, an envelope with cash and a check attached to it, and a small shoe box wrapped in rubber bands. Everything was in order. At 8:15 a.m., the phone rang.

Krasnoff deliberately let it ring three times before picking it up. "Mr. Krasnoff, I will meet with you at the Sheraton Jerusalem that overlooks Gershon Agron, room 503, in thirty minutes. Agreed?" Ishmael said trenchantly.

"No problem," Krasnoff rejoined as he replaced the phone. Ishmael could not see the smirk on Krasnoff's face as he took inventory of his attaché case one more time.

Krasnoff drove his rented car into a remote corner of the YMCA parking lot on the corner of Keren haYessod and Gershon Agron diagonally across from the Sheraton Jerusalem. He went to the trunk, pulled out some old clothing along with a pillowcase-sized canvas bag, then returned to the front seat. First he managed to don a worn herringbone jacket that went over his cardigan sweater, then he put on a woven skullcap. Next, he substituted his wire-rimmed glasses with black, heavy-rimmed glasses, and then fastened a thick black artificial mustache to his upper lip. Convinced of his Palestinian likeness, he stuffed his attaché case into the bag, climbed out of his vehicle, and walked to the hotel with the bag under his arm.

An amalgam of people both scurried and tarried in the lobby as Krasnoff slowly strolled toward the bank of elevators, making a point to nod to the bell captain on the way. Israelis, Americans and Europeans were among the more conspicuous, with a few Palestinians consorting with the concierge. He hesitated until the elevator nearly filled, then annoyedly jumped into the crowd just before the door closed. He made sure the passengers took notice of him.

When the elevator reached the fifth floor Krasnoff pushed his way out, mumbling audibly. Irritated at his behavior, two guests sneered at his back as they stepped out and went down the corridor toward their room. Krasnoff waited several moments until the floor cleared, then stealthily stepped into the vending machine room where he quickly exchanged his disguise for his business attire. He placed the costume into the canvas bag, which he then tossed into the trash barrel. With the task accomplished, Krasnoff peeked at his reflection in the window of the candy machine, then hurriedly walked to Azin's room.

Ishmael ben Azin answered the door, glanced at his watch, then motioned for Krasnoff to enter. "I admire a prompt businessman," Azin remarked with a tight smile as he looked at the attaché case.

Krasnoff gave Azin a thumb-up as he walked into the room. His eyes scanned the room as he announced the half-truth, "*I* admire a *young* man who knows *his business*." He held the attaché case up in the air and added with a twinkle in his eye, "We have run our tests on the fragment and have found it to be authentic. The agency has agreed to your requests."

Azin silently strutted over to the hallway closet, took out his saddlebag, then went to the kitchen table where Krasnoff had laid his attaché case. His eyes widened as he smiled and replied with the colloquial English of a New York drug dealer, "Let's deal!"

Krasnoff shot a look into the bedroom and adjoining bath, paused for a millisecond to listen for noise, then set his briefcase on the floor and sat down to the table. He motioned for Azin to unpack his bag and said curiously, "Let's see what you've got."

Azin grabbed a dishtowel off the sink, placed it on the table to cushion the gems, then with punctilious care withdrew them, one at a time, placing them on the cloth in a circular pattern. Krasnoff's eyes broadened in amazement. When the stones were together, whether the light refracting through them be daylight or incandescent, refulgent rays shot out in rainbow fashion and filled the room. Krasnoff fluttered his eyes several times to adjust to the dazzling display, then picked up the emerald. He held it to the sunlight, bounced it in his hand as if to estimate its quality and size, then inspected the rest of the gems in the same way. Azin watched every move he made.

Krasnoff rubbed his sweaty palms on his thighs as he mentally rehearsed his plan. "The linen and headstone?"

Azin fished them out of the saddlebag and placed them on the table next to the array of gems. "The documents and funds?" he countered with raised eyebrows.

After unwrapping and checking the grave marker, Krasnoff nodded in assent and reached into his briefcase. He paused momentarily and asked, "The jar?"

Azin pointed to the closet. "I even washed it up for you since it is..." he chortled, " as Americans say, a freebie."

Part of Krasnoff's plan employed leveraging the young aspiring businessman before him. "I know they're in here..." he said jokingly while shuffling the documents around inside his attaché case for several moments.

The Bedouin's brow furrowed as he focused on Krasnoff's attaché case. "Problems?"

"Here they are." With his left hand, Krasnoff slowly lifted out the manila envelope with a blank check clipped to it while picking up the headstone with his right hand. With one sudden plunge he slammed Azin in the back of the neck with the grave marker. The youth's head tilted sharply as his neck snapped. His eyes rolled backward while he reflexively reached for the gems, then he fell in a heap to the floor, clutching the diamond.

Krasnoff walked over to Azin and kicked him. "That's for Naomi and Gershom." He recovered the gem out of his hand, then gathered the remaining jewels from the table, carefully enveloping them in the towel and placing them into his attaché case. "And these are for me," he sneered as he kicked the body one more time. He re-wrapped the marker and placed it next to the stones; the linen fragments he placed in the top file compartment.

Reaching into Azin's saddlebag he located the cash deposit; counting it later he found only five hundred dollars missing. Next, he walked to the closet to fetch the jar, making sure the lid was intact, then positioned it near the door. Methodically removing the small shoe box from the attaché case, he set it on the floor next to Ishmael's body, then picked up the telephone and called Israeli police. "Hamas is the hand of Allah!" he shouted into the phone in Arabic. Quoting from the Quran he yelled, "'Who fights in the way of Allah be he slain or be he victorious, on him we shall bestow a vast reward'...I am at the American-owned Sheraton Jerusalem which funds the satanic Jews, and we are taking vengeance for the desecration of our land!" He slammed the phone down, grabbed his attaché case and walked to the door to pick up the jar. Satisfied that the corridor was clear, he retrieved his disguise from the vending machine trash can, then placed the jar into the bag before making his way to the stairway. On the other side of the stairwell door, he paused to listen for footsteps. *Safe*, he thought.

Within one minute he changed back into his disguise, then slowly carried his belongings down one more level where he came to a stop. He opened up his attaché case and removed a remote triggering device wrapped in brown paper. Looking up he said through clenched teeth, "And this is for my people." With that he pressed the button that closed the circuit to the detonator attached to the shoe box of Amatol he had placed next to Azin's body.

The initial concussion of the high explosive rocked both the fourth and fifth floors of the hotel. The force from the blast momentarily pinned Krasnoff against the stairwell wall when the fire door burst open. He quickly regained his composure. "Time to go, Revi!" he told himself.

Just as he planned, the lobby was a frenetic nightmare. Guests were screaming as they ran out every door while the hotel staff frantically attempted to guide them to safety. Israeli secret police arrived in an unmarked van just as Krasnoff blended into the mainstream of guests pouring out the door. Within seconds he was sitting in his vehicle in the parking lot.

From his vantage point, Krasnoff could see the massive hole in the exterior wall that extended into the upper and lower floors. Concrete block along with ornamental figures broken off from the building lay scattered on the ground at the base of the hotel. Electrical conduit and water pipe lay atop several cars in the perimeter of the blast zone. Mangled and disfigured bodies lay strewn in the street as airborne debris circulated above them like vultures descending over dead cattle.

Krasnoff shook his head in disbelief at the size of the hole. For a brief second he felt remorse over the deed, but the sensation left him when his fingers tightened around the handle of his attaché case.

Twenty minutes later the news bulletin announcing the bombing came over the radio on Krasnoff's desk. Officials of the Islamic terrorist group Hamas, denied involvement in the senseless bombing at the Sheraton Jerusalem where 22 Jews had been killed and 18 seriously wounded. The number was still climbing. One Palestinian had suffered a concussion. Israeli officials vowed an investigation and retaliation if the terrorist claim proved true.

Krasnoff smirked with the thought that Ishmael ben Azin had achieved his objective: Worldwide recognition and martyrdom in perpetuity.

CHAPTER

3

Athens

At first only beads of perspiration appeared on his forehead as he napped in his recliner. Then faint traces of a morbid and spasmodic twitch came over his face, until suddenly his hands and feet began to tremble as his mind groped for some semblance of consciousness. Across a cosmic gulf devoid of form emerged the figure of a man trespassing in the hidden vaults of the Holy Land. The man walked into a cave then kneeled on the ground and pulled out a jar from the earth. As if possessed by some infinite force beyond all Nature, he opened the jar and released a white dove that flew away, but not before flying throughout the cave filling it with multi-spectral light. Then the man fell headlong into the pit.

"NO!..." Gregory A. Kavidas cried out from the eerie depths of some nefarious nightmare that refused to release him. "...The *lights* will destroy us!" Fluttering eyelids gave way to a frenzied visage while he attempted to regain control of his intellect. He bolted upright in the chair, massaged his neck and looked at the clock on the wall. It was 3:15 p.m.

He walked over to the massive desk punctiliously placed in his Gothic style office, then pressed the intercom button. "Stephanie, ask Mr. Stein to come to my office," he ordered. *Our plan is endangered,* he realized.

It was at times like this that Kavidas had to draw upon all his spiritual resources to interpret the dream. He knew that his photographic memory and genius brain, both natural gifts, could not help him with matters affecting his future. He closed his eyes, and after several moments of dedicated prayer the answer came. It was not an answer from the God of Heaven, but from his god, the anointed cherub who attempted to usurp the Holy One—Satan, the interim god of this world.

Refreshed in his spirit, he turned to look out the window.

At the touch of a button the drapes parted to reveal a beautiful vista of the timeless Acropolis and the Greek city named after the Olympian deity, Athena. Though the city had been inhabited since Neolithic times, it was in the 450s B.C. that the prestigious statesman Pericles transformed Athens into a famous city. His influence had raised public funds to build the Parthenon, the temple of Nike, the Erechtheum, and other magnificent monuments. Partly surrounded by mountains and embraced by the beautiful waters of the Aegean Sea, Athens dominated the political, cultural, and economic life of Greece, the perfect backdrop for Gregory A. Kavidas to be born.

Beautifully situated near Constitution Square to capture a magnificent view of the Parthenon ruins on the Acropolis, the Kavidas Enterprises building represented both an eponym and a tribute to his family dynasty that was destined for greatness. Built to emulate classical architecture, his building represented something of a fortress. The executive offices occupied the third floor, the clerical offices the second, customer service the first. Unbeknown except to a few, a subterranean floor housed the supercomputers for MASTERLINK, the worldwide credit system developed in America by Kavidas and his partner, Mortimer Stein, five years earlier.

There was a quick knock at the door.

"Come in, Mort," Kavidas said as he closed the drapes.

Stein entered and sat in the stuffed chair decoratively placed on a Persian rug in front of the hand-carved floor-to-ceiling bookshelves lining three walls. His lean athletic body with its sharp chiseled features was accentuated with an expensive American suit. He prided himself with the notion that no one noticed his bald head as long as he perpetually dressed the part of a successful businessman. Many argued his logic. Divorced after 20 years of marriage, at 43, Stein had decided that a celibate life would enable him to devote all his time to Kavidas' purpose.

"We have a problem," Kavidas began trenchantly. "You must go to Israel to investigate the possibility of a device that could hurt us."

"A device?" Stein fretted, detecting Kavidas' determined tone.

"I had a dream that someone recently unearthed an ancient appliance that could be used to unmask us unless it is destroyed first." Kavidas' composure was always undeniably towering and resolute in times of crisis, except when forces beyond his control appeared threatening.

Stein blinked several times as Kavidas' statement penetrated his mind. He was well familiar with Gregory's informative dreams. "How could that be, Gregory?" Stein asked incredulously. "Wouldn't we have known about its existence before now?"

Kavidas shook his head and pointed up. "Obviously, powers greater than ours have allowed this to be found."

"How much time?"

A suppressed smile appeared on the handsome face of Gregory A. Kavidas as he ran his fingers through his thick black hair, somewhat peculiar to a man of 56 years. "Fortunately, no one knows how to operate it yet, so we have a little time." He moved to sit in his highbacked swivel chair while he calculated their position. His eyes seemed to bore holes through Stein as he added, "Our mission is in jeopardy as long as this device is allowed to exist. We must give it our highest priority."

"Do we have a place or a name?" Stein probed.

"Not really—the dream was not specific. However, it is apparent you should begin your work with any recent archeological discoveries." Kavidas' eyes suddenly brightened. "Nose around and use all our assets and your special abilities to find it."

Stein nodded with a cryptic smile, knowing exactly what Gregory meant, and said as he stood up, "I'll have Stephanie book me on the next flight to Tel Aviv."

Kavidas watched Stein with piercing eyes as he walked out. Stein had always been an invaluable asset to him, not only in business enterprises, but more importantly in spiritual warfare. Whatever the assignment, be it the challenging and warring of enemy angelic forces or the removal of earthly adversaries, Stein was dependable.

Fully confident that Stein would handle the development, he flipped the CD player switch on his desk console. He closed his eyes for his second power nap of the day while the sounds of Vivaldi's *Four Seasons* filled the room.

Three levels beneath Kavidas, his Cray-IV supercomputers whirred, scanned, and calculated while monitoring the world's most advanced electronic transfer/financial service and medical identification system, MASTERLINK. MASTERLINK had become the trademark of a joint venture between Mortimer Stein, founder of the Florida-based national credit clearing and background check organization, REDISEARCH, and Gregory A. Kavidas, founding father of Rainbow Pharmaceuticals, the drug research firm that had developed the vaccine for AIDS during the '90s. Meanwhile, the rival pharmaceutical company, Lane Drugs, under the management of CEO

Matthew Lane, publicly accused Rainbow of giving the population a false hope—Lane Drugs research proved the AIDS virus could return within three years of the inoculation. Battling a tarnished image, Kavidas had sold off his drug company and relocated to his native Athens. He then moved into the political arena where the mushrooming resources of MASTERLINK continued to provide unlimited funds necessary for him to reach his destiny.

Using REDISEARCH's enrollment files along with the names of the worldwide recipients of the AIDS vaccine, Stein developed the successor to REDISEARCH, MEDLINK. MEDLINK incorporated all the information from REDISEARCH, the subscriber's personal and credit description, then added all their medical history to provide emergency information. Data storage was in a non-transferrable, pinhead-sized 15-megabyte microchip permanently imbedded on the subscriber to prevent accidental loss and eliminate theft. The chip was always on the person. Within three seconds of waving an electronic scanning wand over the chip designed to replace the elusive conventional plastic card, the satellite link provided any medical facility the necessary data needed to save any subscriber's life. Any surgical or prescription activity was automatically updated.

In the final stage, MASTERLINK, encrypted information was available not to a financial/commercial facility or medical service provider, but only to law enforcement agencies who must first get authorization directly from MASTERLINK in Athens. This data included asset information—real estate, bank accounts, pension funds, insurance policy cash values and tax return status—as well as the individual's political and religious affiliation. Overwhelming public demand for a system designed to ultimately replace all cash and check transactions dictated the need for a global network. With nearly two-thirds of the population now enrolled in MASTERLINK,

Kavidas' goal of a one-world financial system was rapidly becoming a reality.

The weekday traffic on Sederot Ruppin and Giv'at Ram, once again, slowed to a crawl as a multitude of wearied workers drove out of the famed Knesset building that housed Israel's Parliament to their respective destinations. As an aspiring intern working in the legislative branch of the Israeli government, Leah Krasnoff rarely had time for social events or even dating for that matter. Occasionally she would break from her routine and go to Syd's Gym for a workout before going home to the condominium she shared with her father on Shomeron street. Tonight, however, was an exception. Tonight she would dine with Shlomo Rubin, the nephew of the prime minister.

The modest three-bedroom condo on the second floor featured a balcony overlooking a country arboretum where young school children frequently took their field trips to explore the world of botany. It was here that Leah and her father often strolled in the evenings to discuss current events and the dreams of their lives. It was here that her dad spoke of his love for her mom and how he saw so much of his late wife, Naomi, in Leah. Reaffirming his love for Leah came naturally to him.

In the master bedroom, sweat dripped off Krasnoff's brow onto the gems he had strategically placed on a card table set up under the large window overlooking the park. Three hours of experimentation had ended in frustration and failure. Something was radically wrong. He carefully reviewed the stack of diagrams he had made to avoid duplicating the secret combination, but they did not reveal any new method. Overpowered by frustration he yelled out an expletive, "You—!" then threw his chair against the distant wall.

The front door opened and slammed shut.

Adrenaline swept through his body like a sudden gust of wind as he scurried to conceal the gems.

"Hello, Father...home early...have a special date tonight," Leah yelled out matter-of-factly in staccato as she pranced into her bedroom.

Krasnoff was thankful she hadn't heard the crash of the chair against the wall. "Okay, honey!" he replied as he quickly vaulted to close and lock his bedroom door. He abruptly gathered the stones into a felt-lined jeweler's case and hid it under his bed. The jar and headstone remained covered under a pillowcase in his clothes closet. Confident of their safety, he walked out into the living room.

Twenty-five minutes later Leah emerged from the bathroom in a stunning evening dress with her hair in a French twist that accentuated her high cheekbones and long neck. The long dripping diamond earrings that had belonged to her mother sparkled as she walked. Her father took one look at her and saw a mirror image of Naomi. "You look beautiful, Leah!" he exulted.

"Thanks, Daddy," she beamed as she rotated in front of the hallway mirror.

"Your mother would be proud of you," he added warmly as he hugged her.

Her face lit up with a nice smile. "I won't be home late."

With a shrug of the shoulders he said, "No problem. I'll probably still be up." As she opened the front door he added as an afterthought, "Always remember, honey, no matter what happens—I love you."

"I love you, too," she blinked, and walked out. Once outside she paused and thought that melancholia in dads must come with aging.

Krasnoff stood staring at the door for several moments as he strengthened his purpose. "I'm doing this for you, Leah," he muttered. "I only want the best for you—besides, it's what your mother would want too." In the inner recesses of his heart, a voice whispered to him that he had just lied.

He gave the inaudible voice a dismissive wave of the hand, looked toward his bedroom door, and with a deep-seated resolve said aloud, " 'I must keep going until it works."

After another hour of experimentation part of the solution came to him.

"Why didn't I think of this before?" he said to himself. With eyes blazing, he walked to his bookshelf and grabbed his Masoretic text Bible then returned to the table. After checking the Bible's concordance, he turned to the section that described the special garments worn by Israel's high priest when he presided at the altar. He focused on the breastplate, a square piece of cloth made of linen wrought in the same fashion as the ephod, the priest's apron worn over his robe. The breastplate was doubled so as to form a pocket approximately eight inches square.

" 'And they set in it four rows of stones...' " he read aloud from the Book of Exodus, " '...the first row was a sardius, a topaz and...the second row, an emerald, a sapphire, and a diamond. And the third row...' " He carefully noted the placement in the rows, then his eyes dropped down to the distinction, " '...and the stones were according to the names of the children of Israel, twelve according to their names, like the engravings of a signet, every one with his name, according to the twelve tribes.' " First he covered the tabletop with linen, then he laid out the stones on the table according to his interpretation of the description in the biblical passage. He smiled in triumph.

Excitement reigned as his heart raced, only to be crestfallen once again. Laying out the twelve stones in four rows of three, he suddenly realized once again that something was wrong. *Which stone represents which tribe and is the placement right-to-left, or left-to-right?* The placement order of the gems corresponding to the tribes had to make a difference, but how would he know what the arrangement of the tribes was? *When they were encamped or marching?* The combinations were almost infinite. Then he looked at the smaller stones and shrugged his shoulders. *What possible sequence would make these work?* he wondered.

Krasnoff sighed and squeezed his eyes shut to think, then referred back to his trial diagrams once more. Suddenly an idea flashed through his mind. He went to the passage in Numbers that referred to the arrangement of the twelve tribes in relationship to the tabernacle when they were marching, since that fit the pattern of rows. He studied the text for several moments, then revised the formation once again. This time, the lead or primary tribes—Judah, Reuben, Ephraim and Dan—were on the top; that established the proper orientation. Then he assigned Issachar, Simeon, Manasseh, and Asher to the second row and the remaining tribes of Zebulun, Gad, Benjamin and Naphtali to the final row. Together with the sequence of twelve stones listed, he was able to match the stone with the tribe in its proper configuration on the breastplate.

"Okay, so far, so good," he said optimistically, then proceeded with the next step. The three smaller, rounded stones, were quite distinct from the other twelve. One was iridescent blue, which Krasnoff assumed to be a variation of a sapphire; one, a dark purple that resembled amethyst; and the third, a bright scarlet that was obviously a jasper.

Krasnoff closed his eyes in momentary meditation as if seeking spiritual guidance, then laid out the three gems above the twelve stones already in place. Once again, he reminded himself, the proper layout would ensure operation. Initially he set them in a triangular shape with the sapphire at the apex, since he remembered that blue represented God's heavenly nature. Then he put the purple amethyst in the left corner, representing God's royalty, and the scarlet jasper that symbolized blood sacrifice (a summation of his own) in the right corner. He waited several moments for some sign that the sequence was right.

Nothing happened.

Carefully noting the formation, he further experimented by aligning the smaller stones in a circle, then horizontally, then vertically, changing the combination with each attempt.

Nothing happened.

Four hours later, when exhaustion took over, he went to bed.

The next morning, sunlight through his bedroom window bounced off the stones on the table and generated a quasi light show. Spellbound, he stared at the dancing light on the wall until it came to him what was missing. For the next 30 minutes he lay in bed making plans to resolve the problem. Then he telephoned Ze've Mazor, his friend who worked as a tourist guide.

CHAPTER

4

Tel Aviv

The security at El Al airlines represented the highest in the world, an aviation industry reality born of an age of terrorism and conflict. It was reality that Stein could live with and it made his short flight to Ben Gurion airport from Athens quite enjoyable. Once in Tel Aviv, he rented a blue Mercedes Benz SL 500 convertible coupe for his driving while in the Holy Land. Spiritual significance had nothing to do with his stopping at the Wailing or Western Wall on the way to his hotel; it was simply a matter of deference to his heritage as a Jewish-American. In fact, it was merely to keep up appearances.

Intrusive to the sanctity of the Temple Mount area was the excessive presence of military police, ever vigilant to suppress any Arab uprising or political threat to the reverence of the hallowed site. The presence of tourists also represented an intrusion, while the *Hasidim*, enshrouded in their shawls as they dahvened in prayer, seemed to be the only people who really belonged there.

Dating back to the time of the Roman-backed king, Herod the Great, the Wall was the only remaining portion of the second Temple, destroyed when the Roman general Titus sacked Jerusalem in A.D.70. Solomon's Temple, the first Temple, had stood for four hundred years before the Babylonian king Nebuchadnezzar destroyed it in 586 B.C. After the Babylonian captivity, during the reign of the Persian king Darius in 445 B.C., the Temple had been rebuilt by Zerubbabel, a descendant of David. The massive foundation blocks below the Wall that dated from the first, or Solomonic Temple, were quarried in Lebanon and floated down the Mediterranean Sea in rafts by King Solomon's architect, Hiram, in 960 B.C. After three thousand years, they remained as a silent memorial to Solomon and the indomitable spirit of God's people, Israel.

Stein donned his yarmulke, then walked up and put his hand on one of the huge blocks of stone that made up the Wall. After a moment of mock admiration he reached into one of the crevices between the stones and pulled out one of the innumerable scraps of paper with prayer requests left by the faithful. He read the petition, shook his head, then crumpled the paper and stuffed it in a tiny hole above the crevice. "Keep wishing," he whispered to the anonymous supplicant. He looked at his wristwatch and, realizing he had spent enough time entreating God, departed for his hotel, the Renaissance Jerusalem. Once unpacked and refreshed, he went directly to the Israeli Antiquities Authority.

Golda Rokach loved her position as the receptionist for the IAA. Content with her wages, yet reveling in modest raises over the past 20 years, she felt most rewarded when she was allowed to participate in an archeological expedition, the latest being the search for David's true Jerusalem under the direction of the noted archeologist and historian, Ephraim Stern. This afternoon, she was functioning as the receptionist.

Stein walked in, stepped over to her desk to read her ID tag, then looked into her eyes as she talked on the phone with a site inspector.

She was really quite beautiful. He estimated her age in the fifties, not knowing that her frequent climbs, strenuous exercise program, and vegetable juicing concealed her true age of 64.

"Yes, sir?" she asked cordially as she replaced the phone.

He glanced at her name tag once again, reminding himself that his first impression could favorably maneuver her response. "Ms. Rokach, my name is Mort Stein," he smiled, "and I represent MAS-TERLINK, the financial network out of Athens..."

She waved him off and reached into her handbag. Two seconds later she flashed her MASTERLINK card in his face. "I know who you are," she grinned with raised eyebrows. "With your low interest rates, I'm 'melting' this plastic!"

Pretty soon, there will be no plastic to melt, he didn't say, *there will be only a small dot on your hand.* "You should update with the new microdot system," he said as he reached for her hand. "I am quite confident it will not mar your beauty."

She beamed. "Won't it come off? I mean, my hands are always in dirt," she sighed.

"One would never know it," Stein charmed as he rotated her hand. "Your hands are so smooth—your nails, exquisite." He looked into her eyes as if invading her soul and added softly, "No, it will never come off."

With her mouth hanging open, Golda slowly retracted her hand. "How can I help you, Mr. Stein?"

He pulled a chair next to her desk and sat down. "Well, Golda, we hold a number of museum franchises around the world," he lied, "and we are looking to expand our inventory with antiques or arti-facts from the first century B.C.E. It is our design to fund private grants for newly developed areas where we..."

"Golda!" A voice approaching from the next room interrupted. "Where is our file on Beth Shean?" Krasnoff turned the corner into the receptionist's office, saw Stein next to Ms. Rokach, and came to a sudden halt. "Oh, sorry. I didn't know you were with somebody."

Golda stood up and addressed Stein. "Mr. Stein, meet Mr. Krasnoff, our northern and central division chief. Mr. Krasnoff, Mort Stein of MASTERLINK." The men exchanged handshakes and greetings.

"I'll get with you on this, later," Krasnoff said as he turned on his heel and returned to his desk in time to receive a phone call from his friend Ze've Mazor.

Stein's eyes remained riveted on Krasnoff until he was out of sight.

"Now, where were we? Mr. Stein?" Golda asked curiously. No answer. Stein was preoccupied, processing what had just transpired. A strange feeling had come over him the minute Krasnoff walked into the room, a feeling that he would have to explore afterward. "Mr. Stein?" she repeated an octave higher.

Stein snapped out of the daze. "Oh, yes, Golda," Stein resumed, "as I mentioned, we are looking to invest in any discovery from the first century B.C.E. period." Stein leaned closer to Golda and asked above a whisper, "Do you know of any aspiring archeologist who may have recently made a discovery and needs additional funding?"

Golda gleefully turned to her computer keyboard, typed in several commands, and waited for the results to appear on the monitor. After scrolling down the list for several minutes she said, "There have't been any recent discoveries. However, we just assembled our combined Israeli-British team to begin excavating near the earthquake zone next week."

With Kavidas' concern, Stein had forgotten about the earthquake. "That's very interesting," he said inquisitively. "What area would they be looking in?"

"Of course in Israel, any time someone digs a hole, we hope to find some long-lost treasure or skeleton," she said with a wink, "and in this case, a major upheaval really causes a stir in the archeological community. Our concentration will be in the Jordan Rift Valley—in the Dead Sea area—where the quake did the most damage."

Stein stood up, touched the monitor, then rested his hand on Golda's shoulder. "If I wanted to explore a location in that region that would benefit the cause of archeology, who would I ask to guide me?"

Golda glanced back toward Krasnoff's office and whispered, "Get yourself an Arab Bedouin; they know the deserts of Judea better than anyone."

"You are *one* special lady, Golda," Stein said with a smile as he walked out.

Krasnoff finished his call then went to Golda's desk to get the Beth Shean file and announced, "I'm taking a late lunch. I'm meeting a friend of mine."

Golda took another bite of her sandwich as she waved goodbye to him.

Trude's Bagel Joint on Bezalel street was as good a place as any for Krasnoff to meet his tour guide friend, Ze've Mazor, a frumpy middle-aged Israeli with a long black beard, who claimed to be an expert on every attraction in the Holy Land.

"Do you want an inside booth, or an outside table?" the hostess asked Krasnoff the very moment he stepped into the restaurant.

Krasnoff surveyed the interior for Mazor and then said, "I'm meeting someone; we'll sit outside." The hostess led him to a table. Three minutes later Mazor slowly walked in, sporting a new cane, pulled up a chair and sat down.

"Good to see you once again, Revi," Mazor began in Yiddish, the historic language of the Ashkenazi. Mazor was a childhood friend who had helped Krasnoff refocus on life after Naomi died. Every week for one year he had called Krasnoff to inquire of his well-being, something his own family members never thought to do.

Krasnoff smiled and replied in the same dialect, "Good to see you too, Ze've. How is your family?"

Mazor shrugged his shoulders. "As good as can be expected. But, thank God, we'll get by." Mazor had accidentally fallen into a dig site the year before and still had a noticeable limp. Two months' sick leave while he convalesced had taken its toll on the family budget. However, to capitalize on his injury and receive better gratuities, Ze've told the tourist trade that he had taken a bullet in the Yom Kippur war of 1973. Krasnoff secretly planned to remedy Mazor's financial woes when the newly-found revelatory device was operational. It was his way of saying thank you.

"That's the spirit," Krasnoff replied cheerfully. Seconds later the waitress came to take their lunch orders.

"Here is the list of tour members you asked for, Revi," Mazor said. It was a roster of members on the tour he was conducting, made up of Americans, Britons, and Australians. Israeli law required a registered guide to accompany every tour, even if the tour had brought its own experts. Mazor looked at Krasnoff curiously and asked, "Why do you want these names?"

"My department is compiling a list of possible descendants, both in Israel and abroad, from the ancient Levitical priesthood. A research project born of the emerging interest by some splinter groups to rebuild the Temple. The administration thought we should jumpstart it, so I thought it a good idea to make some firsthand interviews myself before I staff it out." Krasnoff didn't take note that his competency in lying was steadily improving.

Mazor didn't have a suspicious cell in his body. He rubbed his belly in anticipation of lunch then said, "Tomorrow, as I told you over the phone, we will be at Beth Shean, and I can introduce you to anybody you choose."

Krasnoff nodded as he scanned the list of 33 names. The roster identified their hotel, country of origin, and duration of tour. Four names stood out immediately. As he had hoped, they were Americans who fit his criteria. He smiled as lunch arrived.

Back at his office, Krasnoff ran a number of background checks on the four hopefuls. He first accessed a Department of Religious Affairs family lineage search used in the Temple rebuilding project records. Then he contacted Atara L'yoshna and Ateret Cohaniam, two activist organizations dedicated to restoring Jewish life to its former state through the rebuilding of the Temple and training of priests for future Temple service. Next, he ran a credit search of the four candidates through Internet inquiries. Then he examined three CD-ROMs listing the name and family heritage of every person in the United States. These trials allowed him to study the family tree back far enough to narrow the choice to two. It was either the American-born Levy or Cohen. He called Mazor after deciding to go with Cohen.

The El Khanqa Mosque on Khanqa Street, adjacent to the Christian Church of the Holy Sepulcher at the edge of the Muslim quarter, was a place reported to be frequented by faithful Bedouins. Less than half a mile away, the Arab community had converted a mini-mall into a modern day bazaar, a place where Stein believed he would find some answers.

A bearded mullah stood by the entrance to a Muslim book store expounding on a *sura* from the Quran while a horde of Bedouin shepherds sat attentively at his feet. Scores of other Bedouins lolled around the restaurant porticos, while still others entered into heated bargaining debates with the merchants over the price of their wares.

Driving up to the entrance of the Summit restaurant in his Mercedes didn't gain Stein the attention he had hoped for, since many modern petrol-rich Arabs had luxury cars. Nonetheless, several turned their heads toward him as he emerged from his car in a Western dungaree outfit. Almost immediately, several street urchins approached him, begging for money. It was quite obvious they were neglected and possibly homeless. He distributed American five dollar bills to the group while attempting to assess their level of discernment for his own purposes. He selected the shortest one, a child with deep inset eyes who projected a rugged look. He spoke with a lisp and yet displayed what Stein called *chutzpah* or arrogance. The fact that he wore a designer sweatshirt that smacked of entrepreneurship was another consideration. The boy looked about 11 years old.

Stein motioned him toward the rear of his car. "I need your help," Stein said in succinct Arabic.

The enterprising young Bedouin nodded, then held out his hand before replying. Stein grinned and crumpled another five dollar bill into his palm while waving the others away from the area.

"Anything for American," the young Bedouin finally replied with labored speech.

Stein put his hand on the boy's shoulder in an attempt to win his favor and asked, "What is your name?"

"Avraham!" he replied with eyes that blazed when he became excited. Avraham, Stein quickly learned, possessed the ability to negotiate a deal if and when needed.

"My company is searching for *antikas* in the area where the earthquake hit. Can you show me where to look?"

The youngster kicked the dirt under his feet for several moments while he mulled over his response. "My people do not go into that area. The Ta'amireh know the land there," he breathed apologetically as if his income suddenly had been shut off.

Stein looked around the bazaar compound. "Is *anybody* here from that tribe?"

The youth looked at his five dollar bill once again and replied ruefully, "My friend Yasir is, and I guess I could find him for you."

Seizing the moment of opportunity, Stein pulled a twenty dollar bill from his pocket and dangled it in front of the boy. "Well, suppose you locate your friend Yasir, and bring him to me." The lad grabbed the bill and ran off. Five minutes later Avraham reappeared with Yasir, a stocky teenage Bedouin, whom Stein recognized as one of the shabbily dressed urchins he had shooed away earlier. He invited both boys to lunch with him at the Summit.

"Two weeks ago, my cousin, Ishmael, journeyed into the desert early one morning scouting for *antikas* and did not come back," Yasir reported in somber tones with his mouth full of food. "Our whole tribe searched the familiar region for three days until we found some camel droppings and fresh footprints leading to a new cave, but there was no sign of Ishmael. My older cousin said they used to explore that area and that he thought Ishmael may have accidentally fallen down into a newly-formed crevasse or been buried in a landslide."

Stein thought on the predicament and the overall blight of Arab hardships in a moment of sympathy, then pushed another sandwich toward Avraham and Yasir while offering, "If you show me where to go, I'll charter a helicopter and we can search for Ishmael by air."

Their eyes suddenly brightened.

"You mean we get to go up in your helicopter, Mister? Sir?" Avraham asked wishfully with deteriorating speech. He turned to Yasir and gave him a playful nudge.

With a cryptic grin Stein replied, "It will be our secret—just the two of you—okay? After our adventure, you can tell your parents, okay?"

They nodded in unison while digging into bowls of ice cream.

Stein sighed in relief, believing that he would beat out the IAA expedition with plenty of time to spare.

Located between the Jezreel and Jordan valleys in northern Israel is the biblical city of Beth Shean, or Tell el-Husn, inhabited almost continuously from 3500 B.C. to the time of the Crusaders. The one-time fortress/city features the ruins of several towns that include evidences of early Egyptian, Canaanite, and Philistine occupation. In a battle against the Philistines on Mount Gilboa, King Saul was slain and beheaded. The Philistines then carted his body to Beth Shean where they nailed his body to the wall and hung his armor in the house of their god, Ashtaroth.

During the Hellenistic, Roman, and Byzantine periods, the city was known as Scythopolis, "City of the Scythians." Scythopolis was the chief city of the Decapolis, or ten-city region that was traveled by Jesus, cited in the Book of Mark. Remains of ancient mud brick temples, granaries, shops on basalt slab streets, and sidewalks paved with mosaics had been excavated successfully. Stables, and a row of stone pillars for tethering horses, as well as floors paved with cobblestones used during the Israelite conquest, were also found.

Eighteen levels of occupation had been unearthed, ranging from the Chalcolithic period (c. 3500 B.C.E.), to the the time of the Byzantines and Arabs who conquered Palestine in A.D. 637, to the Roman subjugation that ended in A.D. 324. The Roman legacy included a theater, hippodrome, aqueduct, and various public buildings. It was at the ruins of the theater that Krasnoff waited for his friend Ze've Mazor to bring the tour group.

Moments before the bus pulled into the parking lot of the long-abandoned ruins carved out of stone, Nathan Cohen recalled a conversation with his sister back home in Florida: "Why would you want to visit a land of rock where every tourist attraction has to be protected by a soldier? Where hostile forces still vie for territory—where terrorism reigns? If you are really interested in documenting history through photography, why not go to Rome or Turkey where the terrain and people are friendly?" But to Cohen, touring Israel was much more than the exploration of old bones or bricks. It was the land of his Jewish heritage; a land of spiritual awareness; a land that, once visited, left an indelible mark on your soul; a land where he hoped to find God and a meaning to his life.

"You will notice, my friends, that many areas have been cordoned off by the authorities," Mazor announced to the sightseers in broken English as they filed off the bus. "Please remain with the group, and pay particular attention to the areas with the bright yellow ribbons—these areas are for government officials only." Cohen nodded in halfhearted compliance, then scanned the landscape to scope out the potential positions where he might have the opportunity to guardedly slip away from the tour and photograph the historic site.

From the entranceway he looked into the distance. A massive tel consisting of layers of evidences of lost civilizations filled the horizon behind the ancient ruins. The tel provided an arresting backdrop to the remnant of roadways, homes, pillars, and colonnades that remained standing after eons of time. Cohen stood motionless for several moments to gaze at the view and pick out strategic locations to set up his camera tripod.

"Mr. Cohen!" Cohen heard. He turned and saw Mazor walking toward him with another man. "I would like you to meet an associate of mine who works for the IAA, the Israeli Antiquities Authority. He has been asked to give special attention to certain Americans with Jewish ancestry; to rekindle Jewish-American interest in Israeli tourism through archeology. We thought you might be curious enough to want in." Krasnoff was impressed with Mazor's gift of embellishing the truth.

Nathan Cohen, born and raised in Queens, New York, had relocated to Florida with his widowed mother two years earlier while his married sister remained behind. At his mother's insistence he finished an associate degree in a local community college; his passion, however, was not in academia but in nature and landscape photography. One day, he hoped, he would snap the *big one* and rise to world acclaim.

Cohen shot his eyebrows up. "What did you say was in it for me?" he replied sarcastically with a thick New York accent.

Krasnoff heard Cohen's response loud and clear. He looked the husky, athletic man with a shock of black hair and bushy moustache before him in the eye and said, "We will pay your air fare and accommodations here in Israel. How's that for starters?"

"I'm interested," Cohen countered as he playfully kicked a dirt mound at his feet. For a man of 23 years, most of which he had spent negotiating life in New York, he believed he could fend for himself when it came to cutting a deal.

Krasnoff detested bargaining, especially with an arrogant Americanized Jew, but for the sake of his mission, he would endure the trial. He surveyed Cohen's photography equipment and added, "We will give you the opportunity to present to our archival department any quality photographs you take. Your name will be recorded as the *eminent* photographer."

"Now you have my attention," Cohen said as he crossed his arms over his chest.

Krasnoff strolled the short distance toward the Roman amphitheater ruins and motioned for Cohen to accompany him. Mazor took the cue to leave the scene while Cohen lifted his camera bag and followed. "Listen, Mr. Cohen, we are on the brink of an important discovery that will change your life," he stated as if it were fact. "If you have a heart for adventure…and I perceive you do…" he paused for Cohen to acknowledge by nodding, then continued, "and the guts to take risks, then you're the man we are looking for."

Cohen's eyes bored into Krasnoff's as he searched for discernment and direction. Suddenly his mother's voice echoed through his mind, *You're so gullible and wishy-washy, anybody could sell you the Brooklyn Bridge!* He quickly dismissed it, since she only said it when angry. His inquisitive personality needed challenge to feed on. The challenge dictated his response. "I'm in," he said definitively.

Krasnoff smiled. "Here's my card. When you're finished here at Beth Shean, come to my home and we'll get started."

They shook hands.

Flying at an altitude of 2,300 feet above the northern rim of the Judean wilderness at a speed of 140 knots in an American-made Bell 206B3 helicopter was a thrill that few Bedouins would ever enjoy. Sitting in the backseat, Avraham grabbed Yasir's hand and pointed down when the aircraft descended abruptly and rolled his eyes every time it yawed left or right. Swooping between the canyons of the forbidding landscape brought tears to their eyes. Scores of alluvial fans leached out into the canyon floors from centuries of scorching heat baking the soft marl, interrupted only by flash rains that etched monstrous crevasses into the hillsides.

Stein sat in the co-pilot's seat guiding the pilot while waiting on Yasir's directions. Fifteen minutes after they had lifted off from a small private airport near Jerusalem, Yasir gestured to Stein that they were in the area of Khirbet Qumran and that they should reduce their air speed and lower their altitude for closer inspection. The pilot seized the moment and did a fly-by of the settlement ruins moments before Stein advised him to drop to 250 feet and slow to 75 knots in order to survey the terrain in greater detail.

From the air, Yasir pointed to several indicators of the recent earthquake in the barren land. Mountain goat and ibex paths were misaligned, and newly-formed catch basins were evident. New mountain cleavage that lacked debris or silt, or any plant growth, was another sign they were in the right area.

"Over there!" Yasir yelled to Stein, pointing to a cave. Stein nodded and commanded the pilot to land at the base of the mountain.

Suddenly a curious feeling overpowered Stein as he stepped out of the helicopter onto the valley floor. He sensed they were in the proximity of the spiritual phenomenon Gregory Kavidas was concerned about. Almost simultaneously Yasir grabbed his hand and started up the slope toward the cave. Avraham lagged behind, carrying the flashlights.

Soon they were at the entranceway to the cave.

Stein crouched down to inspect the ground. Nike sneaker imprints leading to the interior of the cave were evident inside the entranceway. Wind and other climatic changes had covered over the exterior footprints. He waved the boys over to join him.

"My cousin always wore Nikes!" Yasir exclaimed as he began to cry.

Stein patted him on the back while consoling, "It will be all right, you'll see." He clutched Yasir's hand, grabbed two flashlights from Avraham, and walked into the cave. Within moments Stein concluded by examining the prints that the cave had been undisturbed with the exception of one unknown intruder. Avraham dawdled slightly behind with his own light, curiously scrutinizing the walls and ceilings as he walked.

Suddenly Yasir darted ahead nearly eight yards, then came to an abrupt halt and yelled out, "Mr. Stein, come quick! I think there is a grave here!"

When Stein arrived he closely analyzed the area for several moments. Yasir noticed a queer look on his face. "What do you see, Mr. Stein?"

Stein shook his head while bending down into the grave that had a depression in the earth where a headstone would have been. He ran his fingers through the loose topsoil then closed his eyes and mumbled as if he were praying. Suddenly the topsoil started vibrating as eerie howling noises emerged from the inner sanctums of the cave. It was as if a passageway to a bottomless pit had been opened to release demons to join in Stein's incantations.

"Mr. Stein, is everything okay?!" Yasir cried out.

Stein's head rotated toward Yasir as if on a mechanical axis.

"Look at his eyes!" Yasir yelled to Avraham. "He is under a spell!"

Stein glared at the boys as his mouth hung open, but no words came out. He was hearing a voice that no one else heard. It was the voice from the spirit of an Arab Bedouin named Ishmael when he first unearthed the tomb. "The *lights of...*"

"He shakes!" Avraham yelled out as they jumped backward.

Stein's body convulsed for several seconds then fell limp over the grave. Then he bolted upright and turned with glazed eyes toward the cave entrance. In his mind he saw a replaying of the moving images of the Bedouin named Ishmael lifting twelve stones from an earthen pot. Then in an instant he saw the spirit of the Arab Bedouin named Ishmael descending to an abysmal place in the lower part of the earth. It was there that he would make his abode until Judgment Day.

Adrenaline swept through Yasir's body like a flash flood. He darted over to Stein and shook his shoulders, screaming, "Mr. Stein!

Mr. Stein!" Slowly, Stein's eyes refocused on the Arab boy before him. "What did you see, Mr. Stein?!" Yasir breathed with eyes ablaze.

"I saw your cousin, Ishmael," Stein reported somberly.

"Where is he, then?" The boys asked almost in unison.

"A faraway place—" Stein replied, fumbling for words.

"If he is far away, then he is doing well!" Yasir opined gleefully.

"He is in the land of his fathers," Stein lied compassionately.

Sudden realization of Ishmael's fate came over the boys; they began to weep. Stein embraced them both, then walked them out of the cave and down to the helicopter.

Now, after confirming the discovery of the stones, Stein comprehended Gregory Kavidas' concerns.

Back at his hotel, Stein called Athens on his encrypted cell phone to tell Kavidas that *the ancient lights, the very lights of God* had been found.

Next I give you the test, Krasnoff thought as he watched Nathan Cohen pay the cab driver in front of his home. The preliminaries had been accomplished, but Cohen still had to be conditioned and evaluated. Once he passed the *security* stage, the plan would proceed with breakneck speed.

"Nice evening," Cohen said as he greeted Krasnoff at the door.

Krasnoff simply nodded, his mind racing. "Looking forward to starting the next phase of our mission," he began.

"Sounds military," Cohen quipped.

"Well, it might just as well be 'military' since it is 'top secret.' Can you keep a secret?"

"Sure," Cohen rejoined.

"Come with me." Krasnoff escorted Cohen to the dining room table where he had a variety of 8 x 10 color drawings displayed in three rows. He pointed to a series of four drawings of a high priest and asked, "Have you ever seen anything like this before?"

Cohen looked at Krasnoff with a smirk. "I saw *Raiders of the Lost Ark* with Indiana Jones three times."

"Hmm, you got me on that one," Krasnoff noted with a chuckle. Then he pointed to the breastplate the priest was wearing and asked, "What about this, do you know what this is?"

Cohen picked up the drawing for closer inspection. "Interesting. I remember seeing it in some books when I was in yeshiva." He smacked his head with his hand to awaken some distant memory. "What was that called again?"

"The breastplate," Krasnoff instructed.

"Yeah, I remember that, but there was another name associated with the breastplate..." He paused while running his fingers around the drawing of the breastplate, stopping on the twelve stones. "It was a name that had to do with the stones—a weird kind of name—reminded me of my thumb," Cohen ventured while holding up his hand.

"The Urim and Thummim?"

Cohen grinned. "Yeah, that's it."

Krasnoff then picked up a computer generated chart off the table and placed it in Cohen's hand. "This family tree diagram goes back several hundred years, showing a history that could link a Jewish descendant up with the ancient tribe of priests in Israel. Of course, exact records dating back to the Temple period when the priests officiated have been lost in antiquity, but this gives us a starting point—"

"Wait a minute!" Cohen interjected. "My name is on the top of this chart."

"That's right, Cohen."

Cohen's voice rose. "Then the whole business you were selling me at Beth Shean was really a ploy to get me here."

Krasnoff nodded sheepishly. "True, but the claim to fame is real."

"Meaning...what?" Cohen felt abused and manipulated, yet interested.

Krasnoff grabbed his arm and held it. "Meaning, if you are willing to keep your mouth shut—and not breathe a word of our research project to anyone—I believe we will revolutionize archeology and who knows what else."

"I think I see it in your eyes," Cohen observed. "We're talking notoriety and wealth, aren't we?"

"Yes, lots," Krasnoff replied with a devilish guffaw.

"Tell me more about the *project*," Cohen queried, his eyes pleading for understanding.

"In time, in time," Krasnoff replied, quoting the now immortal Ishmael ben Azin. "But first we need to test your blood."

"You what?!"

Krasnoff explained with the half truth, "There is a new DNA analysis that we are developing that helps us to settle claims on ancient property disputes or confirm family heritage, you know, lineage, back for centuries. I want to check yours." Krasnoff knew within himself that the experimental test was being used to help determine ancestry to the priesthood, but Cohen didn't need to know that now.

The young man went silent for a moment.

"Cohen?" Krasnoff asked.

"I'm thinking."

"I need you to make this project work!" Krasnoff pressed.

Cohen thought he heard his mother's voice in his mind warning him again. He shrugged his shoulders, then held his index finger out.

Krasnoff smiled, knowing that Cohen would keep the secret. He was willing to seal the covenant with his blood.

CHAPTER

5

Jerusalem

Krasnoff carefully studied Nathan Cohen's DNA fingerprinting and mapping test results. The tests concentrated on serology and genetic encoding, primarily used in crime detection and human trait determination—hardly reliable for confirming *ancient* family heritage—but it would be added evidence of his priesthood ancestry.

Anticipation mixed with hope when he read that the tests were positive. His preliminary inquiries and trials pointed to Cohen's candidacy, but now with a positive hit on the DNA test, he was ready to proceed. The final test, however, that of successfully operating the stones, would be the determining factor.

Rap-rap-rap-rap. Cohen impatiently knocked on Krasnoff's door. "What's up?" he asked Krasnoff as the door opened. Slightly out of breath after scaling the stairs to Krasnoff's condo, he added, "Your message sounded urgent." He had not heard from Krasnoff for three days.

Krasnoff invited him in as he beamed, "The blood tests are favorable! That's a go-ahead for us!"

Cohen raised an eyebrow. "Okay, sounds good, but what does it mean?"

Krasnoff walked him to the kitchen table for coffee and bagels. "It means that there is a high probability that you are a descendant of the high-priesthood of ancient Israel. Of course, as I alluded to before, no one but God knows for sure—since Herod destroyed all the temple records—but based on available data and testing techniques, the findings are good enough for me."

"I can't believe it..." Cohen fumbled for words as his eyes filled with tears. "You're telling me that there is royalty in my family?" A smile broke out on his face. "My mom is going to flip when she hears this. To think that her son, who just squeezed through college with an associate's degree, would be heir to the priesthood." He shook his head in disbelief.

"Ahh, I thought we covered that item." Krasnoff said with his arms crossed over his chest. "You can't tell your mom about this. In fact, you can't tell anybody—just you and I know about this—our secret, remember?"

Cohen looked annoyed. "How long is this *stuff* to remain a secret? I mean, sooner or latter I'm going to have to tell my family why I'm staying on in Israel."

"Agreed," Krasnoff replied, "but for now, we need to keep this enterprise under wraps until we develop the equipment." *And after the stones are operating, who knows what will happen, Mr. Cohen*, he didn't say. "Then, there will be plenty of time for celebrating and notoriety."

Cohen nodded in assent. "Okay, then what is next on the agenda?" He was now of the persuasion that since there was a *blood covenant* between them, Cohen could treat Krasnoff like a partner.

Krasnoff rolled his tongue in his mouth while he collected his thoughts. The time of decision to move forward with progressive revelation, as he called it, was now. Could he trust Cohen? Up until now he had made no real investment in Cohen, but once he showed Cohen the stones, there was no turning back. Of course the matter of acquisition—how he had acquired the stones—would never be disclosed, but still, Krasnoff thought, the onus was on him. Cohen had nothing to lose. He sighed and pondered, *But where else can I go? Start all over? Too late. This Cohen has the key to operating the mechanism—I have to trust him.*

"It's time for the unveiling," he replied smartly. "Sit tight." Krasnoff went into his bedroom, returned after several moments with the earthen jar and headstone, and placed them on the table.

"What in the world—?" Cohen muttered.

"If you were impressed with the drawings I showed you three days ago, you're going to love this," Krasnoff began with a twinkle in his eye. He pulled the stones out of the jar and carefully set them on the linen cloth.

"Oh my God!" Cohen gulped, "...what are these?" He fell into staccato out of sheer amazement as he fingered the gems. "Are these real? I mean, they look and feel real..." He turned to the earthen jar and held it in his hand while trying to make out the inscription. Next he held up the headstone. "What is this?"

Krasnoff clutched it carefully. "My research shows it to be the actual headstone marker used on the grave of the high priest." He turned the headstone over and pointed, "See this menorah? It is the symbol used in ancient Israel for the high priest." Then Krasnoff ran his index finger over the four dots engraved above the menorah. "These four dots serve as substitutes for the four-letter Hebrew name of Israel's God: *Yod heh vav heh*, normally spelled Yahweh in modern texts..." Krasnoff paused and thumped his foot on the floor to dramatize his point. "That's how I know these things are genuine." He smiled like a Cheshire cat and added, "The real thing." Then he picked up several of the gems and continued, "The problem is with these stones. They are from the high priest's breastplate and the Urim and Thummim."

"The gizmos in the drawings?"

"Right." Krasnoff then rearranged them carefully on the cloth.

"How do they work?"

"That's the problem." He placed the drawings on the table as a reminder. "You can see my preliminary drawings showing the arrangements of the stones, but alas, they do not work." Then he placed on the table several sketches and photocopies of lithographs from old periodicals and trade magazines. "These show the alignment of the stones worn by the high priest. With the Bible's description, I hope to duplicate the setting in the breastplate, and ultimately the Urim and Thummim. Then we can get down to business."

"But one important question comes to mind," Cohen asked curiously while tumbling one of the gems. "How—"

The phone rang.

Krasnoff quickly reached for the phone on the wall with a sigh of relief. He had no intentions of going any deeper at this time. "Shalom."

"Daddy, I called you at work and they told me you took the day off," Leah said. "Is everything all right?"

Krasnoff took his eyes off the jewels momentarily to focus on his daughter's voice. "Everything's fine, Leah. I just needed a break from the office to concentrate on a dig in Galilee that is giving me some trouble." He shot a look to Cohen, who didn't hear the lie since he was concentrating on the stones on the table.

"Well, okay, I was just concerned for you."

A thin smile broke out on Krasnoff's face. "Thanks, darling."

"I won't be home tonight," Leah said. "I going down to Eilat with Shlomo. I'll be back tomorrow."

"See you then," Krasnoff replied as he replaced the phone in its cradle.

"Who's Leah?" Cohen asked.

"My daughter," he replied in a guarded tone.

"Sounds like you two are real close. That's nice," Cohen observed.

Krasnoff dismissed Cohen's remark, lifted the diamond, and said, "She's my heart since her mother died." Then he replaced the diamond. Cohen looked at him, expecting more information.

"Sorry to hear about that," Cohen said.

Krasnoff turned, stared at a spot on the wall, and added with vehemence, "She was killed by a Palestinian terrorist attack."

"Ugh," Cohen uttered. He paused to dwell on that horror, then began fiddling with the smaller stones. "There is a question that came to mind before your daughter called. It's about all these things..." he motioned to the artifacts on the table. "In the last three days, while you were doing your thing with my blood, I've been doing some research on my own, and I'm a little confused about something."

"And that is?" Krasnoff asked guardedly.

"After seeing your drawings, my curiosity was piqued so I bought a few books on the subject. Most of them state that the high priest's garb and equipment have not been seen since the time of David. And by my reckoning, that's nearly three thousand years ago! Then, one book in particular quoted the Talmud as saying, 'Five things were lacking in the rebuilt Temple: (1) The Ark of the Covenant (2) Holy Fire (3) The Shekinah Glory (4) The Spirit of Prophecy and (5) the Urim and Thummim.' " He looked Krasnoff in the eye and concluded, "So how in the world did they survive, and how did you manage to get them?"

Krasnoff had already rehearsed this question and answer in his mind, so he was not surprised by Cohen's inquiry. He just hadn't expected it so early in the game. "Two weeks ago I was out on a dig at

Murabba'at, a remote desert area twelve miles south of Qumran on the western shore of the Dead Sea. The region had just been hit by an earthquake. In my experience, that's a good time to explore. As luck would have it, I found both the jar containing the priest's apparatus and the headstone in a remote cave. It was a newly opened cave— probably from the recent earthquake.

"As to how they have lasted all this time: My theory, and much of it is based on archeological experience, is that the high-priesthood took precautions to preserve the line by squirreling away the Temple 'hardware' in nature's 'safe-deposit' box, the Judean desert, where the climate preserves things like they were in a vacuum."

"For nearly three thousand years?"

"Well don't forget, the remnants we have are all *stone*. We have the *earthen* pot, the *headstone*, and the *precious stones*, all made of rock that doesn't decompose. Then, the jar had a wax seal on it that prevented any moisture or air from entering in. So these factors seem to account for their preservation. Then of course, it is obvious that no one could find them because…" he paused and pointed upward, "God sealed the cave until the day that I would be exploring."

"Sounds plausible," Cohen said with a nod.

"It is possible that thousands of years ago," Krasnoff continued, "they were put into the cave by a group of priests to prevent them from falling into the hands of the Assyrian, Babylonian, or even Greek conquerors. Just because they are not mentioned in the Bible after David's time doesn't mean that they were destroyed—they just haven't been seen." He teetered forward in his chair and opined, "Who's to say that God didn't supernaturally hide them for such a time as this?" Cohen had no way of knowing that only Krasnoff's last words were true.

Cohen mentally started gearing up for the challenge. He toyed with the stones for several minutes, then picked up the diagrams and

pulled a pen from his shirt pocket to begin sketching his own config-
urations. "Can you get me a Bible?" he asked. "I want to examine the
passages dealing with the high priest."

Krasnoff quickly deduced Cohen had made his final decision.
"One more thing. You need to move in here with me and my daughter
as soon as possible."

Cohen's brow furrowed. "Why, so you can keep an eye on me?"
he said defensively. "Don't you trust me?"

"It's not that. For one thing, we need to concentrate on getting
the stones operational. That's going to take a considerable amount of
time and a concerted effort on your part. Next, and take this in the
proper spirit, there is a huge amount of wealth involved here. I mean
these jewels are worth a fortune, so I view it as a security matter. We
need to minimize our public exposure until we achieve the desired
success."

Nathan Cohen thought on Krasnoff's words for a moment then
snickered. "Is that your idea of the promised *accommodations?*"

Krasnoff patted him on the shoulder. "Let's get to work."

Standing under the awning of the IAA building holding a bouquet of long-stemmed roses as a thunder and lightning storm raged in
the distance seemed to have a calming effect on Stein. He watched the
intense energy being displayed in the sky while remaining at a safe
distance. He felt protected. In a way it was a portent of what lay ahead
for him and Kavidas. The world would soon undergo a God-ordained
cataclysmic change, but they would remain secure. The only danger
he saw on the horizon was *the ancient lights…*

With him it was not a hunch, nor was it intuition or a gut feeling.
In reality, it was independent of reasoning. It was an internal voice

directing him to pursue this line of investigation. There was some connection with the lights of God and the IAA, he was sure of it.

"Good afternoon, Ms. Rokach," Stein said happily as he greeted the IAA receptionist once again. "I thought you might enjoy these lively beauties..." he abruptly paused and waved his free arm around, "amidst all the dead bones your agency digs up."

Golda Rokach gave out with a roaring laugh, then blushed. "You're very thoughtful, Mr....?" She remembered his face, but had forgotten his name.

"Stein. Mort Stein."

"Ah, yes, I remember now. The man from MASTERLINK in Athens. Right?"

"Right." Stein propped the roses on a corner of her desk and said, "I thought I'd stop in to see you once again, Golda. To have a chat and maybe do lunch."

Golda fussed with her hair as she fidgeted in her chair. "I'll pass on lunch," she said modestly. "What's on your mind?"

Stein pulled up a chair and said, "I took your advice and hired a Bedouin guide to explore the area at Qumran affected by the earthquake, but I really didn't find anything worthwhile. So I was wondering if the Israeli-British team you mentioned ever found anything?" Stein unwittingly squinted as he watched Golda's facial reaction to his carefully worded question.

"Hmm, let me see," she replied, nibbling on her index finger. She turned to her computer station and typed a command on the keyboard. Ten seconds later she pointed into the next room and said, "That project is being headed up by Rehavam Krasnoff, our investigator..."

Stein waved her off as a jolt of adrenaline swept over him. "I remember who he is—your northern and central division chief."

Golda blinked and slowly nodded as Stein's face took on a concerned look. He began to stare at the wall. "Is everything all right, Mr. Stein?"

Stein bit his lip, seeming to see through the wall with X-ray vision. In his spirit he knew that something was here but he couldn't identify it. *Is Krasnoff the one?* he wondered. *If only I could hold his hand.* He nodded and said, "Fine," then pointing toward Krasnoff's room added, "I'd like to meet your boss someday."

"We can accommodate you." Golda picked up her phone and pressed the intercom button. "Mr. Krasnoff, someone would like to meet you. He's sort of a celebrity—Mr. Mort Stein, one of the heads of MASTERLINK. Do you have a minute?"

Moments later Krasnoff walked out of his office.

As soon as Stein's eyes met Krasnoff's, a spirit of disquietude came over Stein. Stein stood up as Krasnoff walked toward him and extended his hand. "It is a pleasure to meet you, Mr. Krasnoff," Stein began, clasping Krasnoff's hand. "Ms. Rokach tells me you are supervising the explorations in the earthquake zone in the Dead Sea area. As an avid follower of archeology, I am always anxious to hear if there have been any recent discoveries." He strengthened his grip and added with a chuckle, "Of course I wouldn't expect you to divulge any *national secrets* or anything like that, but did you find any newly opened caves, fossils, or artifacts?"

After several seconds of hesitation to process Stein's lengthy introduction, Krasnoff tugged his hand free and replied, "We have been excavating at Murabba'at, recently. When the earthquake hit, we found some surface displacement that could lead to discovery and several new fissures that have possibilities, but nothing substantive."

Stein shook his head and replied kindheartedly, "Oh, that's unfortunate. I was rooting for you to be written up in the *Archeological Review* or some other trade magazine for uncovering a piece of Solomon's Temple or something like that."

Krasnoff did a double take. "Well, if we had, the news media would have been alerted." He turned to leave and added flippantly,

"But who knows? One day you may hear about my digging up Aaron's Rod." He waved and said, "Nice meeting you." Golda looked up when she heard the lock on Krasnoff's door close.

Stein's eyes were transfixed on Krasnoff's space when he had vacated it. He looked down at his right hand and began rubbing it, then shut his eyes for a moment as if he were listening to a recording.

Golda noticed a queer expression on Stein's face. "Mr. Stein? Can I get you a cup of coffee?"

Stein snapped out of twilight and sat down again. "No, I need to be going," he said and abruptly stood up and walked out.

Behind the door, Krasnoff stood holding his hand. He felt emotionally drained, as if his soul had been violated.

"He has an aura about him that smacks of deception," Stein reported to Kavidas over his encrypted cell phone. "I held his hand until there was a transference; I was able to sense a disturbed nimbus that I read as a sign of his involvement. Together with his position at IAA where he has accessibility to heretofore unknown archeological locations—I'm ninety percent sure that he is the one with the *lights*."

"Has there been any evidence pointing to its operation?" Kavidas probed. *Finding the apparatus is one thing*, he thought. *Making it work to reveal my identity is quite another*.

"None that I'm aware of. He's probably in the experimental stage."

"Good, then we still have some time," Kavidas replied in mild relief.

"I detect a heightened sense of urgency. What is our timetable?" Stein asked poignantly.

"Because of MASTERLINK's unique position in the world economy, the board of directors of the European Economic Community

(EEC) have asked me to take the presidency in ninety days. You will be needed here, so you must complete your work by then."

"Hmm, yes, but I may have to resort to some drastic measures in order to resolve this quickly. For now, since my contact at IAA is proving profitable, I'm only considering having him followed, but that may change."

"You have full authority, Mort, you know that," Kavidas reassured in somber tones. "Just make sure that the *lights* are destroyed." *Click*. The phone went dead.

Cohen rubbed his sweaty palms on his pants, then rolled his tongue in his dry mouth as if he were about to perform brain surgery on a head of state. He assembled all of Krasnoff's diagrams on the left of the table, the stones atop a linen cloth that would simulate the breastplate in the center, and an open Bible to his right. The table, now relocated to his bedroom, would be his work station.

Beginning where Krasnoff left off, Cohen assembled the twelve large stones, representing the twelve tribes, in the marching formation during the wilderness journey described in Numbers chapter 2; three vertical rows of four stones each. Based on the diagrams and text, he had every confidence that the alignment for the large stones was correct. The proper configuration for the smaller stones that made up the Urim and Thummim would take some work, since there were no existing diagrams or sketches of them. Fortunately, the ratio of possibilities was small since there were only three stones. But getting them in the proper pattern troubled him.

His first attempt was to place the small stones in a horizontal pattern directly above the breastplate, with the blue sapphire on the right, the purple amethyst in the center, and the scarlet jasper on the left. He then gulped as he read a Bible passage where the Urim and Thummim had been used, held his breath, then asked it a question.

Nothing happened.

Next he reversed the sequence of the stones and repeated the question.

Nothing happened.

"Sure, we have all day," he sarcastically muttered to the stones, then realigned them into a vertical pattern with the blue sapphire on top, the purple amethyst in the center, and the scarlet jasper on the bottom. Once again he asked it a question, only to have the same answer, nothing.

It occurred to him that an L-pattern representing Lord or a Y-pattern representing Yahweh, with the same color order, blue/purple/scarlet, might work, but to no avail. Finally, after two more hours of trials, he shook his head in disgust and abruptly stood up. He walked into the kitchen to have lunch.

As he opened up the refrigerator he looked up and said, "God, why can't You make this easy?" The thought suddenly came over him that he had better not be concerned with what God really thought of the whole matter. "Never mind," he added and made himself a sandwich. Moments later he heard a key slipping into the front door lock.

"Back early," Krasnoff announced as the door slammed closed. "I hope you made some progress!"

Cohen swallowed hard. "In here having lunch."

Krasnoff joined in the sandwich making process as he waited for Cohen to give him an update on his work with the stones. "Well...?" he asked after several moments of silence. "Anything to report?"

"Nothing yet."

"How many patterns did you try?" Krasnoff asked impatiently.

"Many patterns, many hours," Cohen replied wearily.

"You're not ready to give up, are you?"

"Of course not. Just getting away from it for a while—a man's got to eat, you know."

Don't push, Krasnoff reminded himself. It was not a good plan to aggravate Cohen when he was just starting on the experiments. He bit his lip, nodded, and then worked on his sandwich.

"I've been thinking about something and I would like a straight answer," Cohen finally said after several moments of deep thought. "During my experiments I began to question in my mind something you told me about the Urim and Thummim."

Krasnoff loosened his collar. "Such as?"

"Well..." Cohen began inquisitively as he stood up to walk back into his bedroom, "considering you work for IAA, how come they didn't demand you surrender the gems, headstone, and Urim and Thummim over to them? I mean, after all, they are national treasures of a sort."

Krasnoff followed him to the doorway, then paused for a moment to search his mind for a suitable answer. "You have to understand something of what's going on here in Israel," he explained passionately. "There are political factions right here in Jerusalem, namely the Palestinians, and even the Goyim—Gentiles—that are vying for control of our holy sites, and ultimately our homeland. As a Zionist, I am committed to reconstituting a Jewish state, and I believe that if I gave over these jewels along with the Urim and Thummim, somehow the Arabs would make claim to them and then use them as a weapon against us. They would probably wind up on display in the Dome of the Rock." He studied Cohen's reaction and added, "So as central division chief, I exercised my prerogative to hold on to them for a while in the interest of 'national security.' "

Cohen stared at Krasnoff then scratched his head in bewilderment. Krasnoff seemed to have an answer for everything, but his answers did not ring true. "Is that really the reason? Are you telling me the truth?" he pleaded.

Krasnoff held up his right hand. "As God is my witness."

Cohen shook his head in disbelief at Krasnoff's oath. In his heart he believed that self-interest had something to do with Krasnoff's motives, something he conveniently had never mentioned. "Fine. Let's get back to work." He took five steps and shouted, "Oh my God! Look!"

Krasnoff raced to the table and with eyes blazing exclaimed, "The stones are lighting up!"

Cohen peered at the Urim and Thummim stones that were now in a triangular pattern above the breastplate stones. He quickly assessed what had happened: When he stood up to go into the kitchen he must have knocked against the table and rearranged the stones. The blue sapphire was now at the apex of the triangle, the purple amethyst in the left corner and the red jasper in the right corner. The scarlet jasper shone brightly while the other two were growing dark. "Holy—!" Cohen blinked. "What does it mean?"

"It means you found the right pattern! Hallelujah!"

"A triangle?"

Krasnoff scratched his chin then said, "The triangle is an ancient diagram for the Trinity."

"Get out—!" Cohen gulped. "You're kidding, right?"

"No. In graduate school I researched symbols and numbers cited in the Bible." Krasnoff pointed to the three small stones and continued, "The number three is considered to be the symbol for the triune Godhead in both Old and New Testament commentaries, while the triangle stands for the Christian's belief in the Trinity." He waved his hand over all the stones and added, "The Urim and Thummim is a symbol for the mind of God."

Cohen fell into his chair. "Whew! This is heavy!" He tapped the table for several seconds as he gazed at the glowing stone, then said, "You mean that way back in *time...*" he gestured backward with his hand, "they believed in the Christian concept of the Trinity?"

"Apparently," Krasnoff halfheartedly agreed.

Cohen needed time to digest that hunk of meat. "Yeah, but what triggered off the lighting?" he asked rhetorically. He stood up, looked squarely at the Urim and Thummim stones, and asked curiously, "What was the last thing we were talking about?"

"My holding on to the treasure for 'national security purposes,' remember?"

"Yeah, right," Cohen recalled. "Then I asked you the question, 'Are you telling me the truth?' as we walked into the room." His jaw tightened as he meditated on the development. "It must respond to questions asked." He stared at the stones once again for a moment then snapped his fingers and reached for his Bible. "I just read about this yesterday," he added as he turned in the Bible to First Samuel 14:41. "Here it says in this version that quotes Saul out of the Septuagint after he made a rash vow before God concerning a battle against the Philistines, 'If the fault is in me or my son Jonathan, respond with Urim, but if the men of Israel are at fault, respond with Thummim.' So let's use that language." He glanced at Krasnoff suspiciously, then back at the stones and rephrased the question, "Did Rehavam tell me the truth? If yes, give Urim, but if not, give Thummim."

The red jasper illuminated brightly while the other two stones remained dim.

Cohen shot a look at Krasnoff then tried the experiment again to differentiate the two. "If these are from God, give Urim—turn blue; if not, give Thummim—turn scarlet."

The blue sapphire illuminated.

"You dirty—" Cohen breathed, "you lied to me about where these stones came from!"

"I had to," Krasnoff confessed as he walked out into the kitchen. "If I had told you the truth, you wouldn't have helped me."

Cohen followed him. "Then *where* did you get them?"

"I bought them from an old Bedouin. He didn't have a clue as to what they were. He didn't even think the stones were real." He pulled out his wallet to dramatize his point. "It cost me every shekel I had, including my pension money and a second mortgage on this place."

"Oh, so they really belong to the Arabs, then," Cohen surmised indifferently.

Krasnoff sharpened his approach. "As a Jew, would you want this device in the hands of the Arabs?"

Cohen was reminded once again of Krasnoff's hatred for the Arabs. "No."

"Well, then, you can understand why I had to make up the story."

Cohen shrugged his shoulders. "I suppose."

Krasnoff reveled in his temporary triumph, not knowing that God had heard the lie: The scarlet stone shone brightly, but no one saw it.

The front door opened and closed.

"My daughter!" Krasnoff warned as he gestured toward Cohen's bedroom. "Make sure everything is put away." Cohen nodded and slipped into his bedroom as Leah rounded the kitchen corner.

"Hello, darling. How was Eilat, the tourist capital of Israel?" Krasnoff asked warmly.

"Great," Leah said with a smile. "Shlomo and I snorkeled and partied a little. The rest of the time we just rested."

He put his arm around her waist and said, "Wonderful." Then he ushered her into the living room and said, "I'd like to introduce you to one of my research associates. We are working on a project to-gether so he will be staying with us for a while." He walked to Cohen's bedroom and knocked gently on the door. "Cohen, can you come out for a moment?"

Anticipating the meeting, Cohen brightened his appearance. Krasnoff was taken by surprise when he saw how good he could look. "Nathan Cohen, my daughter, Leah."

Cohen was struck by her Semitic beauty. Long black hair cas-caded over her petite shoulders, bringing out a low luster to her pure textured skin flowing smoothly toward flared black eyebrows that fell naturally around large blue eyes. With a height of over five-feet-five, augmented with three-inch high heels on a slender body, Leah was a knockout.

"Whoa!" Cohen said with a leering smile, "Talk about national treasures!"

Leah raised an eyebrow as Cohen continued to survey her. "Nice to meet you, Mr. Cohen."

"Please call me Nat," he insisted.

"Leah has been dating Shlomo Rubin, the prime minister's nephew," Krasnoff announced to douse the spontaneous combustion in Cohen's mind.

"Oh, you're seeing somebody." He rolled his eyes. "Too bad."

Leah turned on her heel and said, "I have to get ready for my date tonight. Are you both eating in?"

Krasnoff and Cohen traded looks. "Yes," Krasnoff answered for both of them, "we have important work to finish."

Cohen looked disappointed, but accepted his sentence graceful-ly. "Maybe we could have lunch sometime," he suggested.

"Maybe," she replied coquettishly and dashed off to her bedroom.

Cohen gave her a thumbs up as she vanished in a whirlwind of commotion. *She likes me, and I could easily like her*, he said confidently to himself as hormonal enzymes surged in his body.

"We should return to our task at hand," Krasnoff reminded Cohen. "Time is slipping away." Cohen agreed. As they stepped into his bedroom, Krasnoff added, "Leah is not to know about this. Clear?"

Cohen was getting the picture in puzzle form; each piece fit together to mean complete secrecy. "Understood."

Krasnoff walked to the radio on the dresser and turned it on to muffle their conversation. He said, "We need to experiment with the 'UT' as I call it to familiarize ourselves with it. Let's set it up." He went outside to the next room for a moment then returned with a book in his hand.

Cohen pulled the breastplate and Urim and Thummim from his end table drawer, walked to the portable table, and assembled the stones in their proper order. "Ready," he said nervously as if he were about to launch a rocket.

Krasnoff tapped Cohen's hand with his finger to calm him down as he thumbed through the Bible. He stopped in Deuteronomy chapter 33. "Way back *when*, as an aspiring archeologist, I learned this verse from a colleague in passing. Now I would like to find out if my hunch is correct. It says here in verse 24, 'And of Asher he said, Let Asher be blessed with children; let him be acceptable to his brethren, and let him dip his foot in *oil*.' " Krasnoff then opened up the Bible atlas he had brought in. He turned to the Tribal Distribution of Palestine chart and put an 'x' on a town in western Galilee by the name of Karmiel, located almost halfway between the seacoast city of Acco and the Sea of Galilee. Krasnoff turned with a smile to Cohen and said, "The area of Karmiel is the modern day location of the ancient land of promise to the tribe of Asher, the son of Jacob." He drew a circle that encompassed the seacoast of the Mediterranean Sea from the northern city of Tyre in Lebanon to Nazareth in the south. " This whole region is where the tribe of Asher settled." He paused to rub his palms together then said, "Now ask the UT if there is oil under the ground in Karmiel."

Cohen squirmed in his seat, then rubbed his eyes in an attempt to actualize what his ears were hearing. "You think there are oil deposits there?"

"Yes, I do. Ask the question."

Cohen looked at the array of stones before him and suddenly felt inept. He put on a pious look and said, "If there is oil in Karmiel, give Urim—turn blue; if not, give Thummim—turn scarlet."

Suddenly the stones began vibrating slightly. A wave of fear swept over Cohen as he abruptly pushed himself away from the table. He covered his mouth with his hand and mumbled, "Oh my God, they're alive!" He could not get used to the idea that God could communicate with His creatures in such a profound way.

The blue stone shone brightly.

"The blue sapphire is definitely yes," Krasnoff concluded correctly, "while the red jasper must be no."

"The purple amethyst must be either maybe, not now, wait," Cohen noted dryly, "or like with the traffic signal, caution."

"Good guess," Krasnoff replied tersely.

They heard a knock. "Is everything okay in there?" Leah shouted through the door. "You guys are making a racket."

Krasnoff gestured to Cohen to quiet down, then said aloud, "We're fine, honey!" He grinned at Cohen and added, "We're just making a breakthrough! See you tomorrow." They heard the front door close as Leah walked out.

The following morning Krasnoff went to a neighborhood realtor and purchased two hundred acres of vacant land in the low-lying area of the hilly region of Karmiel and put it in Leah's name. Then he contracted a commercial petroleum scientist to survey and test it.

It was mid-morning when Cohen realized he was not alone in the house. Through Internet access he had been preoccupied searching and downloading a multitude of documents relative to the Temple priesthood and the ancient operation of the sacred breastplate along with the Urim and Thummim. He quickly discovered that little information was available when he used a search engine that bypassed the Bible, but when he accessed the various names regarding the garments worn by the high priest through Christian or biblical sources, a vast quantity of information came up. He was surprised to learn that some Bible scholars who focused on eschatology believed that in the final days of man on earth there would be an outpouring of knowledge and revelations, and that this increase would be one more facet in God's program that would signal the nearness of the Messiah's return.

He heard rustling in the kitchen while he mentally tried to sort out this information. *Could it be that God has allowed the discovery of the UT at this time because of what these Christian scholars claim? And what about this Messiah business? They speak about His "return" as if His first appearance were an established fact.* His head was swimming in a whirlpool of computer bytes and CD-ROMs that brought him this confusing data. He shook his head as he pushed away from the computer console and walked out of his room, but not before making sure the door was locked.

"Good morning, Nat," Leah said gleefully.

Startled, he replied, "What are you doing here? No work today?"

She pointed to the window and the dreary rain it kept out. "Taking a 'rain' day for myself."

"Do you mind if I sit down with you and have a cup of coffee?"

Leah waved him over to the table and asked quaintly, "Tell me about yourself, Nat. What brought you to Israel?"

Cohen realized that he would have to embellish on the truth to avoid divulging any information relative to her father's mission, one that had now engulfed his entire life as well. "Photography. I do professional photography, specializing in archeology."

"That's really interesting," Leah replied as she went into reflection. "I suppose with my father being a division chief over at IAA I should take more of an interest in that stuff, but I don't." She raised her eyebrows and added, "I want to pursue a career in politics. Right now I'm only an intern at the Knesset, but I shoot high."

"We need more beautiful politicians," he returned with a smile while his eyes brushed over her loveliness.

"Thanks."

"How's Shlomo doing?" Cohen probed, hoping for a negative report so that he might make some inroads.

"He's doing great. His uncle is the prime minister, you know, and I expect Shlomo will run for office in the parliament next term."

"You're not serious," Cohen gulped in amazement. "That's fabulous."

"Well, not exactly. We sometimes clash over our political views, but mostly argue about our religious positions; he is a liberal, I am a conservative. We get along wonderfully, provided we avoid the controversial issues that I believe threaten our nation."

Cohen took a sip of his coffee then asked, "What kinds of issues?"

"Well, the hot topic is the increasing volume of 'completed Jews' that are popping up all over. The girl next to me at work is one, and I have a real problem with it. She's always trying to convert me."

"Isn't that the term taken by Jewish people who believe Jesus is the Messiah?"

"Yes. They claim they remain Jewish, and have found *completion* in him. My co-worker insists she is more Jewish now."

"Doesn't Shlomo see them as a threat?"

"Not really. I've become the bad guy because I believe they are no longer Jewish—they're Christians now. Further, I maintain that the movement is hypertrophying—growing by the day—and metastasizing into some kind of uncontrollable disease that will inflict Eretz Israel, the land of Israel, unless something is done. Shlomo, on the other hand, believes 'live and let live.' If the 'movement' should reach an abnormal proportion, according to him, then the administration will enact policy to deal with it.

"But in my mind, it will be too late by then. They will be too big. I believe in 'preventative medicine,' but he talks as if he can't be bothered with the viral strain until it reaches epidemic proportion— like with AIDS—then we would do something about it. He would probably hope for a wonder drug or pray that those *Christians* mysteriously disappear."

"That sounds familiar," Cohen replied woefully. "We've gone on that merry-go-round in America for years, on that very issue, AIDS, with devastating results."

Leah bobbed her head in dismay. "I do admit that this lady at work is different, however, so there must be some truth to her faith. I mean no matter what happens, she is always at peace, praising the..." she paused to make imaginary quotation marks in the air, "...Lord."

Cohen gave out with a titter. "Do *you* think there's any truth to her claim?"

"Well, when I used to study the Bible I was always troubled about the messianic passages during the time we celebrated Passover. When I would read Moses' account of Passover in Exodus, then sneak a look at Isaiah 53, which the Christians claim refers to Christ, I thought our rabbis gave us the wrong scoop. It reads like Jesus Christ *is* the Passover Lamb.

"Last Passover, this girl at work started a debate with me when she said that God allowed the Temple to be destroyed by the Roman government in A.D. 70 because it was no longer needed once Christ died on the cross. That his death satisfied the requirements of the Levitical law, that's why there is no Temple today, and according to her, we cannot receive forgiveness of sins on Yom Kippur for that very reason—we cannot satisfy the law of sacrifice."

"So in her mind, believing in Jesus satisfies this predicament?"

"I guess."

"You sound like you're really doubting what we have been told to believe, that Jesus cannot be the Messiah."

"Hmm, well, maybe some other time we could talk about it."

Cohen felt challenged by Leah's remarks. What's more, her observations, answers, and thought processing excited him, giving rise to the potential unleashing of passion. He swallowed the rest of his coffee and returned to his room with the notion of looking to the Bible for answers to some hard questions. In his mind, "the Leah thing" as he put it, would unfold on its own.

It was four days before the results of the oil exploration tests at Karmiel returned. The petroleum geologist's report indicated a vast presence of oil 13 hundred feet below the surface of the undeveloped land. Krasnoff then went to his bank and placed the report and the bill of sale in his safe deposit box. His design was to hold the property until oil prices rose once again, then he would take action. But for now, his land and the oil were secure.

"Your interest in the land at Karmiel is thirty percent," Krasnoff advised Cohen at the breakfast table on the morning after placing the documents in his vault. "Since my personal resources are depleted I had to bring in Leah's inheritance money to put up the capital, so together our share should be larger than yours. However, as we discover more sites that bring in money, we will renegotiate the percentage. Fair enough?"

Cohen puckered his lips as he thought on the matter while buttering a bagel. For him, the deal was sweet since he had invested no cash, only his time. But there were other risks worth considering. Was there a divine curse that went along with tampering with God's UT? He wasn't really sure about that, but he had been thinking along those lines recently. The more he studied the Bible the more apparent it became that in the Old Testament economy there were certain things you didn't mess with regarding God's holiness. He remembered reading in Leviticus about Aaron's sons, Nadab and Abihu, who made a profane offering on the altar of God and how they were consumed by fire on the spot. Then there was Uzzah in Second Samuel who, when the oxen carrying the ark of the covenant stumbled, causing it to shake, attempted to steady the ark, and in turn was struck dead. *I suppose I would have been struck dead by now if what we were doing was evil*, he concluded. "Sure, fair enough," he agreed. "You know, I was taking the UT through some 'drills' if you will, the other day," he explained in the next breath. "Together with the Bible, I discovered some interesting information."

"Uh-oh," Krasnoff replied as if Cohen had secretly meandered into his 'authorized personnel only' security zone.

"Well, oddly enough, when I was talking to Leah about the subject of the 'completed Jews' here in Israel it started me thinking—"

"What?" Krasnoff interjected. "Where did that topic come from?"

"According to Leah it's a problem that the Jewish community is really concerned about."

Krasnoff shrugged off the controversy as irrelevant. "So."

"*So*, when I asked the UT about the validity of their claims, it answered affirmatively." He then stood up and shook his head. "Soon afterward, I began to get the impression that the UT is some form of revelatory device where God is progressively communicating something to humanity, so I was thinking about asking it a question about the future."

Krasnoff gulped and spit out his coffee on the table. "You what—?"

Cohen cracked a smile and said, "I was thinking of asking it if Leah is going to marry me."

"You're not serious!" Krasnoff exclaimed.

Cohen laughed and said, "Just teasing." He turned serious and added, "That would probably be blasphemous, and I'm not taking any chances."

Krasnoff grunted in disbelief and finished his breakfast.

Cohen immediately recognized the sacred object the four chief priests were carrying. It was the ark of the covenant. It had two angelic statues with outstretched wings that stood opposite each other on the gold cover, both glistening from the torchlights lining the passageway to the underground vaults. The ark itself was made of a dark wood overlaid with gold. It had four rings of gold attached to it through which the priests inserted carrying poles. He could not see inside the ark, but remembered his Yeshiva teacher telling him that it once contained Aaron's rod, the golden pot of manna, and Moses' stone tablets—the Ten Commandments. The four priests each wore trousers, a coat, a girdle, and a cap, while the high priest directing them through the subterranean labyrinth wore the full regalia befitting his office.

The high priest gestured for them to hasten their work as the stone masons were standing by to seal up the doorway to the vault as soon as the ark came to rest. Rome's Tenth Legion, poised to attack, had surrounded Jerusalem under the direction of Titus, the son of Titus Flavius Sabinus Vespasianus, so the ark had to be preserved in a more secure remote chamber in the tunnel system.

Once the ark was placed on the newly prepared rock platform in the vault, the priests scurried out of the tunnel back to the Temple, while the high priest remained to supervise the entombment process that would ensure its security indefinitely. The masons, sworn to secrecy, then departed for the surface.

The high priest stood outside the sealed vault, then fell to his knees in prayer. For over 30 minutes he made supplication to the Lord to protect the ark in the ages to come, then looked up to the ceiling of the tunnel. It seemed he could see the giant rock that stood directly above the tunnel as a permanent marker for the hallowed chest, the remnant from the Holy of Holies where God had met with man.

Cohen bolted upright in his bed and rubbed the sleep from his eyes before turning on the light; it was 3 a.m. With a brisk step he walked to his closet to get the precious stones. He quickly returned to his bed, where he recklessly assembled the UT amidst the ruffled covers. Departing from his normal procedure, he bowed his head as his heart raced and prayed, "Lord, if this is a dream from you, give Urim; if not, give Thummim."

The blue stone turned an iridescent azure in the low lamp light of the room, skyrocketing Cohen's anxiety. "My God," he uttered. A wave of fear came over him when he realized the power that God was unleashing into his hands.

For nearly an hour Cohen sat atop his bed and watched the display before him as the blue 'yes' stone slowly dimmed into silence.

At 4:30 a.m. Cohen knocked on Krasnoff's door to inform him of the latest revelation. Three minutes later they were both standing above the breastplate and UT stones as Cohen retold his dream and the UT's answer. Afterward Cohen noticed a sudden change in Krasnoff's countenance.

"Why aren't you excited about this?" Cohen snapped. "After all, this will eclipse the discovery of the Dead Sea Scrolls!"

"I'm excited," Krasnoff said dryly, "but—"

"Oh, it's money, right?" Cohen retorted. "Well, we'll be rich! If the Dead Sea Scrolls could bring in $250,000 back in 1947—"

Krasnoff waved him off. "It's not about money, it's about politics."

"What do you mean?" Cohen countered curiously.

"Well, the Israeli government has guardedly excavated over twelve hundred feet of tunnels underneath the Temple Mount, and many of my colleagues believe that they know where the ark is—in some secret chamber deep within the subterranean passageways. But, and this is the problem that I see, back in 1981 the chief rabbi of the Western Wall, Yehuda Getz, entered a passage that acts as a cistern for the Temple Mount today, and saw a big room along with numerous vaults near a tunnel that he believed led to the Holy of Holies. Later they discovered an antechamber in which he believed the ark and other Temple artifacts were being stored and, we might say, divinely protected. So they began digging and came no more than thirty or forty yards away when they were attacked by Muslims."

"Ugh," Cohen groaned. "I think I know what's coming next."

"Well, the Muslims were afraid that if the Israelis found the ark it would be a sign of the Jews' ownership of the Temple Mount, and that Israel would rebuild the Temple. Today this is what they continue to fight against. So, in essence, the discovery was so politically explosive that they sealed up the entranceway and allowed the Arabs to block off the corridor."

Cohen shook his head in disbelief. "Are you saying that we can't announce to the world where the ark is after being hidden for over two thousand years because of some ridiculous in-fighting between the Arabs and Jews? What about the rest of the world—don't they deserve to know about this?" He believed politics and racial barriers stood in the way of God's blessing His people.

Krasnoff pondered the question for several moments, then threw his hands up in the air and said uncharacteristically, "We'll let God be the heavy. We'll make an official report to the IAA director that we have uncovered archeological evidence pointing to the ark's location beneath the Temple Mount. This way we will receive credit for confirming its location, while placing the onus of responsibility for unearthing it on the agency and the nation of Israel..." he paused and pointed his thumb upward, "...and ultimately God."

What they did not know was that Cohen's dream was really from the Lord.

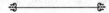

Seconds after Leah closed her car door her eyes made contact with Cohen, who had been waiting for her to come home from work. He sat perched on the railing of their condo patio watching her. His eyes followed her every move. "I need to talk to you," he began as she approached. "Are you staying in or going out tonight?"

Leah set her handbag down and pulled up a patio chair next to him. With increasing curiosity she recognized that the chemistry building between them was unlike her relationship with Shlomo. With Cohen, she felt relaxed, safe, and womanly. "I'm staying in," she replied with a smile that signaled affection. "Maybe we can continue the conversation we began several days ago," she added, opening up an invitation.

Cohen reached over and gently caressed her forearm. "I would really enjoy that." *How important the act of touching is*, he thought.

It builds a bridge that transcends mistaken emotions. As she rose from the chair he asked solicitously, "Can I help you with dinner?"

Leah glowed. "Sure."

The fading twilight provided just enough illumination for them to walk the meandering footpaths that laced the park outside the condo complex. After several moments of commentary on the beauty of nature, Cohen turned to Leah and said admiringly, "I find myself looking forward to seeing you whenever possible. I believe there's more to that feeling than just living in the same home as you and your father—I mean, it's much more than a fleeting feeling of building an acquaintance..." He stopped walking, turned and looked into her eyes and continued, "I find myself thinking of you very often in terms of romance. Is that too abrupt for you?"

"Bulldozing is the word that comes to mind," Leah joked with a girlish grin. *It must be the American way,* she thought, *always in a hurry, even when it comes to dating.*

He once again touched her, this time on the shoulder, as he attempted to defend himself. "I can't keep my New York background from emerging unexpectedly," he quipped, then quickly turning serious added, "but there are times when it serves me well."

Their eyes and hearts seemed to connect. "You mean when it comes to not taking 'no' for an answer, right?" Leah rejoined.

"Exactly," he agreed with an air of conquest.

I suppose I could date a thug from New York, Leah thought. With an exchange of glances, she put her hand in Cohen's and pulled him along down the path, then broke out whistling an American love song she had heard on the radio.

CHAPTER

6

Jerusalem

"We cannot as much as carry a shovel into the tunnel without a dig permit approved by the rabbinic council—you know that, Revi," Director Yigael Ben-Tor said trenchantly. "What's more, it could cause a national incident with the Arabs." He contemplated the ramifications of Krasnoff's suggestion as he paced back and forth in his office, pausing momentarily to gaze out his window overlooking Sderot Ben Zvi street to the splendor of the rooftop garden of the Tirat Bat Sheva hotel.

Krasnoff looked at the austere man who had been his superior for the past 15 years. He had learned to respect Ben-Tor for his diplomacy with government officials and his unabashed tenacity to hold onto Israeli ground. "I know the ark is there, Dr. Ben-Tor," Krasnoff asserted.

"How can you be so sure?"

Krasnoff read him a newspaper clipping from 1981:

" 'This gate, and the Coponius gate, a little bit further from it in the Western Wall that we discovered ten years ago is a secret. The big vault that we saw [inside it] is one of the entrances to the Temple. And as far as the ark of the covenant, we know exactly where it is!—Yehuda Getz, chief rabbi of the Western Wall' "

Dr. Ben-Tor whirled on Krasnoff. "So? We already know there is a possibility that he could be right. We've suspected that for years. But do we dare risk a war based on a *possibility*? That's the big question."

"The time is right for us to examine the tunnel vault to know for sure..." Krasnoff's jaw tightened as he began fumbling for words. "...I just know it's down there." His hand locked around the handle on his briefcase as he mentally wrestled with what to say and do next. "It's more than a *possibility*—"

"What?" Ben-Tor broke in roughly.

"It's a certainty."

Ben-Tor pulled up a stuffed chair next to Krasnoff and said haltingly, "You sound as if you have proof."

"I do." Krasnoff then opened up his attaché case and pulled out a large freezer bag containing several leaf fragments of an ancient document. He placed them on Ben-Tor's desk. Then he pulled out the high priest's headstone and handed it to Ben-Tor.

"What in the world is this?" Ben-Tor asked incredulously.

"After the last earthquake I went on a personal expedition to the quake zone in the Dead Sea area. You're holding in your hands an ancient tombstone of a high priest that I found in a recently opened cave near Qumran. For the last month or so I have been rummaging through files and researching any documentation relative to the Qumran dig site. Those parchment fragments on your desk were unearthed by our archeologist, Dr. Sukenik of the Hebrew University here in Jerusalem, back in the '40s and '50s when the discovery of the Dead

Sea Scrolls was so hot. They were in a separate cave along with hundreds of other manuscripts, but the interesting thing is…" He paused to open the freezer bag and carefully placed two pages in Ben-Tor's hands. "Nobody ever linked the narrative by an Essene scribe, Josiah, until now. He wrote that a high priest by the name of Amariah came to stay at the settlement back in 32 B.C. to flee Roman persecution, and that Amariah said the ark was hidden beneath the Temple Mount. Josiah added that the priest was murdered. The rest of his account has been lost in antiquity."

"This is unbelievable," Ben-Tor remarked, his mouth hanging open.

"But it was not until I found this tombstone that all of that had any meaning and credibility," Krasnoff said with intensity.

"The tombstone verified the presence of the high priest at Qumran, which in turn confirmed the presence of the ark under the Temple Mount," Ben-Tor agreed with a nod.

"Exactly."

Ben-Tor carefully examined the fragmented pages, then inspected the tombstone. "Revi, this could very well be the archeological find of the new century. The discovery of the Dead Sea Scrolls was the highlight of the last century, but together with the ark, you will be credited with the biggest find in the past thousand years." He stood up and extended his hand. "Congratulations."

"What do we do about digging?" Krasnoff asked curiously.

"I'm going to secretly petition the prime minister for permission to dig."

Krasnoff followed up his question. "The rabbinic council?"

"You let me worry about them. If I get the go-ahead from the prime minister, then on his authority, we can begin excavations at night to minimize our exposure. As far as the Protection of Holy Places law that supports the Muslim edict not to dig near the Mount, we'll just have to trust God on that one. I'm sure they'll never find out. We probably would only need several days anyway because we'll center our attention directly under the Mount."

"Fortunately, the Arabs don't have sound detection devices in the ground above the tunnel," Krasnoff quipped as he rose to leave.

"Prayerfully, all their snoops and 'ears' will be on holiday while we're under there. Once we locate it, then there's nothing they can do. We'll own the place without incident." The director then slapped Krasnoff on the back as he opened his door. "Good work, Revi. We're proud of you."

Golda Rokach smiled and nodded at Krasnoff as he left Dr. Ben-Tor's office. She was quick to realize that something unusual had transpired and that she had been left out of the loop.

Krasnoff left Ben-Tor's office elated with the assurance that the recognition he longed for was forthcoming.

"That was a masterstroke if ever I heard one," Cohen said with a luminous smile after hearing Krasnoff relate his visit to Ben-Tor's office. "What made you think of retrieving those scroll fragments?"

"I had written a paper on the Dead Sea Scrolls in grad school, and once the UT confirmed the location of the ark, a lightbulb in my head went on reminding me of the scribal narratives by the Essenes."

"I was surprised you were willing to give up the headstone," Cohen said in wonder.

"I viewed it as an investment. The notoriety of the ark will far outweigh the value of the tombstone. Besides, it will go to the agency and then on to the Jerusalem museum. Maybe they'll make a special building for it like they did with the Isaiah scroll." He cast his eyes off in the distance, envisioning his name as the archeologist who had discovered the famous grave marker.

Cohen intentionally avoided the question of Krasnoff's lie to Ben-Tor about finding the headstone. He reasoned that the outcome would benefit mankind significantly, thus justifying the half truth.

The phone rang.

"Shalom," Krasnoff answered as Cohen walked away.

"Revi," the friendly caller announced, "this is Ze've. I thought I'd call you to see if we could meet for lunch this week…try to catch up on a few things."

Krasnoff didn't have time for this now. His concentration was restricted to Cohen and the UT. He shook his head. "I'll have to pass."

"Next week then?" Ze've pressed.

Krasnoff relented after remembering how Ze've had helped him with the tour roster. "Well, okay, mid-week."

"Done. I'll see you at the Renaissance Jerusalem at noon on Wednesday. I'm buying." Krasnoff shot his eyebrows up in disbelief. "My, my, elegant dining. Well okay, fine. See you there."

He replaced the phone and surmised that the angel of good fortune had finally found his way to Mazor's doorstep.

The following afternoon, carrying a bouquet of roses and a small shopping bag from the King David Mall, Stein dropped by the IAA building with the sole intention of visiting with Golda Rokach. He was stopped at the concrete barricade blocking the front entrance by an armed security guard.

Hmph, something new has been added, he thought. "Mort Stein to see Ms. Rokach," Stein informed the guard.

The guard smiled when he saw the roses and shopping bag, then made a phone call. Seconds later he smiled again while nodding approval and wrote out a visitor's pass. *Time is running out if security is being tightened*, Stein reasoned. *This building is ordinarily low-risk security unless there is the threat of terrorist activity, so something must have happened recently.* A wave of urgency swept over him as he walked the steps to the second floor office of the director, Krasnoff, and his target for today, Golda Rokach. It was an urgency brought on by the realization that Krasnoff must have cracked the code on the *lights* and made them operational.

"Good afternoon, Mr. Stein," Golda bubbled as he rounded the corner of her office.

"So nice to see you once again, Ms. Rokach." He held up the roses as if they were a meal offering to a god and added, "For you."

Her gaze narrowed on his face as she replied, "You are really scoring the points. Thank you." She rose to place them in a vase and asked, "What brings you here today?"

"Just a friendly visit." He then motioned down and asked, "What's going on outside? The last time I came you had the standard terrorist barricades; why the armed security?"

Golda's lips pursed in a soundless whistle. "Something's going down around here, but I really don't have a handle on it yet. You know, Mr. Krasnoff was credited with—" She retreated to thought, wrestling with the notion of befriending Mr. Stein with inside information and her personal observations or keeping quiet.

"Something wrong, Ms. Rokach?" Stein sensed weakness. He pulled the small shopping bag out of his pocket and placed it on her desk. "A special gift to mark our friendship."

Golda's eyes widened, then she blushed. "Oh, you didn't have to..."

"Shush," Stein whispered as he registered the pleasurable look on her face.

"Oh, my God!" she exclaimed upon opening the felt-covered box.

"Just a little something for yourself."

She pulled one of the diamond earrings out of the case and pressed it to her ear as she stood up and looked into the reflective glass behind her. "They're gorgeous."

Stein seized the moment. He gestured toward Krasnoff's closed office door and asked, "Mr. Krasnoff on holiday?"

"Dr. Ben-Tor gave him two days off," she whispered sardonically as she slipped the jewel case into her handbag. She gave a furtive glance around the room and went on. "Interestingly, he was recently involved in a land purchase up in Karmiel that later proved to have oil reserves on it. It's almost as if he's a psychic—maybe even a second Uri Geller. I mean, somehow he got inside information from some geologists or *something*."

Yeah, "something," Stein thought, *is right. And that "something" must be the lights.* Stein bent in closer to Golda. "That is really interesting."

"Now that I think about it," she continued flippantly, "Revi has been acting strange lately. He comes in late and leaves early, and when it comes to his work—" she paused and pointed to the boxes stacked both on top and at the foot of his desk, "...he's definitely preoccupied with something." Then she shrugged her shoulders and added, "But Dr. Ben-Tor doesn't seem to mind so I'll keep my mouth shut."

Stein needed more information, and if a lie would yield the information, then it was justified. "I can understand where you're coming from, Ms. Rokach..." He paused and gazed into her eyes. "Is it all right if I call you Golda?"

"Of course."

"Well, Golda, several years ago when I had my credit clearing business in Florida, my partner secretly developed a software program designed to siphon off my clients to start up his own company and ultimately destroy mine."

"The dirty—" she breathed.

"Exactly." Stein agreed as he carefully drew her in to his web. "But I was given divine favor when an insightful employee learned about the conspiracy and accessed my partner's computer files. In the interest of internal security, I didn't think it was wrong, nor did I believe there to be any grounds to prosecute her. In fact, if it weren't for her taking this risk, I would have been betrayed and my business wiped out."

With a shake of her head she said, "Unbelievable."

Stein read her well and asked, "Do you have access to the central computer files?"

"Of course," she replied. "I have top clearance."

Stein glanced toward her monitor and suggested, "I wonder what hidden files are in Mr. Krasnoff's directories?"

She shrugged her shoulders and said, "I wouldn't be surprised if he's conducting some top secret experiments." She rotated her swivel seat in front of her computer keyboard then typed in two commands: the first a password, the second, Krasnoff's directory. She scanned the listing then announced, "Nothing unusual or suspicious."

Stein stretched over her desk to view the monitor. "What about in his 'removable disk' directory?"

She nodded and said, "Oh, the ZIP disks. Yeah, he has a few in his desk that he keeps for his personal files."

Stein retreated back to his chair and said subtly, "Sounds *very* interesting."

"Do you think I should—?" she hesitated, looking for a signal of approval.

Stein sighed then shrugged his shoulders. "There's nobody around."

Abruptly rising from her desk while looking askance at the front door, she slipped into Krasnoff's office and returned within seconds holding two ZIP disks.

Stein smiled at her achievement.

She quickly inserted the first disk into the removable disk drive and opened it up. There were over 40 folders, all of which were connected to archeological discoveries made in his districts from the years 1995-2002. "No good. Nothing here."

With anticipation she inserted and opened up the second disk.

She called out the titles of several folders as her finger went down the list, stopping on the one labeled 'UT.' "Here's an odd one," she mouthed aloud.

Stein stood to look at the monitor. "That's the one," he said. "Open it."

She double-clicked on the 'UT' folder. A pop-up window flashed: PASSWORD PROTECTED.

"What is his wife's name?" Stein said quickly as if supernaturally prompted.

"His wife is dead—killed by an Arab terrorist."

"Do you remember her name?" Stein asked curtly.

"He speaks of her often. Her name was Naomi."

"Key in Naomi."

PASSWORD ACCEPTED appeared on the monitor.

"How in the world did you know that?" Golda asked in wonder.

"A good guess. Many people use their wife's or children's names for passwords."

"What would UT stand for?" she asked curiously.

Stein ignored the question. He gave her a dismissive wave of the hand to quickly proceed. "Jackpot!" Golda exclaimed as the folder opened up. There were only ten documents in the folder. She scrolled down two documents and stopped. "Here's a file entitled Karmiel."

"The oil discovery. Keep going, we're on the right track." Stein insisted.

"What about this one: 'RabTunnel,' what do you think that involves?"

Stein's brow furrowed. "Could be interesting. Open it."

The document filled the screen in the form of a memorandum. "It's about his meeting with Dr. Ben-Tor," Golda said softly as she continued to read it. Suddenly she swallowed hard and exclaimed, "Oh my God! They found the ark of the covenant in the rabbis' tunnel under the Temple Mount."

With eyes transfixed on the monitor, Stein simply nodded in silence as he read the entire memo.

Golda gulped and said abruptly, "They're going to secretly excavate the tunnel—"

Stein tapped her on the shoulder as he looked around the room and said, "Shush. Not so loud." *That accounts for the heightened security,* he quickly realized. His eyes caught hold of another file entitled, 'HiPriest.' He pointed to it and said, "Highlight and click on this."

The file expanded into a subdirectory. Golda read some of the documents off: "The mitre; the ephod; the robes; the shoulder pieces; the girdle; the breastplate—"

"Hold it," Stein said with intensity. "Double click on breastplate."

"They're descriptions of the high priest's sacred dress," she explained as the file opened. "This is really crazy..." she started to say as she read the report, "...look, he has diagrams with test data and then he explains how he finally discovered how to make the Urim and Thummim operate—" she paused mid-sentence, "...but how could that be, Mr. Stein?"

"I'm thinking," Stein temporized as his mind absorbed what his eyes raked in on the monitor. His hands clenched into fists at his side as he realized his predicament. *Looks like we ran out of time, Gregory. It won't be long before he will turn his attention to us.*

"Mr. Stein?"

"What we have here, Golda, is a man who has spent too much time under the hot sun in the Judean desert digging up dead things.

He must have flipped out." He motioned for her to remove the disks and return them as he continued to suppress her curiosity. "You should know from your affiliation with the agency and your own archeological background that the Urim and Thummim—as well as the other elements of the priesthood—were lost in antiquity. Why, they haven't been seen for thousands of years."

"But what about Dr. Ben-Tor?" she asked after returning from Krasnoff's office.

"Oh, I believe the part about the ark is true." He pointed back at Krasnoff's office. "But, I'm afraid the loss of his wife and his desire to make a name for himself has finally pushed him over the deep end." He gestured toward his head, "He must have some hidden psychological problems, because the business about the high priest and the Urim and Thummim is mere fantasy."

"Well, the loss of a wife can bring on heavy emotional problems," she agreed.

Stein nodded then reemphasized the point. "I discount the element of the priesthood entirely. I suggest you don't take that part seriously."

Golda shook her head gravely. "The poor man, he must be going through hell."

Stein frowned and nibbled on his lower lip to signal his concern, yet it was imperative that he disarm her. "You're right. If I were you, I wouldn't mention our discovery to anybody because it could cost Mr. Krasnoff his job."

She quickly ran her hand over her mouth and said, "My lips are sealed."

Stein smiled broadly at Golda, then departed with the vital information he needed to present to Gregory.

Predestination was a theological term that came to Kavidas' mind as he stood with arms crossed over his chest at his office window waiting for Stein. *As it was with my forefathers, so too will it be with me.* Out of Grecian aristocracy had been born great statesmen and philosophers who had affected the entire world with political science, culture, architecture, language, and thought. All of them had been ordained by God for the welfare of man. Kavidas knew too that his actions were foreordained from eternity past and that both he and Stein would merely act out the parts of the designer, but his predilection for success came with the realization that great multitudes would unwittingly follow him to that destined abode. *Such will be my crowning glory.* Apart from threatening and harassing the elect of God, he could not touch them. They were not his, but belonged to the One who had redeemed them and promised to protect them. So, there were innumerable others who were inescapably his. *Such will be my crowning glory.* For his portion, he would make their lives enjoyable, for a season; it was for them, his disciples, that he would demonstrate his power and greatness so as to garner the faith that he deserved. *Let no one call me the idle shepherd, for once their faith in me is established, I will guide them to their rightful place.*

A friendly tap-tap at the door, and in walked Stein. He went immediately to Gregory and embraced him in fellowship. They walked to their strategic planning table and sat down.

"You can give me an update on your progress to seize the *lights* later, Mort," Kavidas began trenchantly, "but first I want to show you a video of an infomercial we will air internationally next week. It's about the favorable results the last oil price hike has had on MASTERLINK." He pressed the 'play' button on the DVD remote control and the MASTERLINK logo filled the TV screen. The disc contained selected excerpts from CNN broadcasts with current and archival footage displaying angry, disgruntled customers at the gas pumps throughout the world. Close-ups were presented of commuters with gloomy facial expressions pointing to the price on the pump. Furious customers, fraught with frustration brought on by oil company executives pledging to end the crisis, were picketing stations and hurling expletives at the news reporters. Cameos showing movie celebrities and bank executives were next. They too were protesting what they called a feigned shortage, claiming that once again the oil companies and the petrol-rich Arab bloc countries were rigging the prices. Next were interviews with customers complaining of the general unpreparedness of the government, city utilities, and large oil corporations. Unable to procure their vitally needed gas to get to work, people were in a state of hysteria. The recurrent theme, "We need oil, not Jews" reappeared on the bumper-sticker market.

Midway through the presentation Kavidas appeared in front of his corporate headquarters in Athens holding a MASTERLINK card up to the camera. Through a photographic lap dissolve, the card suddenly appeared as a microchip that was to be non-surgically imbedded in the top of a shapely model's right hand. To demonstrate the easy procedure the model placed the chip on her hand, then rubbed on top a dab of absorption ointment from a small tube. After that she simply placed a band-aid over it. A flashing pop-up window stated that in three days the microchip was safely under the skin like a tatoo. After simulated fast-forwarding the model smiled and held up her hand to reveal the imbedded chip that could not be stolen, lost, or misplaced. Then she was seen at a gas station, momentarily placing her right hand under a scanner while waving to her girlfriend in a passing sports car with her left hand. The model triumphantly drove out of the station. Fade out.

Kavidas then returned to the scene accompanied by a group of popular financial icons from around the world. They were discussing the monetary ramifications brought on by the gas shortage problem, and how the boycott by the worldwide MASTERLINK credit system would put sufficient pressure to bear on the oil magnates to roll back the prices. MASTERLINK would be the very leveraging device to force the oil-rich superpowers to capitulate.

Further, with the added perks MASTERLINK offered, the computerized system would be the rightful successor to the age-old coin, bill, and paper currency method.

"This is superb!" Stein reveled.

"It gets better," Kavidas chortled.

The background music began to wane, giving the viewer the impression that the infomercial was over, but Kavidas reappeared with his right hand held up in front of the camera once again, displaying his imbedded microchip. Then a collage of children's pictures with the title "MISSING" in a circle with a diagonal line across it appeared on the screen. A commentator explained the innovation.

"What's this?" Stein asked curiously.

"The latest addition," Kavidas exclaimed proudly as the viewing came to an end. "We now boast of being able to locate any lost children, or for that matter, lost criminals—fugitives from justice—as well as tracking invalids who may have strayed from their custodians. The MASTERLINK chip also acts as a global locator with our own satellite network."

Stein shook his head in wonder. "The system is fully operational?"

"Fully." Kavidas beamed and added, "What's more, we are now integrated with D.I.A.N.E, Direct Information Access Network Europe, the European hi-tech search system that emulates our earlier REDISEARCH credit system. Since it is already in place, we don't have to build an infrastructure here in Europe; we just took them over."

"So our financial side is now complete," Stein noted.

"Yes. I predict by next year MASTERLINK will control the way the public buys or sells everything. Of course we stand ready to make any adjustments the monetary climate may dictate, but for now we can concentrate on our other objectives as the system runs itself."

Stein's eyes brightened with expectation as he probed deeply into Kavidas' for direction. "I've been away. You need to bring me up to speed on our political and religious objectives."

Kavidas made a sweeping motion with his hand and replied, "We're on pace to meet those objectives as well. Through MASTER-LINK we will be able to monitor all our subscribers' political and religious affiliations, since that is imbedded info and updated annually at renewal." Pointing to Stein and himself, he added, "Once I am installed as president of the EEC in two months, we will aggressively seek clandestine alliances with both Israel and select Arab bloc countries. Tomorrow I am going to make a large financial contribution to Israel to start the process going. The Arab crescent is on the rise, and we will need them to meet our political and religious goals. We will work on an amalgamation in the near future." Stein nodded in awe, cracking his knuckles as if he were about to enter a fist fight. Kavidas' eyes raked Stein's face. He held up his hand in a halting motion and continued, "I know you're anxious to move things along, Stein, especially in the religious domain, so you can participate more visibly; but we must wait until the appointed time. Remember, as long as the Holy Spirit restrains us, our operation is extremely limited. In time, we will seize both political and religious control. That is certain!"

Stein looked crestfallen, but acquiesced to Kavidas' wisdom.

A muscle jerked in Kavidas' right cheek. "Now tell me about *the lights.*"

Stein stood up from the table and walked silently to the wall-to-wall bookshelves, then whirled. "I'm concerned," he said with intensity. "This IAA division chief, Krasnoff, somehow has them functioning and they are providing him with information that leads to important discoveries. So far he has claimed ownership of hidden oil deposits in Karmiel, and I just found out yesterday that he confirmed the location of the ark of the covenant."

"I can see where this is going," Kavidas groaned, squeezing his eyes shut as if envisioning the future. "Before long he will make inquires about prominent people and the *lights* will expose us. Then we could take some whopping hits; recruitment will be hampered and our final numbers will be affected."

"We can't let it happen," Stein asserted.

"No, we cannot," Kavidas said with clear precision as he stood up to join Stein at the bookshelves. "You have to destroy this apparatus as soon as possible," he instructed once again, "but you must be careful, since it is quite possible that Krasnoff by now has an accomplice who knows as much as he does. You mentioned having him followed. Well, get on that immediately, and find out if anybody else is involved. Then eliminate them and destroy the *lights*." His gaze narrowed on Stein's face. "Remember, we must have this business in Israel and all the loose ends tied up before I ascend control of the EEC."

Stein nodded in agreement, then gave Kavidas a brotherly kiss before departing.

CHAPTER

7

Jerusalem

Krasnoff awoke at 5:45 a.m. with a killer cluster headache that brought a throbbing pain over his right eye, stuffed nasal passages, and overall malaise. He peered out his bedroom window to see drizzle dripping down the outside glass and decided that the inclement weather only added to the dreary outlook for his day off. It would be hours before the headache drug would bring any sign of relief, and even then, the symptoms would linger for another day. He was in a foul spirit.

Dragging himself out of bed, he walked to his bathroom and took two capsules of his prescription drug, turned toward the bed, and stopped short midway. His eyes caught and fastened on the earthen jar stored in his closet. A wave of anger came over him. He turned to look at his bedroom furniture in disgust, then went to his closet, pulled one of his old suits off the hanger and threw it on the floor. With a stomp of his foot on the aging suit he showed his contempt for his low estate in life. This is not what he had imagined for himself or Leah. It was nearly seven weeks since he had acquired the Urim and Thummim and to date he had nothing to show for it. Not one shekel in his hand. Sure, there would be fortunes to be made sometime in the future when he was able to exploit the oil reserves, but that was allocated for his retirement. What about now? The confirmation of the ark would bring fame and ultimately endorsements that could be converted into cash before it was turned over to the government, but even that was shrouded in a veil of secrecy with the potential of a war with the Arabs. No! He needed remuneration that he could take to the bank tomorrow. It was time to buy a new home for Leah and, he thought as he looked down at the suit, new clothes for himself.

By early afternoon Krasnoff sat at the kitchen table, somewhat relieved of his headache, nursing a cup of coffee with two newspapers in front of him: The *Jerusalem Post* and the *Wall Street Journal*. After quickly reviewing the sports pages and advertisements in the *Post*, he began to study the *Journal*. For over an hour he meticulously scrutinized computer stock listings then finally circled four that showed promise—two in the field of American aerospace research, two in American software manufacturers. He listed them on a writing pad, then refilled his coffee cup as he waited for Cohen to return from running his errands.

Two hours later Cohen walked in happily while Krasnoff sat rubbing his temples to help alleviate the migraine. "Where in the world were you?" Krasnoff asked, bristling.

"Taking care of some personal business," Cohen countered defensively, his gaiety vanishing. Somehow Krasnoff always had that effect on him.

"I thought you went back to Florida," Krasnoff added sarcastically.

"Not yet. What's up?"

"Have a seat," Krasnoff ordered. As Cohen obeyed, Krasnoff opened the *Journal* in front of him and explained, "We've been enriching the archeological world since we've discovered how to use the

UT, but now it's time for us to utilize this God-given gift for our advantage—to enrich us." He tossed the list in front of Cohen and continued, "My share of the oil in Karmiel is for Leah, but we need something for you and me, right now." He pointed to the pad and said, "I want to invest in one of these four promising stocks: Grantham Aerospace; Radial Satellites; SolarPower Technologies or Micro-Prism Software. Ask the UT to choose one."

"What?" Cohen blinked. "But, you said you were broke...second mortgage and all."

Krasnoff fidgeted in his chair. "I am," he lied, "but I can max out my credit cards and I have a friend I can borrow some money from. Together the two will enable us to buy the stock. After we make our money, I'll simply repay it."

Troubled in spirit, Cohen stared at him in bewilderment for a moment. It was becoming increasingly difficult with Krasnoff to separate fact from fiction. "I see your sinus condition is acting up again—sorry," he began subtly. "Correct me if I'm wrong, but I was of the impression that we would be using the UT to further the science of archeology—and make money doing that; now we're pushing the envelope to include the stock market?"

Krasnoff gave him a lethal glance before he forced a smile. "We're going to do both. We can advance the field of archeology and use this gift from God to help us in life." He stood up and walked to the window. "For years I've wanted more of life for Leah. Is there anything wrong with that? And besides, this is my chance to make a mark in the world and become a *somebody*." He turned and said roughly, "Cohen, don't resist me on this."

Cohen sighed and threw his hands up. "Fine. I can go with this." He walked to Krasnoff then put his hand on his shoulder and confessed, "Now is as good a time as any. You might as well know that I have been seeing Leah secretly outside of the house and that we're in love with one another. In fact, we were talking about marriage at lunch today; that's why I was gone so long."

A wave of astonishment washed over Krasnoff. "I'm shocked. Why didn't she tell me?"

"She adores you and is afraid you wouldn't approve."

"What happened to Shlomo?" he asked as his dreams of political aspirations for his daughter disappeared.

"She let him down softly."

Krasnoff shook his head in disbelief. Then a sudden realization swept over him. "Did you tell her about us," he gulped, "I mean the Urim and—"

Cohen nodded and waved him off. "I had to. She was suspicious anyway. Let's face it, how can you keep a two thousand-year-old urn in your closet a secret? She found it one day when she was vacuuming the carpet and asked me about it. No big deal. She's on our side."

Krasnoff nodded wearily in relief as he massaged his forehead to help soothe his headache. After ruminating for several moments he finally said, "Well then, shall we return to business?" Thoughts that Cohen would be good for his Leah encouraged him.

Into Cohen's mind drifted images of wealth and fame that included pictures of him and Leah sipping cocktails as they cruised the Mediterranean Sea on their yacht. "Ready."

Ritualistically, yet reverently, as Krasnoff looked on, Cohen set up the breastplate and Urim and Thummim stones in preparation for the questioning session. Suddenly the thought of God flew into Cohen's mind, but he immediately dismissed it as imaginary. He didn't need a relationship with God in order to recognize that supernatural powers were at work when he was operating the revelatory device. In fact, neither one of them gave God a second thought during their exploratory episodes unless they needed help. To use His name in the chant to invoke His guidance by Urim and Thummim could never be viewed as blasphemous if they really didn't believe in Him.

"If Grantham Aerospace is approved of God, give Urim, turn blue; if not give Thummim, turn scarlet," Cohen's voice vibrated with intensity.

The stones did not respond.

"Check the configuration," Krasnoff grumped.

"It's right. I ought to know by now."

Suddenly for the first time the purple amethyst in the left corner of the triangle-shaped arrangement began to illuminate.

"Uh-oh," Krasnoff exclaimed. "What does that mean?"

"It can mean many things," Cohen instructed with a wry expression. "Either not now, or answer refused." He scratched his head and added, "Or possibly the question is impertinent."

"You think—?"

Cohen shrugged his shoulders. "Let's not forget that this instrument was used by the priest of the Most High God."

"Don't get sanctimonious with me, Nat," Krasnoff clucked reprovingly. "Try the rest of them."

Cohen stiffened under the rebuke. "If Radial Satellites is approved of God, give Urim, turn blue; if not give Thummim, turn scarlet."

Again the purple stone brightened.

"We're in trouble," Krasnoff realized with a frown. Cohen went on to ask the Urim and Thummim about SolarPower Technologies and MicroPrism Software, but the answer was the same.

"Hold it, hold it," Cohen abruptly announced as a jolt of adrenaline passed through his body. "I see a pattern here." He looked around the room. "Get me a Bible."

With rising irritation Krasnoff replied, "What for?"

"To confirm my newfound theory." Krasnoff handed him a Bible wherein Cohen turned to Psalms. He read the title on a Psalm then sat upright to address the Urim and Thummim on the table before him and asked, "If David is the author of Psalm 22, give Urim, turn blue, if not, give Thummim, turn scarlet."

The blue stone answering "yes" shone brightly.

"That's what I thought," Cohen said solemnly as he began to meditate on the development. Moments later he said, "Let's try another, only this time we'll flip it." After reading out of Exodus he asked, "If Moses received the Ten Commandments on Mount Ararat, give Urim; if not, give Thummim." He smiled as the scarlet "no" stone lit. "See, the UT knew it was on Mount Sinai."

Krasnoff crashed his fist on the table, propelling the stones up and down in the air. It was enough. "Who cares?!" he screamed as the veins on his neck began to bulge while his face turned red. "I'm not interested in 'Bible trivia,' I'm interested in making this *thing* work for *us!*"

Cohen glared at him with malevolent eyes and retorted, "Is that what this is all about? Money? Well, it's obvious there is another plan in place since this *thing* only works when asked questions about the Bible or related themes."

Krasnoff grabbed the stones off the table and held them in his hand as he screamed in Cohen's face, "Then you better get with God and make these rocks work right, or I'll sell them to the highest bidder!" After dropping the stones on the table, he rotated on one foot and bolted out the front door.

Cohen paced the room for well over five minutes until he stopped cold and suddenly rehearsed his last sentence in his head. *Related themes.* "Hmm." *Now what does that include?* He went to his research files and pulled out everything on the breastplate and Urim and Thummim, then sat down with the Bible and a commentary. He carefully compared passages and subsequent texts relating to the high priest's use of the ephod, then referred to the commentary for additional insight.

After 30 minutes, the front door opened and slammed shut. Krasnoff had returned.

"I think I'm being followed," he rasped as he went to Cohen's bedroom window to look outside. "Right after I started strolling in the park I noticed a bearded American man carrying groceries walk by me. Fifteen minutes later as I sat on a bench eating an ice cream, I saw the same guy behind a bush snapping a photo of me with a telephoto lens. When I stood up, he took off."

"Why would anybody be following you unless your discovery is known?"

Krasnoff shook his head wearily then nibbled on his lower lip. "Nobody knows about it."

"Could be a coincidence, but we better be careful," Cohen warned, "especially when I'm operating the stones."

Krasnoff nodded in agreement, then sat down on the end of Cohen's bed. "I'm sorry I blew up at you," he began. "I just want things to work out for us. If we could only figure out what the real purpose of the UT is, there isn't any reason why we can't be successful."

Cohen walked to Krasnoff and patted his shoulder. "All's forgiven. We all have our bad days." He returned to the table then pointed out the window and added, "While you were doing your thing out there I studied up on the UT and I believe we can make some money after all, simply by adjusting our thinking."

"Oh," Krasnoff said, elated. "How so?"

"Well, everything I've read points to the use of the UT to reveal the cause of a national crisis, or to select a king—you know, political decisions; or to warn of an impending disaster."

"But how does that square with the oil at Karmiel, or your question about the 'completed Jew' and the ark?"

"Well, just be patient and hear me out. My theory is that the UT confirms biblical truth or themes. In other words, it was true according to the Bible that there was oil in Karmiel. We just asked the right question. Obviously the 'completed Jews' have legitimate biblical claims, and the UT affirmed the location of the ark along with the questions about Moses and David. But when it came to your stock selection, since it is not a biblical theme, it wouldn't answer. Remember, it's not a Ouija board."

"All right," Krasnoff ventured, "let's try it on…" He reached for the *Post* and glanced down at the front page, "…the prime minister. After all, he's related to the Bible as Israel's leader."

Cohen scratched his head as he pondered the challenge. "I guess so…" he replied sheepishly, "…but I think it's a stretch—"

"Just try it."

"Phrase a question to ask it."

Krasnoff squeezed his eyes shut momentarily. "Okay, ask it this way: 'If Prime Minister Rubin is to be re-elected, give Urim; if not, give Thummim.'"

"But that's more of a prophetic question."

"Just try it," Krasnoff repeated the command.

Cohen asked the Urim and Thummim the question then slowly pushed himself away from the table, not knowing what to expect.

The blue sapphire illuminated the answer affirmatively.

"You did it!" Krasnoff yelled aloud. He jumped up off the bed triumphantly and did what looked like four steps to an Israeli folk dance, then suddenly stopped. "Now we just have to figure out how to—"

"Make money from it," Cohen inserted with a chuckle.

Ignoring the jab, Krasnoff said, "While we're making history, my boy, while we're making history." He pulled out a folded index card from his shirt pocket and made a note to send a donation to the prime minister's reelection campaign fund, plus make inquiries as to his other financial interests.

Swept up in the excitement of the moment, Cohen picked up the *Post* then turned to page 2 and said, "Here's something a little obscure that we can experiment with: 'Greek Humanitarian Gregory Kavidas of MASTERLINK Donates $3 Million to Israel.'" Cohen dropped the paper on the table. "Sounds like another Rockerfeller or Baron Rothschilds in the making. Let's ask a question about him."

"Let's see that!" Krasnoff blurted out. He grabbed the paper and voraciously read the article. He slapped the paper and frowned. "A man by the name of..." he paused to grind his teeth momentarily, "...Mort something...Stein, that's it. Yeah, he was from MASTERLINK too. He came by my office a few weeks ago...very interested in archeology."

Cohen shrugged his shoulders. "So? Coincidence?"

"Could be."

"Well, let's frame out a question about this character." *Remember, Cohen*, he reminded himself, *related themes.* "How about we ask: 'If Kavidas is to become a big player in Israel's economic game in the future, should we invest in him?'"

"It needs to be streamlined and rephrased, but that's what we want to know."

Cohen bit his index fingernail while he pondered the dilemma. "If Kavidas is going to be good for Israel, give Urim, turn blue; if not, give Thummim, turn scarlet."

The red jasper suddenly gave off a garish luminosity.

Krasnoff took a step backward. "Huh? Now that's weird. Look at the strange color of red, it's almost as if it's saying a loud NO!"

"That's the first time the scarlet stone reacted that way." Cohen's voice vibrated queerly.

"It's a cinch we're not investing *in* him…" Krasnoff paused to gaze at an imaginary spot on the wall for several moments, then snapped his fingers and said, "but what about investing *against* him!"

"What do you mean?"

"Think about it," Krasnoff said impulsively. "The way things are going in the world today, this MASTERLINK corporation will gobble up all other credit systems and dominate the entire financial and economic world before long—maybe even create an international disaster, like you said. Who is to say MASTERLINK wouldn't become another debacle like Enron or Worldcom back in the States? And because of these failures, let's say there are people out there who don't want to buy into MASTERLINK? They don't like this Kavidas or Stein? Where do they go?"

"Are you suggesting that we start our own credit card company to compete?"

"Absolutely not! Hear me on this…" He smiled and patted himself on the back. "This is fantastic. What we must do in the interest of commerce and fair competition is invest in a commodity that has endured since time began. One that will be universally accepted as an alternative to the MASTERLINK credit system."

"Return to the barter system?"

"No, you schlemiel. What is Israel's second most important export next to citruses?"

Cohen rubbed his ear while searching for an answer. "Minerals from the Dead Sea?"

"Good guess, but, *dong*, wrong. Diamonds, you nudnik, diamonds." Krasnoff thumped his foot on the floor and repeated his solution, "Diamonds."

"Can you elaborate a little?" Cohen queried as if he were still in the dark about the plan.

"Well, up the coast of Israel in Netanya there is a diamond industry that holds the title of the world's number-one exporter of polished diamonds. They buy the raw gems from Africa and Asia. In turn, Israeli companies are making zillions of dollars each year, especially from tourists.

"Historically, diamonds were always used by the Jews as a form of security, either to buy themselves out of Roman or Nazi prisons, or to hide and transport to other nations to rebuild their lives. Diamonds are enduring, portable assets, negotiable throughout the world."

"Well, so is gold for that matter," Cohen objected.

"Gold is enduring, but not portable," Krasnoff corrected. "One cannot swallow a gold ingot and recover it later in a bathroom when all is safe. No, only diamonds can be easily hidden or smuggled in a time of conflict, and I am convinced that we must invest heavily in them in view of what I see on the financial horizon—possibly some kind of national crisis."

Because he was so convincing, Cohen thought for a moment that Krasnoff had received some kind of revelation. "Then that's what we'll do," he affirmed.

"Ask the UT the question," Krasnoff instructed.

Cohen strategically positioned himself in front of the stones to exhibit some semblance of reverence and said, "If we are to invest in diamonds for the welfare of Israel, give Urim, turn blue; if not, give Thummim, turn scarlet."

The blue sapphire glowed brightly.

"Hallelujah!" they yelled in unison. Krasnoff smirked triumphantly at Cohen and left the room a contented man, but the dramatic session left a great void in Cohen's heart.

Golda Rokach teetered forward in her desk chair as she stared in shock at Krasnoff, who gayly sauntered past her into his office. Obviously preoccupied, he didn't as much as give her a wave. Once inside he started whistling several stanzas from a vintage American musical. *What happened to him?* she wondered. *He sure sounds happy.* Fifteen minutes later a surge of relief came over her with the recognition that he obviously didn't detect that his document files had been disturbed.

With deliberate care Krasnoff began telephoning diamond brokers in Netanya to begin his purchasing negotiations. Twenty minutes into his calls Golda beeped him on the intercom and summoned him to Dr. Ben-Tor's office.

"Our courier just handed me a confidential letter signed by Prime Minister Rubin authorizing us to dig in the tunnel," Ben-Tor began, "but I must tell you that I am very apprehensive about this. The prime minister is allowing us to excavate under a cloak of secrecy, but he cannot divert any security to help us keep this from the public, especially the Arab sector. If the undertaking were discovered, he would be implicated as having approved of it, and he cannot allow that. Naturally we must protect the project from leaks—"

"Only you, the prime minister, and I know about it," Krasnoff broke in. He could never divulge the truth that Nathan Cohen's use of the Urim and Thummim had determined and confirmed the location.

"Very good. We must keep it that way." He gave Krasnoff a dismissive wave of the hand as he walked to the phone, but Krasnoff didn't move. "What else?"

"What about the headstone, where is it?"

"It is in a sealed box in our archival vault here in the agency basement. I have labeled the project 2002-K. You may be pleased to know that the 'K' is for Krasnoff. It will remain there until we see how things develop. In time, as you know, all the findings relative to your discovery will be studied, cataloged, and ultimately placed in the museum." He grinned and added, "They'll probably make a separate museum just for the ark. Once again, good work."

Krasnoff sighed blissfully and walked out. Ben-Tor then picked up the phone to contact his prized excavation foreman to head up the task. He instructed him to hand pick, under high security, the engineers and laborers to begin the work. The whereabouts of the ark, he feared, was becoming known, if only to a select few.

The arboretum in front of the Krasnoff home provided a picturesque fabric of nature in a complex matrix of surrounding turmoil. It reminded Leah of a sanctuary where life's needs were met by God amidst a struggling culture attempting to satisfy their needs on their own.

The paths were lined with rare Madonna lilies that formed lush blankets bordering random clusters of Jerusalem pines. Several almond and acacia trees were strategically placed within the perimeter of the inside garden where rose of Sharon and narcissus bloomed. Visitors picnicked while future ornithologists watched and listened to the songbirds chirping, warbling, and peeping. In the ecological corner, fallen pines, covered with lichen and mushrooms, enchanted school children as they journeyed through the small reserve.

"This is a favorite place of my father and me," Leah reminisced while strolling hand-in-hand with Cohen along the winding footpaths. "We often spoke of my mother and the deep emotional grief he suffered after her death."

"The pain is still in his heart," Cohen observed compassionately. "I could see it the first day I was here when you called on the phone and I asked him about your mother; the hatred for the Arabs is unmistakable. But not only that, he's angry at God for allowing it."

Leah nodded in assent then looked at him in dismay. "My, my, you sound like you're an aspiring counselor or something." She paused and wondered where Cohen's sudden influx of discernment came from. "I suppose that's true. Do you think the discovery of the UT has changed his heart any?"

"Well..." he fumbled for words as he put his arm around her, "...he's concentrating on making a name for himself while he makes money. I see that he's preoccupied and not thinking of the issues that he has suppressed over the years, but honestly, no, I don't see a change. He is very driven toward his own goal."

"That sounds like a nice way of saying he'll do whatever he has to in order to get his way."

Cohen stopped and walked her over to sit on a bench. "Leah, I'm committed to you, your dad, and the UT project—you know that. But after the last episode with your father I came away with a change of heart. I am beginning to think that God allowed us to find the UT to benefit humanity, not ourselves. That we should use it to promote public welfare, not private enterprise." He gazed off at several storks nesting in an acacia tree and added as an afterthought, "Somehow I don't see your dad grasping that vision."

An unexpected surge of respect gushed forth from Leah's heart. She hugged him and said, "I'm beginning to see, once again, why I've fallen in love with you."

Cohen's eyes suddenly brightened. "Can you imagine the good that can come out of this? Why, we could ask questions like, 'Are we on the right track for an AIDS vaccine?' Or, 'Are we on course for peace here in Israel?' "

"What about 'Should we elect another woman prime minister, like Golda Meir?' " Leah quipped while pointing to herself.

"Very funny," Cohen replied.

"Excuse me—" they heard from behind. They turned to see a bearded American man holding a street map of the city. "Can you direct me to Independence Park; I seem to have lost my way." He pointed down at the map and added, "I thought this was the park..."

"You're a few blocks off," Leah explained as she abruptly stood up. She looked at his map and reorientated it. "You're here," she said while pointing to Shomeron Street, "and you want to be here," she instructed while drawing an imaginary line to Independence Park.

The man nodded profusely, thanked them, and walked away at a brisk pace.

Leah walked around the bench to pick some lilies as Cohen stretched out. Several moments passed, then without warning he jumped to his feet. "Leah!" he exclaimed as he gestured down the path, "that must be the man your father said was following him yesterday."

"A man was following my father yesterday? Why didn't someone tell me?" she said in reflexive alarm.

"No need. No need, doll. We poo-poohed it away," he replied in a lame attempt to disarm her. "Now we'll have to take a second look at this." He sprinted after the man a short distance to a rise in the footpath, then stopped short. Seconds later he held his arms up in the air, indicating the man had vanished from sight.

The phone in room 1134 of the Renaissance Jerusalem rang six times before Stein picked it up. The irritated American on the other end, who went by the name of Sam, advised Stein that he had violated his normal surveillance procedure by moving in close to his mark to observe. Sam confirmed that there was another young American man living at the Krasnoff home, and that he apparently was romantically involved with the subject's daughter. Stein instructed Sam that he would bonus him out when his surveillance reports detailed what went on *inside* the Krasnoff home. Sam agreed to stepping up the monitoring of Krasnoff's home using hi-tech equipment. Stein replaced

the phone and reminded himself that Gregory was right after all; there were others involved with Krasnoff.

***

"That settles it!" Krasnoff said to Cohen through his teeth. "From now on we will keep the drapes drawn, the doors locked, our mouths shut, and maintain a very low profile until I can figure out our next move."

"We need to relocate—get a fresh start in a different town," Cohen suggested.

"I'm working on that. As soon as I get some return on my investments, we're out of here," Krasnoff assured. "But the nagging problem is, who is this bearded nut, and why is he following us?"

Cohen shrugged his shoulders and shook his head in consternation. "Only you and Leah know anybody here in Israel. Remember, I'm only visiting."

A cloud of fear that his plans were being threatened suddenly drifted into Krasnoff's mind. "I'm going to apply for a gun-carrying permit and buy myself a pistol."

"Do you think our lives are endangered?"

"I'm not taking any chances with our lives or *my property*," he instructed with a definite resolve.

Cohen quickly discerned that the stakes for concealing the UT were rising in direct proportion to the level of revelation. The more they were told, the more security was required to keep the information confidential. "I'll only use the UT at night," Cohen offered as a precautionary measure, "and I'll brief Leah about this so she only goes outside when I'm with her."

"Good idea, that will minimize exposure," Krasnoff nodded. "I'll be vigilant to avoid contacts with agency personnel as well as strangers." He paused and raised his eyebrows defensively and added,

"I'm committed to protect the UT at all costs, and for that reason I'm going to find out who is behind this."

The Fisheries restaurant at the Renaissance Jerusalem boasted of gourmet seafood from the Mediterranean as well as from the Sea of Galilee. Multiple interior designers had labored tirelessly to sustain the European look while pointedly adding the right touch of Judaism to attract the *sabras* and touring Jewish people alike. It was a favorite dining place for the Jewish aristocracy because of the restaurant's strict adherence to a kosher menu.

"Looking good," Krasnoff complimented Mazor as he walked in the front door. He touched Mazor's jacket lapel and courteously added, "Nice suit! You're really coming up in the world." Krasnoff was not used to seeing the unkempt, balding, 46-year-old, man who ordinarily shopped for his clothes in bargain stores, dress so meticulously debonair.

Mazor modestly received the tribute and replied, "I've decided to take the high option on my retirement pension and have some fun. You know the adage, 'I'm spending my kid's inheritance.' "

Krasnoff muffled a laugh as they sat down then said, "I'm happy for you." Krasnoff slowly scanned the restaurant with a deep longing, then pointed to a table across the room and said to Mazor, "Naomi and I used to come here once a month; that was our table. Of course I haven't been here since..." His voice trailed off as he reflected on the good times.

"So tell me, Revi, how are things going down at the agency?" Mazor asked to move the agenda and direct the conversation.

"Real well," Krasnoff rallied. "We are conducting some extensive excavations out in the Judean desert near the earthquake zone. It should prove interesting."

"That's nice," Mazor replied, then folded his hands on the table and said with a wink, "Naturally, in my former work of guiding tourists through hundreds of ancient ruins one hears many rumors and innocent prattle about" he gestured with his fingers, " 'secret discoveries.' How the 'government' has unearthed ancient treasures and property settlement documents in some cave and is keeping them to use as a weapon against the Arabs or something like that."

"That's preposterous," Krasnoff countered with a smile. "Any find, whether it be government or private, is duly recognized by the IAA and made public soon thereafter."

"Then they're not hiding anything?" Mazor smirked as he snapped his fingers to attract a waiter. Seconds later the jovial waiter appeared with menus in hand.

A blip suddenly appeared on Krasnoff's radar scope. "Not that I know of. Why, have you heard anything?"

"Specifically, no. But in my community, there is a groundswell that has emerged from rumors that your agency either has, or is about to make, an important archeological discovery."

Krasnoff began to wonder who made up Mazor's community. "Pure speculation," he replied cooly while his stomach churned on the inside. "Any rumor as to where the discovery would be?"

Mazor shrugged his shoulders nonchalantly. "You know how rumors are, no specifics, just idle chatter that sometimes sprouts legs." He then smiled jubilantly as the waiter arrived to take their orders.

"Well, if this rumor continues to evolve so that it starts walking around," Krasnoff met his gaze, "then the agency will probably make an official statement to dispel the myth."

"Aahhh," Mazor sighed, "a myth! That is a good way to put it. Perhaps this is simply a myth, or wishful thinking. If that is the case, then there is no alarm." Mazor grinned and switched the subject to catch up on family matters before lunch arrived, but Krasnoff was disturbed by the subtle interrogation—even though Mazor picked up the check as promised.

As Krasnoff exited through the revolving door in the hotel lobby, out of the corner of his eye he thought he spotted Mort Stein at the front desk.

By the time he reached his car, Krasnoff's recurrent reflux esophagitis was at an all-time high.

CHAPTER

8

Gaza Strip

Abdul Ayyash, the brother of Yahya Ayyash, the Hamas master-mind (aka "The Engineer") killed by Israeli secret agents in 1996, thumbed through his intelligence reports on the Sheraton Jerusalem bombing that had killed 26 Jews, and compared it with his acquired copy of the Israeli General Security Services study on the so-called terrorist attack. The Israeli General Security study noted that Hamas (an Arabic acronym for Militant Islamic Resistance Organization) never used the explosive Amatol, but only Semtex in their terrorist activities. No corroborative evidence pointed to Hamas as being responsible for the bombing, despite the phone call recorded by Israeli police on that fateful day. Nevertheless, the media maintained that Hamas was to blame, and Israeli General Security conveniently remained silent on the attack.

The aggravation of the trumped-up claim and false accusation knotted in Ayyash's chest as he replaced the reports in his attaché case and recited one of his creeds: "If we get the blame, we *will* get the fame." *There wasn't one of my men within five miles of the Sheraton that day*, he reminded himself with a shake of the head, *but I guess the war must go on.*

Relegated by choice to a nomadic, criminal life, Abdul Ayyash enjoyed the intoxication that accompanied the strategic planning of blowing up buildings owned by Jews. In fact, the buzz kept him on top of his game, for he was very good at what he did. Admittedly his brother Yahya, now a martyr with Allah, was skilled at organizing suicide bombings that killed Jews, but Abdul prided himself with sparing his brothers. Accordingly, his modus operandi was reclaiming property. The property rightfully belonging to Islam.

Ayyash possessed a large frame and muscular physique for an Arab. At an early age he had resolved to emulate Western men by turning his tall scrawny body into one rivaling a Hollywood body builder. After a decade of manual labor for a private road construction company in Hebron during the formative years of the Hamas, he emerged as a formidable brute who climbed the brotherhood ladder to head up the organization. Preferring the comforts of the affluent West, he frequently flew to Eilat on vacation with funds siphoned off financial aid from Iran and arms trafficking revenue that were designated for covert operations. The leader needed to get away every now and then to clear his head.

Home to Ayyash was a misnomer. While he networked, home was living in squalor outside a Palestinian refugee camp in Gaza to protect his anonymity and movements; but in his heart, home was Wadi Nisnas, one of the oldest neighborhoods adjacent to Hadar in Haifa. Amid its mosques, schools, clinics, arched doorways and window grills, haunting Arabic music, and exotic food, Ayyash's extended family found peace and safety.

Looking through the security bars on his fiancé's apartment window to the courtyard below, Ayyash patiently waited for his contact to show. Arab women in long black robes with baskets carefully balanced atop their heads walked through the streets amongst school children being herded up and funneled into their classrooms. He wondered how many of the youngsters would join him one day in a *jihad*—a holy crusade, against the Jews.

Ten minutes later Mazor arrived. This was their third meeting in two weeks.

Mazor gave Ayyash an acknowledging nod as he walked into the apartment. Stealthily he walked to the window and peeked out at his car and the surrounding neighborhood.

"You and your new car are safe here," Ayyash remarked perfunctorily. "It's too bad I can't say the same when I'm in your community," he added with a tinge of sarcasm.

"Need to keep my eyes open," Mazor replied with a slight titter. "I can't afford to be seen here."

"The Mossad and Shin Bet (General Securities Services) try to avoid this place," Ayyash said as he jerked his thumb over his shoulder. "It reminds them of pens of *chazir* (swine)." Mazor jingled his car keys inside his pocket and decidedly overlooked the remark. Ayyash's calculating eyes scanned Mazor up and down with disdain. Any man who would turn on his own people for money repulsed him. "What further information do you have?"

Mazor shrugged his shoulders. "Not too much. Krasnoff is very tight-lipped about any recent finds or excavations. He speaks in generalities, and when I attempted to draw in the net he used the term 'myth' to dispel the idea of any activities around the Mount."

Ayyash's hatred for the Jews was more than cultural inbreeding; it was in his blood. He remembered his father telling him of how Abraham's firstborn, Ishmael, was deprived of his rightful blessing and how it went to Isaac instead; Ishmael and his people were sentenced to live in the desert of Paran. Thousands of years later, Arab blood was still being splattered on desert sands throughout the Middle East. The

Jews treated them as misplaced, unwanted nomads who should remain wandering the dunes. This philosophy boiled the life-sustaining fluid circulating in Ayyash's veins, convincing him that only bloodletting would cure the age-old condition.

The only bond he had with the Jew who stood before him was money. Money in exchange for services. He pulled a fat white envelope from his knapsack and dropped it on the floor in front of Mazor. Mazor grunted, seemingly impervious to the degrading stunt, picked it up and shoved the envelope down his shirt. Ayyash grinned, bobbed his head in petty triumph, and said succinctly, "We need hard data from you to corroborate our intelligence-gathering reports about any subversive activities in the tunnel. If the Jews are digging, we want to know why, and we want to know about it fast—clear?"

Mazor nodded sheepishly. "I can't call you, so where will I meet you next week?"

To avoid detection, Ayyash changed cell phone numbers every ten days. "I will contact you."

Mazor nodded in assent and departed.

Sam methodically planned his work before starting the next phase of the Krasnoff job. He learned that the owners of the condo above Krasnoff were Sephardic Jews from Spain who were vacationing in Barcelona for two weeks. Plenty of time. Then he field tested the equipment from a distance of 50 feet to ensure its sound sensitivity and video clarity. Excellent!

Claiming to be a cable TV repairman, he quickly gained access to the condo. Within minutes of his entry, knowing the room layout to be the same for the Krasnoff condominium below him, he inserted a $\frac{1}{16}''$ carbide-tipped bit into his electric drill and strategically bore five holes through the floor down into Krasnoff's ceiling—one for each of the bedrooms, one for the living room, one for the kitchen. The holes emerged directly next to the ceiling light fixtures in each room. Into each of the tiny openings he placed a wireless DH200 MKIII pinhole high resolution fish-eye video camera—exercising caution so as not to damage their antennae. Then he filled in the holes. The video transmitter was hidden behind a shopping bag in one of the closets. To record the sound he would use a laser/microwave receiver pointed at Krasnoff's window from his van. Both of the devices were linked to a VCR to tape their activities. Within 25 minutes he emerged from the condo, bade the security guards farewell, and drove off. In a secluded alleyway two blocks away he removed the magnetic cable TV signs from his van, discarded them, then returned to Krasnoff's condo parking lot to continue his surveillance.

On the morning following the meeting with Mazor, Krasnoff finally met up with Cohen. "Yesterday was a bummer for me. I'm very uncomfortable with the whole thing," Krasnoff began at the breakfast table. "First I met Mazor for lunch—he more or less interrogated me—then I saw Stein in the lobby, the man who keeps 'showing up' down at IAA, and then there's this guy following us."

"But who are they working for? That's the question," Cohen asked with increasing perception.

"That's right. Could they all be consonant with one another? Who knows? As far as Mazor is concerned, my gut feeling is that he is on the take—but from whom?" Krasnoff wondered, mystified by the recent developments.

"It's time to move." Cohen repeated a suggestion he had made several days earlier as he nervously nibbled on his fingernails.

"I'm closing my diamond deal tomorrow, then we'll plan to move," Krasnoff agreed. "By the way, my gun-carrying permit should come in the mail tomorrow." He reminded Cohen of his pledge of protection. Patting his belt, he added, "Tomorrow night I will buy a pistol."

Cohen sighed and observed, "Who could have guessed that discovering the UT would lead us to this?" His mind suddenly went into neutral when he remembered his mother's advice on the folly of chasing fame and fortune.

Krasnoff swallowed hard. "Don't get melancholy on me, Nat. We'll be up and running once we straddle the hurdle of the watchful eyes—whoever they may be."

Cohen nodded sluggishly, then walked silently into his room and slowly closed the door.

In the van in the parking lot below, Sam reviewed the video recording and carefully appended his diary of the Krasnoff case.

Shortly after sunset, Cohen closed the shade on his bedroom window then set up the Urim and Thummim. This time, unlike his previous sessions, he needed therapy. With the stones in place before him, Cohen folded his hands and bowed his head in prayer for the first time in over ten years. His mind was cluttered with the debris of Krasnoff's plans and the forces trying to pry themselves into their lives. Apart from that, his heart was burdened for truth and freedom from guilt. His mother had warned him how a man's conscience can be numbed to evil, and that man needs a basis of authority apart from the conscience by which to gauge his actions. Few of the world's role models measured up. Cohen needed a basis of authority that had endured time and proven to be reliable. A flashback of his mother's handing him a Bible three months before his Bar Mitzvah made him smile. Both his mom and dad had insisted he study it and prepare to read the prophetic portion of the week—the *Haftarah*—before the adult congregation at Sabbath service. Recalling the festive celebration that followed made him smile, but then a wave of sorrow washed over him when he thought of how far he had drifted from reading the sacred text. Truth had become relative. He had to get back to the Bible where truth was absolute, he knew, but how? "Lord," he prayed aloud, "if you are God, then hear my prayer. I know I shouldn't use the Urim and Thummim for my own personal needs, but I pray that in your infinite mercy, you would make an exception just this one time. I need guidance and assurance because my heart is heavy about my life and where it is going. I need to know that my life…" his voice trailed off momentarily when he thought of Leah, "…my life together with Leah that is, will amount to something—" Another wave of sorrow came over him, but this time his heart corrected his thinking, "…amount to something in *Your* eyes."

Sam glared at a monitor as the scene before him unfolded, heightening his anticipation as Cohen neared the end of his prayer.

"Lord, if all this business with the UT has a purpose and Leah and I are going to be used as vessels of truth in your divine plan, give Urim, turn blue; if not, give Thummim, turn scarlet." Emotionally exhausted, he laid his head down on the table before him and closed his eyes.

Through his eyelids he could see blue light from the glowing sapphire filtering down into his soul. The answer was yes. His heart was overjoyed as he rested awhile with thoughts of God filling his heart.

Sam ejected the videotape from the VCR and quickly inserted a blank in readiness for the next session. Then he called Stein from his cell phone and throughly described what he called the "ceremony." They agreed to meet the following night at their usual rendevous to exchange the tape for another installment payment.

With a package under his arm, Krasnoff walked in his front door to see Cohen and Leah embracing on the sofa. Reluctantly accepting his daughter's choice, he offered a muted smile and walked into the kitchen. Grabbing a beer out of the refrigerator, he sat at the table. From the package he pulled out a gun, a snub-nosed .38 Smith & Wesson revolver. He fingered the mechanisms for several moments, then removed two boxes of shells from the package and set them next to the gun.

"How did you manage to buy the gun without a permit?" Cohen asked as he stuck his head in the doorway.

"I went to the post office this morning, picked up the permit, then went to the gun store," Krasnoff explained. "I need to be prepared for any contingency." He loosened his belt and threaded it into the holster, then inserted six bullets into the revolver's cylinder and one in the chamber. Then he holstered the weapon.

Cohen looked down at the empty package and excess bullets in dismay as Leah popped her head in the doorway next to his. She gazed at the weapon then cast her eyes upon her father's face. She noticed that his eyes appeared to be calculating and cold, his resolve steeled against adversity. She wondered about the attitude of his heart. She ran to him. "Daddy, do we really need to do this? I'm frightened."

Krasnoff repositioned his jacket to cover the weapon and said, "It's very necessary, darling. There's a lot at stake now. Not only do we have to protect the UT, but—" he paused to pull a small felt pouch out of his jacket pocket, "...these as well." He pulled open the pouch drawstrings and slowly poured out four diamonds on the table. "Returns on my investment," he announced proudly in an effort to divert the conversation.

Leah sighed in resignation at the latest development in her father's quest for something that she really didn't understand. The thought, *What is he trying to prove?* continued to assail her. She looked into his eyes and hugged him. "I love you."

"I love you back, you know that," he replied tenderly. He scooped up the diamonds and replaced them in the pouch. "I'm going to have them made into a brooch for you," he added as he looked at Leah, "for when you two get married."

Everyone smiled, then went their own way.

Sam was not moved by the encounter. He replayed the tape to study the gun, dismissing any fear from a novice like Krasnoff, then grinned when he realized that he could demand a higher fee from Stein now that the subject was armed. The gun raised the stakes considerably.

Lying on his bed in the solitude of his room, Cohen reviewed in his mind Leah's reaction to his personal encounter with the Urim and Thummim that afternoon. She didn't seem overly enthused. *I guess I need to show some spiritual backbone*, he argued with himself, *then maybe she'll take more of an interest in spiritual things.* He glanced at the Urim and Thummim table where his eyes quickly focused on the Bible he used for reference. "Someday," he whispered, "I'll really get into you, but for now..." he turned to look up at the ceiling and beyond to the heavens, "...I'm just going to leave our lives in Your hands for You to guide, and when Leah is ready, we can walk down the path together."

Staring at the ceiling, Cohen slowly realized that next to the light fixture was a small hole that he had never noticed before. He instinctively rubbed his eyes for a moment, then pretended to yawn as his mind raced to catch up with what his eyes thought they saw. He reached over and turned off the table lamp, then meandered over to the doorway and turned off the overhead light.

Sam looked at his monitors and realized that the Krasnoff household was in darkness. They had retired for the night. He switched off the monitors and VCR and switched on his portable TV. Then taking a wine cooler out of his mini refrigerator, he propped his feet up on the monitor console. Time to relax.

Cohen stealthily walked out of his bedroom into the kitchen where the only illumination came from a low-wattage bulb in the range exhaust hood lamp. In the near darkness he quietly lifted up a kitchen table chair and placed it under the ceiling light. Standing on the chair, he ran his fingers around the light, stopping on what felt like a hole with a convex surface slightly larger than a B-B. It appeared to be identical to the one he had seen in his bedroom. Moving closer to the light fixture, he squinted to sharpen his visual acuity, then ran his index finger over the opening. It was glass. He left the chair in place, then inspected the living room fixture and found it to be the same. He peeked into Leah's room and saw the lens in the glow of her nightlight. An alarm sounded in his mind.

"Revi, wake up," Cohen whispered in Krasnoff's ear. "We have company."

Krasnoff bolted upright in his bed and reached for his gun on the night table. "Who?" he exclaimed and reached for the light.

"No!" Cohen whispered with a gesture to remain silent. "Someone has installed camera lenses of some sort in here." He pointed to the ceiling. "They're next to the lights in all the rooms."

Krasnoff jumped out of his bed, quickly donned his clothes, and grabbed his gun. He motioned for Cohen to follow him into the bathroom, then jerked his thumb up. Cohen jumped on top of the toilet and felt around the ceiling fixture. He shook his head, then closed the door softly as Krasnoff put on his holster and gun.

"We must be under surveillance by someone," Cohen spoke sotto voce while jerking his hand wildly, "but how—?"

Krasnoff grabbed his aimless hand then motioned up and whispered, "I know my upstairs neighbors are away. I bet the culprit somehow finagled his way in and set the cameras in place." He paused and bit his lower lip as he tried to sort things out. "Today, most of the video and audio surveillance equipment is wireless, but severely limited in range..." His whispering trailed off as he squeezed his eyes shut momentarily, then added, "The dirty spy must be around here somewhere, monitoring our activities." They both tiptoed to Krasnoff's bedroom window and peeked out behind the shade. Nothing. His window overlooked the park and man-made lake used for irrigation. They went to the kitchen window next, but the condo's patio was fenced, making it impossible for anybody or anything to get close. Suddenly they exchanged glances and dashed to Cohen's room, which overlooked the parking lot. There were over 20 automobiles, 2 pickup trucks, and 3 vans in the lighted field. Two of the vans were commercially lettered, the third was not.

"Hmph," Krasnoff rasped then said gruffly, "let's go for a walk." He stroked his holster and headed for the front door. Cohen nodded his head gravely and followed him out.

Stark incandescent light bounced off the surfaces of the vehicles in the parking lot, casting bizarre shadows that fell between the cars and vans. An eerie darkness separated the unmarked van from the others so that Krasnoff and Cohen were able to creep up to the blind side unnoticed.

They crouched down and moved to the rear where Krasnoff stopped and pointed to the license plate, whispering, "Out-of-town tag."

Cohen stood up momentarily then dropped back down again and whispered, "There are many antennae on the roof and I can hear sounds from a TV inside."

Krasnoff's hands clenched into fists at his side as he nodded his understanding. *This must be some kind of mobile receiving station.* He tapped Cohen on the hand and whispered, "Go around the driver's side—sneak a peek and come back." Cohen nodded and obeyed.

Moments later Cohen returned. "There's a man asleep in front of a TV! It's the guy who followed you and stopped to ask Leah and me a question when we were in the park."

Krasnoff nodded his understanding and said, "No doubt the doors are locked. We need to flush him out. Go around to the driver's side again and scratch on the door, then scoot back here."

Cohen's heart jumped at the prospect of encountering the creep who had intruded into their lives. He nodded halfheartedly and crept around to the door once again. He ran his fingernail laterally across the door. Suddenly feet crashed to the floor of the van, then the TV went silent. Adrenaline swept through Cohen's body like a jolt of electricity when he heard fumbling inside the van. He dashed to the back of the van as the man sat in the driver's seat. Then they heard the window roll down. The man looked into the rearview mirror but saw nothing.

They held their breath, hoping he would open the door.

Seconds later they heard the door latch open and the man step out.

Krasnoff motioned to Cohen to stay put, then he stooped down and circled around the other side to the front of the van and stood motionless while the man held onto the door surveying the perimeter. Cohen's nervous system switched on as if an unseen hand had thrown a power switch. He blinked when he thought about the risk, then stuck his head out from behind the van to divert the man's attention. The man lunged for him as Krasnoff leaped and slammed the van door on the man's arm. The man cried out in pain as Krasnoff pulled out his gun and pressed it to the man's temple. "Hold it right there, mister," Krasnoff commanded. The man froze as Cohen frisked him. Krasnoff locked eyes with the man then kicked his right leg, pushing him against the side of the van. "Who are you, and what are you doing?" he growled furiously.

The man gazed off into the darkness and said nothing.

Krasnoff pressed the gun closer to the man's temple, then pulled the hammer back and deliberately shook his hand. "I've had a bad day, and I'm not used to this gun, mister."

A curious neighbor behind them put on his condo patio light, then opened his door and popped his head out

Cohen reflexively turned. "Somebody's coming!" he whispered to Krasnoff.

"Inside!" Krasnoff demanded roughly as he pushed the man inside the van. The man reluctantly climbed in while Krasnoff held the gun on him. "Move over and open the other side," Krasnoff instructed. The man sluggishly complied.

Cohen jumped into the back of the van and began looking around at the equipment. A large bank of miniature TV monitors were wired to a central VCR. Cohen threw the master switch on and illuminated the monitors. Fish-eye views of the insides of all the rooms in the Krasnoff home appeared on the screens. In the right corner were several scopes monitoring the sound sensitivity, and behind him was a console to handle an omni-directional antenna that was not in use. A hand-held microwave parabolic antenna lay inside a bin with a light blinking on and off. Cohen gulped and said, "This looks like a CIA covert operation!"

Krasnoff elbowed the man in the side then clenched his teeth and said, "Who are you working for?!"

The man remained mute.

"There are several tapes here with your name on them," Cohen said in dismay as he rummaged through the overhead bins.

"Play back a portion of one of them, quickly."

Within seconds they were watching Cohen operating the Urim and Thummim on one of the monitors.

"You dirty—!" Cohen breathed then yelled, "WHO ARE YOU?!"

Before the man could respond, Krasnoff hauled off and pistol whipped him twice. The man grabbed his head and fell over on the seat, groaning. Blood filtered through his fingers as Krasnoff reached over to hit him again.

The man winced and held up a hand. "Wait," he moaned, "no more."

"Who are you?" Krasnoff repeated the demand.

"Sam," he muttered. "My name is Sam."

Krasnoff gave him a glowering look then throttled him with his free hand. "Who sent you to spy on us?"

Sam's eyes bulged and his face reddened while Krasnoff tightened his grip. "Nobody," he gasped. "I work for myself."

Krasnoff instinctively knew he was lying. "I'm warning you, Sam," Krasnoff snarled as his face contorted with rage, "I'll kill you if you don't tell me the truth! Who put you up to this?"

Sam struggled to free himself from Krasnoff's grip as Cohen squirmed into the passenger side to assist. At the same time, Sam realized that Krasnoff's fury was out of control and that his life lay in the balance. "Mr. Stein," he finally mumbled. Krasnoff slowly relaxed his hand, allowing Sam to swallow repeatedly.

Krasnoff put his hand to his forehead and closed his eyes for several seconds to absorb the information. Then he turned to Sam and bared his teeth through a smile. "Give me the keys, we're going for a drive."

Sam's mind seized up in panic as an ominous foreboding swept over him. He passed the keys over to Krasnoff and looked through his bloody fingers at Cohen. Cohen's heart sank as he returned the look; he was not able to comprehend the violence and brutality he saw in his partner and future father-in-law. Sam read Cohen's look like a cornered animal senses an escape route.

"What are you doing, Revi?" Cohen asked nervously.

Krasnoff started the engine and replied, "I'm going to put an end to this business once and for all."

Sam's eyes locked on Cohen's, pleading for mercy, as Krasnoff's resolve heightened.

Rap-rap-rap. A pounding on the driver's side window. Krasnoff bolted up in his seat. "Is everything all right?" an elderly man's voice crackled.

The windows were fogged, so Krasnoff lowered the window several inches while he jammed the gun's cold muzzle into Sam's gut as a reminder to remain silent. He smiled at the elderly gentleman and said, "Everything's just fine. We're just having a little disagreement," he looked to Sam then to the man, "but we've settled it now." The man nodded, waved, and walked toward his condo. Krasnoff immediately handed the gun to Cohen to keep guard over Sam, quickly put the transmission in drive, and pulled away.

A muscle jerked in Sam's left cheek as he studied the street layout before him. It was slightly over one block from the parking lot that he made his move. As Krasnoff neared the busy intersection at Agrippas Boulevard and looked left to pull out, Sam jammed his foot on the brake. Krasnoff slammed against the steering wheel and Cohen hit the windshield, dropping the gun on the floor. Sam then jammed the gas pedal while reaching over to open the passenger door. Taking advantage of centrifugal force and vehicle momentum, he pushed against Cohen, propelling him out the door where he tumbled to a stop in the road. Krasnoff and Sam struggled for several seconds, then Krasnoff hit the brake and veered toward a curb as Sam groped for the gun on the floor. Seconds later the van came to an abrupt stop when it hit the curb.

With his eyes on Krasnoff, Sam grabbled frantically for the gun, and when his hand found it he inadvertently looked at it for a split second.

Whack! Whack! Whack! Krasnoff seized the opportunity and repeatedly punched Sam in the bloody side of his face. Sam groaned deeply but quickly rallied. He raised his hand and brandished the gun at Krasnoff. "Now it's my turn, Krasnoff," he growled. "You got lucky back there, but your luck just ran—"

Without warning the passenger side door flew open.

Sam reacted by spinning around, allowing Krasnoff to grab the gun. Cohen stood there gaping and gulping for air with his face scraped and his shirt torn and hanging from his body. "Revi, are you all right?"

"I am now," Krasnoff said with a vengeance. He felt his chest then wiped his hand over his forehead as he gazed at the scene for a moment. He turned and focused on Cohen's face, then glared at Sam with malevolent eyes and yelled vehemently, "You want blood?! Then you'll get blood!" Krasnoff then fired two shots into Sam's torso. His body convulsed then teetered forward on the seat. Making a soft, gagging sound, he fell backward with eyes dilated and fluttering wildly. After several seconds he stopped breathing.

The color drained from Cohen's face. "Revi, was that necessary? Couldn't we have threatened him and let him go?" he said, numbed with shock.

"No! We needed to get rid of him and send Mr. Stein a potent message at the same time," he replied with clear precision.

Cohen glared at the dead man's body and said, "We'd better get out of here. Now!"

They opened their windows and saw that the melee had stirred no interest in the passing motorists. "We'll leave the van and walk casually back to the house," Krasnoff instructed as he retrieved the videotape and holstered his gun.

Cohen blinked in torpid agreement as the realization crashed in on him that his partner was mutating into a monster.

Cohen's life and habits were changing, turning him into a morning person. The horror of the past few nights was unraveling him. At 6:30 a.m., he sat at the kitchen table staring at the wall, entranced as it were, pondering the events of the previous night—the disturbing events that had brought on a severe nightmare.

The thought of his future father-in-law killing a man in front of him was repugnant and utterly unforgivable. Self-defense was arguable; nonetheless, in his mind, it was murder. Did that make him an accomplice?

Twenty-five minutes into his morning, Krasnoff walked nonchalantly into the kitchen shuffling his feet while whistling a radio commercial jingle through his teeth. "Before Leah wakes up," he began as he opened the refrigerator door, "I wanted to bounce my security leak theory off you."

Not a sign or hint of remorse over the death of a human life, Cohen realized painfully. He set aside his coffee and looked at Krasnoff with inquiring eyes. "And that is?"

"Someone must be feeding information to Stein. He in turn responded to that information by sending the man Sam to spy on us to confirm or deny the reports. It must be internal. In my mind, Director Ben-Tor is incorruptible, so that leaves Golda Rokach. She must be the rat." For a fleeting moment he thought of Ze've Mazor, but assigned him to external sources of trouble. Mazor couldn't know about the UT yet, but might become a matter to be dealt with in the future.

"Are you going to kill her too?" Cohen asked discordantly.

Krasnoff glared at him and bristled. "I would only *kill* someone if I had to defend myself or the UT. No, I will not *kill* Rokach, but I will prevent her from talking again."

Tears welled up in Cohen's eyes. "No more killing, Revi, under any conditions, or I'm out of here. Understood?"

Krasnoff nodded and said gruffly, "Not a word of this to Leah. She doesn't have to know about last night." Retaining his uncorrupted fatherly image was important to him.

Cohen shook his head. "If she asks me about anything, I will not lie to her. My relationship with her must be built on a truthful foundation."

"I admire your pristine attitude," Krasnoff said blissfully, then added seriously, "You should be truthful with my daughter." The fact that he himself knew nothing of truth would come back to haunt him someday.

"What do you plan to do about Stein?" Cohen probed. "In my mind, he's your real enemy."

Krasnoff crossed his arms over his chest, raised his eyebrows and nodded in assent. "Not sure yet. I'll hold off on him until I meet with Rokach."

Cohen said nothing. The rest of the day he mentally rehearsed several of his mother's mottos that pricked relentlessly at his conscience.

Ze've Mazor lit up an expensive American cigar as he sipped his after-dinner cordial at the Lamplight, the elegant restaurant in the Seven Arches hotel, located one mile south of the Church of Mary Magdalene in the old city of Jerusalem. After only three puffs on the cigar, his appointment arrived, a man called Nahum, a one-time associate while Mazor was a tour guide. *Good timing*, Mazor thought, *now I'll only have to buy him a cup of coffee.* Nahum Lederman, an Israeli-Arab living in Nazareth, was half Jewish, half Muslim—and more importantly to Mazor's current needs—a government contracted excavation engineer. Lederman managed to walk the cultural and religious tightrope between Arab and Jew by attending an Israeli university and earning a master's degree in anthropology. Normally Israeli Arabs were ineligible for state jobs, but because of a shortage of Arab anthropologists who knew historic Jerusalem, he was awarded the position. As a retired Israeli tour guide, Mazor had many friends and contacts with high security clearances who were involved in government-funded archeological digs and the unearthing of national treasures.

As Lederman pulled up a chair and sat at the table, Mazor flagged down a waiter and took the liberty of ordering. From a side profile, Lederman was a handsome middle-aged man. His black eyebrows and moustache gave his face contrast, while his chiseled features gave it character. He wore his traditional kaffiyeh, held in place with an agal wound around his head, augmented by a blue blazer, turtleneck shirt and white pants. It was the typical outfit worn by affluent Israeli Arabs aspiring to the haberdasher of the Western world.

Mazor clasped Lederman's hand to embrace him in friendship. "You are looking well!" Mazor began robustly. "The government is treating you good?"

Lederman nodded modestly. "Somewhat, yes, life has been good to me." As he put on his wire-rimmed glasses, the waiter brought his coffee. "Your call sounded urgent. What is this all about?"

Mazor bent in closer to him, looked around surreptitiously, and spoke just above a whisper. "Since my retirement I have found new employment with a group dedicated to the protection and preservation of certain ancient monuments here in Israel—the most important being the Temple Mount." He paused to place his hand on Lederman's shoulder and added, "You can appreciate, that can't you?"

Lederman nodded suspiciously. "Go on."

Mazor chose his words carefully. "The heart of an Israeli-Arab can be torn in many directions. Part of the heart wants what is best for Eretz Israel, while the strings of the heart often tug in another direction—to better the Arab world." He placed his right hand over his heart and continued, "As for me, I am a Jew, but I feel for the cause of my Arab neighbors because—" he paused to thump his hand over his chest, "the blood running through my veins cries out for equality! There is plenty of land here for us to share. And that is what this meeting is really about, sharing."

"I'm listening," Lederman said sympathetically.

"Well, we should not only share our land, but information as well. When we consider what is best for our land, we need to consider that a balance of power must exist, and since information is power, we need to keep it in balance." He pointed his finger in a westerly direction and added, "That's what keeps the Americans and the Russians in check, the exchange of information. Whether it be overt or covert, it acts as a deterrent against aggression. It works for them, it should work for us."

"Your point, Ze've, please."

Mazor could see that Lederman was growing impatient. He snapped his fingers to attract the waiter standing by. "Bring my *friend* a lunch menu, please." The waiter handed Lederman the menu, but he quickly waved it off. "I shall get to the point. I have heard rumors that the government is digging around the Temple Mount, and in your profession, I thought you may know something about it."

"It is a breech of security for me to discuss it," Lederman intoned.

Mazor intuitively deduced that Lederman was indeed involved. "Yes, yes, I know that it is a sore subject," he soothed wearily, "since it is such a volatile site. But if something is going on there, and the Arabs find out about it—it could mean war."

"You mean the Temple Mount ownership thing?"

Mazor nodded solemnly. "Let me appeal to your ultra-high level of reasoning with this comparison," he complimented. "Consider what is meant by the nuclear non-proliferation treaty. It is designed to prevent the spread of nuclear weapons among member countries who have agreed not to further enrich reactor-grade uranium to the 90 percent plus concentration necessary to make a bomb. The sharing of this agreement acts beneficially for global welfare. In other words, the exchange of information necessary to build a nuclear-powered electrical generating station, with this agreement, will theoretically prevent a thermonuclear war between member countries."

"Are you suggesting that I share information about our research project on the Mount for the purpose of preventing a war?" Lederman asked incredulously.

Mazor read Lederman's admission of the project as an opportunity to strategically place his queen and rook on the chess board to bring about a checkmate. "My Arab constituents have expert field agents who already know that there is a dig in progress on the Mount."

"They do?" Lederman gulped. "I find that hard to believe!"

Mazor shook his head. "Dismiss the truth if you will, but regardless of your acknowledgment, my constituents are aware of the activities on the Mount and want to be a part of it. If they are advised of the nature of the project, it will defuse their concerns and thus prevent a catastrophe."

"Might I ask, who are your *constituents*, Ze've?"

After a few seconds of concentrated thought, Mazor replied with the half-truth, "They are made up of Israeli-Arabs like yourself, who have taken up the crusade of protecting Arab sites from desecration by the Israeli government. I as a Jew believe that many high profile politically disputed sites—such as the Temple Mount—should be shared as national assets like the Americans shared their discovery of the polio vaccine or the way Arab bloc nations share their oil with each other."

"You make it sound like it is the patriotic thing to do," Lederman quipped.

"If you are participating in a project that will mutually benefit our nation, then what's the big deal? It really is your duty to share this information with your Israeli-Arab compatriots, especially if you are the chosen person to avert a potentially explosive incident." He clasped his hands while his voice vibrated with feeling and added, "You will be heralded as another God-appointed vessel of peace." Mazor moved his knight into position to bring about the tour de force. "We are prepared to pay handsomely for the information."

Lederman stood up from the table, thrust his napkin down to his plate, and said trenchantly, "I resent the implication that I can be bought, Mr. Mazor."

Mazor's face flushed under the embarrassing moment. "Please, Nahum," he entreated, "I apologize and withdraw the remark."

Lederman slowly retook his seat. "My interest is solely out of allegiance to my homeland and the furtherance of peace and scientific studies."

"And I admire that," Mazor said in contrition.

"Any information that I would give you would be motivated by my concern for the betterment of our nation that would improve domestic tranquility."

"Yes, yes," Mazor agreed, crossing his fingers under the table to invoke some mythical god who could grant wishes.

"Any information would be kept secret by the responsible parties aforementioned?"

"Naturally. You have my promise."

"My name could never be revealed."

"You have my word on that," Mazor said as he tightened his fingers.

Lederman made a cryptic gesture to bring Mazor closer to his mouth. "The authorities have located the ark of the covenant under the Temple Mount, and we are presently digging at night to unearth it. We should be finished in about two days."

Perspiration began dripping down Mazor's face as he paused to digest the information. He simply shook his head in bewilderment at first. *I suspected something big, but not this big.* "But the ark hasn't been seen for thousands of years. This has been confirmed?"

Lederman nodded curtly. "By the highest authority. The IAA knows exactly where it is; the agency ordered the excavation."

Mazor closed his eyes and put a hand to his forehead. In his mind's eye he saw this discovery as being potentially dangerous as the Yom Kippur War. His lips pursed in a soundless whistle. "This is overwhelming."

"You have been privileged to hear secret information, Ze've," Lederman said, then patted the top of Mazor's hand and added, "Keep it that way." He rose from the table, walked out of the restaurant, and faded into the crowded street.

Mazor stared at Lederman's vacant seat for several moments while he collected his thoughts. The mystery of why God would allow the ark to be found after all these years came to mind first, followed by the thought that Ayyash would agree that he had really earned his pay today.

Three hours before their appointment, Stein inadvertently found out about Sam while scanning the TV channels. The newscast showed a clip of a van filled with surveillance equipment hung up on a curb on Agrippas Boulevard. An on-the-scene reporter flashed Sam Madler's passport photo before the video camera as she explained that the bearded American, a one-time private investigator from Rhode Island, had been shot dead at close range and that Israeli police were investigating. Stein realized that it was time for him to go after Krasnoff personally.

CHAPTER

9

Athens

Gregory Kavidas carefully appended his speech for the EEC installation ceremony. It had all the hallmarks of a literary masterpiece. He cunningly crafted the speech so as to embrace the conservatives by his acceptance of traditional policies. Throughout the introduction and halfway into the body, he spoke about renewal of the free movement of labor and capital; the abolition of trusts and cartels; and the development of joint and reciprocal policies on labor, social welfare, agriculture, transport, and foreign trade. With the formation of the European monetary system in 1979 that had developed the European Currency Unit, often considered the precursor to the Eurodollar, and the Maastricht Treaty of 1992, that provided for a central banking system, history proved it was a simple task for the EEC to adopt his MASTERLINK system throughout Europe. He predicted that his economic system would continue to bring new meaning to the word *prosperity*.

But as the speech unfolded, he subtly wove into the fabric aggressive policies that he would implement in time—policies that would attract the hawks who clamored for change. Since the founding fathers envisioned the EEC would eventually evolve to include political unity, he would take it one step further, and adopt religious unity as well. Yes, he would explain, this would take time to institute, but the way the world was going, ecumenism was a realistic goal that would contribute to global well-being. Something the nations needed to consider for the future.

Looking at his calender, Kavidas reminded himself that in seven days he would be the president of Europe's most powerful economic union, the former Common Market, with a current membership of fifteen nations, his homeland, Greece, having been admitted in 1981. In time, the multi-national group would break off and settle in with only ten member nations.

In preparation for his new position, Kavidas commuted four times a month to EEC headquarters in Brussels, but that would change to permanent residence once he ascended the presidency. Mort Stein would then take control of MASTERLINK while Kavidas attended to the matters of the Community.

He set aside his speech and picked up his research brief on Executive Orders, the instrument used by American presidents during a national emergency. In 1933, at the request of President Roosevelt, the U.S. Congress had passed the War and Emergency Powers Act, amending the Trading With the Enemies Act of 1917. It granted the president full authoritarian control of citizens of enemy countries, and their property, who were living or working in America at the time. In effect, the 1933 revision allowed reclassification of U.S. citizens when they could be considered enemies of the federal government during a crisis. In 1978 Congress enacted the National Emergencies Act of 1976, which terminated any existing decrees of national emergency, but did not affect the 1933 act. Accordingly, Executive Orders could be declared in the event of an emergency by the president, not Congress, enabling the president to suspend the Constitution at will. All the president needed to justify this act was a national crisis.

Executive Orders had been used historically during wartime, but modern domestic E.O.'s now allowed the president to enforce the involuntary registration and relocation of U.S. citizens into labor groups under government surveillance and for the executive branch to take over labor, services, and manpower resources if needed.

What interested Kavidas most, was the E.O that allowed the government to take over health, education, and welfare programs as well as the mechanisms of production and distribution, energy sources, wages, salaries, the flow of money, and credit. He made a mental note of the presidential prerogatives, knowing that the day would come when he would give Executive Orders involving the whole world's financial system.

Satisfied with his morning planning session, he called for his chauffeur to take him to the airport where he boarded his personal jet to fly him to the island of Rhodes. To get to this favorite vacation spot he routinely passed over the breathtaking Cyclades, a group of islands of southeast Greece in the southern Aegean Sea. From there the flight was simply another 60 nautical miles. Upon landing, Kavidas took a cab to Faliraki for his scheduled planning meeting with Stein.

The Hotel Atalanti at Faliraki was located by the hillside of St. Amon, overlooking the popular Faliraki Bay. It was a short drive from the town of Lindos, the birthplace of Chares the Lindos, the architect of the Colossus of Rhodes. After defeating Poliorcetes in 305 B. C., the townspeople of Rhodes wanted to use their booty to build a thank offering to their divine patron Helios. Lindos designed a bronze statue of the nude young god, wearing a sun-ray crown, to stand on a promontory beside the harbor, looking out to sea. The giant monument stood over 120 feet high on a 25-foot white marble base. Although the

Colossus was reinforced with stone and iron, it broke at the knees and fell in an earthquake in 365 B.C. It remained one of the Seven Wonders of the World up to the Arab invasion of A.D. 653, when it was broken up for scrap metal. Today, there was no surviving evidence of it.

Kavidas and Stein sat at an outdoor table overlooking the breathtaking view of Faliraki Bay. For the first few moments of their meeting, they silently sipped their drinks and took in the scenery. Champion roses adorned.a safety railing that prevented hotel guests from straying too far over a ledge. Beyond lay a sloping grassy hillside that contained many hillocks studded with large rocks. Wild bougainvillaea jutted out from under the rocks, creating a colorful foreground, with the sparkling blue water surrounded by mountains in the background.

Kavidas smiled expansively as he set his glass of lemonade down, "Nice, isn't it?"

Stein nodded glumly in response, apprehensive over the disappointment with the Krasnoff fiasco.

"You needn't be concerned about Sam Madler," Kavidas began intuitively as he patted Stein's hand gently. "You just have to take care of Krasnoff and Cohen yourself. Then the problem will go away."

Stein recognized that Kavidas was drawing upon his gift of awareness and perception more openly now that events for the completion of their mission were progressively unfolding. He had never mentioned Madler's or Cohen's name before. "That's what I get for delegating," Stein replied with a clenched fist.

Kavidas intended to use the failure as a learning experience to monitor the level of Stein's spiritual discernment. "Krasnoff and his accomplice Cohen are being used as instruments to draw our fire, Mort, don't you see that?" He paused to allow Stein to dwell on his words as he retrieved a file from his attaché case. "God is purposefully allowing them to use this device as a means to expose us, but it won't work," he predicted. "Nobody will ever believe them."

"You think I'm spending too much time in Israel dealing with the *lights*?"

Kavidas nodded with a cryptic grin. "I think the time has come for you to use the powers you have been endowed with to bring this nuisance to a speedy end." He momentarily busied himself leafing through the file, then turned toward the bay and added, "I know how intractable Krasnoff and Cohen will be unless you call upon the resources that are available and put your own natural abilities on the shelf for now."

"Are you saying that this is strictly a spiritual battle? Is that all you see here?"

"It was from the beginning, Mort," Kavidas clarified. "From the time of my dream that alerted us to the discovery of the *lights*, I knew that it would come down to a battle between us..." he paused and pointed up, "...and Him. Krasnoff and Cohen are mere tools while the Urim and Thummim are simply a revelatory device that will be used in an attempt to warn the world of our mission."

Stein's lips curved sardonically. "Okay, but He wins."

"Yes. But before that appointed time, we have been given authority to use our defenses. We can thwart, minimize, contain, or eliminate the threat of the *lights* before they can hurt us with large numbers of followers."

Stein needed the exhortation to remind him of their purpose once again. He raised his hand and with a halting motion replied, "Enough said. I'll take care of the problem as soon as I return to Israel."

Kavidas stared at Stein for several seconds then blinked his eyes in recognition. "Let's move on," he said as he pulled out a report and placed it on the table. "Through the Freedom of Information Act of 1967 that allows us access to U.S. government files, we are now gathering information on subscribers' religious denominations and political parties."

Stein picked up the report from the FOIA board that explained how the information was obtained. "How is this being done?"

"I have connections with both the FOIA and the IRS back in the States. When taxpayers take deductions for donations to religious organizations, whether they be charities or churches, we are notified. When they make a political contribution, we are notified. In turn, we input the information as to their religious and political affiliation into our MASTERLINK database for future use."

Stein slowly shook his head in amazement as he looked at Kavidas, the man destined for greatness by divine decree long before the world was formed. Aware of his place in history from the age of reason, he remained unobtrusive until he reached his thirtieth year, then with what Stein called 'divine' permission, his latent gifts slowly began to emerge. From that point, attributes reserved only for gods began to emanate from him, convincing Stein that Kavidas had been chosen by Providence to become a world leader. First in successful entrepreneurship, then economic control, then political finesse—and now with a view to world domination.

The domination will not be accomplished through military conquest, although conquest is a fitting word, Stein thought. *No, it will be accomplished through voluntary worship of their messiah, Gregory A. Kavidas, brought on by the satiation of man's lusts, predetermined by the counsels of God as recorded in His Book. Yes, quoting Gregory's motto, such will be his crowning glory.*

"And what about our international strategy?" Stein asked as he snapped out of his reverie.

"As the head of the EEC I have the authority to initiate trade agreements with non-member countries, Israel being my prime concern. Accordingly, I have already drawn up such a compact to be presented to Prime Minister Rubin after my installation. This agreement will promote equitable product traffic between the EEC, thereby generating nearly one billion U.S. dollars in annual revenue for the Holy Land."

Stein smiled, knowing that Rubin had no idea of the price tag he would pay for the agreement. "And of course, we know he will agree to it."

"He has no choice. American favor toward Israel has soured for good now that Arab oil cartels are controlling prices at the gas pumps. Americans need gas for their cars, not Jews. Arab financial influence in U.S. markets has turned the hearts of the West to favor their oil-rich sand over the troublesome Chosen Ones. Remember, Mort, it's no accident that God placed most of the earth's oil reserves under Arab soil. Through petrol dollars, the Arab world is purchasing sophisticated military hardware from Russia, China, and even the U.S. that will fortify their offensive posture and bring them to the point of attacking Israel. It's prophesied. So by ingratiating ourselves to Mr. Rubin with trade money, we will, in the not-too-distant future, persuade him to readily accept our advice when it comes to other matters, such as national security."

"By endearing yourself to him in bolstering up his economy, you win his confidence."

"That's the plan for Israel. Now when it comes to the Arabs, the prophecy calls for an amalgamation of numerous countries—namely Iran, Syria, Egypt, Libya, and probably Iraq—who will form an alliance with Russia, Armenia, and Turkey to invade Israel soon after the Tribulation begins. Then—"

"—our time will come!" Stein finished the sentence.

"Yes. Therefore, we will make secret trade pacts with these nations to keep them supplied during their period of conflict. This will strengthen our grip on Europe. Once Israel is defeated and overtaken, we will move into Palestine, displace the Arabs, seize control, and then set up our administration in Jerusalem."

"What a plan!" Stein shot his eyebrows up. "Whew! It can be a little overwhelming when you think about it, but on the other hand, we cannot fail." Stein's analytical mind replayed the eschatological tapes that foretold of both him and Kavidas reaching world acclaim before the fateful day when time would come to an end. A day of dread that he suppressed in his subconscious, refusing it entrance into his daily life. Random thoughts of the appointed date occasionally escaped through his internal safeguards, forcing themselves upon his thinking patterns. Over the years, however, he exercised spiritual restraints that reminded him of his need to strengthen his resolve. Visiting Kavidas and uniting with his spirit in worship always assuaged Stein's fears.

Because of Kavidas' command of destiny and his innate ability to control the environment of life, Stein placed complete trust in him. There never had been, nor ever would be even a hint of aspiration to usurp his role, for Stein was perfectly content to be the precursor, the number two man. His fulfillment in life would come by seeing Kavidas catapulted to world adoration as the Christ, while he remained nothing more than the vessel that pointed men to him.

Kavidas nodded in agreement, then quoted the words of Joseph Addison from *Cato*, " 'Tis not in mortals to command success, But we'll do more, Sempronius; we'll deserve it.'"

The phone rang in Ze've Mazor's home at 2 a.m. He placed his pillow over his head to shut it out, but the ringing continued. After eight rings he finally lifted the phone. "Who is this?!" he said roughly.

"This is Ayyash," the grating voice said. "What have you to report?"

Mazor sprang up in his bed and quickly collected his thoughts. "You were right when you said they were digging under the Mount. I spoke to an engineer. The IAA has discovered the ark of the covenant!"

No response.

"Did you hear what I said?" Mazor exclaimed into the phone.

"Control yourself, Mazor," Ayyash replied, "I heard you perfectly."

Click.

It was 3 a.m. and Lederman was fast asleep, when the call came on his cell phone from the excavation foreman. He was told to report to the tunnel, for the ark had been found precisely where Krasnoff predicted.

By the time Lederman arrived, the tunnel section under the Dome of the Rock was fully illuminated with floodlights that bathed the ark in white light. IAA director Ben-Tor, the excavation engineers, and Rehavam Krasnoff stood looking at the ancient container where at one time God had chosen to deposit the sacred instruments given to Moses and Aaron.

They were astonished at its state of preservation. The Israelite ark that represented God's presence to the world, the very ark that led God's people in the deserts of Sinai and accompanied the Jewish warriors at Jericho, the very ark that David brought to Jerusalem after defeating the Philistines, and the very ark that was transferred into the Holy of Holies in Solomon's new Temple, stood before them.

Both Dr. Ben-Tor and Lederman looked at Krasnoff, then back at the ark, then began to whimper. Their whimpers led to cries of unbelief and exultant joy as they gazed at the gold chest hammered out by Israelite craftsmen at Moses' instructions around 1490 B.C.

Ben-Tor examined the hollowed-out vault that housed the ark and found it remarkable in nature. It was lined with a compound that appeared to be made up of agate, quartz, and sand flint. These formed a primitive drying device similar to modern silica gel, which was used chiefly as a dehumidifying and dehydrating agent. The platform that the ark rested on seemed to be coated with the same substance. They were all amazed over the absence of dust or dampness.

Reaching into his pocket, Krasnoff pulled out a tape measure and held it up to the ark. It measured 3 and 3/4 feet long by 2 and 1/4 feet wide by 2 and 1/4 feet high. Ben-Tor delicately and reverently ran his finger over the gold overlay that covered both the cover and lower compartment, which were made of acacia wood. He estimated the modern monetary value would easily be in excess of eight hundred million dollars. He stepped back several feet to gaze at the angelic figures, the cherubim, that were fastened at each end of the cover. They too were made out of hammered gold, facing each other, connected at their wingtips, overshadowing the cover. One of the engineers motioned to Dr. Ben-Tor for his permission to touch the ark. He nodded, then the engineer placed his hand on the cover and said just above a whisper, "The mercy seat. May the God of Israel grant us mercy and forgive our sin for disturbing His sacred ark." They all remembered learning about how the high priest ceremonially sprinkled the blood of the slaughtered bull on the lid or mercy seat to atone for sin, thus *covering* the condemning testimony of the law therein, and effecting reconciliation between God and His people.

In unison, they all said, "Amen."

Krasnoff stepped outside the vault momentarily then returned with the agency's camera equipment. "We need to document the discovery as soon as it is unearthed," he said in an official tone. Ben-Tor nodded then motioned the others out of the vault. Krasnoff meticulously photographed the ark from every angle, paying particular attention to the cherubim on the mercy seat and the gold-covered carrying poles that were inserted into the gold rings fastened to the sides of the ark.

Dr. Ben-Tor waited until Krasnoff completed photographing the outside, then waved in the rest of the crew to accompany him to the ark. He walked to the ark and, raising his eyes heavenward, mouthed a silent prayer. Then, with every eye fastened on it, he slowly lifted the cover.

The inside of the ark was completely empty.

"Just as I expected," Ben-Tor lamented with a tear. Scripture and tradition explained that the articles once contained in the ark were lost in antiquity at the time of the Babylonian captivity, never to be seen again. "Regrettably, we shall never see the Decalogue, Aaron's rod, or the gold jar of manna in this life," he instructed. "We shall have to wait until we get to Heaven to see the original." He was referring to the fact that the earthly ark and its contents were fashioned by Moses' craftsman Bezalel after a heavenly pattern.

Remembering Cohen's dream, Krasnoff had formed the suspicion that the ark would be empty. He feigned disappointment, then for the record took multiple photographs of Ben-Tor and the rest of the staff next to the ark. After stuffing his camera equipment into the carrying case, he then walked to the ark, leaned over, and gave it what appeared to be a sacred kiss. Dr. Ben-Tor went to his side and put his arm around him. "Revi, my heartfelt congratulations," he said as tears welled up in his eyes. "This is an historic moment and you have made the agency proud."

Krasnoff expelled a sigh. "It's almost too good to be true." In his heart, he cared nothing for the agency, only for the glory the find would bring. He turned toward Ben-Tor and asked blandly, "When will you inform the prime minister?"

Swept up in the enthusiasm, Dr. Ben-Tor unwittingly had forgotten about his letter from the prime minister. "I will contact him this morning. Naturally, we cannot even as much as lift the ark off its pedestal without his permission." Ben-Tor looked askance up at the top of the vault as if to see the Dome of the Rock several meters above them and added, "I only pray that he doesn't delay in authorizing us to move this out of here."

An ominous feeling swept over Krasnoff. "An unnecessary delay could prove disastrous."

Dr. Ben-Tor surveyed the crew then shrugged his shoulders. "So, what then?"

Surveying military vulnerability in the Golan Heights with Defense Minister Ussishkin, Prime Minister Rubin did not receive the private call from Dr. Ben-Tor until six hours after the ark's discovery. Lacking complete faith in the project from the beginning, and overly concerned with political and religious repercussions, Rubin advised Ben-Tor to leave the ark untouched until he had time to confer with his cabinet and decide its disposition. That time lag, along with Rubin's directive to squelch exposure by avoiding security, meant that the ark would be unprotected in the vault. This reality would prove to be a critical catalyst in the course of events.

It was early afternoon when Krasnoff picked up his developed film at the photo lab. He boasted to himself that the photographs of the ark and the staff in the tunnel were of professional quality, the kind that the agency would use for publication once the prime minister gave his approval. On the way to his office, he mentally reviewed his suspicions about Golda Rokach. *She has to be the leak.*

Flushed with apprehension, Rokach gave Krasnoff a bright and cheery smile the very second he opened the office door. She stood up from her computer console, walked to him, and attempted to hug him. "Good afternoon, and congrats for the ark discovery, Revi," she said. Krasnoff said nothing, but turned and sat down in her chair. She stood looking at him. "What's the matter?" she asked with a nervous giggle.

Krasnoff looked around to confirm their privacy then crossed his arms over his chest. "Three days ago my associate and I were nearly killed by a man who had wired our home with audio and video surveillance equipment. He was recording our every move from inside a van parked a short distance away. Fortunately we discovered him before he could do us any harm." He turned to her computer monitor and clicked on the Explorer to review her files. "What puzzles me is who would put this man up to such a deed, and for what purpose?" He scanned the files, then turned back to her. "Any idea as to who or what?"

A muscled jerked in her left forearm. She quickly rubbed it as she unwittingly looked into Krasnoff's office. "No."

Krasnoff saw the look and followed her gaze. "Are you sure, Ms. Rokach?" he pressed. He followed up the question four seconds later. "Does the name Mort Stein mean anything to you?"

Her knees felt wobbly so she held onto her desk and said numbly, "He was here asking question about you and your work."

Krasnoff's voice vibrated with intensity, "And what did you tell him, Ms. Rokach?"

She fidgeted for what seemed like several minutes. "Well, he asked me if there were any excavations going on in the tunnel, and…" her voice trailed off as she groped for words. "…Well, you know how rumors spread around here. And the rumor about a secret dig going on in the tunnel had surfaced in the past few days, so I—"

"…blabbed to him," Krasnoff waved her off and completed her sentence with a sardonic grin. "He in turn decided to take it a quantum leap further and get secret information directly from me…" he ratcheted up his volume and yelled in her face, "…in my home!"

"I'm really sorry, Revi," she begged with rapidly flowing tears. "He just had a way with me that led me down a path where I couldn't refuse him."

"What else did he learn from you?" he demanded.

She sniffled several times and said with a shrug, "He asked about the ancient Urim and Thummim, but I don't know anything about that." She blinked and thought a quick prayer of repentance for the lie, then asked God to intervene and not have Krasnoff ask any more questions.

Krasnoff was momentarily stunned. He swallowed hard, turned on his heel, and walked into his office. He slammed the door with tremendous force.

Golda sat at her desk for 30 minutes before she moved an inch. Then she quietly and methodically wrote out a letter of resignation stating that she would be going to Egypt to pursue her passion for archeology. She placed the letter in Krasnoff's mailbox, cleared out her locker, and departed.

Krasnoff never noticed she was gone until he left to go home. He had spent the afternoon pondering how to get to Stein before Stein got to him first.

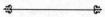

"Hamas must act for its own interests!" Ayyash shouted at his elder and followers. "If we bring in the Palestinian Authority they will try to peacefully negotiate with Israel for the ark and Temple Mount, and then we will lose our place in history. No! We cannot allow the Jews to get the ark!"

"But Abdul, in effect you are asking for *jihad*, a holy war," the elder Muslim argued.

Ayyash knew what he believed. "According to Muslim belief, all men of military age must rally to fight in the event of a holy cause, whether or not it leads to war." He looked the elder in the face and added, "This is a holy cause. Any of my warriors who gives his life for Allah will die a martyr and secure a beautiful place in paradise and receive special privileges!" All seven loyal followers shot their arms up in the air and gave a victory gesture as they chanted aloud, "Praise be to Allah! He will protect us!"

The elder, attempting to interject a semblance of rationality, raised his hand in disagreement as his eyes panned the group. "You think, Abdul, that you and this small band of disciples will be able to seize the ark and claim the Mount for Islam—and not have Israel fight against you?"

Ayyash looked at him with unabashed fury. "We have the strength of an army as long as we are united! Remember the words of Hannibal the conqueror: 'I find a way or I make one.' Yes, we will win."

"You may win, but at what cost?"

"At any cost!" Ayyash stormed out of the elder's room with his seven followers in tow. The elder sat shaking his head in disapproval.

Thirty minutes later, Ayyash and his small band of men were in his networking hideaway, a run-down apartment in the Gaza Strip.

"Remember, my brothers, Hamas means *zeal*!" Ayyash thundered at his men as they sat on folding chairs in his makeshift apartment auditorium. "This very *zeal* for Allah has consumed me so that I can say unequivocally that I am prepared to do as my brother Yahya did—die to protect our land from desecration! While this is a departure from our way of sparing life where possible, the stakes are much higher now, so we must in faithful conscience prepare to raise the price. We must take the initiative and destroy the ark before the authorities move it into the public eye. We only have two days, so we must act swiftly!"

"We are ready to die for Allah, Abdul!" A representative for the group said aloud as the rest of them nodded in agreement.

"Allah be praised! Our rewards will be great in paradise," Ayyash promised. With that everyone raised their hands heavenward, then fell to their knees in prayer. After the twenty minute prayer meeting, Ayyash called his men to accompany him to a small table in the kitchen area where he drafted his plan to destroy the ark.

Two men were assigned to outside security that included standing watch at the Temple Mount and tunnel area. Another two men were assigned to inside security at the tunnel entrance to guard against possible intruders while the demolition team penetrated and set the explosives. The three remaining men would follow Ayyash into the tunnel. All teams would be armed with automatic weapons.

The task of overpowering any Israeli security would be accomplished as they had done many times in the past—covertly. They would wear Israeli military camouflage to fool their enemies, then kill the unsuspecting guards in their path. Their dependence on stealth and speed to acquire the target would be vital.

Resistance inside the tunnel would be minimal, Ayyash knew from Mazor's reports. But they still had to be prepared to neutralize any potential threat they might encounter inside the underground labyrinth. To do so, Ayyash made up six bundles of Semtex in two-pound quantities. These would be divided up and carried by two of the three men designated as protective shields for the main task force. The charges would be linked together with detonating cord and strategically placed along the tunnel system as they progressed toward the objective. This phase of the plan would seal off the tunnel on both sides of them in the event they were unexpectedly attacked. Naturally, an explosion would destroy the target at the expense of their own lives.

The remaining man, Fahim, was carefully chosen as the trusted one who would accompany Ayyash to the ark and complete the mission if Abdul were killed prematurely. Both he and Ayyash had 20 pounds of Semtex strapped to their bodies, wired to a hand detonator.

Ayyash and Fahim dismissed the others and concentrated on the explosive, Semtex. For over 12 years Ayyash had experimented with Semtex until he mastered its full potential. It carried a greater destructive force than TNT. It was cheap to produce, being made up of inexpensive RDX (Cyclonite) and PETN (Pentaerythrite Tetranitrate), and simple for a chemist to manufacture in a basic laboratory. Also, since it was relatively stable until a blasting cap or detonating cord was attached, it was easy to handle. It had become one of the most powerful plastic explosives developed. First made in Czechoslovakia, Semtex found many commercial uses in mining projects and building demolitions, as well as legitimate military uses. Since the substance was overlooked by X-ray machines and not readily sniffed by trained dogs, it was an ideal bomb for terrorism. A car bomb carrying one hundred pounds of Semtex could blow the front off a three-story building.

In Brussels, the council of ministers unanimously voted to appoint Gregory A. Kavidas as the new president of the commission. The council passed their acceptance on to the European Parliament for final approval, knowing that it was strictly a formality.

The council applauded Kavidas' inaugural address, especially the part that he penciled in on the flight from Athens: That he envisioned the EEC as a superstate, calling for a European defense force as a vehicle to effectively handle foreign affairs. His vision embraced the expansion of EEC into central and eastern Europe. As a means of endorsement in recognition for his visionary views, the council changed the designation of the EEC to European Union to commemorate a change of command. The council also gave the president more power that included curtailing the rights of the member nations' veto power.

Kavidas marveled at the development, since it followed a pattern he had designed for eventual global government that would be

based in Europe. He disdained the U.N. as strictly an American enterprise, domiciled on U.S. soil and financed by wealthy Americans. If that weren't reason enough, he believed their record of failure was overwhelming. It really was time for a change.

Once Krasnoff contrived the plan to reach Stein, he forced himself to put the scheme out of his mind, if only for one evening. He needed to celebrate the discovery.

"We're going out for the evening—my treat," he triumphantly announced to Leah and Cohen as he marched merrily into the house.

Leah jumped up off the sofa and ran to her father. "Congratulations on the find!" She put her arm around Cohen and added, "We're really proud of you." Krasnoff soaked in his daughter's approval.

Cohen closed the Bible he had been reading, snuffled and said, "It's about time you sprang for a shekel!"

"Where to, Dad?"

"How about we do dinner, then take in a show at the Jerusalem Center for the Performing Arts on Marcus Street? Itzhak Perlman is playing Tchaikovsky's Concerto in D, op. 35."

Leah shot her eyebrows up then looked at her fiancé and smiled luminously. "Who's Tchaikovsky?" They all laughed uproariously as the tension of the day drained out of them.

"This was the first time I heard Perlman," Leah confessed to her father as he drove around the corner from Marcus Street onto HaNasi. "I have to admit," she marveled, "he is superb, and a wonderful testimony to the handicapped. Imagine being crippled and playing a violin like that?"

"The human spirit is indomitable when it wants to be," Cohen said trenchantly.

Krasnoff nodded at Cohen's remark and wondered about the testimony he would leave. *What will be said about me?*

Suddenly the engine died and the car rolled to a stop in the right-hand lane.

"Dad, didn't you remember to buy gas?" Leah chided playfully.

"Shush!" Krasnoff shouted nervously as he peered at the slightly visible fuel indicator. The needle was still on full.

"Oh–oh." Cohen muttered from the back seat after peeking at the darkened instrument panel.

A bad feeling swept over Krasnoff. He sat motionless for several moments, then scanned the nearby vicinity for anything suspicious. What he saw was nothing but uncaring, high-speed traffic whizzing by them. Yet, despite the appearance of normalcy, the muscles in his stomach began to tighten.

A heavy rain squall started up and blasted their car from all sides.

"Where did this bizarre rain come from?" Leah exclaimed in disbelief.

Krasnoff tried the ignition again. Nothing. He pulled the switch for the headlights in and out repeatedly. Nothing.

"I don't like this, Revi," Cohen said with controlled alarm.

A severe wind evolved from the squall, picking up nearby debris and slamming it against the car. Street trash, empty soda cans, and even a refuse container crashed into the sides as they recoiled in heightening terror. Krasnoff took hold of the door handle and pulled it up.

"Revi, don't go out there!" Cohen shouted. "Wait until the storm passes."

But Krasnoff sensed this was no ordinary outburst from nature. There were other factors in control. "Stay here!" he ordered as he opened the driver's side door. The gale force winds immediately clutched the door and drove it against the car body, snapping one of the hinges.

"Oh, my God!" Leah yelled in fright. "Get back in the car!"

Krasnoff ignored his daughter's command and forced the door closed behind him. Then he put his glasses on to shield his eyes from the driving rain and cupped his hands like binoculars over his glasses in an effort to survey his surroundings. He looked into the fury of the storm then up into the sky. He could see stars shining through the evil maelstrom. The occurrence seemed to be confined to a small perimeter where his car was. "How could this be?" he shouted aloud. He stepped back into the car, threw his hands up in the air, and screamed, "We're being attacked by some queer force!"

He never noticed the blue Mercedes Benz SL 500 convertible coupe standing idle with its lights off just over a hundred feet behind them.

Turning into HaNasi and accelerating well above the speed limit, a propane tank truck driven by an overworked father of five rapidly moved into the righthand lane where Krasnoffs car stood stranded. The driver saw a metallic reflection in the roadway and decided to change into the left lane, but an unseen hand turned the wheel so that the truck swerved back into its deadly path. Although the driver panicked and slammed his foot on the brake pedal, the truck continued unabated. Then he rammed his hand on the horn, but no sound came out. He reached down and turned off the ignition only to find that the heavy truck continued to coast at a threatening speed.

Cohen saw headlights flashing in the rear window. Turning around, he screamed, "Oh, my God, a truck is going to hit us!"

Leah froze in place when she saw the truck bearing down on them. Cohen clutched her hand and cried out, "Lord, save us!"

Something snapped inside Krasnoff. He braced his feet against the floor and pushed his body against the seat to brace himself, then clenched his hands around the steering wheel. "NO! Let God be cursed!" he yelled out.

A wave of calm washed over Cohen. In one sweeping motion, he opened the back door and hauled Leah out as he screamed, "Revi, get out or you'll be killed!"

The truck driver stuck his head out the window and screamed a warning that went unheard.

Cohen pushed Leah safely onto the sidewalk, then in a split second vaulted to Krasnoff's door and pulled on the handle, but the door jammed. He lifted his leg to the side of the car for added leverage and yanked on the door as Krasnoff pounded on the window in sheer terror. "Push, Revi!" Cohen screamed.

The door opened ten inches allowing Krasnoff enough clearance to begin wiggling out as Cohen pulled on his arm.

Voosh! A deafening rush of air sounded. *Crash!*

The truck collided with the rear of the car with tremendous force, hurtling Cohen almost 15 feet into the lane of oncoming traffic. Shaking uncontrollably, he looked back at the car and saw it burst into flames from the impact. The truck driver shouted, "Gas! Get clear!"

Cohen peered at Krasnoff lying on the ground next to the car. He rallied and jumped to his feet as the oncoming traffic veered to avoid the unfolding disaster. "Revi, I'm coming!" he shouted and leaped to Krasnoff's side.

A loud hissing noise started up from the truck. "The tank is going to blow!" the truck driver yelled at Cohen from the sidewalk.

Cohen grabbed Krasnoff's left arm as he lay unconscious and dragged him clear. Then he looked back at the car door. "Oh, God!" he exclaimed in horror when he saw Krasnoff's right arm dangling from the doorjamb.

Three seconds later the propane tank exploded.

CHAPTER

10

Jerusalem

Four surgeons at the Biqqur Holim Hospital on Nathan Strauss Street labored five hours to reattach Krasnoff's arm, but the prognosis was unfavorable. The lead surgeon informed Leah that she should make inquires about a prosthetic device for her father in the eventuality that his body rejected the limb. The thought of her father wearing an artificial arm for the rest of his life was repugnant to her.

She slowly walked around the hospital bed and thanked God that her father was alive, but cursed the truck driver when she looked at the maimed man lying before her fighting to keep one of his body parts. The skull bandage and massive bruise on his face told of the concussion he had sustained when the truck impacted, while the reattached arm lying bundled at his side told of his narrow escape from death.

Krasnoff lifted an eyelid and toughed out a meager smile when he realized his daughter was hovering over him. "Hi, Dad," she said softly as she patted his chest.

Krasnoff painfully blinked several times in bewilderment. "How long—?"

"You've been out since last night." She finished his question in an attempt to limit his talking. Cohen came from behind Leah and simply touched the bed rail.

Krasnoff gazed at them and asked with a garbled voice, "What happened to me?"

Cohen tapped Leah on the shoulder and pulled her away from the bed. He leaned over Krasnoff and whispered, "You lost your right arm, but the doctors reattached it."

Krasnoff shook his head violently in a vain effort to minimize the effect of the anesthesia. "No! This can't be!" he sobbed as he turned to look at his right arm lying numb at his side. Leah covered her eyes with her hand as she turned and retreated out of the room.

"Revi," Cohen soothed as he sat on the bottom of the bed, "we are all lucky to be alive." He nodded to the door and continued, trying to console him, "Leah and I were only bruised, it was a miracle."

"For you, yes, but not for me," Krasnoff groaned as he turned his face into the pillow in anguish. Moments later the added pain reliever took its course. He fell fast asleep.

Cohen sighed deeply and sat down in the chair next to the bed.

Krasnoff's hospital door opened slowly, awakening Cohen from his restless nap. "Hello, I'm Dr. Ben-Tor," the visitor announced in a low whisper. "I work with Revi at the Institute."

Cohen waved him in and stood up as he motioned for Ben-Tor to take his seat. Ben-Tor dismissed the offer and walked to the bed. He glanced down at Krasnoff's bundled arm and shook his head. "Terrible thing." He gestured for Cohen to walk with him to the back of the room and added, "I saw Leah out in the hall; thank God she and you are all right."

"We were very fortunate. We could have been killed."

"What happened?"

"We were on our way back from dinner and a concert when our car died and then we suddenly encountered weird and abnormal weather. Then before we knew it, we were hit from behind by a truck."

"It all sounds so crazy!"

Cohen stared him in the eye and said through his teeth, "It was more than crazy, it was…" his voice trailed off to search for a word, "…more like demonic. The way the wind and the rain came at us—"

"Dr. Ben-Tor?" Krasnoff's weakened voice croaked out.

They turned to see Krasnoff attempting to push himself up in the bed. They rushed to his side. "Easy, Revi," Ben-Tor entreated, "you shouldn't be trying to move just yet."

Drawing upon hidden strength, Krasnoff grabbed hold of Cohen's arm and said to him through clenched teeth, "I know in my gut it was Stein. You can't let him get to us."

Ben-Tor's eyebrows shot up. "Who's this Stein he's talking about?"

Cohen shot a look at Krasnoff as Ben-Tor glanced down at him and gestured for Krasnoff to zip his mouth shut. "We have a hunch that the secret on the ark may be out."

Stupefied, Ben-Tor turned to Cohen and asked, "You know about the ark?"

Cohen smiled and pointed to the door. "I'm Revi's future son-in-law. He told me about the discovery."

With a sigh of relief, Ben-Tor continued, "Of course Revi swore you to secrecy."

"Of course," Cohen replied, "and Leah as well." He winked at Krasnoff to signal that their secret about the Urim and Thummim was still safe.

Krasnoff raised his left arm for attention.

"What is it, Revi?" Ben-Tor asked as he bent over to hear Krasnoff's feeble voice.

"The prime minister?"

Ben-Tor shook his head. "Still no decision."

Krasnoff squeezed his eyes shut and mumbled, "We need to move…time is critical."

Ben-Tor threw his arms up in the air. "My hands are tied," he lamented. "We have to wait for Rubin to make the call."

"I have a bad feeling about this," Cohen interjected. "You should take extra precaution to protect it."

"We thought we would have had approval from the prime minister by now, but it looks like the bureaucracy of his cabinet is getting in the way. So I've made arrangements to add extra guards as soon as they're available."

Cohen nodded in approval. Ben-Tor looked at Krasnoff then raised his arm in a victory gesture and walked out.

Seconds later, Leah walked in and asked Cohen, "Did my father have a nice visit with Dr. Ben-Tor?"

Cohen's breath caught in his throat. "Real nice."

"What's the matter, Cohen?" she queried.

"Your father mentioned Stein in front of Ben-Tor and nearly connected him with the UT, but I was able to camouflage and divert it. But it is ironic that I came to the same conclusion as your dad about Stein being involved." He gazed out the window and added, "Call it intuition if you must, but I just know he was behind the whole attack."

"Nat," Krasnoff said as he swallowed hard, "I need you to do some checking on Stein." With his left hand he massaged his face to keep awake and instructed, "My staff at IAA knows Leah, so you and she can get into my files with my password. Tomorrow morning before Ben-Tor arrives, go to my office and access the same program I used on you. Run a background check and full trace on Stein. We've got to get to him before he gets to us again."

Leah pulled out a pad from her handbag and wrote down the passwords to access IAA's search programs. "You need to rest," she offered to her father as her eyes filled with tears.

With wakening resolve Krasnoff tugged on Cohen's arm and said, "And do a search on Stein's partner at MASTERLINK, that Kavidas fellow. I'm sure he's in on this too."

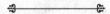

Tradition had identified Mount Moriah as the mount upon which Abraham had prepared to sacrifice his son Isaac. David, toward the end of his reign, bought the desolate hilltop of this mount, which Araunah the Jebusite had used as a threshing floor, and built an altar to the Lord. David in turn pledged to build a temple to God upon the mount. However, this noble task was completed not by David but by his son Solomon, whose artisans labored for seven years to construct the greatest monument to Jehovah ever recorded in the Old Testament. Solomon's Temple was destroyed by the Babylonian king Nebuchadnezzar in 586 B.C., and later rebuilt under Zerubabel. Later, Herod the Great, hoping to expunge some of his crimes against the Jews, reconstructed the Temple on a large scale. This was the Temple Jesus Christ visited and prophesied that it would be destroyed. That prophecy was fulfilled by the Roman general Titus in A.D. 70.

Early Christendom viewed Mount Moriah as a place cursed by God and accordingly let it go to ruin where it became a heap of rubble. When the Muslims conquered Jerusalem in A.D. 636, they cleared the Mount under the direction of Khalif Omar, and built a mosque on the site, claiming that from that site the prophet Mohammed had gone to Heaven on his winged horse. Then in A.D. 691, Adbed El Malik Ben Marwan, the Omayad Khalif, replaced the mosque of Omar with the present one, which was considered to be one of the most beautiful of Muslim shrines—the Dome of the Rock.

Stein sat on the steps of the western entrance to the Dome of the Rock, just gazing at the hordes of tourists who found the shrine particularly interesting as a way of exploring the religious rites of Islam. For him the mosque was nothing more than a means to an end. He knew the day was quickly approaching when the entire configuration of the mount would be changed to make room for the temple that the prophets predicted would herald the return of Christ—who would usher in the consummation of all things and set up His Kingdom. But before He came, Stein reminded himself, humanity would for a season worship their self-appointed god on this very mount.

Because of this guaranteed appointment with destiny, Stein refused to allow any thoughts of failure regarding Krasnoff to permeate his thinking and dissuade him from staying focused on Kavidas' master plan. The plan was certain to succeed, despite the presence of the Urim and Thummim, so obviously in time the device would be rendered ineffective by divine decree. Until that time, he decided, he would persist in his attack to shield their identity and minimize any exposure through the efforts of Krasnoff and Cohen, by discovering and pushing the limits of their obvious protection.

Early morning admittance into the IAA building for Leah and Cohen was a simple task. The archeological and antiquities community had quickly learned about Krasnoff's accident. With Leah's face being known over the years, their entrance into the building was readily approved by security.

Once inside the office, Leah took notice that Golda Rokach's desk had been cleared. She shrugged her shoulders in dismay, then proceeded to her father's computer console where she quickly went into his search engines using the passwords he had provided.

The IAA computers were linked to the Internet and a highly sophisticated central network in the Department of Ancestry and Property needed to trace claims and settle disputes on ancient lands. Confident of success, Leah keyed in the logo MASTERLINK, then the proper names Gregory A. Kavidas and Mortimer Stein.

The monitor screen quickly filled with enrollment data and subscription instructions on MASTERLINK. When Leah probed for more information, the report added the location and fundamental functions of the company along with public information regarding its founders, Kavidas and Stein.

"The report doesn't say much," Leah grumped as the file continued to load.

"Where's the info on—?"

"Uh-oh," Leah said as the flashing words, ACCESS DENIED, came up on Gregory Kavidas' and Mortimer Stein's names.

"Looks like we have two slimy fish on the line," Cohen added as his eyebrows furrowed.

"Maybe, but watch this," Leah said with a twinkle in her eye. She moved out of the Internet program and into a highly secured program.

"How did you manage that?" Cohen asked curiously as the screen began revealing classified information.

"I work for the Israeli government in the Knesset, remember? I have special clearances." Cohen marveled at her resourcefulness.

One minute later Leah remarked with a tight smile, "Looks like a small hit."

"How small?"

"Cursory information only. There are no religious, political, or financial facts in the archives." Leah placed her finger on the monitor and read off the scant information: "Kavidas was born in Athens in 1946, to parents of aristocracy; father, Greek; mother, Italian. Entrepreneur, former Owner/CEO of Rainbow Pharmaceutical out of Wellington, Florida. His..." Leah's voice paused as she peered at the screen. "...now this is interesting: His drug company developed an AIDS vaccine—"

Cohen snapped his fingers to interrupt. "Sure, I remember reading about it in the papers. A great hullabaloo ensued when a rival company, I think it was a Miami-based firm called Lane Drugs, blew the whistle on him after the vaccine went awry. Soon after that, he sold the company and bailed out to Europe."

"There's nothing more on him," Leah sighed with resignation. Then she ran a search on Mortimer Stein that brought the same brief results.

Cohen crossed his arms over his chest in dismay. "There's something blocking us from accessing them."

"If there is any data on them, it must be encrypted or embedded so that it can be retrieved only by them."

Cohen scratched his head. "Even with your availability to secret information, we can't get to them."

"There's something diabolical about all this. They must have something to hide," Leah postulated.

Cohen gazed at the monitor and slowly shook his head. "I have a gut feeling you're right."

Leah shut down the computer. "What do you suggest?"

Cohen put his arm around her as she stood up and said, "We'll use what God has placed in our hands to find out who they are."

Leah knew immediately what he meant.

The telephone was ringing as they entered the house. Leah raced to the kitchen and picked up the phone as Cohen prepared the Urim and Thummim. Three minutes later she walked slowly into his bedroom as he set the stones in place. He immediately sensed a problem. "What's wrong?"

"That was the hospital," she said numbly. "They called to advise us that there is a snag with my father's insurance. When I suggested they simply place his medical expenses on one of our charge accounts until it was straightened out, they further advised me that there is some kind of hold on our credit lines. We can't use any of our credit cards."

"That's impossible!" Cohen argued. "There's some kind of mistake."

"No mistake," Leah shot back. "I had them confirm it three times."

Leah dropped down onto Cohen's bed and began to whimper. "What's happening to us? Our whole world is crumbling around us."

Cohen raced to her side and embraced her tenderly. "Now, now, we'll be all right. Don't worry," he consoled, "your dad has funds from the diamond investment that we can use if we need to."

"I know, thank God." She paused momentarily to collect her thoughts then added as her whimpers escalated into sobs, "I think this UT thing has become a curse. We've had nothing but trouble since it came into our home."

"God must have allowed it for good, we just have to find out for *what*," he replied halfheartedly.

"I wouldn't be surprised if Kavidas and Stein of MASTER-LINK shut us down," Leah croaked out between sniffles as they jointly theorized.

Cohen looked at his fiancé in amazement. "I'll bet you're right! Even though we don't have a MASTERLINK card, they must control other credit houses and dictate subscribers' approval."

"And if you dare to come against them, or just make inquires about them, they cut you off," Leah said fiercely.

Cohen's concerns were heightening. He simply nodded at the suggestion, then went to his work table and busied himself with his apparatus as Leah lay back on the bed. Within seconds her anxiety sought relief and she fell asleep.

Cohen prayed that God would enable him to ask the UT correctly so as to invoke a divine answer to the worsening conditions that had embraced their lives. Then he meditatively set the gems in their rightful place on the table. *Now, how do I phrase these important questions?* he thought. *Are Kavidas and Stein responsible for the attack in the car on the way home from the concert?* He thought about the question, rephrased it, and wrote it down on a pad. Then he closed his eyes in an effort to recall all the events over the past two months.

Suddenly surreal images raced through his mind that initiated the exploitation of chance effects. Fragments of reality drifted through some time portal and then paused in front of him. He saw Krasnoff walking away from a smoking building with the Urim and Thummim under his arm. Then through a simulated lap-dissolve photographic technique, he saw Krasnoff talking with the tour director, Ze've Mazor, before he was recruited at Beth Shean. A replica of Krasnoff's smirking face when he learned about the diamond investment appeared on a grotesque bogey man who danced triumphantly in the background. The last fragment that floated by was the worst. It was the evil look on Krasnoff's face as he shot Sam.

Cohen opened his eyes as his knees began to knock. He was truly puzzled. *God, why are you showing me this stuff about Revi?* he asked himself. He shook his head in an effort to clear the mental debris that seemed to linger, then forced himself to look down at the pad on the table. "What else do I want to ask?" he thought aloud. He remembered asking the Urim and Thummim if Kavidas would be good for Israel and how the *lights* answered with a resounding no. Now, in view of the recurrent suspicions that haunted him, he felt compelled to ask the same question of Krasnoff. *Remember, Nat*, he reminded himself, *related themes*.

With the gems in their proper orientation, Cohen glanced at his pad and asked softly, "Are Kavidas and Stein evil agents, being protected by evil principalities, and are they responsible for the recent attack? If the answer is yes, give Urim, turn blue; if not, give Thummim, turn scarlet."

The blue sapphire glowed brightly.

Cohen nodded as if the stones simply confirmed his suspicions.

He turned to check on Leah, who remained asleep, then bowed his head and prayed just above a whisper, "God, you must be doing something in my life. You have given me some vision about Revi that troubles me. Help me to understand its meaning for my life." After several moments of silence he lifted his head and with his eyes still closed said, "God, if Revi is not from you and he is out to harm us, give Urim, turn blue; if not, give Thummim, turn scarlet."

"Oh my God!" Cohen heard from behind. He turned quickly to see Leah pointing to the blue stone, which was shining luminously. She had heard everything.

He turned and clutched her hand. "I thought you were sleeping; otherwise, I wouldn't have asked the question," he offered in defense.

Leah cupped her face in her hands and began crying uncontrollably.

Cohen rushed to her side to embrace her, and held her tightly until the pain subsided.

"My hunch is that Kavidas and Stein are both part of some gigantic plan to dupe the world into believing something that we haven't seen yet," Cohen theorized. He looked at Leah and added, "With their worldwide financial conglomerate already in place, and now with Kavidas as the president of the EEC, it seems to point to a master plan, one that is satanic in origin. They see the UT as a threat to expose them, so they are after it. That's the way I see it."

"I agree," Leah affirmed with a slight catch in her throat. "And my father?"

Cohen gracefully stroked Leah's face then pulled her head to his chest. "Your father has me deeply troubled. I don't know how to tell you this. Do you remember the night your father came home with the gun?"

"Precisely, it was the night before I went on the ten-day seminar for my work."

"Well, that night we had an unexpected visitor who was hired to spy on us. I uncovered the plot. Your father and I surprised him and overpowered him in his surveillance van. I thought we were just going to scare him off, but your father turned violent, pistol whipped the man into confessing he worked for Stein, then took him for a drive. While we were driving, the man seized the opportunity to escape and pushed me out the door of the moving van where I rolled on the ground and scraped my face—"

Leah touched his face and interjected, "I was away and didn't know…"

Cohen acknowledged her concern but quickly dismissed it. "I was all right, but when I reached the van the man had your father's gun on him. Then in a flash the tables turned and your father had the gun. In anger he shot the man twice, killing him." He scratched his head in contemplation then added. "Even though he took the surveillance video, it will only be a matter of time before the police connect the dots and come after him."

Leah gasped then covered her mouth. Through a muffled gag she lamented, "Saving his arm isn't going to help. I'm afraid he's changing into something dreadful."

"I believe he already has," Cohen groaned.

"What are you going to do about it?"

"I've already thought about it and decided to leave it with the very one who started this whole thing. The one who seems to be calling me."

"Who's that?"

"God."

⁂

It was 3:15 a.m. and drizzling when Abdul Ayyash dropped the rope ladder over the northernmost wall adjacent to the Ha-Kotel, the Western Wall, some three hundred feet away from the eyes of the Israeli military sentries who stood guard at the main entrance to the holy site. He believed it a good omen to start the mission with inclement weather. The security personnel would seek shelter from the elements and therefore reduce the chance of hostile encounters. Nevertheless, he was prepared for any contingency.

He signaled to his trusted friend, Fahim, to have the team check their weaponry and demolition charges, then motioned for them to pull down their camouflage ski masks and descend the ladder. Within 20 seconds, all eight men were crouching in the darkness inside the small archways lining the adjoining wall that led to Wilson's Arch, contiguous with the Western Wall. He surveyed the area and realized that Allah was truly watching over them: There was a conspicuous absence of guards. He stealthily walked to the entranceway and peered into the exhibition hall that led to the rabbinic tunnel. There was only one civilian with a holstered pistol patrolling the front entrance. *Where is the military?* he wondered. *If the ark is a national treasure, why aren't they protecting it?*

Ayyash waved his marksman to his side. That one immediately took his sniper's stance with a high-powered rifle sporting a 15X scope and silencer. In one sweeping motion, the sniper put a round squarely through the heart of the armed civilian, who fell down dead without so much as a grunt. Ayyash smiled; his marksman patted his rifle and retreated to the rear of the team. Neither of them bothered to check the body; thus they missed the two-way radio on the dead man's belt.

Ayyash and his three men quickly broke the lock on the door to the entranceway and walked through the doorway. He motioned two of his security men to remain just inside Wilson's Arch, while he stationed the remaining two inside the exhibition hall at the tunnel entryway.

As they moved through the entrance to the tunnel they came upon the Master's Course, a section of the wall named such by scholars because it contained the largest single building stone ever found in Israel. The stone was 40 feet long, 10 feet high, and 10 feet deep, and weighed 458 tons. It had been installed in the foundation during the second Temple period to stabilize the structure during earthquakes. Ayyash kicked the stone and whispered bitterly, "Place two bundles of Semtex at each end of this rock. We will make a statement to our Jewish intruders." The demolition expert strategically wedged the bundles into the sides of the rock, then ran the spooled connecting wire down the tunnel after the advance team heading for the vaulted area.

At nearly five hundred feet into the tunnel, Ayyash paused and grabbed hold of one of the reinforcing timbers that uniformly lined the sides and ceilings of the long passageway. The interior of the tunnel reminded him of a mineshaft. He turned to Fahim and said through his teeth, "This will be like the inside of a pipe bomb. The concussion from the blast will eradicate any Jewish presence." He pointed to a joist and said, "Two bundles here." Fahim delegated one of the demolition men to act out the order as the main assault team continued to advance toward the objective. Forty-five seconds later they were within visual range of a corridor that led to the vault containing the ark.

A voice from the vault, checking security with the sentry at the entranceway on the two-way radio, resounded off the tunnel walls. Ayyash and Fahim froze in their tracks. The rest of the task force dropped to the tunnel floor immediately.

Fahim made a fist at Ayyash and whispered, "We forgot to check the body for a telephone. Damn."

Ayyash set his jaw firmly and motioned forward as he said, "It doesn't matter. We're not leaving here until our objective is reached and the mission completed." He looked back and waved the rest of his men to follow him as he dropped to the ground. Then they all began inching themselves on their bellies toward the vault.

Seconds later he heard the same voice again, this time talking to what must have been his companion assigned to watching the vault with him.

At the end of the corridor, Ayyash pulled a small mirror out of his jacket pocket to look around the corner. He turned to his men and held up two fingers. The team leader acknowledged with a nod. Two civilians, both armed with assault rifles, stood in front of the ark, which was cradled in what looked to Ayyash like a small cave. The man with the phone looked concerned when there was no response from the outside sentry. Ayyash heard him say to his fellow guard that he wanted to go check on him. His companion warned him not to, but suggested calling their central number for instructions and help. Ayyash would not let that happen.

"Now!" Ayyash exclaimed in a hoarse whisper to Fahim.

The sentry indexed the central telephone number and pressed the Send button one second before the sniper's bullet slammed into his forehead, killing him instantly. He fell backward against the ark then slid onto the ground in a heap with his head lolled to one side.

A spray of automatic weapons fire from the other sentry's rifle filled the corridor.

Fahim fanatically grabbed Ayyash and pushed him back into the corridor to protect him as he jumped out into the open brandishing his gun and yelling, "Allah be praised!" As he ran to the ark he pulled the trigger on his weapon while the untrained sentry returned fire. A random bullet found its mark in Fahim's neck. He lunged toward the sentry in a desperate maneuver, but fell dead a few feet from the ark, with his hand within inches of the detonator attached to his body.

A lull in the fire allowed Ayyash to hear the voices coming from the telephone. He gave his loyal friend a quick parting look then turned to his remaining men and cried out, "We have company coming!"

The sentry jumped for cover behind the ark as armed figures began to stand up in the gunfire smoke that floated throughout the corridor and into the vault. Ayyash's two men stood and stared at the ark in awe and bewilderment for several seconds until Ayyash screamed, "Shoot!" By then, the sentry had opened fire and cut them down mid-stride. Suddenly Ayyash realized he was alone with the sentry.

Calculating that he needed the 20 pounds of Semtex on his body to destroy the ark, Ayyash fired several rounds around the arch of the vault to keep the sentry at bay, then stretched and reached one of his fallen men to drag his body back into the corridor. He removed the bundle of Semtex from the body then threw the explosive toward the vault. The bundle landed about 15 feet from the ark. Once it hit the ground, Ayyash braced himself against the wall of the corridor and, covering his head between his legs, closed the switch on the detonator.

The concussion from the thunderous blast sent a shock wave through the tunnel that stunned Ayyash's senses and nearly deafened him. He immediately heard screaming coming from the vault. When the smoke cleared somewhat, he saw the sentry wandering aimlessly around the ark, holding his ears. The ark was not damaged. A glance at his watch told Ayyash that time was running out; his security team was instructed to blow the tunnel in seven minutes.

As the unarmed sentry meandered out into the open corridor, Ayyash, feeling no compassion, pulled a trench knife from his pocket. He stealthily walked up to the momentarily blinded, agonizing civilian and cut his throat. The man dropped where he stood as blood gurgled out of his carotid artery onto the ground. Within 30 seconds he was dead.

IAA director Dr. Ben-Tor had no choice but to notify the General Security Services, the internal security and counterintelligence arm of the Mossad, the instant he was informed of the invasion. Within six minutes of the telephone call the ever-ready squad were on station at the Western Wall, looking down at the Wilson's Arch, the entrance to the tunnel. Using infra-red scopes on high-powered sniper rifles, GSS marksmen immediately took out the two Hamas guards standing watch at the entrance before they could detonate themselves. Not knowing whether or not their confederates were dead, the two inside attackers counted down to the agreed time, then prayed together to Allah to receive them into Heaven. They pressed the switches on their detonators simultaneously with the line to the tunnel charges. The combined explosion was like a shotgun blast that blew a chunk of rock out of Wilson's Arch and hurtled it at the Western Wall as a giant plume of smoke rose into the rainy night sky. In a moment the rain suppressed the smoke, revealing the courtyard in front of the Wall to be cluttered with rock fragments and various kinds of debris ejected from the mouth of the arch. GSS agents quickly scrambled to search and destroy any possible survivors at the tunnel entrance. Seconds later they announced to their task force leader: *Clear.*

The thrust of the internal explosion acted like a giant ramrod, jamming Ayyash against the wall of the tunnel. It was followed by a recoil effect that immediately sucked him into the vault, hurling him at the platform that supported the ark. For over a minute he lay, stunned from the hammering assault, then pushed himself up into a sitting position only to writhe in agony at the sight of his shattered right leg. He looked forlornly at his leg, then turned his head slightly to hear the eerie silence that permeated the vault. For what seemed like an interminable period he sat stupefied, looking up at the winged cherubim on the mercy seat of the ark. Flash images of his life darted through his mind as the realization that the vault had been sealed off by the explosion came over him. *I am alone with Allah now.*

He shook his head in brief periods of sanemindedness. He stared at the angelic creatures crafted into the top of the ark. The fact that he was within 30 yards of the sacred Holy of Holies where the ark had stood originally would never be revealed to him.

He looked back at the macabre scene where his fellow soldiers lay dead and knew that he would be with them and Allah very soon. With one hand on the ark and the other on the detonator switch, he looked up at the ceiling of the vault, then closed his eyes and quoted a verse from the Quran, "How disbelieve you in Allah when you were dead and He gave life to you! Then He will give you death, then life again, and then unto Him you will return" (al-Baqarah 2:28.21). With that he extended the hand holding the detonator into the air as a final offering to Allah and closed the electric circuit to the explosives strapped to his body.

Krasnoff set the *Jerusalem Post* down on the hospital bed as a teary-eyed Dr. Ben-Tor walked into the room. "Unbelievable, just unbelievable," Ben-Tor said with a shake of the head. "The most important archeological find in three thousand years and some fanatical Arab fundamentalist group goes and blows it up right in front of our eyes."

Krasnoff, groaning under intense pain, forced himself to sit up and asked bitterly, "Where was the security?"

"We only had our own men in there. We never received the military protection I was hoping for." He threw his hands up in the air and added, "So now, and I'm sure you've read about it, Rubin is threatening to resign as prime minister. He secretly blames himself for stalling and delaying the action we requested."

"Good, I hope the bum does resign!" Krasnoff replied hotly.

Ben-Tor simply nodded. "It's not in the papers yet, but the Mossad has ferreted out an Israeli who was linked to Ayyash, the mastermind who led the attack—a man by the name of Ze've Mazor. He's in custody as we speak."

Krasnoff gulped when he heard Mazor's name but said nothing about him.

Ben-Tor reached for Krasnoff's newspaper and said, "This too is not out yet, but this fool Ayyash blew up the ark not realizing that the vault that contained it is almost directly under the Dome of the Rock, right off Warren's Gate. The explosion was inside the tunnel chamber—confining the displacement area—and was so intense, it destabilized the shrine's foundation. The Arabs have engineers studying it now and from what I've heard, it doesn't look repairable. The gold-plated dome drooped at least fifteen degrees off its axis, scattering thousands of the Persian tiles from the exterior walls all over the mount, and on the inside, the rock of Mount Moriah sank twelve feet into the ground when the underlying rock platform collapsed from the blast. The mosque is a mess." He snuffled nervously and summed his fears. "If there's anything that could ignite a *jihad*, it would be touching their mosque."

"Small consolation in comparison to the ark," Krasnoff sighed with resignation.

Ben-Tor nodded in agreement. "Of course, no one will ever know about the ark now that it's been demolished into smithereens.

But on the bright side, it looks like the Arabs will be relocating and rebuilding their place of worship off the Temple Mount area."

Krasnoff knew enough about his religion to make the connection. "I'm sure the Zionists will be elated. Now they can proceed with rebuilding the Temple, and then the Messiah can come."

"You know what, Revi," Ben-Tor marveled, "I never thought of that."

Three days after the *Jerusalem Post* carried the news of the attack in the tunnel, it ran a follow-up story that brightened the spirits of the people of Israel. The ex-pharmaceutical magnate and entrepreneur of MASTERLINK, now turned EEC president, Mr. Gregory A. Kavidas, announced that he would contribute four million dollars to help the Israeli government deal with their latest catastrophe.

The chain-link fence surrounding Krasnoff's condo patio afforded him the luxury of observing the arboretum while restricting the volume of passersby considerably. For the present, he enjoyed some semblance of privacy. He adjusted the sling on his arm then wiggled his fingers in utter amazement, marveling at the advances in surgical and neurological technology that enabled him to do so; the prognosis for his body's accepting the re-attachment of his arm had been changed to *guarded*.

Off in the distance his eyes caught the glistening and sparkling effect brought on by the early morning sunlight bathing the dew-moistened leaves. "Real pretty, isn't it?" Leah asked as she walked out onto the patio.

He shrugged one shoulder as he looked up at her and replied, "Especially this morning."

"What's so special about this morning?" she wondered. She was about to clutch his hand, but her heart was changing toward her father, into an attitude of distrust.

"Well, we need to clear out of here, so I've decided to sell this condo and move to a suburb of Netanya that's close to our diamond investment."

"To shake off Kavidas and Stein?" Cohen put in as he joined them.

Krasnoff nodded. "Yes." He gestured with his good arm and added, "We'll take ourselves and the UT and put it where they can't find us or it." He gazed at Cohen then back at his arm in the sling and ordered curtly, "I need you and Leah to deal with the realtor and pick out two or three nice homes as soon as possible and then I'll come and look at them with you."

Giving Cohen an expression of disinterest, Leah walked back up to their condo to dress for work.

Cohen seized the opportunity, pulled up a patio chair, and sat next to Krasnoff. "Revi," Cohen ventured, "I think now is as good a time as any to clear the air about a few matters."

Krasnoff squirmed in his chair and carefully massaged his bad arm. "Can't wait?"

"No," Cohen said with clear precision. "I'm concerned with our relationship, and I don't want it to spill over and interfere with my love for Leah."

Krasnoff raised an eyebrow as he registered the look on his face. "Okay, what's troubling you?"

Cohen had deliberately mentioned Leah to bring Krasnoff around to the realization that the erosion of trust could impact Leah, as well as all others who came in contact with him. Leah would act as insurance to pull the truth out of him. "This whole thing with the tunnel and the ark started me thinking," Cohen calculated carefully. "I think we could have prevented this disaster if we had told the IAA about the UT in the first place. It could have saved lives and—"

"Absolutely not!" Krasnoff yelled in his face. "There's no way in hell that we could have nor will we ever go public with the device."

Cohen motioned with his hand. "Calm down, Revi, calm down. Your anger is getting the best of you." He stood up and walked toward the fence, then turned to continue as Krasnoff fidgeted in his chair. "Just for the record, can you tell me once more how you acquired the UT?"

"Why? I already told you what happened."

"The truth?"

Krasnoff refused to look into Cohen's eyes. "Yes."

Cohen heightened his probe. "Well, I don't believe you. I think you may have committed a crime to get it."

"What? That's ridiculous!" Krasnoff asserted as his tension increased exponentially.

"Oh, really? Then let's test the veracity of your thinking process to arrive at the *truth*! As a citizen of Israel, if the means by which you came to possess a 'national treasure'—that could help the nation religiously, militarily, politically, economically, and socially—were honest and above board, then why wouldn't you want to share it with all Israel and all mankind?"

Krasnoff set his jaw and refused to reply.

His non-answer answered for him. Cohen whirled on him. "That's what I thought. And another thing, how long are you going to keep Sam's killing from Leah? Don't you think she's entitled to know that her father is…"

"…a murderer. Is that what you were going to say?" Krasnoff shot back.

Cohen shook his head. "No. I was going to say, dishonest."

"Yeah, sure."

"My love for Leah does not allow me to hurt you," Cohen pleaded. "I only want the truth, please."

Krasnoff pushed himself up with one arm, circled the chair twice, then took a meditative stance. Moments later he stared at Cohen and said in mock contrition, "I'll tell her if that'll make you feel better."

Cohen nodded, knowing he had the leverage he needed. He stared Krasnoff down and asked, "What about the UT? Did you acquire it honestly?"

Krasnoff's face went pale. A sudden wave of abandonment washed over him as if he were about to lose the only thing that really mattered to him, Leah. He had to tell the truth. "I killed a Bedouin to get it," he finally choked out.

Cohen swallowed hard as he shook his head. "I think God already told me, Revi. I had a dream of you walking away from a smoking building with it under your arm. It was very lifelike."

Krasnoff stifled a whimper as he spoke in short sentences. "The Sheraton Jerusalem. The place where I met Ishmael ben Azin. He wanted to sell it to IAA, so I took it."

"The smoking...?"

"A bomb. I killed him with a bomb."

Cohen fell into a chaise lounge and cupped his face in his hands.

After a long period of silence Krasnoff asked in a voice just above a whisper, "What are you going to do, Nathan?"

Once again, Cohen found himself giving the answer, "I'm going to leave it with God."

CHAPTER

11

Jerusalem

His mental faculties were well intact as he resolutely walked through the busy labyrinth of the netherworld that led to the abysmal sanctum of the damned hidden well beneath the surface of the earth. It was the very abode of monstrous things that lurk in the dark and the shadows, inaccessible to prayers and sacrifices, a dreary place with cheerless passageways, tenanted by fallen angels and fully conscious disembodied spirits. These were reserved in punishment and misery, co-existing in torment until they would be surrendered up for judgment on the last day, only to be cast into the lake of fire by a holy God.

Vast smoke-filled antechambers connected cavern after cavern that served as holding stations for the miserable denizens of the underworld who had both rebelled and rejected God's salvation. The place was called *sheol* or *hades*, but to those who inhabited the dungeon of the wicked and the dead, it was hell.

His journey took him deep into the infernal regions, the very bowels of the earth where unquenchable fires sear and burn the souls of the captives locked up in the terrible house of confinement. It was a blasphemous dwelling place where the dragging sound of ankle chains never ceased—a place of anguish and pain where the horrible howls and squeals of the victims were never heard by the living.

But to this visitor, the searing heat, foul odors, and torturous cries meant nothing, for he was not yet consigned to the prison of the condemned. That day for him was still in the future.

Soon he found himself at his destination, an isolated area designated for the *Shedim*, a hidden race of creatures not akin to the rest. Evidence of their existence was reported among the ancient writings, yet not given to legend but to the domain of the supernatural. Some of the creatures resembled gnomes, hobgoblins, elves and sprites; still others, if released, assumed human form and frequented dirty places at nighttime. For his purpose, he would choose the mother of Hormiz, Lilith, the queen demoness of the *Shedim*. Reported to be of regal ancestry among the angelic, therefore holding dominion over the community, she was represented as a very fair woman with long, wild-flowing hair, and deformed feet. She was supposed to be capable of inflicting fatal diseases.

Amidst the cacophony and pandemonium she paid obeisance to him in respect for his rank, and in turn he silently gave her a scroll with her assignment, sealed by the highest authority to validate the order. The laws of hierarchy mandated her compliance.

Anticipating complete victory, he turned and departed for the surface.

Krasnoff displayed signs of irritation as he waited his turn with the therapist at the Golda Meir clinic attached to the Biqqur Holim Hospital. Regaining full strength of his arm would require many months of rigorous treatment and exercise. Today his irritation was not due to the inconvenience of waiting, but rather to anticipation—anticipation of Leah's reaction to his killing Sam. Today, he resolved, he would both salve his conscience of the deed as well as satisfy Cohen of his promise to come clean with Leah. He relegated the task to the ride home. The murder of the Bedouin never entered his mind.

Krasnoff fidgeted in his chair for over 15 minutes before Leah approached the receptionist to inquire about the delay. The receptionist blamed it on the fact that one of the regular therapists had met with an automobile accident the day before, necessitating the drawing of a substitute from the labor pool, a woman named Leona.

Moments later Leona opened the door to the waiting room and called Krasnoff's name. He looked up to see a vivacious looking woman in a nurse's uniform holding a chart. He was taken aback by her voluptuous smile and the long red hair that flowed over her shoulders. He estimated her age to be about 42. He manipulated his body in the chair to avoid hitting his damaged arm as he attempted to stand. Leona ran to his side to help him up. Leah watch, surprised at Leona's overzealous spirit.

"Here now, Mr. Krasnoff," Leona blurted out softly, "let me assist you into the therapy room." Krasnoff blushed from all the attention, then began relaxing as the tension oozed right out of his body. Leona quickly went to work by slipping her shapely body behind him and tenderly lifting him until his body momentum enabled him to stand up. She placed his good arm over her shoulder and escorted him out of the waiting room and into the corridor that connected the therapy room. Leah cracked a smile when she saw the gleam in her father's eye. The look turned to dismay as she glanced at the remaining male patients, who hoped for the same treatment when their turn came.

"Oh, how horrible!" Leona remarked impulsively as she stared at the suture marks encircling Krasnoff's arm. Ordinarily, therapists refrained from making any kind of comments on a patient's condition, but Leona's exuberant personality would continue to violate hospital policy. "Are you in a lot of pain?" she asked after removing his outer shirt.

"It's getting better," Krasnoff replied bravely.

She placed a five-pound dumbbell in his hand and motioned for him to exercise as she moved to rub his chest and arms down with lanolin. "Your record stated that you sustained this injury in an auto accident. Was anybody else hurt?"

Krasnoff was not used to dialoging with his therapist; this was a welcome change. This woman Leona seemed to have an endearing voice and gentle touch. He was really enjoying the session. "My daughter and future son-in-law received only minor injuries."

She tapped him on the back and then patted the massage table. He smiled and gingerly obeyed. He closed his eyes as her fingers dug into his chest muscles, relieving the pressure exerted from the surrounding skin as it continued to tighten and heal. "Oooh, this feels good," he sighed.

"You have powerful shoulders," she added as she began massaging his shoulders while occasionally running her skillful hands up and down his neck.

"They're from lifting rocks out on digs," he replied boastfully.

She stared at him with a penetrating look then smiled expansively. "I hope you don't mind but I read your file, and was fascinated by your profession. You're an archeologist with the IAA?"

"I was..." he replied with a leering smile then paused as he raised his injured arm. "But this qualified me for early retirement." Apart from being enraptured by her effusive personality, he realized he was beginning to watch her body moves very carefully. He felt himself slipping into a romantic daze that suspended the nagging pain in his arm.

"I've always been extremely interested in antiquities," she ventured, snapping him back into reality, "so maybe when you're feeling better, we could trade a therapy session for a lesson in archeology."

"I've always been fascinated by the barter system," Krasnoff chortled, "and I can't think of a better way to spend a Saturday evening."

"Then it's settled," she said with a luminous smile, "we'll firm it up when you come back for your next session in two days."

"I'll be here early."

"It sounds to me like she was hitting on you, Dad," Leah teased as Krasnoff related the session to her on the drive home.

"I guess," he replied with a grin. "To tell you the truth, it felt pretty good. It's been a long time."

To hear her father mention *truth* disrupted her thoughts. She decided to change the subject. "Cohen and I found two nice places for you to see in Netanya—actually, about two miles away from your diamond business."

Krasnoff smiled at his daughter. "That's superb! Let's go see them tomorrow when you get off work."

His jovial spirit, no doubt the fallout from his explosive meeting with Leona, seemed out of character. "Okay," she replied blandly.

"What's the matter?" her father asked, detecting her uncommitted tone.

"Nothing."

He touched her arm and cleared his throat, then after a moment of silence said in an apologetic voice, "I have something to tell you."

Leah's muscles tightened as she braced herself for a verbal exchange with her father that could only drive a wedge between them. She pressed her foot down on the accelerator and replied, "Oh?"

Krasnoff motioned for her to slow the car down. She mechanically complied. "It's about something I've kept from you, something that needs to be explained."

"I'm listening."

The words came hard to Krasnoff. He stammered in his lame attempt to confess his deed. "I know there is a conspiracy to steal the UT from me, and the persons responsible sent a man by the name of Sam to spy on us. His spying, as the videotape we recovered revealed, was to locate the device, but Cohen uncovered the plot before he could pass the video on to his superiors." He stopped and waited for her to respond.

She pulled the car over to the side of the road and turned the engine off. "Then what happened?"

Krasnoff clasped his daughter's hand. "He would have ruined everything for us," he said. "He had to be stopped."

Leah looked nonplussed. She said nothing.

"It was self defense, really," he argued to himself aloud. "He would have killed us both if I hadn't killed him first."

Leah knew that was the best her father was capable of. He just was not an honest man. She simply nodded as he looked at her sheepishly, hoping for absolution. But absolution was not hers to bestow. Pity was the only thing that came to her mind as she reached over and turned the ignition on. She would have pity on him, but forgiveness was something she would leave to God.

Seconds later she pulled out into traffic. She would never bring up the issue again, nor let on that she had already known about the murder.

"He never once said he was sorry, or that the taking of a human life bothered him," Leah lamented to Cohen.

He squeezed her hand and pulled her along one of the paths in the park they frequently strolled outside Krasnoff's home. With a shrug of his shoulders he consoled, "He's just not himself any longer. He's a different man from when I first met him." The thought of telling Leah that her father also murdered a Bedouin to secure the UT flashed into his mind, but he knew that would push her over the edge. It was not for him to reveal her father's sins. "Hopefully, in time, he'll change for the better."

Leah agreed with Cohen's assessment of her father, but that didn't salve the wound in her heart. In fact, she began questioning the integrity of her heart. How long would they continue to make excuses for her father's behavior? One thing was certain, she could no longer trust him. Her mind started to go into overload with the onslaught of pain. She decided to erect a mental wall between her father and herself to protect her from future hurts. Conversations from now on would be brief and noncommittal. "Things will be different when we move out of here," she finally replied optimistically.

"I hope so," Cohen said with a shake of the head, then added woefully, "but, things seem to be getting worse no matter where we turn."

Leah stopped short. "You're frightening me, Nat."

"I don't mean to, but realistically, Leah, look at the political and economic scene with this Kavidas and Stein at the head of MASTERLINK, for example. The power they are wielding in the financial world, and right here in our own lives, is all encompassing."

"You mean their shutting off our credit?"

Cohen had investigated the mysterious melee surrounding Krasnoff's hospital bill and confirmed that MASTERLINK had put a block on all their credit lines. He looked at Leah incredulously. "Isn't that scary enough?"

Leah gazed off into the distance. "And then there's the aftermath of the destruction of the ark and the whole Temple Mount thing; who knows what that will bring?" She put her arm around his waist for temporal security, then pulled him along the path to venture deep into the park.

Looking over his shoulder into the mirror, Krasnoff pulled the loose fitting shirt over his healing arm, then tucked the shirttail into his pants and fastened his belt. He prided himself on being able to fully dress himself once again. It was important to him to show his therapist progress toward physical and emotional independence. He needed her approval. After a final 180-degree turn in front of the mirror, he walked into the kitchen.

"I'm driving myself to my therapy session," he announced to Leah and Cohen as they enjoyed breakfast together.

Leah glanced up at her father but said nothing.

"You feel up to it already?" Cohen replied as he traded a look with Leah.

"Getting stronger every day!" he boasted cheerfully. He lifted his injured arm with his good arm and added while wiggling his fingers, "Six more weeks of therapy and I'll be as good as new."

Leah simply raised her eyebrows at the proclamation, then after a moment of contemplation said, "It will be nice to see you fully mended."

Krasnoff decided to ignore his daughter's lack of enthusiasm. "Leah, can you try to get home early today so we can go see the houses you looked at?"

Disjointed, but controlled, Leah replied, "I'll try." With that she kissed Cohen goodbye and stood up. Cohen's eyes followed her as she walked out the front door. Her father simply shook his head and haphazardly fixed himself a bagel and coffee.

"Aahhh! You're half an hour early!" Leona gushed as Krasnoff rounded the corner of the receptionist's office. Seconds later she waved him into the therapy room. He was delighted she recognized him immediately.

"I was really looking forward to my next session," Krasnoff replied gleefully as he lifted the shoulder of the injured arm.

Leona stopped in her tracks, stared into his eyes, and said, "I was too."

A warm fuzzy feeling overcame him as he met her gaze, then he broke off the eye contact and proceeded to take off his shirt.

"Now, now, now. I'll help you with that," Leona proffered with a sensuous smile. Krasnoff nodded and allowed her to remove his shirt as he carefully surveyed her body. Once his shirt was off, she touched the massage table and said, "Lie on your back so I can work the chest muscles today." As if in a stupor, Krasnoff silently obeyed. Moments later her gentle rubbing of the soothing liniment onto his chest brought immediate comfort. He closed his eyes and began to fantasize about the woman above him—who he hoped would soon seize his body and carry him off to a remote cave where they could spend the night lovemaking.

Breaking into his fantasy, Leona asked curiously, "The receptionist tells me you paid cash for your last session. Isn't that a little unusual in today's economy—I mean with medical insurance and all that stuff?"

Krasnoff kept his eyes closed as his mind groped for a glib answer to the MASTERLINK problem that remained unresolved. "A little glitch with my insurance coverage. So until it's straightened out,

I'll pay cash; they'll reimburse me later." Leona shrugged her shoulders, then raked the hair on his chest with her hands.

Time seemed to slip away quickly. After ten minutes of massaging his chest, Leona leaned over and whispered in his ear, "Turn over so I can work your back muscles."

He slowly opened his eyes and began to turn when he felt her hand on his waist. She proceeded to carefully manipulate his body so as to minimize any pain to his shoulder. "Thanks," he said, stifling a wince. A second before he closed his eyes to continue his blissful slumber his mind registered she was wearing black stockings. "Nice," he moaned.

"I didn't forget about your offer to teach me about archeology in trade for therapy," she said. He could not see the gleam in her eyes.

"I was hoping you would ask," he replied with a sigh of satisfaction.

"Suppose you come over to my apartment Saturday evening so we can begin the bargaining process."

Krasnoff's senses lit off like a rocket. He felt the surge of inner forces that dictated he was every bit a man. "Where and when?"

"I'll write down the address and directions before you leave."

Krasnoff smiled and dozed off.

Passing over the Poleg River, an uncontrolled body of water turned nature preserve, the Krasnoffs and Cohen approached Netanya, their future home. Netanya, with a population of over one hundred thousand, boasted a charming beach and promenade and a universe of both expensive and inexpensive hotels, shops, and whatnot that were often filled to capacity with vacationing Europeans and affluent Israelis. The boldly modernistic concrete beach facilities and pleasantly landscaped greenery made Netanya a great place to spend an afternoon of seaside sun and surf.

Immigrants from Belgium and the Netherlands in the early years of Israel's statehood had laboriously endeavored to make Netanya the world's number one exporter of polished diamonds imported from Asia and Africa. Expansive showrooms displaying precious stones, hosted by multi-lingual, well-dressed female guides, lined the thoroughfares.

Just north of Netanya, overlooking the Valley of Hefer, was the house Leah believed her father would want. They walked the elevated wrought-iron fenced veranda that ran across the front of the house, and marveled at the spectacular view of the valley below. It was truly breathtaking. "There's no need to look at the second house, Leah," Krasnoff said jubilantly. "This is where I want to live!" He made the decision after a careful two-hour survey of the house.

"I knew this would be perfect for you," Leah replied, being swept up in the enthusiasm of the moment.

"Besides the nice view, there is ample security here," Cohen added. He was referring to the fenced perimeter surrounding the small estate that included a central station alarm system and 24-hour TV surveillance.

Krasnoff studied the real estate papers in his hand, then said to Leah, "Call the agent tonight and tell them we'll take the house. Make it clear that since the house is vacant, we want to move in right away." He turned to Cohen and instructed, "Make sure the UT and the other artifacts are mobile and ready to go by next Friday. I'm hiring a contractor to convert one of the bedrooms into a special secure room to house the apparatus. This way it will be safe from any predators."

Cohen wondered whether it was possible to hide the UT in a place away from *predators* since it was apparent that the real enemies, Kavidas and Stein, seemed to be capable of penetrating any and all security systems. "Will do," he replied with a nod.

On the way back to Jerusalem, a news report came over the car radio informing the public that Prime Minister Rubin's popularity had rebounded after the explosion in the Rabbi's Tunnel, and that he did not think it in the public's interest to resign, much to the disappointment of the radicals in the Knesset who were hoping for relief. With that news filling the air, Krasnoff did not want to add to the tension by announcing his plan to see Leona that night. He couldn't handle any disapproval from Leah.

Violent lightning strikes followed by deafening thunderclaps and a massive cloudburst severely disturbed Krasnoff's concentration as he drove to Leona's apartment, located just over one mile from the therapy center. With the heavy downpour quickly flooding the streets and restricting passage, he pulled to one side to wait for the storm to pass.

Looking up at the black alto-cumulus clouds that appeared to rise into the upper atmosphere, he saw flashes of light being exchanged between the giant electrical capacitors suspended in the air; and a wave of fear came over him. Frightened by the awesome power of nature being unleashed before his very eyes, he gawked up at the meteorological disturbance and suddenly theorized that a higher power very well might be orchestrating events. Despite the scientific explanation for such phenomena, the thought that something like this might come together by chance puzzled him. He started thinking about God. *If there really is a God, could He be angry with me for my wrongdoing?* he wondered. It was something that he would have to consider and do something about. *But not right now*, he reasoned. *I will make my peace with God before I die. I have plenty of time to correct the balance sheet. I will make large donations to Jewish charities and national humanitarian programs to offset my transgressions.*

Then we'll use the UT to uncover wealth to end much of the poverty and misery that surround us here in Jerusalem. But first I want to pay off the house and stabilize my diamond business. Then I'll tend to these things, he thought with confident satisfaction.

Leona's apartment building took Krasnoff by surprise. It had all the amenities of a posh New York Upper West Side townhouse. Exotic shrubbery garnished the exterior of the European-style housing complex; the interior lobby boasted elegant Mediterranean furnishings. His first impression was that she lived way above her income; a therapist could never afford such luxury. *Perhaps she has hidden assets to draw from or is not who she claims to be.*

Krasnoff's eyes widened in shock when Leona first opened the apartment door. "Wow! This is some pad!" he exclaimed effusively. Quickly surveying the immediate environment he added, "I'm really impressed." Turning on the ball of his foot he scanned her up and down, taking note of how scantily clad she was, and said as his eyes narrowed to a gaze, "But not half as impressed as I am with you!"

Leona watched him with piercing eyes and replied, "You said the right thing." She walked to the sofa and plopped into the soft cushions and added as she patted the space next to her, "I'm the one who should take your breath away, not my furniture. That's only the window dressing."

Unwittingly Krasnoff migrated to Leona's side. "I'm curious," he inquired while giving off a leering smile. "Did you win the Irish Sweepstakes or something? I mean, it takes a lot of 'shekels' to keep up a place like this."

Trying to overlook the friendly probe, she dropped her lower lip and gave him a sensuous smile. "I come from a wealthy family. They take care of me." She bounced off the sofa and walked to the refrigerator. "A glass of wine?"

Instinct dictated that he should not dig into Leona's personal finances any further. "Red if you have it."

"How's the shoulder?" she asked while pouring the sherry into the glasses.

Krasnoff rubbed his wounded arm, quickly deciding not to spoil his chances for advancement. "Fine! Pretty soon I'll have full use..." he stopped short, knowing that was impossible, "...well, almost full use of the arm."

Leona returned to his side and handed him the large glass of wine as she looked deeply into his eyes. "Let's toast to us."

Holding the glass with his rehabilitated arm to gain her approval, he replied, "To Leona, the woman who really makes me feel good."

Three glasses of wine later, Leona had full control of the mood.

"Tell me more about your work," she said coquettishly. "I'm especially interested in your findings that relate to the Temple and the ancient priesthood."

The wine began to take hold of his senses. A bleary look at Leona told him little about her strategy. "You're really interested? Well, then pour me another wine and I'll tell you all about it." He yawned several times and then pushed himself upright in the sofa as she readily complied with his request. Then, for the next 45 minutes he elaborated on archeological themes to satisfy her curiosity. Smiling, she watched him struggle to keep his eyes open.

"Tell me about the Urim and Thummim," she asked, stroking the back of his neck. "What role did that play in the priesthood?"

Various thoughts tumbled through his consciousness as he fought to stay awake. *When are we going to eat?* He scratched his head and continued to wonder, *Didn't we already talk about the UT? Revi, keep your eyes open!* "The Urim and Thummim are ancient high priestly devices used to tell the mind of God over certain things," he managed to eke out while thoughts of her body being close to his drifted in and out.

"What ever became of them?" she asked subtly with eyes pleading for understanding.

Krasnoff smiled then gave her a sly wink and said, trying to keep from slurring his words, "They're in…" he paused and grinned, "…a very safe place."

His answer told her that he knew where the device was. She began unbuttoning his shirt and with eyes fastened on his, continued her probing. "But not destroyed or lost somewhere in antiquity like most people think?"

He gave her an amatory look then closed his eyes and put a hand to his forehead. Within half a minute, he was sound asleep.

Leona pursed her lips in consternation. "Okay," she whispered to the sleeping man before her, "now we go to plan 'B.' " With that she reached over and, gently clutching his hand, uttered a chant in an unknown tongue.

Krasnoff's glazed eyes slowly opened to a stare then came into sharp focus. "My God," he cried out, "it's really you, Naomi!" He reached for her face and began crying. "It's been so long. I really miss you. Why did you go away?"

"You will be with me soon, Revi," Leona said, impersonating his dead wife's voice while rubbing his chest, "and then we can spend eternity together. But for now, I need to know where the Urim and Thummim are. God told me to ask you. You can trust me, Revi."

In his mind's eye, he saw Naomi and his brother Gershom leaving that fateful afternoon on their shopping trip. He reached up and touched the face before him, "Naomi, darling, you know that they are safe with me and Leah. They are secure in our home, you know that."

The woman before him nodded, then kissed him tenderly as he fell back asleep.

Leona stood up, looked down on Krasnoff, and said, "Blubbering fool."

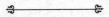

Restlessness finally yielded to exhaustion, and in the early morning hours before daylight illuminated the land, Cohen fell into a deep sleep where he experienced a dream that would forever change his life. The dream that would prepare him to accept his place in the divine scheme and in the seething vortex of time. The place, whose merest mention was overwhelming and paralyzing to the senses, was a place men and angels were not permitted to tell of.

A portal opened in the roof of the Krasnoff house, exposing the blackness of night wherein a fiery chariot of pure gold with a team of six stallions, all with blazing eyes, circled high above, coming closer to the rooftop with every revolution. As Cohen watched in his dream, the chariot came to a halt above the house. Suddenly, as if catapulted out of his bed by some unseen hand, he found himself suspended in space at the rear of the chariot. He stood motionless for what seemed an interminable period, then without warning came the thunderous command of a voice from Heaven, "GET IN!" He obeyed, and as he stepped into the chariot, the horses reared up on their hind legs and snorted flames of fire. In the next instant they were galloping upward at breakneck speed toward the outer canopy of space that led to God's domain.

Unable to calculate the distance or duration of the journey—for in the spiritual realm there is neither—Cohen traveled through three ethereal frontiers of space: the atmosphere, the stellar spaces, and then into the hidden regions of the triune God in what felt like only a fraction of time. Without warning he found himself in the entrance-way of an immense, magnificent throne room located in the center of the celestial expanse of God's habitation. "Oh, the wonder, the transport of God!" he uttered in praise as he stood enthralled, looking off into the distance toward the glory of God. Suspended above the throne were countless numbers of angelic beings standing in ranks of thousands upon thousands, forming a heavenly choir that echoed through the canyons of massive celestial mountains far off in the distance. Cohen quickly closed his eyes and did an internal assessment amidst the splendor of it all. "How can I, a mere mortal—a sinner for that matter—end up here in Heaven? I do not deserve this. Am I dead or am I dreaming?" he asked aloud then felt his body in an attempt to reassure himself.

Around the throne were 24 elders, dressed in white garments, with golden crowns upon their heads, 12 representing the Old Testament tribes of Jacob, 12 representing the New Testament apostles.

"I am Gabriel," said a voice from behind him, "the guardian of Israel, who has been assigned to care for you in the troubled days ahead."

Cohen clutched his chest as he whirled toward the voice. "Am I—?"

"No, you are not dead," the angelic officer of the heavenly host interrupted, "but called up by the Holy One for commissioning." He pointed toward the throne and added, "I will escort you to Him." Gabriel looked very much like a man, consistent with biblical descriptions, except with perfect, chiseled features, and two towering wings. The wings were made of bony frames covered with pure white membranes, then with glistening silvery feathers. They were motionless as he walked. Cohen surmised that he used the wings only when traveling in earthly spheres.

Cohen felt his knees knock together as he trembled in fear of what lay ahead. Flashing lightning bolts emanated outward from the glorious throne, while resplendent, rainbow-colored clouds drifted slowly through the air. In the next instant, the scene changed. He shielded his eyes as a great funnel of flames rising into infinity appeared before him. The fires burned with a fierce intensity, yielding only light. The center of the fire looked like glowing metal, even molten gold, while inside the funnel were what looked like numerous living beasts, slowly ascending and descending as the flaming shaft approached the throne. Cohen was compelled to follow the pillar of fire ever onward. As he walked toward the royal seat his eyes fell upon the beautiful angelic creatures who attended God—the cherubim and seraphim. On the right were the highest ranking angelic beings, the cherubim. Some had two wings, others had four. Their wings were spread upward, each touching the wing of another on either side, forming an angelic crescent around the throne.

On the left were the seraphim, full of eyes in front and behind and possessing six magnificent wings—two covered their faces, two covered their feet, and two enabled them to hover, ready for their next command. "Holy, holy, holy is the Lord Almighty; the whole earth is full of His glory!" they shouted in unison. With every shout the heavens shook and the temple of God filled with a radiant burst of His Spirit.

"Stop!" Gabriel shouted at Cohen then blocked his path with his arm. He pointed toward the glorious figure on the throne and announced, "Behold, the Lamb of God who takes away the sins of the world."

Cohen froze in his steps. There was nothing on earth that could have prepared him for what he saw next.

Sitting on the throne was the glorified Christ, Jesus the Messiah of Israel. It was unmistakably Him, Cohen reasoned, for as he gazed at His presence he saw Him raise his hand to an angel. Cohen's eyes fastened on the nailprints in His wrists. Cohen wanted more. He strained at Gabriel's arm and cried, "I need to go to Jesus." Gabriel looked at the Lord, who nodded approval, and lowered his arm. Cohen advanced ever so slowly toward the throne with Gabriel at his side. While still at a distance, Cohen began to sob as he realized his filth and unworthiness. The closer he walked toward Jesus, the more his heart broke for his sin. He walked another step then fell to his knees and cried out, "I am a sinner with an unclean heart, and my eyes have seen the King, the Lord Almighty." In celebration of his recognition and salvation, a river of fire sprang up from behind the throne and flowed out into the great expanse toward the distant mountain range. Blazing wheels slowly rose from the fiery river and disappeared in the star-lit canopy above.

Taking another step closer, Cohen suddenly saw the person of Christ change before his eyes. He retained the features of the Son of Man, yet a transformation took place where he took on the appearance of the Ancient of Days, the Father, yet manifest in the Son, with a long, flowing, diamond-studded white robe, and white hair that looked like wool. Cohen cowered at the awesomeness of it all.

"My Spirit lives!" Christ announced so that the great assembly could hear. With that the entire horizon behind the throne began glowing, then quickly burst into an enormous dazzling white globe that reminded Cohen of the creation of a star. It nearly blinded him.

He shielded his eyes as an omnipresent voice boomed, "Behold the glory of God!"

"Who is worthy to open the books?" the angelic host shouted.

"Only the Lamb!" came the reply from untold multitudes of voices from behind. Cohen turned to see what looked like millions of men, women, and children—from every nation—clothed in shining white robes walking into the throne room. His spirit immediately identified them as the redeemed, the Bride of Christ. They slowly approached the throne as they sang the Hallelujah chorus.

Then a divine convergence occurred.

The Ancient of Days stood in the center of the throne room, while the Son sat at His right hand while the glory of God, the spectacular globe of light, even the Holy Spirit, came together with Them to form what looked like a tremendously giant triangle, the age-old symbol of the Trinity. "I and the Father are one," the Son declared to the heavens.

The scene changed again.

Cohen found himself before a row of colossal books that stood on massive pedestals made of granite, cut by angelic hands. The row of books extended for what looked like miles. In front of every book, an angel stood as a silent sentry to guard the contents. Cohen began walking down the row then caught a glimpse of some of the books placed in categories: The Books of Life, recording the names of everyone ever created. The Books of Deeds, recording every human act. The Books of Conscience, the testimony of the God-given gift of choosing right and wrong given to every man. The Books of Words, recording every word uttered by mortals. The Books of Secret Words, recording every thought. The Books of Public Works, recording those acts of faith by the redeemed. At the end of the row, an angel stood writing names in one of the books. In a flash, Cohen was conveyed to that book, where he saw his name being written with what looked like red ink. His spirit corrected his thinking: It was the blood of the Lamb by which his name was written. Once the angel had written Cohen's name, he closed the book. Cohen looked to his right and saw only one more pedestal with what appeared to be the last book upon it. He knew in his heart that that meant the end of man's time on earth was very near.

Suddenly the Son assumed the shape of a Lamb, then quickly that of a powerful lion with a full mane. Yes! Cohen realized from his study of the Bible, He was the Lion of Judah! The Son, who was also the Lion, approached the next-to-last book. As the angel stepped aside, the Lion opened the book, then turned to Cohen and said, "I have written your name in one of the Lamb's Books of Life. Now you are My ambassador to prepare the world for My coming. You are of the tribe of Levi, and I have given you the task of recruiting the 12 tribes to fulfill the culmination."

Cohen turned his face down. He felt ashamed to receive the assignment to bring in the 144 thousand Jewish missionaries—12 thousand of each of the 12 tribes of Judah—to the world. They would come during the terrible period known as Jacob's Trouble, the Seventieth Week of Daniel, the awful Tribulation.

The Son of God touched Cohen's shoulder and said, "I have given you My seal; now go, My chosen servant, and be fruitful."

Just as Cohen turned to depart, the great multitude of the redeemed divided, allowing him to walk between them down a path made of pure gold to a precipice that hung suspended in the heavens. He walked to the cliff and stood still in utter amazement as his mind could not fully comprehend what his eyes saw. There were innumerable cities, all with magnificently crafted mansions. The cities were both near and distant, hanging in space, yet connected by a celestial floor that permitted one to journey on foot. Traversing back and forth between the cities were both the redeemed and angelic creatures, singing praises to the Lamb all the while.

Below him he saw quite another scene. As far as the eye could see there were the ongoing actual events described in the Bible for all the redeemed to revisit. Time did not exist here. God lives in the *now*, not the past or future. The events on earth were simply a copy or pattern of what took place in the realms of paradise. It was like being transported back into time and viewing the occurrence, only this was the real thing. Cohen dropped to his knees and gazed out into the vast expanse. There he saw the Garden of Eden, with the Tree of Life in the center surrounded by the most beautiful lush flowers and vegetables ever imagined. Adam and Eve were sitting by the virgin waters of the River Euphrates, naming the animals. Farther down he saw Noah and his family building the ark, with a simultaneous depiction of the

global flood that destroyed all human life except the eight who trusted God's promises. In one corner, Cohen saw David the shepherd boy
standing before the Philistine giant, Goliath, slinging his stone. At
another location, thousands of heavenly inhabitants were visiting
what was undeniably Solomon's Temple.

He stood up to look at the endless procession of events then focused on one: A plateau off in the distance told of the culmination of
all acts of the Bible. He saw the living Christ hanging on the cross at
Calvary with the empty tomb behind him as myriads of angels sang
praises to the resurrected one.

Predetermined future events were also being exhibited as Cohen
gazed beyond the drama of Calvary.

"The time will come when you will remain here," an angelic
voice intoned, shattering his reverie, "but for now, you must go."

"But why—?" Cohen sighed in disappointment, turning to see
Gabriel once again.

Gabriel put his arm around him in consolation. "I know you
want to dwell here, but your work is not finished yet." Cohen's heart
filled with the joy of the Lord as he realized his purpose. Gabriel
walked him out of the throne room to a great ladder that hung suspended in the ethereal world of God. "Before you descend, I will
show you what events must follow." Suddenly a swirling spiral of fire
with flaming spikes darting far into space appeared before them,
bringing Cohen to his knees. He shook uncontrollably and hid his
face in his hands.

"Fear not, servant of the Most High," Gabriel announced,
"behold…"

The spiral of fire slowly diminished, leaving behind a great sea
surrounded by many nations. Out of that sea emerged a hideous beast
that walked on the water until he came to the place called the Beautiful Land, Israel. Once he arrived on the land he became a man, a

master of intrigue who caused deceit to prosper. He overpowered all obstacles.Because of his success, the whole world was astonished and followed him in his endeavors, not knowing that folly and destruction awaited them. His fame was unparalleled in history and he was exalted and magnified above every god, yet in secret he uttered blasphemies against the Most High because he knew his time was short. Out of the Beautiful Land came a second beast who exercised the same authority as the first and performed great and miraculous signs to bring honor to the first beast. He called fire down from Heaven and caused everyone to receive a mark on his right hand or forehead. That number identified the person with the first beast, who was given power to war against the saints.

He set himself up to be as great as the Prince of the Host, yet had no regard for the god of his fathers. All whose names were not written in the Lamb's Book of Life worshiped him. He remained until the time of wrath was completed and the Son of Man appeared in the sky. His number a mystery—666. Even in the dream, Cohen thought he remembered reading about such a person in the Book of Revelation.

"Now go your way, Cohen," Gabriel soothed as he put his hand on the young man's shoulder.

Cohen awakened from his dream, jumped out of bed, then dropped to his knees in prayer and thanksgiving.

CHAPTER

12

Jerusalem

Learned man cannot assign a scientific or rational explanation to dreams, but rather often regards them with a certain degree of superstitious fear. The cultured, too, are not without a superstitious awe and dread of dreams, heightened in mind by the natural curiosity to know the future. Frequently made up of only fragmentary ideas or loosely connected trains of thought, dreams do not come to the threshold of consciousness, except perhaps in death itself. Dreams are to the sleeping state what visions and hallucinations are to the waking state.

Time and space seem vividly real in dreams; the duration in a single dream may occupy but a moment of time for the dreamer. But out of this dim region in which the thinking labors forth to emerge into daylight have come poetical and musical inventions, as well as scientific remedies and spiritual perceptions—born out of the life of genius awakened in sleep.

Dreams have often been regarded in the spiritual realm as the means of direct and special intercourse with God. The Book of Numbers advises that dreams and visions are the two forms of the prophetic revelations of God, His special will often being revealed to men through dreams. Biblical patriarchs indeed received supernatural glimpses of the future in dreams. Jacob saw a stairway to Heaven at Bethel; Joseph saw a futuristic dream regarding Israel while he was in Canaan; Solomon dreamt in Gibeon; and Daniel had a prophetic dream while in Babylon. These all serve to remind us that a fitting dream was one of the three things regarded as marks of divine favor: a good king, a fruitful year, and a good dream.

Apprehension gave way to serenity as Cohen sat on his bed reading his Bible amidst the stack of moving boxes lining his room. At 4:30, the front door opened and his heart leaped with excitement.

"Nat, are you here?" Leah called the moment she stepped in from work.

He dashed to her side and she immediately knew something was different about him. The glow on his face seemed to emanate from within. He hugged and kissed her several times then held her at arms' length and said, "Leah, I had a dream early this morning where I was transported to Heaven! I saw Jesus in the throne room of God!"

"You what?!" she exclaimed incredulously.

He gulped and raved on, "There were angels and believers on Christ—millions of them—and cities floating in the air and then there was the Garden of Eden—" He stopped short and shook his head while reliving portions of the dream. "I saw Noah building the ark, and Solomon directing Hiram as he built the Temple. Then I saw Daniel before the Babylonian king Nebuchadnezzar…then the cross where Christ was crucified—"

Leah snuffled in bewilderment. "Whoa, whoa! Slow down!"

He rushed her to the sofa and held her in an embrace. "It was awesome, really," he began exuberantly as her gaze remained transfixed on his face. "I know it was real," he continued as he clutched his chest. "In my heart, I know it was real!"

Leah couldn't bring herself to believe what he had said, but she did believe that he had had a dream. "This happened this morning?"

He took a deep breath then fell back into the cushions. "I may sound like a prattling fool, but I'm serious! This thing happened. I was conveyed to Heaven and..." he paused again and closed his eyes.

"And—?"

"...and I received my 'commission' ; Jesus gave me a mission. The end times are upon us; and since I am from the tribe of Levi, I have been given the command to begin recruiting the twelve thousand men of each of the twelve tribes of Judah to make up the one hundred and forty-four thousand Jewish witnesses who will emerge during the time of the Tribulation."

"Whew!" Leah shot her eyebrows up. "This is heavy." She stood up and walked to the far end of the room. She crossed her arms over her chest and added, "I guess that means we'll have a son. Then what happened?"

Cohen read her facial expression. "Leah! You must believe me! I gave my life to Christ in that dream—He is the Messiah—my spirit testifies that it's true. He lives!"

"Could this be the voice of your mother that you're always telling me about?" she asked like a atheistic skeptic.

"No, absolutely not!" he said with clear precision. "What's more, Jesus told me to tell you about the dream, so His plan includes you."

Leah's eyes bore holes into the man sitting on the sofa before her. "He what?"

Cohen rushed to her side and reiterated, "He told me to tell you about the dream. Don't you see, Leah, that He sees us as *one*. Together, we are going to be used of God to advance His kingdom!" He reveled in the mere thought of it. With his eyes turned upward he added, "As missionaries to His people; unbelievable!"

"Man, you've really changed!" she rejoined.

Cohen's breath caught in his throat. After a moment of contemplation he said, "God's Spirit is in me and I must obey." He held out his hand and she grabbed it and embraced him.

Several moments of silence passed, then Cohen looked Leah in the eyes and said ominously, "There's something else, Leah."

Leah's body stiffened. "What is it?"

"I was given an encrypted message by the angel Gabriel, a mystery if you will. I've been studying the Bible, but I just don't have the interpretation yet. I believe it has something to do with us here in Israel, and with political leaders who deceive the world. That's all I've been able to figure out so far."

Leah's eyes widened. "Did you tell my dad all this?"

Cohen made a gesture with his hand. "He never came home last night."

"You're kidding, right?"

"No. I waited for him to come out of his room after you left for work, but when he didn't come out at lunchtime, I opened his door and saw that his bed hadn't been slept in."

Leah frowned. "This doesn't sound kosher," she mumbled. "I'll bet he went to see that babe that took a liking to him, that therapist woman."

Cohen agreed immediately. "You're probably right. I told you he's acting weird."

"We've got to find out…"

The door opened wide and Krasnoff walked in.

Cohen and Leah exchanged looks. "Revi, is everything all right?" Cohen asked.

Krasnoff nodded indignantly. "Of course."

Leah noticed that his clothes were terribly wrinkled. She walked to her father and immediately smelled wine on his breath. Her thought to interrogate him vanished when she realized there was another aroma coming from her father, a ladies' perfume. "Are you sure, Dad?"

"I'm fine," he replied with a wave of the hand. He walked to the sofa and plopped down, striking his injured arm against the side of the sofa. He grimaced and moaned, rubbing the wounded area. Within a minute, he began to doze off.

Leah looked compassionately at her father, then glanced at Cohen. He motioned for her to let him rest.

Two hours later, Leah gently stroked her father's cheek. "Dad, I made some coffee for you." He nodded as his eyes slowly opened then followed her to the kitchen table.

Cohen signaled Leah that she should ask her father where he had spent the night. She took the cue and said, "We were worried about you. You didn't come home last night."

A queer look swept over his face. "What do you mean?"

Cohen exchanged glances with Leah. "Dad, your bed wasn't slept in last night. Where were you?"

He scratched his head then loosened the top button of his shirt. He looked at her inquiringly and replied, "I thought I slept in my own bed and just went out for a walk early this morning." He frantically scanned their faces. "This isn't so?"

Leah sighed deeply. "No, it isn't so, Dad." She stood up from the table as a wave of anger suddenly came over her. "Just look at you! You're a disgrace! Are we now to call you a drunk?! Were you in a stupor all night?"

"Leah!" Cohen interjected, "easy on him. I honestly don't think he remembers where he was."

Leah rolled her eyes in disgust and walked to the refrigerator for the cream.

Cohen massaged Krasnoff's hand while he glanced at Leah. "Revi, I have something important to tell you," he began. "It's about a dream I had that really seemed like a vision. It was a dream where I saw a glimpse of Heaven and I—"

Krasnoff held up his hand in a halting motion and said sarcastically, "Spare me."

Cohen bit his lip then changed his tactics. "I know it sounds crazy, Revi, but I saw Jesus and He told me about future things and I'm sure it has something to do with this Kavidas fellow."

Krasnoff choked on his coffee. "What? Have you flipped out?"

While Leah looked on in helpless frustration, Cohen dug in. "No. What's more, I now know my raison d'etre, my reason for being. It's to sound the alarm. You see, the UT allowed us to confirm the historical parts of the Bible that in turn confirm the prophetic parts. The parts that haven't happened yet. This somehow includes the dastardly duo of Kavidas and Stein." A puzzled look came over his face. "God commissioned me to tell His people about Christ being the soon-to-return Messiah, then revealed the future to me in some kind of cryptic fashion."

Krasnoff sneered at him. "You're daft! Too much time with the UT has made you mad." A wounded look came over Cohen. He looked up at Leah and saw her crying. "What's the matter, Leah?" he asked as tears welled up in his eyes in response.

"Nobody could say what you did to my dad with such conviction unless they were convinced in their heart that it was true."

"You mean you really believe me, Leah?"

She cradled her face in her hands. "God, show me this truth," she prayed aloud.

"Don't tell me he's persuading you!" Krasnoff scoffed.

Cohen went to her side and said to Krasnoff, "May God show you His truth in Christ as well."

"The only truth I believe in is that we protect the UT. We need to hide them as soon as possible," he replied, filling the room with tension. "Let's get on with it!"

Leah dried her eyes and walked out of the kitchen. Cohen's heart broke for the blindness he saw in Krasnoff. "Yes, we need to move the UT to a safe place. Leah and I will take the stones to the vault at the diamond store while you rest and clean up."

Krasnoff rose to his feet and yawned. "Good plan," he said callously.

As Leah drove through the unusually heavy late afternoon traffic on the roads to Netanya, Cohen steadied the earthen jar (secured with bubble-wrap) between his legs while holding all the priestly equipment on his lap, the Urim and Thummim on top. The plan was to get to Netanya, deposit the items in the vault, and return to Jerusalem as quickly as possible. Leah took the Nahal Ayyalon expressway northwest to Tel Aviv to connect to the Ha Yarqon turnpike that would bring them to Netanya in slightly over one hour.

They spoke not a word for the first 15 minutes of the trip.

"I've been thinking of everything that went on back at the house, and I can't get it out of my mind," Leah finally began as she glanced at Cohen. She was surprised to see him sitting with his head pushed back against the headrest, squeezing his eyes shut. "What's the matter, darling?"

"It's not just with me. My spirit is really troubled about your father," he said with a voice vibrating with intensity.

"You mean the way he acted back there?"

"That too, but there's much more. I fear for his life. I have been dwelling on my dream, and have come to realize that something must happen to your father. My dream didn't include him…" He paused and elevated the Urim and Thummim slightly to dramatize his point.

Leah writhed slightly and tightened her grip around the wheel, then stepped down on the accelerator. The speedometer moved up to 85 mph. Cohen reached over and rubbed her arm. She turned to him in recognition as she backed off the gas pedal and said with an elevated tone, "I can't take much more of this, Nat, I really can't. I just wish this whole thing would go away!" She looked over at the UT and shook her head. "The damn thing is a curse."

Cohen shook his head. "No it isn't. It's like anything else that God does in one's life. We are either exercised unto godliness or bitterness, depending on our perspective and relationship with Him. If we see all things as coming from Him—recognizing His sovereignty—then we accept them and turn them into blessings. If we perceive things from God as being evil, or as forms of punishment, then they do indeed become a curse."

"Are you saying the UT is a blessing?"

"Until the time that I met Messiah Jesus in my dream, I was ambivalent. Part of me saw it as a means to gain fame or whatever; part of me saw it as a damned thing that brought heartache and trouble. But now, all that has changed." He turned to her and smiled, then said with conviction, "When you make your peace with God, your outlook will change too."

"You really are different!" she marveled.

"I am beginning to appreciate what the Bible teaches about 'being a new creature in Christ.' In fact, my learning process in God's ways has just begun." Cohen was referring to the divine act of regeneration, or *new birth*—the instantaneous spiritual change that occurs through the operation of the Holy Spirit at the time of conversion, forever altering the heart and mind of the recipient.

Leah sighed deeply as Cohen closed his eyes once again. *God, when is this going to happen to me?*

It was after 5 p.m. when they arrived at the newly named Krasnoff's Diamond Exchange building in Netanya. Expediently, Leah negotiated the security combinations and passwords, allowing Cohen to place the high priestly garment and jar into a separate safe within the store's vault, a location that would remain unnoticed by employees or customers. Cohen had resolved that when they relocated to Netanya, he would resume his weekly meeting with the revelatory device in a secret location whose whereabouts he had not yet determined.

"Good riddance," Leah muttered as she locked up the front door.

"Let's go for dinner on the coast before we head back," Cohen suggested, somewhat relieved that he was temporarily excused from being the custodian of the lights of God.

Leah's face brightened expansively. She grabbed his arm as they strolled back to the car. Cohen suddenly stopped short. "Give me your cell phone, quick," he blurted out.

"What for?" Leah exclaimed with heightening alarm.

"Your father is in mortal danger."

Krasnoff's locked door slowly opened without the aid of a key as Leona stepped inside. As an eagle tracks a rodent she quickly surveyed the kitchen and living room for her target, then motioned for her partner to follow her. She stealthily walked to the master bedroom and paused at the doorway. Krasnoff lay asleep on his bed. She turned to her accomplice, who nodded curtly, then she stepped toward her prey.

The phone rang once.

Krasnoff stirred.

Startled, Leona turned to her companion and mouthed, "Sir, what should I—"

Stein waved her to silence as he pointed toward the phone.

The phone stopped ringing just as Krasnoff turned on his side.

In Netanya, Cohen heard the Krasnoffs' phone *click* as it rang, then it went dead. He immediately pressed the redial button.

"What's the matter?" Leah burst out

"Broken connection." Cohen took a deep breath while shooting a prayer up to God. A recorded announcement came through the cell phone, advising the caller that the number was unavailable. Pangs of dread and horror filled Cohen's mind as he envisioned disaster. His gaze narrowed on Leah's face.

"Oh my God!" Leah cried as she read his expression. "What is it?"

"We have to get back right away! They think your father has the UT. They came to get it."

For ten full minutes Stein and Leona searched the house for the revelatory device and found nothing.

Angered, they walked into the bedroom where Krasnoff lay sleeping.

Leona looked to Stein then placed her hand two inches above the left side of Krasnoff's chest. She moved her hand in a circular motion to obstruct the flow of the blood in his coronary artery. He immediately clutched his chest as a severe pain radiated to his left shoulder and down to his arm. His breathing abruptly accelerated and his face began to redden as a necrosis of a region of the myocardium began. He moaned gravely and slowly opened his eyes.

"Rehavam, tell me where the Urim and Thummim are and I will let you live!" Leona ordered. She lifted her hand momentarily to alleviate the internal pressure. Krasnoff gulped in mouthfuls of air as his eyes darted back and forth on the two faces above him.

"Leona, how could you?" Krasnoff choked out. His mind recaptured the past fantasy when this woman had feigned affection for him.

"You idiot," she snarled, "as if I would be interested in a mole like you." She slammed him across the face. "I'm waiting for —"

"You rotten dogs!" he gasped as he took a meager swing at her. She ducked her head and yelled, "Where is it?!"

Krasnoff clenched his teeth. "You'll have to kill me."

"If that's the way you want it, fine," she replied fiercely. She lowered her hand and resumed the circular motion. An acute interruption of the supply of blood to his heart resumed at a measured rate. Krasnoff's eyes rolled back.

As a *Shedim* demoness, Leona, known by the fallen as Lilith, had her strengths: She was able to impersonate and imitate good angels as well as inflict diseases such as angina and heart disease upon mortals. Her powers extended to causing accidents to hurt and even kill the living, but she was unable to project a false reality.

"Wait," Stein said from behind. Leona immediately withdrew from Krasnoff and stepped back, awaiting her superior's next command.

Krasnoff's body went limp.

Stein stared at Krasnoff as if to bore holes in his head and in the next instant, Krasnoff found himself in the park next to his home, the park he always loved, sitting on a bench next to Leah. It was a beautiful day and the birds were singing as the resplendent sunshine glistened off the morning dew that coated the canopy of leaves above them. Leah put her arm around him and asked, "Dad, where are the

Urim and Thummim? Cohen and I need to use them to confirm information that God gave him in a dream."

In the depths of Krasnoff's mind something registered untrue, but he couldn't retrieve truth just now. Years of yielding to lies and compromise prohibited him from calling upon truth at a time of need; it was buried deep in his heart. Spirals of reality blended with unconsciousness and swirled in his mind. They seemed to surround him, causing him to lose his balance as he attempted to stand up and walk away to a more comfortable place. In his mind's eye, he shouted for help, but nothing came out of his mouth. *They know about Cohen's dream?*

"Dad," Leah asked again as she pulled him back on to the bench, "you can trust me. Where is the device?"

He gently touched her face and smiled as he mouthed out, *Cohen has it, remember?*

Stein smiled at Leona.

"Yes, Dad, I remember. But I'm sick and he left without telling me where he was going, and I need to contact him immediately."

Krasnoff nodded. "He took it to our store at Netanya." As soon as the words left his mouth, a wave of consciousness washed over him. He suddenly realized the real truth—that Leah had gone with Cohen and that this was not Leah talking to him. Strength welled up from within as he started to push himself up. He yelled, "Get away from me!"

Stein motioned for Leona to quickly resume her stance over him before he could pull himself together. As he reeled to retain some semblance of sanity, she placed one hand over his head and the other over his heart and chanted a prayer to her god. She glanced over at Stein, who signaled his approval, then she made a fist and slammed it down on Krasnoff's chest.

He stopped breathing and fell limp on the bed. His eyes began to flutter as the realization came over him that his life was about to end. *I will get up!* he thought desperately and tried to move but his body remained inert. *My God, I'm going to die!* His eyes began dilating as life slowly ebbed out of him. *Is that you, Leona, I see?* He struggled to keep his mind functioning by concentrating on images he knew and loved. *Pain, oh, the pain in my chest.* Dazzling lights seemed to fill the room, burning his eyes. *Is this the way to Heaven? No! Wait, Revi!* he demanded of himself. *What about God and my sin?*

"You need not worry about that," a lying voice from the room said.

The thought that something was wrong flashed through his mind in a millisecond of time. *Where is the peace? WHERE IS THE PEACE?*

Blackness followed, total blackness. When his consciousness returned, he found himself in the place of eternal torment.

Stein and Leona didn't exchange another word as they walked out, nor did they look back at Krasnoff's body.

On the Nahal Ayyalon expressway, Cohen pulled the car off the next exit after Tel Aviv and came to a stop on the service road. "What are you doing, Nat?" Leah asked frantically. "We still have twenty-five miles to go."

"It's too late."

"Don't say that!" Leah yelled as her eyes filled with tears. Then she asked in a muffled voice, "How do you know, anyway?"

He sighed and placed the transmission in Park. "I just know."

"That's not good enough for me, Nat!" she retorted.

He embraced her until he felt the rigidity leave her body, then said softly, "The Holy Spirit within me testifies that your dad is beyond our help, and we need to go back to Netanya and get the UT before it's too late. We *must* protect the stones from falling into evil hands."

Leah succumbed. She began sniffling and climbed into the back seat. In seconds she was sobbing.

Cohen starting grinding his teeth as he thought on Krasnoff's death, then placed the gearshift lever into Drive and drove out into traffic. Within minutes he was retracing his way back to Netanya.

It was just after sunset when Cohen drove into the rear alley of Krasnoff's Diamond Exchange building. He immediately noticed a vacant blue Mercedes, parked with its motor running. With heightening awareness of danger and Leah still sleeping, he ran to the front of the store and peeked through the storefront window. At first he didn't recognize the stranger talking to the counter saleslady, then he suddenly placed him from the newspaper article and photographs describing Gregory Kavidas' three-million-dollar donation to Israel—it was Mort Stein.

Cohen's mind began to seize with panic. "Take control, Nat," he commanded himself. "We're not going to allow him to get it." A surge of peace welled up within him, and he knew it was from God. He dashed to the rear of the store and quickly opened the security door. The vault containing the Urim and Thummim was only a short distance away.

"Nat, what's going on?" Leah asked from behind him, totally unaware of the perilous predicament.

He whirled on her. "Shush! Stein is in front, working his way in. He's here to get the UT!" Cohen bobbed his head up and looked through the one-way observation mirror as he waved Leah toward the vault. "You get the UT while I watch him." Leah nodded and stealthily walked to the safe.

Fifteen seconds later she was holding the UT. She looked help-lessly at Cohen as she stuffed it in her knapsack and whispered, "What about the urn?"

"Leave it! Let's just get out of here."

She moved toward him and inadvertently slammed against the end of a jeweler's bench. Several earrings and a spool of silver solder fell to the floor. "Damn!" she mouthed. She blinked apologetically at Cohen then in a split-second thought on his Jesus. *Dear God, please no, please don't let him at me. Dear Jesus, I mean, please don't let anything happen.*

Stein heard the noise and peered through the mirror. His de-meanor immediately changed from a friendly curious shopper to a frenzied animal. "Who's in the back?" he snarled.

"Why, nobody," the alarmed saleslady replied.

"Yes, there is!" Stein snorted as he defiantly walked toward the employee entrance.

"Excuse me, sir!" the saleslady warned. "I will sound the alarm if you take one more step!"

Stein stopped in his tracks and turned to the lady. "Oh, is that so?" His face reddened with rage at the mortal who dared to chal-lenge him. He raised his right hand and pointed at her, then mumbled something under his breath. The woman suddenly grabbed her throat and started choking. Stein smiled triumphantly as her body fell dead to the floor in a crumpled heap.

As he rounded the corner into the rear vault and work space area his eyes saw what his mind refused to register. He clenched his fists and bit his lower lip as he surveyed the scene. Both the vault and out-side doors were open, and immediately he knew his adversary had beat him there by mere seconds. He bolted to the rear door just as Leah's car careened around the corner. The car was quickly absorbed in a heavy stream of night traffic.

Stein stood in the alley and calculated for several moments. "This isn't over," he said aloud in their wake. "I know who you are and where to get you."

Like migrating birds in the night, Cohen and Leah moved surreptitiously from one shopping mall to the next in the old city of Jerusalem until they finally arrived at the Holocaust Museum in the early morning hours. Here they would find fleeting rest for several hours amidst the hundreds of cars in the parking lot. Here they would piece together the strategy that would shield them from the evil predator who stalked them.

Leah rubbed her eyes as the embracing music of the Israel Philharmonic Orchestra with Jascha Hiefetz playing Paganini's Violin Concerto No. 1 in D Major, op. 6 came over the car radio. She wiped the sleep from her eyes and sighed as Cohen smiled at her. "Good morning," he said softly.

She reached over and turned the radio volume down. Her eyes widened as she asked solemnly, "Where do we go from here?"

"I've been thinking while you were sleeping, and I think it will be dangerous for us to go back to your old home or even to try to see your father."

She ran her fingers loosely through her rumpled hair and began to cry. "Are you saying that I can't go to his funeral? That I can't see him for the last time?"

Cohen shook his head and warned, "They will be waiting for us, I'm sure of it."

Silence.

After a moment of contemplation she said, "I want to see if there is anything in the newspaper." Cohen nodded, started the car engine, and drove to the next corner street hawker to get the daily *Jerusalem Times*, then stopped at the Dunkin Donuts restaurant across from the museum for breakfast. On page ten, Leah found what she hoped against, a small article on her father's death. She read the obituary then closed the paper and put her head on the table.

"What did it say?" Cohen asked curiously.

Leah raised her head, and amidst a flood of tears quoted, " '…the famed archeological research analyst, Rehavam Krasnoff, 45, recently retired from the IAA, died suddenly at his home yesterday of a myocardial infarction. Funeral arrangements are incomplete…' " her voice trailed off as she lowered her head once more. "There was nothing wrong with his heart—this is a big lie."

Cohen slammed his hand down on the table. "Damn them! Why do they get everything their own way?" He thought momentarily on his emotional reaction then answered his question, "It's because this is *their* time. But I can see that God is raising us up to be a great hindrance to them—to slow them down as much as possible!"

Leah concentrated on her pain. "What about Shiva?" she asked through a forced smile. "What about mourning for my father?"

Cohen glanced over at the Holocaust Museum that stood as a testimony to the Nazi atrocities during World War II in which over six million Jews were slaughtered and said, "We shall afflict our souls and recite the mourner's Kaddish prayer each morning for the next seven days as a tribute to him."

Leah took a bite of her glazed donut, then sipped her coffee. Her face contorted slightly as she thought on her father. "We need to mount a campaign to get them back for this."

Cohen leaned forward conspiratorially and said, "We will, but it can only be with God's help or we will fail miserably. Their forces are much too great for us to battle in the flesh, for we are dealing with principalities and powers above our comprehension."

That triggered a question in Leah's mind. *If evil, not natural forces are at work here, then there has to be a spiritual explanation.*

"Nat, can demons who are nothing more than fallen angels cause death? I mean, could they have killed my father?"

Cohen thought on the question, then pulled out his pocket New Testament and turned to the Book of Hebrews chapter 2. "I recently read this. Listen. 'He too [Jesus] shared in their humanity so that by His death He might destroy him who holds the power of death—that is, the devil—and free those who all their lives were held in slavery by their fear of death.' "

"So then, they can kill people," Leah concluded. "They did kill him."

In absence of witnessing the event, there was a degree of uncertainty regarding Krasnoff's death. Cohen consoled cautiously, "They can't touch believers in Christ, only non-believers."

Leah dwelled on that truth and placed it in her heart. She finished her coffee and donut, then closed her eyes momentarily and said, "Nat, I want to visit a place I read about when I was a little girl. It's a Christian site in the old city, the Via Dolorosa."

Cohen raised an eyebrow, wondering what God was doing in Leah's heart. "Sure, I've heard about the place. It's the road where Christ walked with His cross." Leah simply nodded with inquiring eyes as if being led by some divine force to a place destined to change her life for all eternity. Cohen went to the counter and paid the check, then escorted Leah to the car, keeping in his mind the knowledge that they had to stay on the move.

In 1855, Father Alphonse Ratisbone from Strasbourg, France, a Jewish believer in Jesus as Messiah, came to Jerusalem and bought land beside the ancient ruins of the Ecco Homo arch, reportedly the place where Pontius Pilate stood when he said to the Roman people of Christ, "Behold the man." The ruins next to the arch were removed and in 1859-64, Ratisbone built the convent of the Sisters of Zion. In

1931-37 Mother Godeleine and Father Vincent of the Ecole Biblique of Jerusalem excavated the site, uncovering the very pavement recorded in the Gospel of John; "He brought Jesus out and sat down on the judge's seat at a place known as the Stone Pavement" (19:13). This pavement, named Lithostrotos in Greek, was the place of the public trial of Jesus Christ.

It was here that Pontius Pilate moved his tribunal to be near the rioting crowd waiting outside the Antonia Gate. It was here that Pilate presented Jesus, after having Him scourged; said, "Behold the man"; finally washed his hands; and condemned Jesus to death on the cross. This road, or pavement, which was at the city's ground level in Christ's time, was the actual courtyard of the Antonia where Jesus was condemned to death and where He started the way of sorrows, the way of the cross, Via Dolorosa.

They walked down the three flights of stairs from the modern street level to the Via Dolorosa, some 30 feet below ground. Immediately Leah was awestruck at the original Roman paving stones where Jesus had walked. The stones were striated in a manner to prevent horses from slipping, and channels in the pavement, for collecting rainwater into the large cisterns beneath the roadway, were still visible.

Cohen grabbed Leah by the hand and led her off to a special section of the pavement and pointed down. "Do you believe it," he marveled, "you can still see the Roman carvings of the games they used to play here." On the surface of the stones were freehand etchings for playing a game of dice, known as the King's game, where the Romans chose a burlesque king, mocked him, and put him to death. It was possible that Jesus could have been used in such a game.

Leah gestured toward the wall. "Look, Nat, at the mural." Cohen looked up from the pavement and cast his eyes on a beautiful full-sized tile mosaic of Christ in front of the city gates, carrying His cross. He looked back at Leah only to see her eyes filling with tears.

"Are you all right?"

She began to sob so hard she could barely get the words out. "Not really." Cohen escorted her off to the side, away from the meandering crowd of tourists. She sniffled several times in an attempt to stifle her crying, then fell silent.

"Leah, talk to me," Cohen entreated.

"Something's happening inside me, Nat," she began in a feeble attempt to explain her emotions. "It's like a spiritual awakening that started when I realized how much you've changed, and then with my dad..." She coughed several times to clear her throat and added, "I want to have what you have, the peace and assurance of salvation that comes with the relationship with Christ that you spoke of."

The feeling of God's power between them was almost palpable. Cohen's face lit up with joy as he gazed into Leah's eyes. He knew in his heart that God was drawing her to Himself. "Just let go and trust God with your life, Leah, it's as easy as that. God does the rest. Simply pray to receive Christ as your Messiah, and believe in your heart that He died on the cross for you personally, and your sins will be forgiven."

She could only nod as she prayed.

Cohen was certain that God had answered her prayer.

CHAPTER

13

Athens

Kavidas had long ago abandoned fundamental excursions into man's understanding of the mind. The intellectual processes that included the mental and moral states of being making up the personality were expatiating mental trysts he had enjoyed in his youth. But as an adult, the totality of his existence, the seat of his thinking as it were, came under the jurisdiction of direct guidance. Guidance he came to love and trust.

Emotions and reasoning faculties, interests and the will, inner powers, lustful desires, knowledge and understanding, thought, memory and the seat of the intelligence—one's entire state—depended on what or who controlled the mind. This in turn dictated behavior. The man whose mind was controlled by the Spirit was led to good; the man whose mind was controlled by the flesh was led to evil.

With a slam of his fist on his desk, Kavidas let Stein know, through the telephone lines, of his disappointment in the handling of the seizure of the Urim and Thummim. Yes, he was relieved that Stein had eliminated the threat of Krasnoff, but the nagging problem of the revelatory device was troubling him. His recognition of sovereign appointments caused him to remember that the time had not yet arrived, but he knew in his spirit that it would be soon. In his heart, he could not fault Stein. "How much longer, Mort?" Kavidas asked trenchantly.

"A matter of days," Stein replied optimistically. "They're on the run, trying to keep the instrument from me, but I'll track them down and *I will* get the stones, rest assured."

"My identity?" Kavidas asked, the question of compromise solemnly on his mind.

Stein sensed a tinge of Kavidas' mortality emerging from his guarded hypostatic union where man and angelic entities are joined together, an infinitesimal crack in his armor. "Security is still very tight; I see to it personally."

"Good."

A moment of silence ensued.

Turning to Kavidas' agenda Stein asked, "When do you return to Brussels?"

Kavidas picked up the wireless phone and walked to view the scenery from the panoramic window in his office. "Tomorrow. The following day I will begin drafting my recommendation to the UN for a Palestinian state with East Jerusalem as the capital." This far reaching recommendation fell well beyond the scope of the president of the European Union and his commission at present, but in the mind of Kavidas, the influence and power of the president's office would change under his command. In time, his office would control the EU's defense forces, which would be used to police foreign affairs. Naturally this would include the Middle East, and Israel in particular. The abrogation of America's support for Israel would be simultaneous with U.S. decline as a global power—Kavidas felt certain of this from his study of the prophecies concerning the four prophetic empires described in the Book of Daniel.

Stein picked up on the theme. "Here in Jerusalem the Jews have a real sour sentiment toward the Arabs since the Arab bloc nations are boycotting any American firms that do business with Israel. It's their way of strangling off and punishing any nations that don't support Islam."

"It must happen in order for the Islamic nations to continue their impetus, their climb up the political ladder where they will build the necessary force to come against the Jews. America is a favorite target of the Arabs," Kavidas added obtrusively. "Remember September 11, 2001?"

"Militant Muslim Arab groups like Hamas and Hezbollah are escalating their war against Israel with their suicide attacks. There were two last month, and one so far this month," Stein noted with a clenched fist that signified approval.

Mere child's play compared to what lies ahead, Kavidas thought.

On Keren haYessod Street the Bet Bernstein hostel stood as a lighthouse for Israel's transient youth. The lodging place historically accommodated bicyclists or walkers and rarely asked any questions. Naturally it was an ideal place for those seeking anonymity to flop for the night. Leah demanded they stop and rest there so she could sleep on a bed and take a shower. "I can't do Dunkin Donuts for breakfast again. I need a change," Leah said wearily as Cohen secured the knapsack that contained the Urim and Thummim for travel.

"We'll go to the YMCA across the street," Cohen offered as an economic alternative. He began ushering her out the door as he kept a close eye on the time. He believed it perilous to remain more than eight hours in the same location.

Leah shrugged her shoulders. "Okay." Several moments passed as they walked out the door of the hostel, then Leah's eyes filled with tears as thoughts of her father's death came over her. "After we eat, I want to go to the medical place where my father went for therapy. I want to see that woman he fell in with."

Cohen stopped short, turned, and registered the look on Leah's face. He saw a glassy stare that reminded him of one overtaken by a lust for revenge. "Leah, that's crazy! Remember, we are being followed; it could be very dangerous, and what's more, we need to let the Lord solve this." He paused to appeal to her spirit. " 'Vengeance is mine, says the Lord...' So, we must let Him take care of her."

"I want to see her squirm here on earth, then see her burn forever in hell," she replied vehemently.

Cohen nodded his head as he realized that Leah's relationship with God was in the embryonic stage and that this was the voice of her old carnal nature speaking. It would be a while before God's Spirit took hold of her heart. "All right, we'll go and check it out if that will make you feel better."

"It will."

The sight of the Biqquor Holim Hospital brought back painful memories of her father. To think that the man she loved and had taken care of for years after her mother died would suffer the horrible accident, then be murdered a short time later, was more than she could bear. She gave Cohen a peck on the cheek, then slammed the car door and walked determinedly to the Golda Meir clinic. She was resolved to accuse the woman who was the last to spend time with her father of complicity in his murder. "I would like to speak to the therapist treating my father, Rehavam Krasnoff, " Leah politely asked the receptionist.

The receptionist looked annoyed, but forced a nod and walked to the file cabinet console.

She pulled out Krasnoff's file, glanced down at it and said half apologetically, "I'm sorry, but the therapist, Leona Rozen, was only a temporary we acquired from an agency. She's no longer here."

Leah's face contorted. "That can't be, I—"

"Excuse me!" a disgruntled woman patient cut in. "I've been waiting to see my therapist for over an hour. I demand to see her now or I'll complain to the doctor."

The receptionist's eyes bore holes in the complainer's face as her stomach bile began to rise. The job was really beginning to get to her.

The complainer stared her down as she tapped her foot. "I'm waiting, dearie!"

The receptionist's face turned red with rage. She turned to signal the nurse and unwittingly set the Krasnoff file down on the counter in front of Leah. Leah watched the scene intently, then carefully lifted the corner of the file and quickly read the temporary employment order assigning the therapist Leona to the office and in turn to Krasnoff. It contained pertinent information on her, including her home address.

Within minutes the cranky patient was escorted into a therapy room. When the receptionist returned, she was delighted to see that Krasnoff's daughter was gone.

One-half hour later, Cohen and Leah were at Leona's address.

Leah ignored the luxurious trappings and proceeded to rap hard on the door as Cohen studied the outside of the apartment and looked for busy-bodied neighbors.

No answer.

Cohen lifted his foot and whacked it against the door.

No answer.

"Hand me your handkerchief," he whispered to Leah. He placed the handkerchief over one of the small window panes next to the door then hit the glass with his fist. The glass fractured and fell inward. He reached inside and unlocked the door. *Nice and easy now, Cohen.* Once inside the living room, they immediately listened for noise or movement. None.

Cohen motioned for Leah to check the bedroom while he quietly snaked himself into the kitchen. "Nobody here!" he said aloud as he picked up several uncashed checks on the counter. They were from the Golda Meir clinic, payable to Leona Rozen. From there he went to the bathroom.

"Nat, come in the bedroom," Leah called.

Leah had pulled out the dresser drawers for inspection, then surveyed the closet. "It's obvious she's gone, but why would she leave all these expensive clothes? What's more, take a look at the drawer where she kept her stockings."

"She didn't even bother to cash her paychecks," Cohen noted as he sifted through the drawer. He paused and gave Leah a quizzical look. "Every one of them is black. Is that normal?"

"Not at all. Now come over here and look at this." Leah walked to the closet and pointed to the row of shoes on the floor. "Notice anything different about her shoes?"

Cohen peered at the shoes for a moment then picked one up. "There's a weird footprint imbedded in the pads of all the shoes. It looks like she only had two large toes, sort of like deformed pincers."

Leah shook her head as she looked on. "I'm telling you, there's something very strange about all this."

Cohen dropped the shoe and walked back into the kitchen. He opened the refrigerator and found it empty and warm. It looked like Leona had never used it. Then he looked inside the kitchen cabinets. They were bare. *She doesn't eat; uncashed payroll checks, and those impressions in her shoe—and then to just vanish?* There was more. The phone was dead. No TV or radio. There were no toiletries or towels to be found in the bathroom. The only evidence that she existed were her uncashed checks, her clothes, and her shoes.

He walked back into the bedroom as Leah was stuffing one of Leona's shoes into her handbag and said, bewildered, "Let's get out of here! This place gives me the creeps."

Looking around for the last time, Leah nodded her head in agreement. "It's almost as if she were an agent from hell who completed her task and returned."

Cohen looked at her as if she had suddenly uttered a divine oracle.

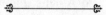

Am I now in a dream? I cannot say. It is too awesome for me to describe. But there is one thing I do know. I believe in what I see; therefore, it must be real. His eyes widened in amazement as they fell upon the being standing before him. It was the anointed cherub who at one time had guarded the very throne room of God and walked the paths of Eden. The beautiful angel who fell to pride and led the heavenly rebellion. The beautiful, powerful angel who was wise in the ways of the world; who drew the unsuspecting to his masquerading light, the ruler of the kingdom of the air.

He bowed down before the being.

I shudder, yet I open my eyes and see the shadow of his wings unfolding before me. They are magnificent in all their splendor and power, towering above his presence as they commemorate his strength, cunning, and wisdom.

"Arise," he commands.

I stand and look into his face, and behold his features are too marvelous for me to gaze upon. I turn away but he bids me to look at him as he raises his right wing and extends his arm toward a multicolored globe that hangs suspended in the blackness of space. I recognize the globe immediately. Then suddenly he looks up and points to an object moving rapidly in a wide arc across the backdrop of space. As I watch, the object leaves a long white streak behind it. I follow its path and see that it is continuing in its endless journey, when suddenly it is diverted into a collision course with the globe. I cringe momentarily and then look into the eyes of the revelator, my master—yes it is proper that I call him this—who then points to the arc of the celestial body, causing it to change its course once again.

He nods to me and fills my mind with understanding.

Kavidas awakened from his dream, called Stein in Jerusalem, and ordered him to return to Athens immediately for an important meeting, one that could not be held over the phone.

Slightly over 24 hours later, Stein walked into Kavidas' office filled with a great deal of apprehension. His demeanor changed radically, however, the moment he saw Kavidas' face. He studied it for several seconds and recognized the look of victory. "The nature of the call doesn't match your smile. You look like an American president who just won reelection," Stein quipped merrily as he closed the door behind him.

"Mort, you better sit down for this one, " Kavidas began with a raised fist. "Yesterday I had a prophetic dream of great magnitude that involves the whole world. I believe this dream will eclipse any other I have had in the past, and I am persuaded that this will advance our cause tremendously by placing us in alignment with prominent world leaders."

Stein watched his leader with piercing eyes. "I thought you already were a prominent world leader."

Kavidas cracked a smile. "Remember where we are supposed to be by this time next year?"

Stein nodded solemnly.

"Well, this will place us there."

The receptionist at the *Miami Star* telephone switchboard had no idea who she was talking to when Stein first called. "Is Jerry Latham still reporting for the *Star*?"

"He is. Who's calling, please?" the woman asked with a strident voice.

"This is Mortimer Stein, formerly of Rainbow Pharmaceuticals in Wellington, Florida. I would like to speak with Mr. Latham."

The receptionist blinked several times while trying to retrieve from her memory any information on Rainbow Pharmaceuticals—or for that matter, Mortimer Stein. She vaguely recalled their association several years prior with the AIDS vaccine, TOI-VAX. Shrugging her shoulders she replied, "Just one moment."

"This is Latham," the voice on the phone answered.

"Mr. Latham, this is Mortimer Stein in Athens, Greece."

Latham's breath caught in his throat. "The same Stein who works with Gregory Kavidas, the EEC man in Brussels? One-time owner of Rainbow Drugs and MASTERLINK?"

"The same," Stein replied. "I particularly liked the favorable coverage you gave us when we were in Florida, and I am calling to inform your paper that Mr. Kavidas has a very important announcement to make to the world, you being the first to hear it."

Stein and Kavidas' reputations did indeed speak for themselves. The veracity of the forthcoming statement would be weighed out with that in consideration. "What's the announcement?"

"You'll need to write it down," Stein directed.

Latham grabbed a pad and pen while raising an eyebrow. "Go ahead."

"Exactly three days from now, the asteroid 433 Eros will skip orbit and threaten Earth. I will call you then and advise you of the outcome."

Latham smirked and thought of cracking a joke in reply, but decided to ask, "How do you know this?"

"Mr. Kavidas is an extraordinarily gifted person and has predicted it to protect mankind from chaos, panic, and widespread hysteria."

"I'll check it out and—"

Click. The phone went dead.

Latham doodled on the pad under his notations, then flicked the pad to the corner of his desk and went to lunch.

CHAPTER

14

Anglo-Australian Observatory,
Warrumbungle Mountains, Australia

A breath of warm night air meandered into the open window of the observatory control room, then softly brushed the wind chime hanging on the building's concrete block wall. The tingling sound caught Rance Bradley's ear, temporarily diverting his attention from his computer monitor, which was linked to the huge optical telescope pointed at an area between the planets Mars and Jupiter. He sighed during the split-second interlude, then returned his eyes to the screen. After 20 years of advanced research, he had developed a sixth sense that signaled when something in the sky was different. He shook his head then massaged his temples; his eyes were bothering him again. He reached for his glasses and muttered, "Nuts."

The Anglo-Australian telescope at the Siding Spring Observatory in New South Wales stood on a rocky outcrop overlooking the Warrumbungle National Park. Inside the observatory dome, which rose nearly 164 feet above the ground, was a 3.9 meter telescope suspended between the arms of a huge horseshoe-shaped bearing. The bearing permitted the telescope to follow the movements of celestial bodies across the sky with amazing precision. The large optical telescope could look anywhere in the heavens more than 20 degrees above the horizon. On the computer's digital readout were the coordinates that directed the telescope at the Apollo-Amor group of asteroids, which occasionally cross Earth's orbit.

Dr. Bradley had an obsession with asteroids. He had been monitoring the life of both Ceres and Eros, two giant members of the asteroid belt, for over three years, watching with anticipation as Eros neared the Earth. By comparing the blurred trails on a current time-exposure photograph of the stars with one of his archival plates, Bradley could track the asteroid's movements with remarkable accuracy. After checking the orbital trajectory he loosened his shirt collar and whispered to himself, "That's what I was afraid of—movement."

His phone beeped, then his technical assistant announced, "Dr. Bradley, in checking with Kitt, the NEAR spacecraft update reported that the multispectral camera imaging detector has indeed sensed a deviation in Eros's trajectory. They're faxing the report now."

Bradley raised an eyebrow. "Okay, Gloria, thanks." Bradley used the Kitt Peak National Observatory in Tucson, Arizona in the Northern hemisphere, with its 4-meter, nearly 160 inch, Mayall optical telescope, as a safeguard on his findings. NEAR (Near-Earth Asteroid Rendezvous) was the first U.S. spacecraft to orbit an asteroid. Launched in 1996 aboard a Delta II vehicle, the spacecraft was designed to make quantitative and comprehensive measurements of composition and structure of the near-Earth population of asteroids. Equipped with an X-ray/gamma ray spectrometer, a near infrared imaging spectrograph, a laser altimeter, a magnetometer and the multispectral camera, the rendezvous mission was to answer fundamental questions of the nature and potential threat of bodies that orbit in

Earth's solar system. The ultimate fate of the spacecraft was to finally crash land on asteroid 433 Eros.

Seven minutes later, the phone beeped a second time. "Dr.
Bradley, the faxes are here. Is this something to be concerned with?"

Bradley glanced down at the upcoming conjunction of planets
report on his console, cleared his throat and said confidently and
calmly, "It's nothing to worry about." His conscience always troubled
him after he lied. An austere man of 52, Bradley loved God and the
way He displayed Himself in the universe. Bradley only indulged
himself when it came to his family; his time was carefully appor-
tioned between his marriage and his work at the observatory.

He stood up to remove his lab coat, thinking it was getting
warmer in the control room, then looked down at the vast array of
buttons, lights, and dials that linked the computer to the telescope. He
gazed out the window. Unwittingly his fists clenched when he remembered the asteroid that had passed within 280 thousand miles of
Earth in 1996. The distance was greater than that between the earth
and the moon, but in astronomical terms, it was a "bullet burn." In
1993, the Gehrels group found an asteroid that had approached to
within 90 thousand miles of Earth, uncomfortably within the moon's
orbit. In 1989, Henry Holt discovered an Apollo asteroid that came
within half a million miles of Earth. Any celestial object coming
within one million miles of Earth was considered a "near miss." In
the recent past, in 1908, a large asteroid had collided with Earth, pul-
verizing and destroying thousands of square miles of forest near Tun-
guska, Siberia. Predating that hit was the meteoroid or asteroid that
had struck Earth in Winslow, Arizona, thousands of years ago. That
iron-rich terrestrial object, at least 164 feet across, had hit planet
Earth with enough force to gouge out Barringer crater, a huge hole
measuring .75 miles across by 656 feet deep. The blast was equal to
the detonation of a 20-megaton hydrogen bomb. The fact was, some

two hundred large asteroids had orbits that crossed the earth's orbit, and all of them had the potential of hitting the earth some day. In space distances were very great, but an asteroid traveling at rates between 11,000 and 25,000 miles per hour could pose a threat in a matter of days.

Bradley quickly dismissed the possibility of such an event. The global devastation that would be inflicted on Earth with its modern population and city structure would be a cataclysm of gigantic proportions.

Bradley walked to his office adjacent to the main telescope room, sat at his desk, then pressed the speed dialing button to NASA in Florida. His clearance password put him in immediate contact with Mission Control. Over the years Bradley had built a rapport with the Mission director, Jim Button, a middle-aged scientist he greatly admired for his perseverence and gutsy risk taking—the very attributes that often saved NASA many embarrassing moments before the public.

Director Button took the call as an opportunity to relax as he scanned the giant screens in front of his command console. He put his feet up on the console and said into the phone, "Rance, how are things 'down under'?"

"Very warm, I guess."

Jim detected concern. "Is everything okay?"

"Well, yes..." Bradley hesitated, "...sort of..." His internal mechanical safeguards prohibited alarmism. "We need to confirm NEAR's last fix on 433 Eros. I suspect the upcoming planetary conjunction has caused gravitational perturbations that may require you to make certain adjustments in the craft's flight trajectory and orbital inclination."

"Hold on," Jim replied as his feet hit the floor. He snapped his fingers and motioned to one of his resident astrophysicists. "Get me the JPL charts on the upcoming conjunctions," he commanded. Within seconds he had the Jet Propulsion Laboratory's charts in his hand.

While carefully reviewing the reports he picked up the phone and said curiously, "They look normal. What's up?"

"That's what I thought at first. But if you check your log you'll see that last month there was another conjunction—Earth, moon and Mars—and together with the upcoming conjunction of the two giants Jupiter and Saturn, there has been lunisolar perturbations. The combination of these events, when coupled with Eros's rate of acceleration as it nears Earth, will cause the asteroid to prefer another orbit."

"Don't say that, Rance," Jim replied nervously.

"Well, there has been a 'tug,' and if you recall, 'tugs' are cumulative with asteroids. We will be looking at a deflection if the trend continues."

Button's face took on a look of concern. "Dr. Bradley, are you telling me that we have to re-task our spacecraft to accomplish the rendezvous?"

"Jim," Bradley soothed, "you know that we cannot predict the path of an asteroid with any high degree of certainty. Although Eros was in the thirteen to fourteen million mile range in 1975, the variables are..." he paused, "astronomical, for lack of a better word. You know that." Bradley was surprised that Button didn't see the real peril. "But beyond the mission and the possible re-tasking, there is another problem."

"What else did you see through your 'looking glass'?" Button asked dryly.

Jim heard Bradley breathe deeply. "I don't mean to get technical, but if you factor in the conjunctions along with Eros's orbit being so close to the earth, then throw in the moon's projected position, there could be a decrease in energy, enough to alter its heliocentric orbit. Friction will then reduce the orbital energy so that it will be captured by the earth and collide with us."

"Hold on, Rance," Button rejoined, "are you saying that there is a danger of Eros threatening us? This thing is millions of miles away." He stood up and then whispered into the phone, "Wouldn't this thing burn up as it enters our atmosphere?"

"Jim, this 'gal' Eros has been clocked at over eight kilometers per second, nearly eighteen thousand miles per hour—sufficient to shatter rock—and it's twenty-four miles across! That's like a small planet! A good chunk of her is bound to get through! We need to do the right math and make the right calls on this."

With that Jim slipped into momentary reflection. Originally discovered in 1898 by Gustav Witt, the director of the Urania Observatory in Berlin, 433 Eros, an S-type asteroid, had come within 23 million kilometers of Earth in 1931. Categorized according to the spectra of reflected sunlight, 75 percent of all asteroids were very dark and were called carbonaceous or C-types; 15 percent were greyish and silicaceous or stony, the S-types; the remaining 10 percent were metallic in makeup, the M-type. "Where's Ceres these days?" he asked with a wry expression in an attempt to shift the magnitude of the issue.

"Thank God we needn't be concerned about her," Bradley replied. "That baby is over a thousand kilometers across! Fortunately, at nearly three AU's from the sun, her orbit would never cross Earth. It's her sister, Eros, that concerns me."

Button was quick to realize that his day was not going to end well. "I'm going to telephone APL right away. I'll talk to you soon." Within seconds, Button was talking to the mission manager at the Applied Physics Laboratory, the contractor overseeing the NEAR project. He in turn notified the National Security Advisor, who briefed President Lasson that there was an imminent problem in outer space.

Forty-five minutes after Mission Director Button got off the phone with Dr. Bradley in Australia, Florida State Senator Randy

Conlon received a telephone call on his secure line. Conlon, a retired decorated wing commander, now serving as the head of the space appropriations committee, loved anything to do with flight. After the Challenger disaster, rumors abounded that Conlon was partly responsible for reallocating the funds to put the space program back on its feet. The president relied upon his experience, thoroughness, and unadulterated reports to help form national space policy.

The president's directive advised Conlon to order a military helicopter out of the Homestead Air Force base and fly from his Parkland home in Florida to the NASA Ames Research Center of the Lowell Observatory Near-Earth Object Search to gather and report back firsthand information on the movement of 433 Eros. LONEOS was a system designed to find Earth-crossing asteroids and comets known as near-Earth objects.

An entourage from Ames Research Center, led by Jerry Nolan, a laboratory director with a Ph.D. in astrophysics, met Conlon and his aide at the helicopter pad and gave them a quick tour of the research facility. Once at the control center, Nolan called in two other staff scientists to review their incoming reports from NEAR. Despite the urgency of the visit, Nolan exhibited a gracious and congenial spirit toward Conlon and his assistant. Drawing on his friendly demeanor, Conlon took Nolan aside privately. He smiled and said, "The president wants to know if we really have anything to worry about."

Nolan, a robust man with a manicured beard and balding head, sighed and looked at the status boards displayed on the far wall. "We could be in trouble."

Conlon blanched then asked, "How much and when?"

Nolan grabbed a nearby stool to sit on while explaining to Conlon his findings. "I called my associates Andy Winson at Palomar and Mike Curr at Johns Hopkins—the APL lab guy who built NEAR—and we all concur that this S-type asteroid or mountain in space, with its iron-magnesium/nickel make-up, now has an erratic orbit that will pose a real danger." He waved his hand in the air and added, "According to Goldstone radar, this asteroid now has an orbit that intersects the orbit of the earth. In fact many scientists believe that the Apollo objects are the main producers of craters larger than five kilometers on Earth as well as on Venus, Mercury, and our moon. That's problem number one. The probability of our Earth colliding with an asteroid can be estimated at one in thirty thousand. But when you add to the equation the alignment of the planets—the conjunctions—and the resultant disruptions that seem to have caused 433 Eros to jump its orbit, well, that's problem number two..." his voice trailed off as if he were making some mental calculation.

"You sound as if there is a number three," Conlon observed bleakly.

Nolan hopped off the stool and motioned for Conlon to follow him to a computer monitor. Once there, Nolan keyed in a numerical sequence bringing 433 Eros asteroid up on the screen. The image rotated very slowly as the NEAR-IR Spectrograph and Multispectral Imager televised the asteroid in real time. Nolan pointed to the monitor and said, "Now you and the taxpayers will see whether or not the funds you're paying for this project is worth it." He moved the pointer and clicked on "dimensions." A pop-up window appeared that read: 14 X 14 X 40 km. He added, "That's problem number th—"

"How in the world do you measure—?" Nolan interrupted as he shook his head in disbelief.

"As the asteroid rotates it reflects sunlight back to Earth at different degrees of luminosity. We carefully measure these variations in magnitude; this in turn enables us to determine its shape and dimensions. Together with the knowledge of Eros that was gathered by extensive observation when the asteroid passed within 0.15 AU of Earth in 1975, we believe we have a good handle on its mass."

Conlon motioned toward the ceiling and asked, "Would you translate the metric numbers for me, doc…what is an AU and how big is 433 Eros?"

Nolan licked his dry lips and said, "I'll answer the second question first. Roughly speaking, Eros is about nine miles deep by nine miles high by twenty-four miles across. As for the AU, it is a term used to measure distances within our solar system. It means astronomical unit. It is the average distance between the earth and the sun, or about ninety-three million miles. So two AU would be equivalent to eighteen million miles—a relatively short distance in outer space with the speed 433 Eros is traveling."

Conlon winced and exclaimed, "Oh my God, that's a monster."

"Yes, it's big," Nolan replied tersely. "Based on our profile calculations, it's not likely that Eros will skip back into space, so we will have our hands full if the trajectory doesn't change."

Conlon gulped and asked, "What kind of damage are we looking at if it hits, and how much time before we know for sure?"

After a minute or so of contemplation, Nolan said analytically, "Right now it is about .10 AU or nine million miles away, so based on its present velocity, it could be upon us…" he closed his eyes when calculating and added, "…in about 21 days."

"Ugh," Conlon grunted. He happened to look down at Nolan's console and noticed a graph marked Eros Close Approach Report. He picked it up and said, "This says here that Eros approached us in 1901 at a distance of thirty million miles; then again in 1931 at a distance of sixteen million miles, and then again in 1975 at a 'close encounter' of fourteen million miles—" His eyes blazed as the realization came over him. "This celestial rock has been coming closer at every pass it makes at us!"

Nolan took the report from Conlon with a curt nod and replied, "Yeah, that makes number four."

After taking a deep breath, Conlon asked, "And the damage?"

Nolan sat down at the computer terminal, then typed in a command to show a simulation. The monitor displayed planet Earth in scale against a black background. Suddenly a fast-moving object entered the screen from out of the black and slammed into Earth. "In 1937, the asteroid Hermes came within about five hundred thousand miles of Earth. Its diameter is under 2.4 miles. If Hermes had impacted the earth..." He paused to page down, "...then this is what would have happened..." The simulation showed the asteroid hitting the Middle East. Nolan sibilated, "This little 'guy,' scientists estimate, would have exploded with the force of twenty thousand one-megaton hydrogen bombs. Enough to take out a country the size of Israel."

The simulation frightened Conlon as he pondered the consequences. "And Hermes is a peanut compared to this thing," he observed grimly.

"Hmm, yes," Nolan agreed, then added, "It is the second largest planet crosser in the solar system, bigger than the Martian moons Phobos and Deimos." He looked up toward the ceiling and quipped, "The asteroid was named for the son of Aphrodite, Eros, the god of love. I wonder if they'll rename it now."

"What else?" Conlon demanded as a tremor of fear began to seize him.

Walking away from the console, Nolan shrugged his shoulders and said, "I hesitate to mention it, but there's the dust canopy thing."

"What dust canopy?" Conlon queried.

"Well, it's only a theory, but scientists have tried to explain the extinction of dinosaurs, and came up with asteroid impact theory. If an asteroid of only ten kilometers collided with Earth, it would have blown enough dust into the atmosphere to form a canopy and block out sunlight for years. The drop in temperature and the adverse effect of the loss of adequate light for photosynthesis would have caused the dinosaurs and all vegetation to perish."

"I never heard that one before," Conlon replied suspiciously.

"Well, it's only a hypothesis," Nolan soothed.

Senator Conlon had heard and seen enough to complete his report to the president.

While en route to the helicopter, he sensed a knot in his stomach. He realized he hadn't felt this way since flying combat missions over Vietnam.

CHAPTER

15

Miami, Florida

Surprisingly, and this was due to her gifted memory, the receptionist recognized the voice of Mortimer Stein the second time. She quickly put the call through to Latham. "Mr. Latham, what have you done with the announcement I gave you three days ago?" Stein asked with rising impatience.

Latham reached over to his computer monitor and pulled off the note he had taped to it. "Nothing, really, Mr. Stein," he replied with a shrug of the shoulders. "I was thinking of talking to the editor about it, but considering the magnitude of this—"

Stein cut him off with a shout. "You what?!" Latham quickly held the phone at arm's length as Stein's voice reverberated through the earpiece. "If you value your job as a reporter you better do some checking fast—we haven't much time left!"

Latham spun around in his chair, then began flipping through his phone directory for a name and number. "I can do that," he said with controlled alarm.

"Listen, Latham," Stein ordered curtly, "write down these coordinates. They represent the numbers concerning 433 Eros, which will threaten our planet."

This can't be a prank. "Yes, sir," Latham replied, this time his voice vibrating with feeling. "I'll pass the information to the authorities."

"They already know by now, Latham, " Stein revealed. "But what they don't know is that the asteroid will be deflected. I want you to tell them, okay?"

"Okay," Latham said sheepishly.

Stein ended the call.

Latham pressed the speed dial on the phone and within seconds was talking to the FBI.

The White House, Washington, D.C.

Wind-swept rain bathed the giant 747 as it taxied down the runway to the Washington National Airport terminal in Arlington. As it neared the jetway, Conlon peered out the jet's portal while the dawning light illuminated the ground crew waiting to service the arriving aircraft. The crew, bundled in foul weather gear, huddled next to the building seeking shelter from the elements. *Dear God*, he thought, *as if things aren't bad enough, I have to move through this slop.* Despite the years of traveling to the capital district, he still could not adjust to the northern climate.

As Conlon stepped off the aircraft, a man in a blue suit accompanied by two airline security officers met him. Adrian Moore was the special advisor to the president. Together he and Conlon moved quickly through the airport to the limousine waiting to take them to the White House.

The rain began to abate on their arrival, giving way to subdued sunlight that shed a dismal grayish cast on the home of the president.

I hope this is not a portent of things to come, Conlon observed sourly as the doors to the mansion were opened. Once inside, Moore and Conlon were escorted to the Oval Office. Moments later they were ushered into the president's presence.

Seated at his massive mahogany desk, the president, who was on the phone, turned toward Conlon, gave him a curt nod, and with a raised hand acknowledged his entry. While President Lasson finished his phone call, his staff filed in and took their seats. With that Conlon massaged his stomach in an effort to ward off the acid reflux that had been building since breakfast on the plane.

As he sat looking at his boss, a quote his wife frequently repeated came to his mind. *It is doubtful that God can use a man greatly unless He has hurt him deeply.* He pondered the statement for a moment before he remembered that it was the Christian theologian A.W. Tozer who first said it. He sighed and studied the profile of the man seated before him. A graduate of Anapolis, a wartime hero, a committed family man, and then to be handsome and president at age 54, was indeed a rare mixture of blessings and accomplishments.

"Gentlemen," the president began as he replaced the phone, "that was Bob Dancig—he is in Tel Aviv with Lester Reilly." Just about everybody in the room had met Dancig, the vice president, and Reilly, the national security advisor. "They're reviewing our foreign policy with Prime Minister Rubin and they're both troubled over the meeting. Something is stirring once again in the Middle East. Rubin has filed a complaint with the UN that the Russians are continuing to supply the Iraqis and Iranians with arms in exchange for oil, and now the Saudis are sympathizing with them. They may ask us to remove our bases from Saudi soil unless we slow down our military and financial support to Israel." He paused to allow his audience to digest the bulletin, then stood up to open the window drapes. "The sky is clearing, that's good," he added cheerfully to move the agenda. Then, yawning, he returned to his chair. Smiling at Conlon he said, "Tell me some good news, Randy. Tell me this thing in space is going to do a 'fly-by' and not return until my term is over."

Conlon traded a look with Adrian Moore, then rolled his tongue around in his mouth. "I wish I were like Polyanna and could make this giant rock in space go away, but I'm afraid it's not that simple, Mr. President."

The president glared at him and then pulled a note from his vest pocket and announced to the room: "Did you know that the FBI received a phone call from a Miami newspaperman saying that Gregory Kavidas, the ex-pharmaceutical magnate turned politician, predicted that 433 Eros would shift orbit and come at us?"

Shock rippled through the group. They were speechless.

Lasson stuffed the note back into his pocket. "Give it to me straight, Randy."

Conlon took a breath and began. "Our planet has really led a charmed life for the past half million years or so. By God's providence we've avoided nearly every major hit from outer space, but now…" he squirmed in his chair and winced, "…it looks like we're in the crosshairs of 433 Eros. Unless there's a radical change in the asteroid's orbit, Earth is going to experience a horrific event very soon."

"But Senator Conlon, my researchers tell me that the chances of our getting hit by a 'doomsday' asteroid are something like thirty thousand to one," Adrian Moore interjected.

"Yeah, I've recently heard that number," Conlon said with a dismissive wave of the hand. "Some equate it to the odds of dying in an airline crash." The group looked at one another, knowing that the airline industry had been plagued with air disasters in the past decade.

Newell, the secretary of defense, stretched his shirt collar in a vain effort to relieve tension, then looked over at Conlon in reflexive alarm. He stood up and placed a file marked Top Secret on the president's desk. He pointed to the report and said, "In November of 1996, a small asteroid hit Honduras and carved out a crater 165 feet across. In comparison—" he paused and pointed to Conlon, "Senator Conlon's report, being confirmed by the U.S. Naval Observatory and the European Space Agency at Noordwijk, the Netherlands, reminds us that 433 Eros is huge—" He paused and shook his head, "...I'm not sure we earthlings are going to make it unless we come up with viable options pretty darn quick."

President Lasson looked down at Newell's report on his desk. "I hope your report details our alternatives, Gary. I'm not ready to turn this country over to a hunk of celestial garbage just yet."

"We have options," Newell and Moore said almost simultaneously.

Leafing through the documents the president read aloud, "NEO Mitigation Options: 1) Deflection to Another Orbit; 2) Vaporization by Detonation of a Nuclear Device—" Then his eyes fell on 'Probable Impact Zones.' He nodded to the group and added, "You guys have been doing your homework." He tossed the report onto his desk and asked, "Where's the impact zone?"

"America appears to be safe," Conlon proffered as he opened his portfolio, placing a file on the president's desk. "We're not totally certain as to the path of the asteroid, but based on NASA, the AAT observatory in Australia, and the NEAR spacecraft in space, we calculate the present trajectory..." he briskly walked over to the wall map, then added as he looked at his charts, "...the predicted path will bring the asteroid to about seventy-five degrees east longitude and zero degrees latitude—" He pointed to the northern end of the Indian Ocean and said, "—about five hundred miles southwest of Sri Lanka.

"It appears that due to Earth's magnetic fields it may favor the equatorial zone." He threw his hands up in the air as a vain gesture and added, "However, as it nears the gravitational pull of our moon, just a minor variation in its trajectory could change its course." His jaw tightened as he retreated back to his seat.

President Lasson pulled the note out of his vest pocked once again. "Kavidas predicted those coordinates…" He paused and waved the note in the air, "…but I'm happy to report that he also predicted the asteroid would be deflected."

"That's not likely," Newell countered. "One shift, yes, but not two."

Lasson held the note in his hand and asked, "Okay then, what about damage?"

"Too soon to calculate," Newell noted. "We anticipate that it should lose over forty percent of its mass as it comes through the atmosphere, but that will still leave enough to really hurt us."

"How bad?" Lasson groaned.

"We have oceanographers and earth scientists across the nation working the numbers now; we should know in a few hours," Newell added.

The president shook his head in disgust.

Adrian Moore slid to the edge of his seat and said, "Mr. President, we need to take a hard look at these NEA Mitigation Options again. We can't let this thing hit Earth." His eyes began to fill up. "I really don't think we can survive a hit from a massive extraterrestrial object of this size. It would be equivalent to or greater than detonating all of the planet's nuclear weapons at once." He pulled a host of graphs and charts from his attaché case and continued, "Here are supercomputer simulations in six stages that show what may happen if sixty percent of 433 Eros deviates and strikes a land mass…" He rushed to place the illustrations in front of the president. "It shows core and mantle displacement that will alter all life on this planet as we know it."

"But—" President Lasson replied with eyes that pleaded for help, "it's going to hit the Indian Ocean, right?"

"Even if our scientists make the right call on this, can you imagine the tidal wave and aftershock of such an impact on the ocean? The tsunami alone would inundate southern India, level Sri Lanka, cover Sumatra, and who knows what would happen to Africa. Countries would be obliterated—and probably every city on the Indian Ocean basin would be destroyed. And that's just the half of it. We can't really predict—even if the ocean cushions it—what will happen if the earth's mantle is disturbed. The impact of Eros could set off a chain of earthquakes and volcanoes that would make the chaos of pre-historic times look like a Sunday picnic," Moore observed bleakly.

The president turned to Newell with heightening concern and said, "Adrian is right. We can't let this asteroid hit us. What about the deflection or vaporization options?"

Newell explained, "In my discussions with NASA, JPL, and the nuclear brain trusts we've contracted, the consensus is that we need to deflect this monster right away. That involves the immediate launching of a high-yield nuclear missile that would be guided to explode near 433 Eros to alter its orbit so it misses Earth."

"But if we do that, then maybe it will come back and bite us in the buttocks a couple of years from now!" Lasson exclaimed impulsively. "What about hitting it—vaporizing it with a nuke—what about that option?"

Newell temporized then replied, "I suppose you're right. There really isn't any other choice if we are to be permanently rid of this thing, but…" his voice trailed off.

"*But*, what?" the president demanded.

"Well, Mr. President," Newell sighed, "there's this 'dust canopy' theory that a Dr. Nolan of the Ames Research Center wrote about in his report brought to us by Senator Conlon." He nodded to Conlon who picked up on the signal.

"The apocalyptic theory, as it was explained to me, Mr. President," Conlon began, "is that because of the mineral makeup of 433 Eros, when it is pulverized by a nuclear weapon, a huge global dust canopy could form on the exosphere, or the outside of our atmosphere, blocking out the sunlight for several years. Temperatures would radically drop throughout the planet, all plant life could die and the food chain would collapse." He grimaced, then scanned the group's faces to see their reaction and added, "It's like the reverse of the biblical 'vapor canopy' theory."

"The *what* theory?" President Lasson snapped.

Sensing their skepticism, Conlon shifted uncomfortably in his chair, then shot a look at Newell and continued, "The 'vapor canopy' theory, Mr. President. My wife has done studies on this at our church. According to the creationists' view, one of the factors leading to the Flood was the collapse of the so-called 'vapor canopy.' It was an envelope-type umbrella that circled the earth producing a 'greenhouse' environment that allowed both flora and fauna to grow to giant proportions. It was like a gigantic cloud suspended above the earth. It was God's way of watering the earth before He brought rain. You know, before the Flood, it never rained. Creationists maintain that the worldwide death of animals and plants, and the subsequent rapid deposition of sediments and soil from the Flood, gave us today's fossil fuel." He paused to scratch his neck while regrouping his thoughts. "But that antediluvian scenario yielded a tropical climate. With the dust canopy, we're looking at something altogether different. The entire meteorological cycle will change." He gulped and concluded, "We could go back to the ice age."

"That's it?" Lasson snarled. "End of story? NO! We're not going to buy into that theory. We'll blast that sucker before it comes close to us and let the solar winds blow it out of our galaxy." With strengthened resolve he commanded, "Adrian, convene an emergency meeting of the United Nations Security Counsel so that we can vote on these two options as soon as possible. In fact, make that a telephone and fax documentation of the vote with our recommendation to nuke it. We don't have time to convene the counsel."

As they slowed to turn the corner on Yemin Moshe by the Montefiore Windmill, Cohen caught a glimpse of the headline on the *Jerusalem Post* held up by a street hawker. He quickly pulled the car to the curb and honked the horn to buy a paper. He sat reading for several minutes, then turned to Leah and said, "You're not going to believe this. Kavidas has predicted that the earth is going to have a near-miss with an asteroid that is threatening us!"

The magnitude of such a prediction swept over Leah like a tidal wave. "Oh, my God!" She grabbed the paper out of his hands and began reading it for herself as Cohen stared out the window in shock.

" 'The expected trajectory should place the asteroid in a path that will threaten Russia...' " Leah read aloud. "It adds that sources close to Gregory Kavidas quote him as saying that it will be deflected, the cause of the sidetracking being unknown at this time." She turned to Cohen and asked, "Now how could he know all that?"

"I'm asking myself the same question. If all the Ph.D.'s on this planet couldn't predict it, how could he?"

Cohen reflected on the question momentarily, then turned to Leah. "When your father and I first started asking the UT questions, we asked if Kavidas were to become a big player in world events, and even Israel..." His voice trailed off and he was lost in deep thought.

"And?...What was the answer?" Leah asked as fear began to ice through her.

"The UT responded in a queer way. It gave off a bright red glare as if—" He stopped short and grimaced while scratching his head to help him with the answer.

"Go on, Nat!"

"...as if it were a warning."

Leah felt her stomach flutter. "Remember the tiny bit of information we accessed through IAA's computer network? I'll bet it was only a fraction of the *dirt* on this guy's background."

"Just business-related data, really," Cohen concurred, "nothing personal. I'm convinced that his MASTERLINK has some way of blocking the *juicy* information from getting out."

Leah swallowed hard. "Let's face it, the UT already confirmed to you that both Kavidas and Stein are evil. So it follows that they would call upon the supernatural domain—like warlocks—and reveal this asteroid thing since they're in touch with demonic powers that know something about the future."

Cohen had to admit that Leah's assumptions made sense. She theorized further. "I'm beginning to see patterns here. The way things are shaping up, it looks like Kavidas is making a colossal move for *control*." She snapped her fingers as she inserted an important part of the puzzle in her mind. "This wizard is acquiring more control with every crisis here on earth. First, he controlled the drug world with an AIDS vaccine, then he mounted a global campaign to reform the world's monetary system with MASTERLINK, and now he's controlling the world's temperature by controlling their fears with this asteroid, 433 Eros." She shook her head, then gazed out the window in deep thought.

"My, my," Cohen marveled as he touched her shoulder and smiled at her. "I can see that God is doing a work here. Perhaps your postulating is really a revelation?"

She turned to him and cracked a smile as she grabbed his hand, squeezing it hard.

Cohen read her signal. "Don't you worry. The Lord is going to protect us, you'll see." He looked at his wristwatch. "Time to move on."

They drove to the nearest ATM machine for Cohen to pull out some needed cash, but the machine rejected his request. MASTER-LINK had intervened.

Presidential advisor Moore returned to the Oval Office after making his calls when suddenly the door flew open. "Mr. President," a high-ranking security officer announced with heightening concern, "we have incoming encrypted traffic from Jodrell Bank. Their radio telescope is tracking a secret Russian launch from the Plesetsk cosmodrome facility. Eros's trajectory changed toward their direction, so the Russian space agency, together with the Russian military space forces, has shot a multiple warhead nuclear device to pulverize it!"

Lasson jumped to his feet and exclaimed, "Oh, my God!" He pointed at Newell with his eyes blazing and yelled, "Get Reilly on the phone right away—he's probably airborne by now!"

The secretary of defense rushed to the security phone and gave an order. Seconds later he was talking to the national security advisor. He nodded several times, then announced, "He's on his way to the airport with Dancig. I'm putting him on speaker phone."

"Mr. President," Reilly's voice began, "just before you called I received a flash message from CIA/Langley. Once alerted by Jodrell Bank, they contacted their Russian operatives who told them what's going on. Here's the situation: The Bolshoi Teleskop Azimutalnyi Special Astrophysical Observatory at Mt. Pastukhov observed another shift in 433 Eros's orbit only two hours ago. They calculated the new trajectory..." his voice faded out.

"Are you there?" Lasson cried into the phone as the transmission wavered.

"...impact...about one hundred and twenty miles south of Tobolsk in southern Russia," Reilly's voice continued, "so their military confirmed it with the Energiya Rocket and Space Complex that operates the mission control center in Kaliningrad that directs the MIR II orbiting space station. Once confirmed, they made the decision to launch. They didn't feel the need to check with anybody—they must have thought it was a case of self-preservation. Now we just have to wait and see what happens. We'll call you again once we're in the air."

Lasson pressed the speaker button and the line went dead.

A long pause ensued, then everyone in the room traded looks.

The president stood up and walked slowly to the window. He motioned to the sky after a moment of contemplation and said, "I guess God took the matter out of our hands."

Senator Conlon's thoughts went beyond. *I wonder if this is the divine match that lights the fuse to the dynamite.*

At 600 thousand kilometers from 433 Eros, Director Stanaslav at the Energiya Rocket and Space Complex ordered a course correction that brought the space vehicle carrying the multiple warhead to within 12 hundred kilometers of the asteroid. Once this close orbit was achieved, he authorized the detonation of the nuclear weapon.

"Senator Conlon," the Marine sentry announced as he stuck his head into the president's office, "there's a call for you on the secured line from NASA Ames Research."

Conlon rushed from the window to the red phone.

The color drained from President Lasson's face.

Silence reigned in the room.

After a minute of listening, Conlon smiled then gave Lasson a "thumbs up." Lasson gave a sigh of relief, not knowing what the call was about. His intuition told him it was good news.

The very second Conlon hung up the phone, the president spoke. "Well?"

"Mr. President," Conlon said with a serious demeanor and shake of the head, "the news is both good and bad." He stood up to address Lasson and added, "The Russians detonated their high-yield nuclear device in close proximity to 433 Eros, which was at the exact point of declination needed to shift it out of its present collision course." He smiled luminously and proclaimed, "The asteroid will miss us—we are saved!"

Cheers broke out in the Oval Office.

Several minutes of tension-relieving laughter ensued.

President Lasson stood erect while patting his vest pocket. He made a mental note to thank Kavidas for his prediction. He then rolled his tongue in his mouth. "And the bad?"

Conlon returned to his seat. "Naturally this asteroid will continue around the sun in an heliocentric orbit, but with the deflection, the duration of its travel has been greatly shortened. It will threaten Earth again within the next seven years."

Lasson slapped Conlon on the back. "Science has once again saved us!"

The statement grieved Conlon, who knew differently. In his mind, God used men to accomplish His will. God alone deserved the credit. "Just a side note, Mr. President," Conlon replied with a tinge of disrespect as he jerked his thumb over his shoulder. "Jerry Nolan, the fellow on the phone at Ames, said that he was jokingly going to recommend to the National Astrophysical Society that they rename

433 Eros, Wormwood, after the falling star described in Revelation 8:11."

"Stop it!" Lasson said through his teeth. "This is a time for celebration, not solemnity."

Conlon nodded passively as the rest of the room applauded the suggestion.

In time Congress passed a bill funding an asteroid defense system, but when Wormwood would return, it would be of no avail.

In slightly less than two hours of travel, Cohen pulled into the parking lot of the Jerusalem Forest, located west of the city. He turned off the engine, dropped his head into Leah's lap and fell asleep amidst the sounds of wildlife that remained peaceful, unaffected by the turmoil and complications of life.

Tap-tap-tap-tap. Tap-tap-tap-tap.

A woodpecker on a nearby tree busily pursuing his lunch awakened Cohen from his nap. He reached over and turned on the radio as Leah yawned and stretched.

In less than one minute, the all-news station based in Tel Aviv repeated the breaking headline: *Russia Saves Earth From Extinction!* The report included several interviews with quick-thinking Russian scientists, followed by a brief statement by the Russian premier explaining his actions. A detailed summary from NASA came next. Their report demonstrated the operation of the Russian rocket and the effect of the detonation. The commentator finished the news bulletin from a human interest perspective by replaying a quote by Gregory Kavidas, who had predicted from a dream the outcome of the near-disaster. He added a postscript by repeating the rumor that the asteroid had been renamed Wormwood.

Cohen turned to Leah and exclaimed, "Wormwood?! That's the celestial body that falls to earth from space and destroys one-third of the oceans and an incalculable amount of human life!"

Leah blanched and grabbed Cohen's Bible off the back seat. "Where?"

"Revelation chapter 8," he said numbly. The frightening thought that global events with prophetic implications were developing quickly flashed through his mind.

Leah quickly located the verse and read it silently. What her eyes saw, her mind could not believe.

"That's a part of the seal judgments that occur during the Tribulation period," Cohen paraphrased.

They exchanged looks momentarily. "Get into the back while I inquire of the Lord with the UT," Cohen said haltingly. Leah jumped out of the front seat into the back and handed him the knapsack containing the UT.

It was irreverent for him to set up the UT in the car, he knew, but he consoled himself with the comparison of the children of Israel inquiring of the Lord during their wilderness journey as opposed to the Temple's permanent dwelling place in Jerusalem. In his mind it was like a battlefield hospital.

He pushed the front seat back and set up the revelatory stones to speak to God.

The warning came through loud and clear as they both looked on in horror at the response.

Cohen reached for Leah's hand as he pronounced, "We need to get to a phone right away. We're going to need help."

CHAPTER

16

Miami, Florida

Lane Pharmaceuticals of Miami, under the skillful direction of founder and CEO Matthew Lane, had received a presidential citation for pioneering in AIDS research in 1995. The antitoxic serum developed by Lane actually arrested the deadly effects of the AIDS virus. Rival drug manufacturer Gregory Kavidas of Rainbow Pharmaceuticals had won world acclaim earlier for initially marketing the TOI-VAX vaccine that temporarily halted the spread of the virus, but six months into the distribution program it was discovered that the ill effects of the disease returned. TOI-VAX was pulled from the shelves, Kavidas sold the firm off, and relocated to Athens with Mortimer Stein. Lane Drugs, for the sake of grieving humanity, had extended a credit to the millions of TOI-VAX recipients and donated huge quantities of their serum to stay the deadly disease.

At a drop-leaf table in a corner of his spacious office overlooking Miami's Bayside Marina, Matthew Lane busied himself with his second love, eschatology. His ongoing study of Bible prophecy filled many hours of his time since he had been widowed at the young age of 61, five years ago.

"I'm sorry to disturb you, Mr. Lane," his demure secretary, Rhonda, said as she cracked open the door, "but there is an urgent long-distance call from Israel for you. A man by the name of Cohen Cohen says he must speak to you."

Matthew Lane, a large man with chiseled features, rose slowly from the table, lumbered over to his desk, and lifted the phone. "Matt Lane," he said unpretentiously.

Cohen had rehearsed his attention-getting opening line: "Mr. Lane, I know you don't know me, but you know about Gregory Kavidas!"

"Go on, Mr. Cohen," Lane said into the phone as he sat down.

Adrenaline swept through Cohen's body like a flash flood. "Thank you for agreeing to listen to me, Mr. Lane," Cohen began nervously. "It's hard for me to explain this, but let me begin by saying that I was living in Florida when your firm developed the AIDS serum and I'm aware of the contention with Rainbow Pharmaceuticals and Mr. Kavidas."

"I'm listening."

"Well, frankly, none of that really had any effect on me until I arrived in Israel and—" A pause ensued as Cohen suddenly realized he had to reveal the source of his discovery. He closed his eyes and shot a prayer to Heaven for guidance to make the right decision.

Lane could hear Cohen taking deep breaths through the phone. "Mr. Cohen?"

"Um. Someday I hope to get a chance to explain this to you in more detail, but I have reliable reasons to believe that Kavidas is an evil agent from Satan and I'm terribly concerned. Can you help me?"

Lane couldn't see Cohen's face, but what he heard sounded interesting. "Tell me more," he replied cautiously.

Cohen went on. "Well, this asteroid thing is really only one event in a string of circumstances that brought me to the conclusion that I needed to find someone to talk to about my findings and dealings on this guy."

"What kinds of circumstances, Mr. Cohen?" Lane inquired.

"Well, there's a man by the name of Mortimer Stein who has invaded our lives," Cohen explained effusively. "He started out by systematically tracking and later attacking—and I believe murdering—my friend, a Mr. Krasnoff, an investigator who worked for the Israeli Antiquities Agency."

Lane cleared his throat, and asked suspiciously, "Now why in the world would he want to do that?"

A long pause.

"Mr. Cohen?"

"Because we discovered something that he wants—something that can betray him and Kavidas."

"Are you at liberty to talk about it?"

"No."

Exercising judgment, Lane asked, "If you don't want to talk about it, then how can I help you?"

"I'm not sure. I only know that God has spoken to me in a very real way (Cohen did not have the confidence to disclose his dream), and I know that I am part of a plan to unmask this faker before he dupes the whole world."

"I will need more than that to go on," Lane argued.

Across the miles, Cohen turned to Leah and shook his head. He placed his hand over the mouthpiece of the phone and whispered to her, "I have to tell him more or he won't believe us." Leah nodded in agreement.

Cohen explained the Urim and Thummim device to Lane.

Lane reached into the depths of his soul and asked God for discernment. After a moment of contemplation he said, "I will need a phone number to call you back on this."

"We're on the run; we are using public telephones."

"Then I will need a place where someone can meet you."

"Uh-oh." Cohen muffled out.

"You needn't be concerned. This is a trusted person who understands exactly what is happening," Lane assured.

"Hold on." Cohen covered the mouthpiece and explained Lane's offer to Leah, who shrugged her shoulders and pointed back to him. It was his decision. Cohen squeezed his eyes shut momentarily, then replied, "Have this person meet us at the ruins of the ancient synagogue at Capernaum, on Lake Galilee, the day after tomorrow."

"I can arrange that."

Leah tugged on Cohen's jacket and mouthed out a question. Cohen nodded. "Who is this person, and how will I know him or her?" he asked.

"The man's name is David Douglas, an American working undercover for the Lord in an undisclosed location in Israel. His wife's name is Kathy. I will have them meet you as you asked."

"May the Lord bless you, Mr. Lane," Cohen said as he ended the call.

Lane replaced the phone and smiled at how marvelous his God was—a God who saw fit to send help to warn humanity of the terrible horror that was about to be unleashed on the world.

At 13 miles long and 7 miles wide, Lake Galilee, also known as the Sea of Tiberias and the Sea of Kinneret—because it is shaped like the Hebrew harp or *kinnor*—is probably the most breathtaking and certainly the largest lake in Israel. Fed by subterranean springs and the melting snow of Mount Hermon, the waters of the Sea of Galilee were where Jesus was said to have walked. The entire coast of the lake was sprinkled with churches marking the miracles Jesus performed in the region. It became His home and, later, the birthplace of Christianity.

At Capernaum, a village on the northwestern tip of the lake, Christ preached more sermons and performed more miracles than anywhere else. Here Christ performed the miracle on the centurion's servant and on Simon's wife's mother and the paralytic. It was here that Christ exorcized a demon from a man, fed the five thousand, and spoke the wonderful discourse on the Bread of Life. Scholars report that Christ taught in a synagogue that apparently had been built by the centurion of a detachment of Roman soldiers based here. The Roman garrison used the village as quarters while operating a customs station where the dues were collected by stationary and itinerant officers.

The ruins of a limestone synagogue overlooking the lake were uncovered by the German Oriental Society under the direction of H. Kohl and C. Watzinger in 1905. The house of worship was later dated back to about A.D. 400. It was at this synagogue that Cohen waited for David Douglas.

Walking hand-in-hand, Cohen and Leah frolicked in a brief moment of reverie between the columns of the synagogue that had stood erect for over 16 hundred years. The columns were silent reminders of past grandeur of the once great city of Capernaum, now left desolate as a mute testimony to the curse Christ pronounced on the unbelieving city. The young people climbed to a ledge overlooking the Canaanite ruins and gazed out over the lake.

"Are you Mr. Cohen?" an English-speaking man asked as he emerged from a small group of tourists.

Cohen froze in his steps and gazed at the man as Leah silently walked to a remote corner of the synagogue. "Yes. I take it you are David Douglas?"

A woman slowly meandered out of the tour group and stood beside Mr. Douglas, who reached for her hand. "We exercise caution wherever we go," he declared, "and I wanted to be sure it was you before I brought my wife out." He acknowledged Leah off in the distance and said, "This is my wife, Kathy."

Wiry, yet muscular with pronounced features, wire-rimmed glasses, and a thinning hairline, Douglas looked to be about 50 years old. Close-up, his skin looked weathered and sun-toughened, taking on more of the appearance of an Israeli than an American.

Cohen directed them to the corner of the synagogue with Leah and said, "We can find privacy over here." Once in the corner, the women exchanged introductions.

"Matt Lane tells me that you've had dealings with Kavidas and Stein," Douglas said curiously, "and that you possess the ancient Urim and Thummim."

Cohen nodded and reached for Leah's hand. For the next 25 minutes he explained how he had acquired the UT. Surprisingly, as if he were expecting supernatural events to occur at this juncture in God's timetable, Douglas simply made several mental calculations while his wife, Kathy, took notes.

"So what do we do now?" Leah asked, speaking Cohen's mind as well.

"Time to check in with God," Douglas said with a wink. "We need to 'fire up' the Urim and Thummim."

Disappointed in the lack of information and instruction, Cohen shrugged his shoulders and led the way back to the car. *Lord, I'm trusting you to put together some of the pieces in this puzzle.* Once at the car, they drove to a vacant field near the shoreline of the lake.

Leah and Kathy then hung clothes over the windows for privacy as Cohen and Douglas sat in the back seat maneuvering the stones into their proper places. Several minutes later, Cohen was ready to speak to God.

"*Awesome* is the word that comes to mind," Douglas whispered in wonder as he watched Cohen position the stones of the high priestly device. He reached over and touched one of the gems. "As good as this is, prayer will always be our direct and immediate link to God."

"Amen," the ladies said in unison.

"Ready," Cohen announced.

Douglas shot a look at Kathy, then with clear precision said, "I want you to ask the UT the following question: Is Gregory A. Kavidas the antichrist, Satan's messiah?"

"What?!" Cohen gulped. "Are you serious?!" He looked at Leah, who suddenly turned ashen and grabbed Kathy's arm. *Evil agent, yes, but the antichrist?*

"I'm dead serious," Douglas replied with a straight face, "and Mortimer Stein is the prophesied false prophet. There's a great deal that you don't know about them. Believe me, they *are* agents from Satan like you said, and much, much more." He pointed at the *lights of God* and commanded, "Ask the question."

Beads of perspiration formed on Cohen's forehead as he paused for a moment to rephrase the question. "If Kavidas is the antichrist..." he hesitated to gain clarity, "give Urim, turn blue..." his voice fell into a feeble whisper then began to vibrate with intensity, "if not, give Thummim, turn scarlet."

"Aarrgh!" Cohen exclaimed and recoiled as his face contorted with fear when God answered. When he looked at Leah, she had her hand over her mouth in disbelief. Douglas and Kathy sat nodding their heads.

Douglas's brow furrowed. "Just confirmation."

"You mean you knew right along?" Cohen asked incredulously. "Before today?"

"You'd better shut down the UT, this is a long story," Douglas replied with a thumbs up. Cohen handed off the priestly apparatus to Leah, who carefully packed the UT into the knapsack. "For several years we've been following Kavidas," Douglas explained, "beginning back in Florida several years ago when he teamed up with Stein. Shortly after he emerged as a pharmaceutical magnate, things began to take on prophetic implications. First came the AIDS vaccine that catapulted him to worldwide notoriety, then the prophetic utterance of the earthquake at Yosemite National Park that heightened his world acclaim. The clincher came with the emergence of MASTERLINK, now modernized with the computer chip in the right hand that is connected to the terminal in his home office in Athens. This system was masterminded by Kavidas and Stein as the final monetary system predicted in Revelation chapter 13. Meanwhile, unbeknownst to him, a small band of Christians, headed by myself, found out about the true nature of his vaccine and credit system. We began a crusade to unmask his real agenda.

"Diabolic forces were unleashed against us at that time—I'm sure at Kavidas' command—bringing great misfortune and tragedy against our group. Of course God is good, giving us divine protection; however, it became apparent to us that we are entering into the final days of the Bible. With that came the realization that Kavidas will gain strength and power—unparalleled in history—until Christ's return. Then He will dispose of him.

"When we began to mount an offensive, Kavidas and Stein conspired to torch our home and kill my family, but, thank God, we escaped unscathed and shortly afterward I relocated to Israel to teach at the Holy Land Institute in Jerusalem. Then Kavidas somehow arranged for the authorities to arrest me on the grounds of being a political dissident and fugitive, so I fled to the Judean wilderness for safety."

Leah listened intently, then scowled. "You're living in the desert?"

"No, not really. I have built a network of believers throughout the Holy Land, including Jordan, where my family—we have three children—can stay hidden until the proper time arrives for us to continue our crusade against the two of them. Until that time, Matt Lane and I are in constant contact, tracking Kavidas' course on our 'plotting boards,' so to speak."

With his arms crossed over his chest Cohen shook his head and said, "And what mortal could have predicted with any degree of accuracy what would happen when that asteroid threatened the planet?!" He threw his hands up in the air and added, "This all sounds so unbelievable."

Douglas pulled a sheet of paper from his shirt pocket while nibbling on his lower lip. "Want more proof? Our conclusions are not based on theory, but facts. Look at this..." He paused to open up the paper, revealing the name Gregory A. Kavidas with a numerical value next to each letter of his name. "Kavidas comes from aristocracy. His father is Greek, his mother Italian or of Roman descent. Painstaking research has produced startling results. Kavidas rarely uses his middle initial together with his first and last name because the gematria in the Greek equals six hundred sixty-six!"

"Uh-oh," Cohen said numbly. He reached over and lifted the paper out of Douglas's hand to read it himself. "Isn't six hundred sixty-six the secret symbol of the ancient pagan mysteries connected with the worship of the devil?"

"Yes," Douglas affirmed, "the biblical number for the antichrist."

"Now I know why the UT gave off a warning when I first asked it a question regarding him," Cohen observed.

Kathy chimed in. "David, tell him about the recent developments going on back in the States."

Douglas nodded and repositioned himself in the back seat so as to address both Cohen and Leah. "Two years ago, a longtime friend of mine who was the pastor of a Christian church in my home town of Coral Springs, Florida, had the foresight to recognize that the MASTERLINK system is the emerging financial arm of the antichrist and warned his congregation not to enroll in it. Well, his church branded him an alarmist, ignored him, and before he knew it, many of the congregants were looking to tithe to the church from their MASTERLINK accounts. He objected to their compromise, they became offended, and either went to another church where the pastor didn't care where the money came from, or they protested and stopped giving altogether. The church had to close due to financial troubles, and today, the pastor is selling used cars."

"You mean MASTERLINK is that entrenched in the States?" Leah asked in dismay.

"Kavidas' MASTERLINK network is unique and innovative," Kathy explained. "The ID chip is designed for all financial, confidential, medical, and what few realize, political and religious data on all subscribers. In other words, Kavidas knows everything about you, and the day will come when as the Bible puts it, '...no man will be able to buy or sell unless he has the mark of the beast...' " She shook her head and added, "...and that mark is MASTERLINK, controlled by Kavdas."

"It's beginning to catch on over here," Cohen observed glumly. "Probably by next year it will have spread throughout Europe and the Middle East."

"The big attraction was consolidation of credit cards, anti-theft features, elimination of cash, and only a one or two percent interest charge. Of course, his system began swallowing up all the competition," Douglas remarked.

"It gets worse," Kathy said numbly. "A girlfriend of mine who teaches in an elementary school in Maryland was informed one day that a gay man was authorized by the superintendent to come into her classroom—mind you she teaches fourth grade—and present the homosexual agenda in such a way that made it sound like they were beginning a recruitment and indoctrination program in the schools. When some of the children voiced their disapproval, the gay man accused them of being homophobic, influenced and conditioned by their parents or church, and rebuked them sharply. What's more, the man brought photos of the child whom he and his partner had adopted, advising the class that this was perfectly normal."

"How can they get away with that?!" Cohen asked Douglas bristling.

"They are really digging in for the long haul," Douglas said as his jaw tightened. "Laws are already in effect giving them equal spousal benefits with the heterosexuals." He flayed his hands and lamented, "This is representative of the spiritual and moral decay enveloping our world today."

Kathy nudged her husband and said, "Tell them of your theory of Christ's return."

Douglas looked at Kathy and then squeezed her hand as a sign of approval in what he saw. Despite the wear and tear on her emotional and physical well-being for the past four years of persecution by Kavidas, she had maintained herself remarkably well. She had the spiritual aptitude of Esther, the discernment of Abigail, and the maternal instincts of Eunice. In addition, godly disciplines in her life were rewarded with the beauty of Sarah. "Well, when I interpret Revelation 6:11—along with passages in Genesis where God destroyed mankind in the Flood and then in Sodom and Gomorrah, I infer that God has a fixed number of redeemed to be saved and when that number is reached, the end comes. Boom—Christ returns! That, together with His intolerance toward immorality, seems to point to the fact that God has a 'divine thermometer' that brings on His wrath."

"The doomsday temperature does seem to be climbing at an uncontrollable rate," Cohen agreed.

"Tell David about your dream, Cohen," Leah prompted.

For 15 minutes they sat with eyes fastened on Cohen's face as he related his dream.

Douglas clapped his hands in exultation the moment Cohen finished. "It's perfect! Don't you see, your dream is—" He paused and reached for his pocket Bible, then quickly turned the pages to Joel chapter 2 and continued, "…a fulfillment of this prophecy that had a partial fulfillment in the early church period, but now it will be fully realized." He cleared his throat and read, "'And afterward, I will pour out My Spirit on all people. Your sons and daughters will prophesy, your old men will dream dreams, your young men will see visions…I will show wonders in the heavens and on the earth…'

"This is an end-time prophecy. It explains why God allowed you to have a dream. We will soon be entering into the final days on earth." He reached over and touched Cohen's shoulder. "The Lord must have an important mission for you, Cohen." With a shrug of the shoulders he added, "Unfortunately, the other side will also have dreams. That explains Kavidas' ability to predict the outcome of the asteroid."

Everyone nodded.

"You're a Bible scholar, David; what's your view of Cohen's dream?" Leah asked quizzically.

David blinked. Interpretation of Bible texts—especially prophetic ones—had always been serious business with God, a ministry that had severe spiritual penalties if improperly used. In point of fact, Moses' law mandated that if a prophet as much as uttered a false prophecy, he was to be executed immediately by stoning. "Fortunately when it comes to interpretation, we can draw from other biblical texts for help, and in the case of your dream, our present political and social environment brings clarity to the explanation.

"The sea is a symbol for the Gentile nations; the hideous beast, a symbol for the antichrist. Kavidas fits the profile as rising from Greece, a Gentile nation, and the Beautiful Land is Israel, the vessel God has chosen to administer salvation and grace to humanity. We expect that Kavidas will ultimately transfer his political headquarters to Jerusalem in the future.

"Intrigue, deceit, and power are the hallmarks of this satanically energized man who will gain worldwide recognition. Again, Kavidas' name skyrocketed with his introduction of the AIDS vaccine a few years ago, then MASTERLINK, and now with the asteroid publicity and head of the EEC—there is little to prevent him from maintaining high notoriety, exactly as predicted. In time he will form a protection pact with the Jewish people, who will be assailed by the Arab bloc nations. The Jewish nation, Israel, in turn will hail Kavidas as the Messiah when Kavidas is credited with defeating the Arabs, after they form an alliance with the Russians and attack the Holy Land."

Cohen picked up on the momentum. "Then the second beast in my dream must be Stein, his henchman."

"That's the way I see it," Douglas agreed. "We can look forward to him performing miraculous signs that will promote Kavidas' agenda. The big one will be when he calls fire down from Heaven—a counterfeit of Elijah's miracle on Mount Carmel described in the Book of First Kings. That will, however, be eclipsed by Stein's demonic feat of bringing Kavidas back to life after he suffers a mortal head wound."

"Probably inflicted by a Jewish radical who sees through the charade," Cohen added.

"Perhaps. By that time, the whole world will be worshiping him as the Messiah," Douglas continued, "this all taking place in a span of seven years known as the Tribulation period. Then Christ returns—He is the Prince of the Host in your dream—bringing in the culmination right after the great conflagration or —"

"—Armageddon," Leah said, finishing his sentence.

"Right again," Douglas affirmed.

An information exchange broke out as Cohen and Douglas discussed theories and facts relative to prophetic events: Third World nations acquiring ballistic missiles with half having nuclear capabilities; 14 or more nations having weapons of mass destruction; 23 or more nations building ICBM's; 66 or more having the technology to field surface-skimming cruise missiles; the effect of such an exchange on the world's food, vegetation, and oceans. China supplying Iran with arms; Russia's need to neutralize Israel's nuclear deterrence before mounting its attack as predicted in the Book of Ezekiel chapter 38. The American abandonment of Israel because of unceasing terrorism and choices surrounding oil-rich Arab countries.

The tension was increasing exponentially until the catharsis was complete. Douglas stopped abruptly and said to Cohen, "I'm starving. Let's get something to eat."

"Amen," he replied wearily. The girls nodded their approval. "Oh, one more thing," Cohen said as he reached into Leah's handbag and pulled out Leona's shoe. "Take a look at the print on the sole and give me your opinion."

Douglas carefully inspected the shoe then paused to scratch his head as he pondered the evidence. "Where did it come from?"

Cohen shot a look at Leah. "Long story. We believe the owner of this shoe was somehow involved in the death of Leah's father."

Douglas wrinkled his nose. "I've seen this impression on extant documents relating to the demonic world. A professor friend of mine at Trinity University did some serious research in ancient Israeli folklore—some of which has its roots in the Talmud and the Zohar—and came up with some interesting findings."

"Such as?" Cohen asked curiously.

"Something about a special breed of fallen angels or demons called the *Shedim*, who did the dirty work for Satan—like his hit men—always in human disguise. The giveaway was their deformed feet. The commentaries speculated that they would show themselves in the last days when the shackles and chains that hold them in the bottomless pit are taken off so they can torment unbelieving mankind."

A chill ran up and down Leah's spine as she placed the shoe back in her handbag.

CHAPTER

17

Jerusalem

Leah sat quietly in the back seat of the car, gazing out at the Judean hillside as they traveled to Kefar, a small town 13 miles west-southwest from Bethlehem. Grazing sheep and colorful farmhouses dotted the landscape and at times became a blur as the vehicle picked up speed on the sloping hills. "It won't be long now," she heard Douglas say aloud from the front seat. "Just a little while longer." *Yeah, Lord, may it be just a little while,* Leah thought. *Cohen and I have been in this car for such a long time.*

The droning sound of the engine together with the rushing of the air outside the car brought relief to her anxious heart, reeling with the horrors of the past as well as the dread of the future. She ran her fingers through her hair and mentally sought a tranquil place where she could be alone with God and talk to Him about her troubled spirit.

"Over there is the Aid-el-Ma, the alleged location of the cave of Adullam," Douglas explained as he pointed to a group of limestone cliffs off in the distance, "where David and his band of four hundred men had their stronghold as fugitives from King Saul."

Leah's eyes brightened as she stared off at the location. For a brief moment she imagined David's men camping out in the numerous small tunnels that connected several mammoth caves in the busy labyrinth. It was a subterranean region with dry, pure air where David could meander along winding narrow passages, with cavities on either side, separating the larger chambers, hallmarked by arches, wells, rock terraces, and fortifications that would provide protection from marauding soldiers and tribes. She envisioned adjoining passages that linked the inner chambers. The whole formed a perplexing city where David could hide out for months, even years, a place where he could dialog with God and write his psalms.

Breaking out of her reverie, she turned to Cohen and asked, "Didn't David write some psalms while in the caves?"

Cohen looked askance at Douglas, who answered, "I believe they were Psalm 57 and 142, if I'm not mistaken."

Leah nodded, then returned to viewing the mountainscape. After a moment of contemplation she asked, "David, do you connect the events of David and Saul with you and Kavidas?"

"In many ways, yes," he replied, "and you will appreciate this in time as well. When you're on the run for doing God's work, with people or principalities chasing after you, you can relate to David when he fled from Saul into the Judean wilderness for those seven years. David's story is told in the Books of First and Second Samuel."

"In a way, it will be like that for those who come to believe on Christ during the Tribulation period when Kavidas and Stein are reigning like kings, right, David?" Kathy observed. She considered her husband an authority on Bible prophecy.

Everyone in the car turned and looked at him.

"Yes," Douglas answered. "Those who become believers during the Tribulation will be persecuted to such an extent by Kavidas' forces—along with the supernatural disasters that will befall humanity, described in the Book of Revelation—that, yes, they will be fleeing into the caves of the earth for protection."

The frightening realization brought a wave of silence that prevailed until they arrived at the Douglas's hideaway house.

It was early afternoon at the Renaissance Jerusalem where Stein sat in a chair on the veranda overlooking the city. Fleeting moments of frustration filled his thoughts as he plotted his next move—his final move—to apprehend the revelatory device and eliminate the opposition. He steeled his mind to accept nothing but victory. He had calculated his losses and acquiesced to them, but now with the time of Kavidas' presentation to the world drawing near, he had to call upon any and all forces to rid the earth of the scourge that threatened their plan.

His head dropped back in the chair as tingling sensations of light enveloped his body. *Relax. Open your mind*, he told himself. When he looked up he saw colored halos and luminous tails dangling in midair before his eyes. Suddenly the veranda became surrounded by clouds, bringing on the realization that contact was about to be made. His heart began to race as his mind began to inform him of the unfinished assignment.

He heard what sounded like a trumpet blaring off in the distance. It signaled a time of judgment that was in the near future, a time when God would bring darkness, clouds, desolation, misery, and gloom upon the earth in payment for men's sinful desires, for their sexual impurity, and for the degrading of their bodies with one another. In the Book of Romans, the apostle Paul described the awful events as punishment for exchanging the truth of God for a lie, and for worshiping and serving created things rather than Him, the Creator. Now they would receive in themselves the due penalty for their perversion.

Fragmented images began to encircle a fixed point before his eyes, rapidly forming a montage with several scenes taking shape simultaneously. One scene showed an enormous shaft running from the earth's surface to an indeterminable depth in the bowels of the earth. Smoke, like that from a gigantic furnace, rose from the abyss, blackening the sky and shrouding the sun in an eerie blanket that immediately brought fear to all the world's inhabitants. Then out of the shaft ascended innumerable locusts—even millions upon millions of them, flying wildly, buzzing and clinging tenaciously to mortals. These demonic insects had mutated over the eons and were now empowered with the sting of the scorpion, to torture those who did not have the seal of God on their foreheads.

Twilight had fallen in one of the scenes, so that no man could witness the next terrible release from the depths of the subterranean pit. It was an unbinding of the *Shedim*, partially concealed by the spectral half-moon shining wanly on the grey desolation outside. Men, unaware of the origin of the shaft, were sniffing in disgust and holding their noses at the fetor that wandered for miles from the damned place. It resembled the rotten stench of burning sulfur. Next to the shaft, weird footprints imbedded in the ground trailed off into every direction as the *Shedim*, the fallen ones who had been locked in the nefarious prison of Tartaros, marched off like soldiers to fight the war man could never win.

A diabolic hatching of different sorts was taking place in another scene. The damned agents from the netherworld were selling their evil wares to the sordid minds of men who sought gratification of the flesh, from the pandering of raucous music that disturbed the soul of youth to the medium of pornography that led to the reshaping of values within their hearts. This alteration brought on rebellion inside the home where the adolescents of the world thought nothing of betraying their parents to the authorities of the MASTERLINK system they refused to subscribe to. Infiltration into the vanguard of the church came easy, since men in the pulpit assuaged the power of the gospel through personal compromise, while chasing the ideology known as accommodation.

The plan, most assuredly, would come together. MASTERLINK would be a global network; Christians would be controlled and Kavidas would become the most important person on the face of the earth.

The imagery began to fade, but not before the faces of Cohen and Douglas came into view. They sat in the living room of a small house in a town called Kefar, formulating plans to publicly expose the very demagogue Stein had entrusted his future to. Stein's face contorted with rage when he remembered his dealings with Douglas, and immediately the specter of discovery reared its ugly head. His hand tightened into a fist, and he slammed it down on the arm of the chair. Seconds later, he saw Leah and Kathy discussing their fears of what the future held in store for them.

Even though his eyes were transfixed, Stein began to smile.

"Everyone is tired from traveling, so we'll make it an early night," Douglas said to the group assembled before him. His and Kathy's home, rented from a member of the Koinonos network of Christians dedicated to protecting the brethren, was an extremely modest dwelling place with three bedrooms nestled in the foothills of Kefar.

Cohen sat on the sofa with Leah snuggled tightly in his arms while Kathy sat on the floor with her three teenagers. In a way it reminded Kathy of a time in the distant past when they had lived in Florida, and David had told Bible stories to the children sitting on the floor around a bowl of popcorn.

"I'm persuaded that we must expose Kavidas and his conclave immediately," Cohen began with a high degree of intensity.

Leah, keeping to herself for the past several hours, sat upright and blurted out, "We need to warn the world about who he is, and we can start right here in Israel!"

"What do you mean?" Kathy asked as she combed out her daughter, Hillary's, hair.

"I have some connections down at the Knesset building; I know who to talk to," Leah said as she swallowed hard with strengthening resolve. "Cohen and David should bring the UT before the parliament and let it rip! With the four of us and the UT, the world will listen to us. There's nothing to be afraid of."

It was only a split-second of time, but in Kathy's mind, the re-playing of events that had led her family to Israel was all too real. The horror of her children being followed from school, the shooting of her husband by their friend-turned-foe who, she later found out, was on Kavidas' payroll. The near-fatal car accident where her family be-came the target of Kavidas' vendetta to get back at her husband, the malicious lies spread about them in a barrage of newspapers articles, and the final blow, when Kavidas and Stein sent their executioner to torch their home while they slept. Miraculously surviving and escap-ing to Israel, they vowed to attack Kavidas only when instructed by God. No, Leah was wrong. With Kavidas and Stein together with the forces they could marshal, there was plenty to be afraid of.

Turning to Leah, Kathy propounded with heightening concern, "Leah, David and I have been through some heavy battles with Kavi-das when we were back in the States, while you and Cohen have had only a skirmish or two. We cannot go against him without an organ-ized plan—he's lethal!"

"You call being under surveillance while we slept and then being attacked by demonic forces where my father lost his arm a skirmish?"

Leah retorted as she whirled on her. "I suppose the murder of my father doesn't qualify for a retaliatory raid then, does it?"

"Well, yes," Kathy conceded, "it most certainly does. But experience dictates that Kavidas knows by now that David and I are part of the problem. Since the stakes are higher, he will take more aggressive action to prevent us from hurting him."

A sudden chill came over Leah as she pondered Kathy's rebuttal. It was a truth she hadn't thought of. A bewildered look came over her face as she sought refuge in Cohen's arms once again.

Douglas waved Kathy off as he moved to the end of his seat and said soothingly, "Whoa, now, let's not give Satan the advantage here. We need to maintain a united front. We all have battle scars that qualify us for combat duty."

" 'Pleasant words are a honeycomb...' " Kathy quoted in reply. Douglas smiled at his wife for her effort to soften the tone of the conversation.

"Let's close out the evening with a round of prayer," he suggested. "Then we can all rest quietly, knowing the Lord will protect us."

Outwardly everyone agreed, but Leah felt the icy finger of fear pointing at her heart.

It was nearly 2:30 a.m. when Leah awakened out of a deep sleep to what sounded like a form of mechanical humming coming from under her bed. It was a metallic noise that bellowed and echoed, giving her the impression that it came from somewhere far below her. Her eyes widened in shock when a dazzling brightness began to radiate from the same location—under her bed. She pulled the covers over her head, but she could easily see the light intensifying and she felt heat being emitted at an alarming rate. She began to sweat profusely but refused to drop the covers. *Cohen*, she thought, *I need you!*

Her heart began to race as fear swept over her like a violent wind-storm. She knew she was in trouble from unseen forces.

The room began to fill with a pungent smelling smoke as the heat abruptly subsided, being replaced with a rapid cooling. She began to shake from the cold as she attempted to cry out, *Cohen, help!* but no words came out of her mouth.

Suddenly the covers were ripped off her by an unseen hand!

Oh, my God! she cried out in her mind when she saw an arm pass through the solid frame and mattress of her bed and hang suspended in the air, holding the covers above the floor. *This can't be!* she reasoned.

She jumped out of the bed and fled to the corner of the room just as two figures began to materialize before her eyes. They appeared to be a man and a woman fixing her with a penetrating stare. With a menacing look they came at her and stopped at her feet as she cowered in the corner.

"Why doesn't your faith in God help you now?" the masculine voice mocked as he kicked her foot. His face was veiled in shadow, unrecognizable.

"It didn't help your father and it will not help you," the feminine voice stated with crisp sarcasm.

Leah's mind could not grasp what her spirit dictated she should do. In her heart she believed it was a lie, but her fear disabled and paralyzed her faith. *Denounce them!* her spirit cried out, but again, she could not utter a word. She sensed an evil influence exerting tremendous force on her mind and soul, determined to dissuade her. As inward pressure began building, she cried out to God in her heart for increased faith, and He heard her. She *would* fight back.

"We've come to claim you, Leah," the masculine voice declared, "so that you can join your father in Heaven."

"You're a liar!" Leah exploded with strengthening resolve. Her blossoming faith erupted, overpowering her fear. Her newly acquired relationship with God and her elementary knowledge of the Bible quickly alerted her to the untruth that her father was in Heaven. "You have no power over me—you are a liar!"

"Damn the Holy Spirit!" a strange voice from out of nowhere muttered aloud.

Changing her course of action, the female vocalized, "David is the one who has lied to you, Leah. He is planning to betray you and keep the Urim and Thummim for himself. He has already made a deal with us."

Leah glared with malevolent eyes and replied fiercely, "David would never do that; he's a man of God determined to unmask Kavidas!" As soon as the words left her mouth, she realized she could not reason with them. "I demand that you leave, in the name of—"

The man stepped forward, cupped his ears, and commanded Leah, "Stop!" He would not hear the ineffable name that would halt his attack. He pointed at the bed, and it immediately lifted off the floor and started rotating. Leah looked on in horror. It moved toward her as if to crush her against the wall. She yelled out, "Cohen, help!"

But the room was somehow sealed; no sounds could be heard beyond the door.

Outside the bedroom, an exhausted Cohen slept on a daybed, dreaming of future days. He and Leah were at the Wailing Wall in Jerusalem, handing out tracts and preaching the unsearchable riches of Messiah Jesus; people were crying out for relief from the terrible plagues that had befallen them, yet they refused to repent of their evil deeds with an irascible vengeance.

For hours Cohen and Leah preached, until the Israeli police were called to arrest them for evangelizing and proselytizing without a permit. They turned to flee when suddenly, in the dream, an unknown man stepped out of the crowd. He came up to Cohen, clutched Cohen's shoulder and exclaimed, "Cohen, Leah is in danger! You must wake up!"

Cohen lifted his head and fluttered his eyes several times before looking over at Leah's door. *Nothing unusual.* He fell back into the pillow and closed his eyes.

The man in the crowd reappeared in his mind. *Cohen, wake up— NOW!* he warned.

Cohen bolted upright and looked at the door once again. This time his eyes ran directly to the ghastly light that appeared to ooze out from the bottom. In the next second he found himself standing at a distance of ten feet away, holding his arm like a battering ram, rushing toward Leah's door; but an unseen force acted like a barrier. The door held fast as if it were a stone wall.

He backed up to try again, paused for a second to think, then yelled aloud as he thrust himself at the door, "IN THE MIGHTY NAME OF JESUS, I COMMAND YOU TO OPEN THE DOOR!" The impact of his body pulled the hinges, doorknob and striker plate clear out of the wall. The door flattened on the floor as he burst into the room.

The scene was hellish.

Leah lay prostrate on the floor with an angelic look of divine peace on her face, while the bed hovered in mid-air over her, as if waiting for the next command. Cohen quickly surveyed the room and spotted the two attackers reeling from a frenzied melee that, he later realized, was due to his crying out the all-powerful name of Jesus. They quickly scrambled to their feet and began to regroup.

His face contorting with rage, Cohen lunged for the man, but the woman figure raised her hand, hurtling him against the wall. He dropped with a thud. Rallying, Cohen shot a look at Leah, who mysteriously remained enraptured and dazed. *Thank you, God, for protecting her!*

Cohen clenched his teeth and slammed his fist against the floor, then regained his agility, sprang to his feet, and started toward the man as the assailant stepped out of the shadow. Cohen stopped short. "I might have known!" he sneered as his eyes fell on Stein. Turning in reflexive alarm, he looked at the woman. "Your executioner?" he growled vehemently as his lips twitched in anger. Cohen's eyes traveled down her legs, taking note of her mutated feet.

Stein's emblazoned eyes announced his fury. He nodded to his accomplice, then pointed to Leah. Cohen registered the look on their faces and began to brace himself for the worst. "We want the Urim and Thummim, now! You're out of time!" Stein demanded. Cohen glanced over at Leah and saw the bed rising perilously. In the next instant, a fire sprang up under her. Cohen wiped his nose as the smell of burnt flesh filled the room. "The device!" Stein rasped with heightening volume.

It's an illusion, Cohen, a voice whispered to his heart.

Cohen's eyes were riveted on Leah as she lay motionless with the flames engulfing her. *This can't be!* "All right, all right," he yelled out in a moment of weakness. "I'll turn it over to you."

Cohen, it's an illusion, the voice repeated. *Trust God.*

"Leah is the weak link in your ministry," Stein lied acidly as Cohen shook his head in an effort not to listen. "She will bring destruction on your efforts," he roared while pointing an icy finger at Cohen. "You cannot win against us, so withdraw or be killed!"

"I know Scripture, Stein, and Yeshua will defeat you in the end, but until then…" He paused and mouthed a prayer to the Lord for added courage, then pointed *his* finger at Stein and continued, "…we will fight you on every front! We will mount up with wings of eagles and publicly announce to the unwary world that Kavidas is really Satan's messiah so they will not take his mark! We will develop our own monetary system—even if we must resort to barter—so that we will not bow down to the idol, MASTERLINK! Our forces will campaign throughout Israel and the West so that your scheme to overtake the free world will be thwarted and turned to folly!"

"Enough!" Stein boomed. He raised his hand at Cohen and brought it down sharply in a slicing motion. All at once, Cohen felt a stabbing sensation in his stomach. When he looked down, his intestines were dangling through a large gash in his side. He fell to the floor, holding his gut as blood spurted out onto the floor.

"You are covered by the blood of Jesus, Cohen!" Douglas yelled out from behind. "It is a trick, do not give in to them!" Douglas ran to his side to help him up, then turned to Stein and cried out, "IN THE NAME OF THE ALMIGHTY JESUS I COMMAND YOU TO LEAVE!"

A howling noise sprang up from nowhere, and in an instant they were gone. Vanished!

Crash! The bed dropped to the floor over Leah.

Cohen looked down at his stomach to see that the injury was nothing more than a demonic fabrication. Douglas helped him up, then they scrambled to Leah's aid. She lay under the bed, dazed but unhurt. They lifted the bed off her and placed her on it, then they fell backward next to her with a great sigh of relief.

In the world of demonkind, Douglas reminded himself after the attack, supernatural abilities rely upon deception. Systematic theology combined with sound exegesis when studying biblical passages revealed this truth. Necromancy or speaking to the dead was when a fallen spirit impersonated, based on the subject's memory, the lost one, often advising him or her to take action that would further the demon's plan of subterfuge. Divination was a human device whereby demonic powers were instrumental in ascertaining the future by magical arts, superstitious incantations, or natural signs arbitrarily interpreted. In the Scriptures, it was often allied with witchcraft and idolatry. Astrology, charming through omens, enchantment through conjurors and exorcising with magic rigmaroles to enlist the aid of evil spirits were not playthings, but a doorway to the occult—heathen counterparts of Christian prayer. Supernatural revelations, fortune-telling, hypnotic regression, and forecasting were correlations with the occult. They influenced the dream state.

Events involving fallen angels or demons in the Bible demonstrate their counterfeiting abilities: Predicting the future, using great strength, displaying treacherous natures, speaking through animals, traveling by supernatural power, projecting a false reality instantaneously, removing and planting thoughts, and manipulating the mind. Demons could lie incessantly, bring oppression and depression if needed, or terrorize their subjects and "strip" them mentally. Often they assumed human form, but could remain invisible while making their presence known in mysterious ways. Many unsuspecting experimenters who toyed with or explored the demonic world did not realize that the demons sought total control and would not hesitate to kill those who resisted.

"The attacks will intensify and end in death unless we do something to protect ourselves," Cohen said bitterly while stretching his arm around Leah. The group clustered together in the living room to assess the damage.

Douglas nodded his head in agreement. "We were fortunate this time. But the next encounter could prove disastrous."

"You mean because of the reinforcements?" Cohen noted.

Douglas looked askance at the girls, then back to Cohen. "Yes. The way I read this situation, I'm convinced that there's been some kind of release whereby the *Shedim*, being nothing more than fallen angels, will now assist Kavidas and Stein in bringing about their sinister plot."

A muscle jerked in Cohen's right cheek as he perceived Leah's anxiety level rising. He held her tightly and smiled luminously at her. "Christ is greater!"

"Amen!" the group agreed wholeheartedly.

"Now, what do we do about the UT?" Kathy asked.

"I think Leah's suggestion of bringing the device before the Knesset is a good one. We can then convince the cabinet of Kavidas' real identity!" Douglas said trenchantly with a clenched fist.

"That's if all hell doesn't break loose on the way there," Leah said discordantly.

"We will invoke God's protection," Cohen reminded Leah with heightening resolve. "We'll be fine."

"Then it's agreed," Douglas affirmed.

Within the framework of the Israeli democratic system, in which there was a separation of powers among the legislature, the executive branch, and the judiciary, the Knesset was the legislative branch, with the exclusive authority to enact laws. One of the functions of the Knesset was to supervise the government of Israel, most of whose ministers and deputy ministers were elected Knesset members. The Knesset could pass laws on any subject and in any matter, as long as a proposed law did not contradict an existing basic law. Every law that the government wanted to enact had to pass the Knesset's approval.

Israel's first government, formed by David Ben Gurion on March 8, 1949, continued to operate without a constitution, but a number of laws passed by the legislature regulated how the government operated. Israel's head of state, the president, served mostly ceremonial functions and was elected by the legislature. The country's chief executive was the prime minister, elected by popular vote.

It was to the prime minister, Rubin, that Leah would bring her appeal.

Leah swiped her ID card in the parking lot security system device and the gate arm lifted. Douglas smiled at Cohen who gave him a "thumbs up" as Leah drove to her designated space. Within minutes the four of them were in the reception area where Leah went directly to the chief of security to clear Cohen's knapsack and determine Prime Minister Rubin's whereabouts. After a quick check of her credentials, the security chief called the prime minister's secretary, who screened all his prospective appointments.

It was no coincidence, but God's providence, that the secretary was now dating Rubin's nephew, Shlomo, Leah's former boyfriend. She bumped Leah up to be next in line.

Prime Minister Rubin, once a robust radical bent on political reform, greeted Leah and her entourage with the official smile and warmth usually reserved for campaign trails. Rumors abounded detailing the trouble in his office and home since the tunnel disaster, despite his party's ardent desire to absorb most of the responsibility and cleanup associated with it. Conspiracy and complicity theories were raised and squashed soon after the tragedy, citing executive clemency laws that paralleled recent American history. It became common knowledge that the PM intended to ride out his term without further confrontation.

Once they were seated, Rubin nodded to Leah and began, "I wish I had the opportunity to meet all our interns here at parliament, Ms. Krasnoff, but with time constraints, unfortunately it is not possible." He motioned a greeting to the others then turned back to Leah and added, "So what brings you to my office?"

Familiarity dictated that Leah would be the spokesperson. She moved to sit on the edge of her chair as if to convey urgency and said, "Mr. Prime Minister, a matter of national security has come to our attention, and we here believe it necessary that you take appropriate steps to prevent..." she groped for words, "...the deliberate dismantling of our society as we know it. In our estimation, a colossal attempt to overthrow the governments of the world through subterfuge is underway by two men who already possess great power and the will to do it."

Rubin's face contorted in disbelief. "*Who* are you talking about?"

"Before I answer that, Mr. Prime Minister," Leah replied, pointing to the group, "I would like to present three individuals who will attest to the claims I am making." Leah waved her hand in a sweeping motion then stopped on Douglas. "This is Dr. David Douglas, a biblical scholar from America who taught in a Miami university before coming to Israel. He taught for a semester at the Institute of Biblical Studies here in Jerusalem. Next to him is his wife of over twenty-three years, Kathleen. Together they have three children. Kathleen held a high-ranking position with a major franchising company back in Florida." She looked at Cohen and smiled. "This is Nathan Cohen, my fiancé, also an American, who was recruited by my father, the late Rehavam Krasnoff, to work on an important archeological discovery." She nodded gravely and added, "I'm sure you know all about my father from your relationship with the IAA."

"Of course," Rubin consoled.

"I prefaced my answer with their credentials," Leah continued solemnly, "to lend credibility to what I'm about to say. We are not a bunch of weirdos holed up in a desert fortress with a particular agenda to further our cause, nor do we purpose to retaliate against these two men for their conspiring to kill us. No! We are simply concerned about the future of Israel and the rest of the globe. Our mission is to disclose their true character to the world—starting right here, since you know who they are."

Rubin fussed in his chair and panned the group. "I do?" he said tersely then shrugged his shoulders. "Who are they?"

Leah stood up and handed Rubin a recent newspaper article containing a photograph of Gregory A. Kavidas and Mortimer Stein together in front of a MASTERLINK logo. The photograph had been taken in Athens.

"This can't be," Rubin groaned. "These men are heroes in the eyes of the world!" His lips curved sardonically. "Remember the asteroid thing? The earthquake prediction years earlier?"

Leah glanced over at Douglas, whose jaw tightened at Rubin's remark, while the rest of the group nodded their heads plaintively.

Douglas stiffened and said, "Mr. Prime Minister, we have ample documentation that both Kavidas and Stein are wicked men with supernatural powers. They are determined to dupe and enslave mankind with a—" he stopped short and pulled from his pocket what looked like a business card with a microdot in shrink wrap attached to it. The label read MASTERLINK. "...a global financial system that will incorporate every form of commerce, medical, and personal information necessary to maintain complete control of every person on this planet. And that is only the beginning of sorrows."

Cohen stood up as Douglas sat down. "Mr. Rubin," he pleaded, "I've had the privilege of hearing from God on this matter. We *must* do something about them before it's too late."

Rubin patted his foot on the floor and remarked sharply, " 'Hearing from God,' Mr. Cohen, is something even the rabbis long to do." A cynical look came over his face. "Is this the kind of proof you expect me to bring before my cabinet? A microdot and some insane cockamamy gibberish about Kavidas' business enterprises?"

Douglas swallowed hard and squinted at Cohen; circumstantial evidence wasn't cutting it. They needed more to persuade Rubin. They needed physical proof. He jerked his head slightly to wave off Cohen's line of reasoning. "Mr. Prime Minister, despite your familiarity with the work carried out by the IAA regarding archeological discoveries, you will be shocked at what we are about to show you." He nodded to Cohen, who slowly and methodically lifted the Urim and Thummim, along with the high priest's garb, out of the sack, then headed for a table in the corner to set it up.

Rubin's breath caught in his throat. He gulped then croaked out, "What in the world is that?"

"It's the—" Cohen started to say as he began assembling it on the table.

"My father discovered it near the ruins at Qumran!" Leah blurted out. "It's the Urim and Thummim—the actual device used by the high priest to determine the will of God!"

"That's impossible!" Rubin flared. "The Urim and Thummim were lost in antiquity." He stood up and pointed to Douglas, whom he assumed to be the leader. "Please take your parlor magic paraphernalia out of my office; I have work to do."

Cohen nodded to Kathy and Leah, who quickly squeezed their eyes shut and zipped a prayer up to God. *If only the Holy Spirit would open up his eyes!* But it was not meant to be, for the plan of God required the nation of Israel and the world to continue in their blindness for a little while longer.

Douglas walked over to Cohen and motioned for him to don the high priest's uniform and start up the UT. He then turned to Rubin and explained, "For years, Mr. Prime Minister, I have been tracking Kavidas and Stein in their quest for world domination with little success, due to their popularity and resourcefulness—also because they were aided by relentless satanic forces. By enlisting those forces they have managed to slip away unnoticed and avoid detection. Their hordes of accomplices pick up every shred of evidence that could incriminate them." He touched the breastplate on Cohen and continued, "But now, through God's providence, we have available to us a revelatory device that will confirm our claims." With that he turned to Cohen and said, "Time to call upon God, Cohen."

"This is blasphemous!" Rubin protested as he reached for the phone.

"This is holy!" Douglas countered as Cohen began invoking God.

"If Kavidas is the wicked antichrist and Stein his false prophet," Cohen wailed, "give Urim, turn blue; if not, give Thummim, turn red!"

The room turned somewhat surreal as the stones began to glow. A strange quiet overpowered the clangor coming from outside.

Rubin's mouth hung open as he slowly replaced the phone. His eyes were transfixed on the gems as they changed colors. The scarlet jasper and the purple amethyst dimmed as the blue sapphire glowed brightly.

"You see, Mr. Prime Minister!" Douglas clamored. "God has answered through the UT—and the answer is a resounding yes!"

"Yes, meaning Kavidas and Stein are the real articles, the genuine antichrist and false prophet?" Rubin mocked as his facial expression went from astonishment to scorn. He walked over to Cohen, lifted the breastplate, and stooped down to look under it. "You easily could have manipulated these lights to flash on your command, so who's kidding whom?"

"But, Mr. Prime Minister," Douglas pleaded as Cohen's face blanched in bewilderment, "we are not contriving this! Kavidas' name has the equivalence of the prophetic six hundred sixty-six! We can prove that if only you would be open-minded."

Rubin wrinkled his nose in contempt. "Listen to me!" he retorted. "For centuries fatalists and the doomsday prophets have accused leaders of being the 'supposed' antichrist." He counted off on his fingers. "Let's see, there were among others, Antiochus Epiphanes and Bar Kochba, then there was Adolph Hitler." He snorted, then added, "Some have even accused the Pope and certain American ambassadors of being the *bad guy*..." His voice trailed off in disbelief, and he walked to the window. With a diplomatic flair he moved the curtain aside to look down the promenade. He had made his decision.

Resigned to the defeat, Leah thought she would make a last ditch effort. "Do the three million dollars Kavidas contributed to Israel for humanitarian purposes and the four million for the tunnel disaster have anything to do with your perspective, Mr. Prime Minister?"

Rubin whirled on her and said nothing at first as his eyes bored holes into her. "I would have expected more from you, Ms. Krasnoff," he said acidly. He turned again to look out the window, then said with finality, "Now if you'll excuse me, the duties of the state require my attention."

Douglas stood up and led the procession out of the prime minister's office. The meeting was over.

CHAPTER

18

Jerusalem

David Douglas knew from his seminary education that a theodicy attempted to explain the evil or justice displayed by God in the world, and that Kavidas' triumphs, although sweeping in nature, would inevitably come to an end when Christ returned. Thus, the wrongdoing would stop and punishment would be meted out according to His divine decree. But to mortals undergoing the defeat in the here and now, immediate justice was preferable. Ironically, humans want justice for others, mercy for themselves. Douglas labored to remind himself of the Scripture that read, "…vengeance is mine, saith the Lord."

"Kavidas' control extends all the way up to the prime minister here in Israel," Cohen observed bleakly as they commiserated over coffee and donuts at a luncheonette across from the Knesset building, "and who knows how far his reach is back in the States." He bit his lip and added, "Before long MASTERLINK will swallow up the entire American and European economies while surreptitiously seizing control of every aspect of one's life at the same time."

"Maybe you should call Matthew," Kathy suggested to her husband nervously, "and explain to him our visit with Rubin and ask him for advice."

"I think that's a good idea, David," Cohen allowed. "Remember, 'in the multitude of counselors, there is safety.' "

Douglas nodded his head. "Good quote. I agree." He called for the check then said, "We'll call him from your car on my secure cell phone—we need to watch our backs."

Lane stood erect after his daily prayer time just as the call from Israel came in. It was early morning in Florida and the chill of the night air meandered through his bedroom window and encircled his feet. A shiver came over him as he picked up the phone, but he decidedly resolved to make it a good day despite the ominous feeling. "Praise the Lord, this is Matt Lane."

Lane couldn't see Douglas's smile on the other side of the Atlantic Ocean as he welcomed the friendly voice. " 'Let everything that has breath praise the Lord,' " Douglas recited in reply. "Hello from Jerusalem, Matt."

"How are things going, David?" Lane inquired.

Douglas took a deep breath and said, "We're in trouble, Matt. Satan is working overtime to keep us, once again, from alerting the world to Kavidas' agenda." Douglas then embarked on an extended monologue relating the entire episode with Rubin at the Knessert building. Lane was not shocked at the outcome.

Surprisingly, a newspaper hawker walked by the car at that moment holding a stack of papers with Kavidas' picture on the front page. Cohen signaled the peddler for a copy and quickly read the article, then mouthed to Douglas while he was on the phone, "Rubin nominated Kavidas for a place in the Hall of the Gentiles!" The Hall of the Gentiles was the nation of Israel's way of recognizing those non-Jewish persons who had contributed to the welfare of the Jewish people since the time of World War II. The Avenue of the Righteous, which led to the Hall of Remembrance commemorating the Holocaust, saluted those who had helped Jews at the risk of their own lives during the Nazi regime. Oscar Shindler was one of the many.

Douglas nodded gloomily at Cohen and passed the information on to Lane over the telephone. It was apparent that Rubin had sold out to Kavidas.

"On another front, some weird problems have just popped up over here," Lane started to explain, "namely, some form of demonic assault. It's sweeping the entire nation. I've had numerous reports from members of my church, and from my branch managers in other states, about intense activity that smacks of the kind of thing going on during Christ's ministry—you know, where the demons really felt threatened, so they let it all rip."

David cupped the mouthpiece and said to Cohen and the others, "Looks like the *Shedim* are emerging all over, not just here. Lane says they're having some kind of demonic invasion in the States." He grabbed a pad to make some notes then said to Lane, "This demonic invasion must be worldwide in scope. Over here we've identified them as the *Shedim*—"

"The *Shedim*?!" Lane broke in. "You mean the evil spirits described in Jewish satanology that take on human form?"

"I'm afraid so," Douglas replied ruefully.

"Then that explains the assault."

"Probably."

Lane went on to relate several incidents that sounded like a correlation of events. In New York City several elementary school boys were deeply engrossed in a toy fad that had grown into a global mania. The toys were supposedly innocent, created by a foreign national who had made his fortunes in pornography and wanted to construct a role-playing game where children trained to become monster masters in the world. The psychological strategy behind the mass marketing was never an innocent fantasy, but a way of stimulating the mystical curiosity in children to bring them to the level of addictive mythological religious fervor.

The creatures in the game had special fighting abilities. Some grew, or evolved into even more powerful creatures that gave children a seductive vision and a tempting promise to advance in supernatural powers. The cravings for more occult cards, games, gadgets, and comic books became insatiable when children began to summon up the game spirits to enter into them and thus give them the supernatural powers ascribed to the innocent characters they attempted to imitate. The cultist role-playing game fueled a quest for personal power and authority. Through identification with the godlike superheroes, the child became the master who then usurped any sovereign ruler, including God, police, parents, or pastors. The game suggested occultic practices and violence, so that the child-hero became an extension of the spiritual powers used to destroy opponents through poisoning and fighting. The toys and games all were a means of anesthetizing the conscience of the nation's youth, opening avenues to the soul, making them easy prey for those *Shedim* to enter.

Douglas temporized, then said to Lane, "Your story reminds me of the account of the boy possessed with an evil spirit in the ninth chapter of the Gospel of Mark."

Lane agreed and added that the *Shedim* were probably becoming the masters in control of the nation's youth, who were subversively banding together to form armies bent on destruction and anarchy. "You know about gay marriages, David. Well, in Vermont, the first state to recognize homosexual marriages on equal footing with heterosexual marriages, there were many accounts of brutal sex slaying events where young boys were involuntarily sodomized and left for dead. In another state, a particular adolescent who did not consent to the nefarious act had his underwear stuffed into his mouth, while the gay attacker repeatedly raped him and even took a break to eat a sandwich. The youth died of suffocation."

Lane connected the scenario to the Bible's prediction in Revelation chapter 9 that sexual immorality would continue to escalate and take on unprecedented proportions in the last days of man. He reminded Douglas of God's intolerance toward acts of immorality and how, historically, immorality had brought destruction on humanity. He cited the Sodomites, the Canaanites, the depraved inhabitants of Pompeii, and then asked him to fill in the blank for the nation that was quickly succumbing and should be added to the list. Douglas snuffled and reluctantly offered America as the likely candidate. Lane agreed and observed that the *Shedim* were fighting on three fronts so far: using the medium of role-playing games to gain access to children and simultaneously using homosexuality to gain access into the adult community. The third avenue was drugs. Yes, they were really digging in.

Lane explained the third form of attack from a personal perspective.

"You'll remember, David, that the Bible predicts in Revelation chapter 10 that drug abuse will intensify in the final years. Well, my son Brandon's wife, Cindy, works as an RN over at Broward General Hospital in the men's drug rehabilitation center, and she has undergone some real hair-raising experiences.

"She had one young married male patient who was diagnosed as a manic depressive and had been addicted to amphetamines as a mood elevator for over ten years. Well, he finally checked himself in for treatment after his wife threatened to divorce him. He himself wasn't convinced that he needed the treatment, so he never cooperated with the nurses or doctors unless they gave him the drugs he wanted. When they would withhold the drugs he would shriek like a banshee and thrash about, becoming extremely violent, throwing whatever he could reach at them, often injuring the nurses severely. On two occasions he took a steak knife off the dinner tray and sliced a gash in his own arms and had to be subdued and sutured. Finally, they tied him with restraining straps. In protest he refused to eat or drink any fluids and began to waste away. When Cindy came to spoon feed him one morning, he suddenly jerked his head up and bit off a piece of her ear! Naturally they began to feed him through an IV, but his will to live began to deteriorate rapidly and they feared for his life.

"Then, I guess it was about the same time that I became aware of an increase in demonic activity over here—the *Shedim* you explained—that things really got crazy in the hospital. Cindy's coworker walked into this guy's room last week to take his morning readings and stopped short in the doorway. The restraining straps were off and he was fully dressed, lying on the bed watching the TV as if he were waiting to be discharged. He looked robust and strong—healthy as a horse—as if he had never been sick! She checked the chart to make sure it was really him, then approached him and asked what he thought he was doing. He responded calmly in a mild tone that he was going on a trip to a special place. Then Cindy unexpectedly rounded the corner and entered the room. His demeanor changed immediately. He pointed his finger at her and cried out fiercely in an uncanny, raspy voice, 'I know who you are—you're one of those followers of Christ—I will not be taken!'

"Then without warning the electricity in the room went crazy. Sparks flew out of the receptacles, the lights went off, his monitoring devices all peaked simultaneously. Cindy and the other girl both saw his body parts pass through solids—his arm passed right through the mattress and came out under the bed! Then he went into some kind of seizure, where—according to Cindy—he bounded off the bed and began beating both of them with his bare fists. They screamed for help, and just as two orderlies appeared in the doorway, he scrambled to his feet, bolted to the window, and jumped to his death. He never even looked back."

Douglas held the phone at arm's length and shook his head for several seconds. He couldn't believe what he was hearing. "That sounds like the work of the *Shedim* for sure. Possessing, controlling, performing supernatural feats—until finally the subject yields totally in death."

"Using drugs as a channel to reach his soul, the entity took residency, remaining calm, concealed, and projecting a false reality—his recovery, until..."

Douglas finished the sentence. "...Until your daughter-in-law, Cindy came in, then it reacted violently."

"The presence of the Holy Spirit in her triggered the response," Lane asserted.

"Right. It's apparent that the *Shedim* have penetrated many drug users. Do you think those events are representative of the entire world?"

Lane paused and then made a calculated assumption. "I don't have many reports just yet, it's all too new right now, but yes, I would speculate the infiltration is worldwide."

"Just the beginning of sorrows," Douglas lamented.

"I'm afraid the world is in for some heavy chastisement," Lane concluded.

"We'll leave that in God's hands for now," Douglas said with a sigh. "So what do you suggest *we* do next?"

"Look, David, both you and Cohen did the right thing by appealing to the authority there in Israel; the Knesset and Prime Minister Rubin. Unfortunately, Kavidas must have gotten to him first, so you have no other alternative but to go to plan B."

"What's that?" Douglas asked curiously.

"You need to go to the people! Go public and expose Kavidas for who he really is!"

Douglas's spirit testified that Lane's answer was correct. He and Cohen would mount a crusade and attack Kavidas on the very grounds he hoped one day to conquer, Israel. "You're right, Matthew, we will formulate a plan and go to the people."

They said their goodbyes and Douglas ended the call.

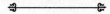

It was an unlikely place for a strategy meeting, but with the high influx of tourists and the multitude of cavernous rooms, the Church of the Holy Sepulcher provided a secure environment for Douglas and Cohen to organize a plan.

Considered to be one of the most sacred places of Christianity, the Church of the Holy Sepulcher stood over Golgotha, the place of the Crucifixion and the tomb where the body of Christ was laid. Since its construction in A.D. 324 the church stood almost in the center of the walled city. Eleven years after the Crucifixion, Golgotha was included within the perimeter of the city by a new wall built in the year A.D. 44 by Herod Agrippa.

In A.D. 135 Hadrian, wanting to weed out all evidence of the Jewish religion and the Christian religion as a Jewish sect, completely destroyed Calvary and the tomb of Jesus by building a Roman temple dedicated to the god Jupiter. This act had the opposite effect; instead of desecrating the place, the temple actually marked the site and preserved it until its triumphant discovery two centuries later by Constantine. Accordingly, in A.D. 326, Hadrian's temple was demolished by Queen Helena, and the ruins of Calvary and the tomb were found intact as described in the Gospel reports.

Constantine, under the direction of his mother, Helena, built a magnificent church over the ruins. The grandiose monument was destroyed in A.D. 614 by the Persians, rebuilt on a smaller scale by Abbot Modestos, and later destroyed by the Khalif Hakem in A.D. 1009. The destruction of the church was the primary reason for the Crusades. In A.D. 1048 the church was restored by Constantine Monomochus, and in 1149 A.D. the Crusaders, after the conquest of Jerusalem, erected the church that was still standing in the twenty-first century in much of its original architecture.

Douglas led his small troop down the stone staircase to an antechamber located below the main sanctuary, to a place where the Jewish tombs were located. Not often frequented by sightseers and travelers, the site provided an ideal location away from the threat of inquiring eyes and ears.

"The first item on the agenda," Douglas began as the others sat atop the sarcophagi set out in rows in the ancient cave, "is to decide *where* are we going to go public with the UT? The second is *when*."

"Rosh Hashanah is next week. The New Year would be a perfect time to cleanse the earth of Kavidas," Leah suggested enthusiastically. Rosh Hashanah ushered in a period of ten days of awe, culminating in Yom Kippur. It was also called the Day of Remembrance; tradition said the world was born on Rosh Hashanah. It was celebrated with the blowing of the ram's horn, the shofar, to call the Jewish people to pray for peace and tranquility for all mankind.

Douglas pointed to Leah. "Perfect. We will use the backdrop of the High Holy Day to arrest every Jewish person's attention."

Kathy raised her hand and pointed up. "What about just going upstairs? I mean this church is like a magnet, drawing hundreds of tourists every day. I think it meets our criteria."

Douglas wagged his head. "Good suggestion, babe, but I don't think it will give us the exposure we really need, especially for the Jewish population. Most of the visitors to the church will be tourists, and probably, Gentile Christians."

"So you're saying you want to make this a show, right?" Cohen said impulsively.

"I believe we will encounter great opposition, so we want maximum coverage for the little bit of time that we will have. Every minute will count, so we need to be in a place that is highly publicized and very crowded with every ethnic and religious mix out there. This will facilitate our exit, our escape."

Suddenly everyone traded looks. The solution as to *where* hit everybody all at once. "I think we all know the place that qualifies..." Cohen's voice vibrated with feeling as he surveyed their faces. "The Wall—the last vestige of Jewish heritage!"

Leah nodded, "David hit it! We need to go to the Wall with this." The others nodded their heads in agreement.

"Praise the Lord," Douglas said with a broad smile, "we're of one accord."

For the next hour, Douglas and Cohen hammered out the details of the plan while Leah, Kathy, and the three children prayed earnestly for God's guidance and protection.

At exactly 9:30 the following morning, the phone rang at the editor's desk of the *Jerusalem Post*. "This is a spokesperson for Project Megiddo," the caller announced. "There is going to be a vitally important meeting next week at the Wailing Wall at sunset on the eve of Rosh Hashanah. It is a meeting that will change the course of history. Be there!" As soon as the line went dead the editor immediately checked with the paper's security officer, who advised that the call had been recorded, but the brief message could not be traced. The editor then picked up the phone to call the General Security Services (Shin Bet), the counterintelligence branch of the Mossad in Nablus, to alert them of a possible threat to national defense.

At 9:35 a.m., the caller placed another call, to Chief Rabbi Ariel Getzen, the director of all holy places in Israel. The aged rabbi answered the phone in the spirit of the upcoming holiday, "l'Shanah Tovah!"

Cohen recognized the greeting and replied, "Happy New Year to you too, rabbi." He cleared his throat and hastily added in a disguised tone, "This is the voice of Project Megiddo who will unmask Satan's messiah, the antichrist, at the Western Wall on the start of Rosh Hashanah! Shalom!"

"Who is this?!" Rabbi Getzen yelled into the phone, but the caller had hung up. The learned cleric deliberated his response to the message for several moments, then called the police. His next call was to his board of directors to call them in for an emergency meeting.

Douglas bent over two out of three fingers he was holding up as Cohen keyed in the next number. It was to the director of the Israeli Antiquities Authority. "Dr. Ben-Tor," Cohen said in a falsetto voice, "this is the voice of liberation for all Israel; the voice of Project Megiddo! You and your constituents must be at the Wall on the eve of Rosh Hashanah because a startling discovery will be revealed! A discovery that will alter the course of the future!" The phone went dead.

Now it was Douglas's turn.

Douglas keyed in the international telephone number, then waited several seconds for the various satellite and computer connections to reconcile. "MASTERLINK Corporate Headquarters," the operator at 1800 Stratonos, Athens, announced in Hebrew. The computer telephone system had immediately identified the city of origin.

Douglas could speak fluent Hebrew. "This is the voice of Project Megiddo in Jerusalem with an important message for Gregory A. Kavidas. Tell him that his true identity will be exposed on national TV next week here in Jerusalem." He pressed the END button on his phone, then turned to Cohen and said trenchantly, "The fuse to the dynamite has been lit."

Cohen smiled, then raised his fist in the air in a victory gesture as their ladies exchanged worried glances.

Stein stood in his hotel room looking out over the old city section of Jerusalem when his cell phone beeped. He read the number off the LCD and raised an eyebrow. "Hello, Gregory," he answered. A pause ensued. "Gregory?" Somehow Stein sensed that trouble was brewing.

"Mort, why didn't you inform me of the disturbance over there at the Wall?"

Stein shrugged his shoulders and answered, "I'm not aware of any. What kind of disturbance?" Kavidas advised him of the telephone call.

"This thing must be so fresh, that nobody knows about it yet," Stein temporized aloud over the phone.

"I'm concerned about this, so I've booked a flight to Jerusalem; I'm arriving tomorrow morning. By the time I get there, I want you to have a complete rundown on this *Wall* thing so that we are prepared to meet this confrontation head on. Clear?"

Stein could read Kavidas' escalating anxiety level across the telephone lines as if he were talking to him face-to-face. "Clear." Stein heard the secure line click off.

The TV room at the Beit Bernstein youth hostel on Keren ha Yessod Street in Jerusalem, with its black and white TV and two soiled sofas, was nothing more than a room to flop in. Douglas remarked, however, that the security was top-notch; nobody would think of looking for them in such a hole.

Douglas and Cohen agreed that there would be greater security in numbers—meaning that the more attention they received, the better their chances of credibility and survival. Historically speaking, the newspapers could not be trusted when it came to Christian truth, and once the media designated Project Megiddo to be of a Christian nature, they would slant their journalism accordingly. Therefore it was imperative that they take to the streets and generate their own advertising of the upcoming event.

"What we will need, ladies," Douglas instructed both Leah and Kathy, "is for you to get several thousand handbills and various posters printed and begin to distribute them throughout the city. Have the children slip a leaflet under the wiper of as many parked cars as you can find. Every passerby you meet on the sidewalk should receive a flyer! Go to the shopping centers and post the placards in the windows. We want to inundate the population with the news that something spectacular is about to happen!"

The fervor was mounting in the group. "It's like some kind of showdown at the O.K. Corral," Kathy quipped.

Douglas chortled then said, "Sort of, but these stakes are much higher. We're not just fighting for what's right, but for the survival of the whole planet."

They fell silent for a moment, then prayed for protection before setting out on their assignments.

Stein's exhaustive intelligence gathering network quickly advised him that Douglas and Cohen were behind the meeting at the Wall. *They will not survive this, for I will smash their crusade and grind them to powder*, Stein said in his heart as he gazed into his bathroom mirror. *This is the last time we will meet!* Yes, it would be a battle of sorts: good vs. evil; Kavidas and Stein vs. Douglas and Cohen; God vs. Satan. *God will ultimately win*, Stein reminded himself, *but the way I read Scripture, that time is still a long way off.*

Chief Rabbi Getzen, considered the spokesman for the religious community in Jerusalem, walked into the Knesset building and demanded an audience with the prime minister. Immediate recognition of one of Israel's hallowed dignitaries allowed Getzen rapid entrance into Rubin's office.

Rubin payed obeisance to the holy man, then sat at his desk and toyed with a file as Getzen pulled up a chair. "Mr. Prime Minister," Getzen began, "my sources tell me that the city is in a state of near hysteria over this 'Wall' thing, and that does not take into consideration the impact it has had on my orthodoxy. To think that our people could be incited by some pranksters attempting to unmask a *mythical* person is preposterous!" He paused to clear his throat and added, "May I ask what is being done by the government?"

Rubin nodded in respect to the rabbi and in a conciliatory tone advised, "Rabbi Getzen, I have been informed by the General Security Services that the *Jerusalem Post* along with the IAA have been notified of this event..." he groped for words, "...or show, if you will—and that it has risen to national proportions. Apart from alerting the media, the so called 'Project Megiddo' people have resorted to advertising by circulating handbills and other leaflets announcing the event. They're all over the place! Knowledge of the event has become widespread, and the TV networks have picked up on it as a media carnival. It has become a national security problem. That of course means that the military will be there on Rosh Hashanah to ensure that the safety of all our people will not be compromised."

Getzen raised his eyebrows and nodded in relief. "Any idea as to who these people in 'Project Megiddo' are?"

Rubin tapped the file on his desk labeled "Project Megiddo" in which were several documents and pictures of Douglas and Cohen, et. al. His meeting with them was still very fresh in his mind. "As a matter of fact we do," he asserted, "but we cannot reveal any names until the GSS brings us positive proof of their intentions."

Getzen was known for his intuitiveness. He stood up and slowly walked around his chair twice, then gazed into Rubin's eyes. "What are they bringing with them? I mean, what could they possibly have that could generate this kind of *hoopla*, if you'll pardon the American expression."

Rubin smiled mirthlessly. "We're not sure yet, but the GSS is concerned that it could be some form of propaganda about the Temple; you know that's a political football." He lied to protect himself, for he could never admit to knowing about the Urim and Thummim in front of a learned rabbi and not be called a fool.

"That's it?" Getzen scratched his head. "What about the part about the antichrist?"

"Well, they might make some connection between some contemporary or future political figure and the Christian character, the antichrist." He shook his head slowly. "It wouldn't be the first time that's happened."

"Hmm, yes," Getzen said as he calculated Rubin's response, "I suppose that's possible." He shrugged his shoulders and added, "So you don't think there's anything to be concerned about?"

Rubin gave him a dismissive wave of the hand. "No, I do not." With that he stood up and walked to Getzen and said with a luminous smile, "Rabbi, the time has come for us to form a committee to begin discussions on the rebuilding of the Temple. Now that the Muslim mosque is not operating because of the bombing, I believe we can rekindle hope in the people of Israel by making plans to bring about the realization of every rabbi's and Jewish person's dream, the Temple." Calculatingly, he didn't tell him that MASTERLINK had secretly donated an additional 15 million dollars toward the rebuilding project to curry favor with Israel.

Rabbi Getzen's heart began to race in anticipation of the prospect. To think that he would be the ruling rabbi when the Temple reconstruction began would be the crowning glory to his career. "What will become of the Dome?"

Rubin knew there was ample room on the Mount to rebuild the Temple, but that Jewish law prohibited construction while another religious monument occupied the space. "The bombing has damaged the foundation of the mosque; accordingly, we have suggested to the Arab community that they move their building to another holy site."

"And they agreed?" Getzen asked.

"Well, let's say they're considering it. This might not happen for a year or two, but we need to begin preparations for the contingency."

"Marvelous!" The thought of the Temple brought tears to Getzen's eyes. *Messiah will come when the Temple is operating!* He walked to the door with his fears allayed and said his goodbye.

Neither Rubin nor Getzen realized their discussion had such prophetic implications.

Being of a kindred spirit, Stein recognized Kavidas' presence the moment he set foot in his hotel room. When he opened the door, his mouth dropped open in shock. The man before him had undergone a considerable physical transformation. His characteristic Greek facial features and complexion—sharp and olive tinted—were now blunt and fairer. He no longer had the commanding profile of a spiritual leader, nor the assuring glow of an international director. He looked like any ordinary Israeli working in an office in downtown Tel Aviv. "You're in disguise?" *Yes, we've come to the point where our operations must be covert until the appointed time*, Stein reminded himself. Yes, masquerade, subterfuge, and deception would be their trademarks. By design, he would resume his identity as Gregory A. Kavidas of the EEC after he settled the blasted distraction at the Wall.

"My political position must be protected," Kavidas said succinctly and moved immediately to the sitting room of Stein's suite.

Stein said nothing until they both sat down. "I've been thinking..." he began then unwittingly paused and loosened his shirt collar, "...we could get hurt at the Wall."

Kavidas nodded. "I know that. That's why I've come."

Serious planning was needed in order to ensure against any interruption in their scheme.

Time to move again.

The hot air was palpable with what seemed like a solid presence. The glare from the burning sun, too, made the sunglass-wearing travelers feel like screwing up their eyes painfully. The southern part of the Dead Sea had partly dried up due to the lack of seasonal rainfall, leaving small scattered pools amidst the salt formations dotting the primordial seascape.

Once again, Leah found herself gazing out the car window as the vehicle sped the group to Ein Gedi, a lush oasis on the western side of the ancient sea, 25 miles southeast of Jerusalem. Here they would hide out until the confrontation.

Weary of traveling, Cohen drove the car over to King David's Spring and stopped for refreshments. A popular site for hiking and bathing that led up to a beautiful waterfall, David's Spring was fringed in ferns. Tradition said David had hid there from Saul during one of the king's maniacal rages. According to the biblical account, David went into the very cave where Saul was sleeping and, as Saul slept, David cut off a piece of the king's robe to prove that he could have killed him. Later, David regretted the act as being tantamount to treason.

The greenery crept up the steep cliffs beside the water springs, providing a scenic backdrop for the large variety of birds and animals that frequented the area. Gazelles, ibex, oryx, foxes, jackals, and leopards were common sojourners. Both couples walked silently along the nature paths for over an hour before continuing on to the guest house.

Adjacent to the Kibbutz Ein Gedi, camping site, youth hostel, and resturant were a guest house and spa for bathing in the Dead Sea water and nearby sulphur springs. The Douglases' group was welcomed without question.

'You really think we were in danger in Jerusalem?" Leah asked Douglas in a whisper as they sat down for dinner.

"Very much so," he replied in a low octave as the rest of them huddled together to hear his response. "Now that we've made our intentions known—we're going to be hunted. We are all targets. Fortunately, there have been no pictures of us, so no one knows what we look like." He tapped his cell phone attached to his belt, then pointed up and added, "They can triangulate on us by satellite, so from the time we left Jerusalem, we are *incommunicado*, so to speak."

"We'll stay here until the big day?" Douglas's eldest son, Alan, asked.

Douglas scanned the blank faces of his two other children and nodded.

"Yes!" they all said in unison. The prospect of finding refuge at a youth hostel with a spa was appealing.

Douglas pointed to his mouth and said, "We must keep a low profile, and speak to no one. Understood?"

They all nodded their heads gloomily.

CHAPTER

19

The Wailing Wall

Douglas led the way into the Temple Mount area through Zion Gate, located at the southern end of the old city. It was early morning on the eve of Rosh Hashanah, the festival of trumpets.

He paused momentarily inside the narrow doorway and wiggled his fingers in the bullet holes that served as a constant reminder of the war in 1948. The rest of the group exchanged glances at his silent commentary on the ever-present hostility in Israel. He waved them into the city.

Once inside the enclosing walls built by the Ottoman emperor Suliman in A.D. 1537, the group quickly and stealthily moved into the Chabad onto Ha Shalshelet, which connected to Jaffa Gate, the main passage into the holy site. The Western Wall stood only four hundred meters from the Jaffa Gate. From there they walked to a yeshiva on El-Wad, adjacent to the Wall. They sat down on the lawn of the yeshiva dressed as Jewish students with their prayer shawls and yarmulkes on. They were now in place until sunset.

The sun climbed above the Wall, casting sparkling light on the Tower of David, or Citadel, then continued until it bathed the courtyard of the Wall. The resplendent light glistened off the dew drops that dripped off the Wall, so that the Wall stood out as if a spotlight were shining on it. An hour later, the hot sun began baking the dust in the Kidron Valley, generating a warm, dry breeze that wafted over the city walls. The breeeze carried a refreshing scent that displaced the morning dampness.

"David, look!" Cohen said excitedly. He pointed to an Israeli Cable Network van with twin satellite dishes mounted on its roof moving slowly into position near the Wall. ICN fed news to the entire nation.

Douglas nodded, shook his head with a cynical look, and said, "The media will treat this like a circus. Prayerfully, we will come up on top."

Ben-Tor glanced down at his wristwatch as he drove by the Temple Mount on the way to the IAA office. He marveled that huge crowds were forming four hours before the much-publicized event and wondered what in the world could be the big attraction. Never once did he give thought to the possibility that it had anything to do with the Urim and Thummim. As a precaution, he would get to the meeting early.

Kavidas stood at Stein's hotel window glancing down at the bustling traffic below him. He shook his head in disgust, raised a fist toward Heaven, and glowered at Stein. "Why can't we find them?"

Stein shrugged his shoulders. For the past two hours they had prayed and petitioned their lord for illumination. This dilemma only fueled their concerns that they needed to find Douglas and Cohen and stop them before they went public. Finally, after a moment of deep contemplation, Stein replied, "There must be some kind of divine shield blocking us from locating them."

"I don't want to hear that, Mort!" Kavidas said as he crossed his arms over his chest. Stein detected an intolerant spirit emerging in Kavidas as he shifted in his chair. Kavidas bit his lip and added, "We don't want any surprises at the Wall…we must take steps to protect ourselves. We'll need reinforcements."

"But surely you're not worried about Douglas and Cohen and a few Christians at this point, are you? I mean, how can they hurt us?" Stein countered. "With our resources, control, and clout, we can virtually exterminate them in no time."

Kavidas starting pacing in front of Stein, then came to an abrupt halt. "This group is just the beginning. I foresee that they will band together to fight us on every front, starting with the Urim and Thummim, then onto MASTERLINK and everything it stands for—jeopardizing our grand plan unless they are stopped.

"They're getting organized. With a little momentum they could seriously weaken our position and require us to shift our emphasis. That distraction will delay our operation, and in turn will mean more souls will be lost to the other side." He renewed his pacing, then added, "Strength in numbers and unification of purpose can present a major threat to our overall strategy. I've seen this before. People like Douglas and Cohen become an army of resistors, digging and burrowing in. Making tunnels in the earth, fortifying storehouses, making ready to engage the enemy, gaining triumph by wearing their opponents down one soldier at a time over a long siege—like what happened at Masada, Vietnam, and Afghanistan. Their tactics sour and spoil the challenge of conquest."

Stein looked at Kavidas, and for a moment, saw weakness. "You do believe we can win, don't you?"

"Our victory," Kavidas temporized as he shot his eyes upward, "is contingent on time. The sooner we act within the time allotted, the better our chances of success will be. *Time* is our enemy while it is their ally, because in time our duplicity will be revealed, lessening our chances to win—and we're in this to win. So we are going to take steps to remedy this problem."

Nodding with a tight smile, Stein knew within himself that Kavidas towered above humanity in times like this. There were no obstacles he couldn't vault while drawing on the inexhaustible power infused in him from the moment of birth by the prince of darkness. Together Kavidas and Stein were unbeatable. Yet, a muscle jerked in Stein's left cheek as the realization set in that this meeting wasn't going to be just a battle but an all-out war.

It was late afternoon and the sun was dropping to the horizon signaling the end of day. A yellowish cast from the golden light of the sun permeated the environs, giving the vicinity a hallowed look. Douglas glanced overhead and calculated by the sun's position that it was approximately one hour before sunset. "Time to move to the staging area," he announced to the group.

They walked discreetly to the excavation area at the southern end of the Temple Mount where a right-angled stairway led directly to the Mount. The hazardous zone, riddled with crumbling archways and holes in the ground, kept all curiosity-seekers away and afforded them relative secrecy.

"Light off the UT," Douglas instructed Cohen. "We need to have God's assurance before we go into the lion's den."

Cohen shot a prayer to God, then pulled various garments along with the high priest's equipment out of the sack. He moved into the shade of one of the archways to dress. *It is such a great honor to wear these clothes. I wonder how many more times I will be allowed to wear them?*

"Look at Cohen!" Leah gulped. He had secretly taken the past seven days to hunt up all the clothes worn by the high priest. To his great delight, he had found the shoulder pieces, the golden crown, the girdle, and robes in a costume shop. Then he painstakingly assembled a makeshift breastplate, ephod, and mitre, or head-covering, thus completing the high priest's uniform.

Several tears appeared in the corner of Cohen's eye. *Lord, I am not worthy to wear this.*

"Look at his face!" Kathy exclaimed. He had inadvertently moved into the sunlight, and his face was radiant. "He reminds me of how Aaron the high priest must've looked when presenting the sin offering in the Holy of Holies!" The women began to cry.

"Stay in the shade so nobody sees us!" Douglas warned. They all backed into the archway out of sight as Cohen adjusted the priestly outfit in final preparation for the presentation. Within minutes they were all crouched in a corner as Cohen readied himself to petition the Lord. "Heavenly Father," Douglas prayed aloud as they all bowed their heads, "we ask at this time for Your divine protection and guidance as we place ourselves in Your hands. Enable us to bring out the truth that Kavidas and Stein are evil agents disguised as angels of light, determined to enslave humanity. Allow Your Spirit to emerge victoriously. We pray this in Jesus' name."

"Amen," they said in unison.

Douglas motioned to Cohen, who stood up and put on the mitre, then pulled the Urim and Thummim from a linen bag inside the breastplate pocket. He kneeled down on the ground to set the gems in their proper order in his lap. Placing the blue sapphire on top, the purple amethyst in the middle and the scarlet jasper on the bottom, he cried out, "O Lord God of Israel, Your servant must come up against the evil forces of Kavidas and Stein. Will they surrender before You?" If yes, give Urim; if no give Thummim."

The scarlet stone designating *no* lit up.

"Uh-oh," Leah said through a muffled cough.

Douglas patted her shoulder, shook his head, and whispered, "Shush." He then nodded to Cohen to ask God's answering device more questions.

"Will the citizens of Israel and the world believe us when we unmask him?"

Everyone exchanged glances then held hands as they awaited the answer.

The scarlet stone lit up again.

"Oh God!" Kathy said as her mind seized up in panic. "We're going to be killed—"

Douglas squeezed her hand in quiet assurance. "God is in control," he said just above a whisper, to remind everyone of His sovereignty.

"Will we be protected?" Cohen asked with marginal confidence as he glanced at Kathy.

The blue sapphire illuminated brightly. A wave of relief washed over them.

Kathy tugged on Douglas's hand and asked, "So what does this mean?"

Douglas looked up at Cohen, boldly called upon his faith, and said, "I believe it means that we are going to be mightily used of the Lord today."

Cohen quickly picked up on Douglas's attempt to console the group and to allay their fears. "Whatever the outcome, we know that God will be honored."

They prayed collectively one more time, then left for the Wall.

Dr. Ben-Tor could sense the energy in the crowds as he looked down on the Wall from his lookout above the courtyard. His position in the IAA bought him clearance designated for security personnel only. In a sweeping survey he noticed the Mossad strategically stationed in four locations: two squads were standing atop the Wall in defense posture, scanning the crowds. The other two squads were walking amidst the swarms of people—one in the men's sector and one in the woman's sector. By Ben-Tor's estimate, at least eight thousand persons were in the courtyard. *Security will be very difficult to manage*, he said to himself.

On the elevated visitors ramp, adjacent to the Wall, he noticed an ICN cameraman with his videocam panning the onlookers as they continued to fill the courtyard. The other cameraman stood in the corner of the Wall, waiting for a signal to start filming. To the rear of the compound, the satellite dish on the ICN van was fully extended, transmitting the event as it unfolded to the network satellite 57 miles above their heads.

At the military police booth just outside the courtyard, Ben-Tor saw over 45 army persons, armed with automatic weapons, waiting for the command to patrol the entire compound. "My God," he muttered, "this looks like the makings of a 1-Alpha battle zone." He reached for his field glasses and began to scan the crowds when suddenly his eyes fixed on a face emerging from the multitudes near the Wall. He recognized her through her disguise. "Leah?" he mouthed in utter disbelief. Then he labored to identify a familiar man walking just ahead of her dressed as a high priest. He gulped when he realized it was the man he had met at Krasnoff's hospital bedside, Nathan Cohen. "What the hell...?" he mumbled. Following directly behind Cohen was another American man, a woman and three children. They were apparently working their way up toward the Wall as well. "This is going to be crazy!" He turned on his heel and quickly ran to the staircase leading down to the courtyard. He had a feeling that he would be desperately needed.

"There's Stein!" Douglas yelled aloud when the man abruptly appeared near the Wall ahead of them. Stein was searching the crowds with a malevolent glare.

"He's looking for us," Leah announced gravely.

Douglas turned around and threw a prayer shawl over Cohen's outfit, then motioned with his hand. "Nice and slow. Mingle in the crowds so you won't stand out. When we reach the dividing fence for the men and women, we'll go our separate ways to the Wall."

Stein stood on his tiptoes and pivoted a full circle. *No sign of them.* He checked his wristwatch. *They must be here by now.* After a leering glance he nodded at Kavidas who stood with a prayer shawl over his head, dahvening at the Wall some 40 feet away from him.

Kavidas acknowledged the look then returned to his prayer posture and whispered to himself, "You needn't be concerned, Mort— I'm in control."

A lone rabbi standing next to the Wall blew the shofar to announce the start of the holy day. The crowd fell silent in anticipation as the Jewish men bowed down before the Wall in supplication.

Suddenly out of the evening shadows, Cohen came to a halt and stood erect in the middle of the crowd. He took off the prayer shawl and put the mitre on his head.

"Look! There's a high priest!" a man yelled out. Thousands of men turned in amazement to see Cohen, then began running toward him in a frenzy as he made his way to the Wall.

The realization of Cohen's presence crashed in on Stein. He shot a look toward Kavidas, who in turn motioned for him to close in on Cohen.

Cohen reached the Wall and turned to face the pressing crowds. His insides were churning. He reached for Douglas's hand for assurance, then they raised their hands in the air collectively and shouted, "Hear O Israel, the Lord our God is One!"

A great hush came over the crowd when they heard the national invocation.

Across in the woman's section, two voices cried out in song, singing the hymn "Redeemed." Douglas smiled when he recognized Kathy's and Leah's voices amidst the Jewish women.

The Mossad pushed their way through the assemblage and began cordoning off the area, waiting for instructions. The military police went on immediate alert and began pushing the crowds to the side as the GSS director, Ben-Tor, Chief Rabbi Getzen, and other officials made their way through the crowds toward them.

Stein suddenly stepped out of the throng and stood directly in front of Cohen. Recognizing him immediately, Cohen called upon God for strength.

"Stand back!" Douglas commanded Stein.

Stein clenched his fists and snarled, "You have no power over me!"

Cohen and Douglas traded a look, agreeing in silent prayer that they needed divine help—immediately. "IN THE NAME OF YESHUA, THE LORD, I COMMAND YOU TO STAND BACK!" Douglas cried out.

Stein crumpled to the ground as his legs gave out from under him. *At the name of Jesus, every knee shall bow.* "Gregory!" he yelled out. "Help!"

Cohen and Douglas heard his plea, then looked around for signs of Kavidas. Seeing only the ICN cameras filming them, they focused on arresting the world's attention. "Listen, people of Israel, to God's word!" Douglas shouted. He tapped Cohen on the shoulder.

Cohen blinked in recognition then pulled the Urim and Thummim from the breast pocket, displaying them in the palms of his hands.

The crowd backed off in reflexive alarm as the stones began to illuminate.

"Do not be afraid!" Douglas cried out as he pointed to the gems. "The voice of God will reveal the truth!"

Ben-Tor and the other officials stopped in their tracks, gaping at Cohen as the drama unfolded.

Stein jumped up and lunged for the stones to silence them, but Douglas quickly made a fist and swung at him, hitting instead an unseen barrier that surrounded Stein. "Oh my God!" Douglas gulped as he massaged his hand. "There's some kind of protective shield around him." *I must call upon the name of the Lord.*

Several Mossad commandos jumped Douglas, wrestling him to the ground as Stein grabbed Cohen's arm. Cohen shook him off. *I may get only one chance to ask a question, so I better make it good.* He yelled out, "If Gregory A. Kavidas and Mortimer Stein are Satan's messiah and false prophet who will lead the world to destruction, say yes, give Urim—turn blue; if not, give Thummim—turn scarlet!"

Stein, along with the crowd, stood frozen in time, gawking at the stones.

Standing alone in the far corner, Kavidas simultaneously raised his right hand above the heads of the crowds and held it there as he closed his eyes to concentrate and bring to bear all the power imbued upon him from Satan.

Douglas frantically maneuvered himself to his feet, but the Mossad held him firmly as he gazed at the blue sapphire radiating brightly in Cohen's hand. "YES!" he bellowed. "See, God has answered YES! Kavidas is the antichrist!"

But the people saw something different. They saw the red jasper light up.

"Something's wrong!" Cohen screamed to Douglas as he watched the onlookers' faces. "The people are not seeing as we do!"

Douglas tried in vain to free his hands from his captors as he surveyed the crowd. "They've placed a blanket of blindness over them!" he suddenly realized aloud. "They're using mass hypnosis on them!" Even the journalists' cameras saw the Urim and Thummim turn red.

Cohen dropped his arms to his sides and slumped his shoulders. "This can't be!" he exclaimed. "We're losing them!" A surge of despair began to rise within him until he remembered God's promise not to leave him or forsake him. He gazed up at the top of the Wall and saw what looked like hundreds of men, not ordinary men, but angelic beings with drawn swords standing ready to fight. Their swords were flaming and left fiery trails as they waved them in the air in expectation of combat. "David!" Cohen gulped. "Look at the top of the Wall—there are angels up there!" He quickly asked God to open Douglas's eyes so that he too could see them.

Douglas peered at the Wall and saw the celestial warriors looking down and watching them. His spirit began to rejoice then quickly stopped. His mind seized up in panic as he cast his eyes on a man who kept staring at him. The man's eyes were piercing and controlling— the eyes of wickedness and evil. He recognized the eyes as the feeling of oppression around him became almost palpable. "Cohen," he gasped while forcefully pulling away from the Mossad guards, "there's Kavidas over there at the Wall! He's controlling everything!" Once free, he stood, pointing toward Kavidas.

Cohen rotated in place and glared at the man. The face was different, but the eyes were the same. *Yes, it is him!* his spirit testified.

But Kavidas was not alone. "David, he has help," Cohen realized with a shiver. "Look around him."

Douglas squinted in Kavidas' direction and saw that what he had thought were hundreds of Jewish men congregating, were in fact, fallen angels disguised as men—the *Shedim*—in camouflage. Their eyes, sunken and darkened from countless centuries in the pit, betrayed them. Douglas quickly identified their pernicious leers and fiendish grins. "Those who are with us are more and mightier than those who are with them!" he yelled out.

"Hold it right there!" the GSS captain commanded as he signaled his men to seize Cohen and Douglas. The Mossad willingly released them into their custody.

"Mr. Cohen," Cohen heard from behind, "what in the world do you think you're doing dressed up in that outfit? Have you taken leave of your senses?"

Cohen turned to see Dr. Ben-Tor and Rabbi Getzen coming up alongside the GSS captain. Ben-Tor stopped in front of Cohen and began examining his priestly garb, while Rabbi Getzen started to remove the breastplate. The GSS captain reached to take the stones from Cohen's hands. "We can have you arrested for trespassing, disturbing the peace, and desecrating a sacred site as well," Rabbi Getzen warned.

Suddenly Douglas jumped in front of them all in full fury. "What about him!?" he hollered in Ben-Tor's face as he pointed to Stein.

Stein stood there smiling. *Fools!*

"What *about* him?" Ben-Tor replied calmly as he motioned for the GSS to push the crowds back. "He hasn't done anything wrong." He nodded to Stein and asked, "You okay?"

With a raised hand, Stein replied, "I'll be fine as soon as they return my property." He pulled a document from his jacket pocket and handed it to the GSS official. The document, on an official IAA letterhead and signed by Rehavam Krasnoff, verified ownership of the ancient artifacts. Mortimer Stein was the rightful owner.

The crowd began to murmur as the GSS official handed the document to Ben-Tor and Rabbi Getzen for authentication. Bewildered, Ben-Tor scratched his head as he read the registered document showing that Stein had purchased the high priest's equipment from a Bedouin who had unearthed them in the Dead Sea area the prior year. The document was a bonafide legal contract.

The skin on the back of Cohen's neck began to crawl, followed by a wave of fear. He remembered that the Urim and Thummim had warned Douglas and him of the outcome. They had to escape. He shot a look at Douglas, who winked at him.

Without warning Cohen and Douglas grabbed the breastplate and the stones, then jerked themselves free and leaped into the crowds. The GSS pulled their weapons out and pointed them at the men, but Ben-Tor clamored to their defense. "Put away your guns!" he yelled as the crowd panicked and scrambled for safety, leaving Cohen and Douglas in the open.

Cohen seized the moment. He looked up at the angelic host and cried out, "Blind them!"

All at once the heavenly messengers cracked to attention with their swords pointed at the *Shedim*. From the tips of their swords came a barrage of fiery bolts that shot out and targeted the eyes of the *Shedim*, instantly blinding them. They all squealed in torment as the light around them was suddenly extinguished. Some dropped to the ground, groveling on the concrete, while others held their eyes and swayed aimlessly as they sought something solid to hold onto. Within minutes they meandered helplessly out of the courtyard.

"Try again!" Douglas shouted to Cohen. "Fire up the UT again!"

Cohen's mind locked up in terror, but he forced his tongue to move as he pointed to the shrouded man by the Wall. "If Gregory A.

Kavidas and Mortimer Stein are the antichrist and false prophet who are deceiving these people, say yes, give Urim—turn blue; if not, give Thummim—turn scarlet!" With that he held the three stones up in the air for all to see.

The blue sapphire shone radiantly, but the master of deception—the prince of this world—the angel of light, working through Kavidas—manipulated the minds of the people.

"You see, they're crazy—even insane!" Stein exclaimed as the red stone blazed brightly, signifying no.

"Boo!" the crowds shouted at Cohen as they dispersed. "Take him away!"

Cohen gave Stein a lethal glance and shook his head. "It's no use," he said in disgust to Douglas. "They put a spell over the people to confound them! Sure, we'll win the war, but they have won this battle."

The GSS official walked Cohen and Douglas out of the court-yard, away from the crowds, then stripped Cohen of his priestly gar-ments and gave them to Ben-Tor. The breastplate along with the Urim and Thummim were ceremoniously placed in Stein's hands. Stein's heart welled up with triumph as he thanked the officials and walked away with the prize.

The Jewish-looking man who had orchestrated Stein's victory from a distance smiled broadly and nodded in exultation. They would meet in Athens tomorrow.

Dr. Ben-Tor called Rabbi Getzen, the GSS official, and the Mossad area director into a corner for a conference as guards watched Cohen and Douglas. In 15 minutes the decision to release them in their own recognizance was made, based on Ben-Tor's recommendation.

Cohen and Douglas walked out of the courtyard defeated.

CHAPTER

20

Athens

Soft drizzle fell upon the archeological complex of the famed Roman Agora, Tower of the Winds, and the Library of Hadrian, located just north of the Acropolis. It was Kavidas' favorite place to celebrate his victories. He had much in common with Emperor Hadrian. The first century ruler had beautified Athens and restored many of the ruined cities; Kavidas' family wealth and philanthropy continued to enhance the city. But in Isreal, Hadrian had banned Jews from entering Jerusalem except on one day a year and also had prohibited the rite of circumcision. The Jews, led by Simon bar Kokhba, rebelled against Hadrian's authority, defeated the Romans, and captured Jerusalem and many other towns. The Romans regrouped and crushed the Jewish insurrection, killing bar Kokhba at Bethar near Caesarea, ending the Jewish war of freedom. Hadrian then returned to Rome and ordered the holy city of Jerusalem plowed under and a new city, the pagan Aelia Capitolina, built in its place. These actions led to the final dispersion of the Jews from their homeland; they did not again have a state governed by themselves until the establishment of Israel as a state in 1948. In this regard, Kavidas would emulate Hadrian's victories. His design was always to destroy Israel and establish his reign.

In front of the wrought iron fence surrounding the ruins of the Tower of the Winds, Stein held an umbrella over both their heads as Kavidas unwrapped the canvas satchel used to transport the breastplate and the Urim and Thummim from Jerusalem. Kavidas held the articles up in the air and triumphantly cried out to God in the heavens, "You have been humiliated!" Then in mock adoration, he bowed down and added the invective, "Yes, I know it is but for a season, yet for this season we shall prevail and conquer!"

Stein stood next to Kavidas in awe at his companion's utter defiance, then reverently took the breastplate and the gems from Kavidas' hands to hold them. He swallowed hard and asked, "What shall I do with them?"

Knowing full well from the beginning that the *lights of God* would operate only in Cohen's hands, Kavidas shrugged his shoulders and said with a snort, "They have served their purpose for the other side in a lame attempt to disclose our mission. They are worthless now, so sell them for their intrinsic value and place the money in the account designated for our contribution toward the rebuilding of the Temple. We'll be using those funds soon."

Stein understood his intentions perfectly. The predestined plan, formulated by God from the beginning of time, dictated their every move. Kavidas would use his political position with the EEC to ascend to world prominence where he would embrace Israel—his ultimate target, because it was the nation that had brought forth Jesus the Messiah—with the continued promise of military and financial support to bolster its national security. This act of endearment would cement the relationship between Kavidas and Rubin. First the Temple would be rebuilt according to the prescribed prophecy, then the West would turn up their noses to Israel in favor of the petrol-rich Arab countries. Then the Arab bloc nations, under the leadership of the Russian militarists, would invade Israel. Rubin would call upon Kavidas to come to his nation's rescue. Triumphantly, Kavidas would return to Israel as the conquering savior—their messiah—the false messiah who would lead the nation to destruction at Armageddon.

Stein bounced the bag containing the precious stones in his hand several times, adding a certain pathos to the scene. In his mind the *lights of God* had suddenly lost their value. "Fine, I'll dispose of them," he said after a moment of contemplation.

Kavidas grabbed his arm. "We're not finished with them yet."

"We're not?" he replied, looking at the bag.

"I'm talking about Douglas and Cohen."

Stein blinked several times. "What do you mean?"

"We must silence their voices," Kavidas said coldly. "They cannot verify anything now that we have their…" he paused to contemptuously flick his finger against the bag, "…'weapon,' but they can still hurt us. We must stop them."

Stein frowned and said, "But at the Wall it was obvious they have some kind of protection from God. We can't get to them."

A broad smirk appeared on Kavidas' face. "True, but we *can* get to their loved ones."

Joyous singing from the Douglas house at Kefar echoed off the nearby foothills on a glorious October morning. Gala trappings of olive tree boughs hung from the front porch and white gardenias adorned the outside railings. It was to be a happy time, the wedding of Nathan Cohen and Leah Krasnoff.

Inside the house, a white runner led to a beautifully embroidered wedding *huppah* that stood in the middle of the living room. To the right of the canopy was a small white table containing two cups of wine and a three-stemmed candelabrum needed for the ceremony. In the kitchen, hallway, and bedroom, turned into a makeshift den, fellow Christians and guests joined in the gaiety to add their blessing to the wedding celebration.

An hour later, the minister, David Douglas, pronounced Cohen and Leah husband and wife, to a resounding "Mazzal Tov" from their relatives and guests.

It was the happiest day of their lives, but it would last only a short while.

It was mid-afternoon by the time the wedding cake was served.

Weary from dancing and celebrating the blessed union of Cohen and Leah, the guests began looking for closure of the gala event. Douglas motioned for Cohen to meet with him privately while Leah changed out of her wedding gown into casual clothes. Plans to protect the ministry had to be made before the newlyweds departed for their honeymoon at Eilat, the resort area in southern Israel.

Douglas put his arm on Cohen's shoulder and escorted him to the outside porch. They sat down together on the hood of a car. "Put everything about Kavidas and Stein out of your mind for the next ten days," Douglas began with a smile, "and concentrate on relaxing and enjoying each other's company. You deserve that."

Cohen nodded in agreement, but his heart still ached over the encounter at the Wall. He jumped off the hood, stooped down to the ground, and doodled in the dirt. "I know that when Christ returns He will administer perfect justice," he began, "but what bothers me is how Kavidas and Stein get away with their evil exploits without society exacting due punishment for their crimes against humanity. They really should get it *now* and *later* at the Great White Throne judgment!"

"It's an imponderable of God, Nat," Douglas struggled to explain, "but a look at history may help us. Historically, we can use ancient

empires that were the enemies of Israel as an example. The Babylonian, Medio-Persian, Greek and Roman empires were all dismantled
by God after they served their purpose of chastening the Jewish nation. Likewise, the Arab countries that are persecuting Israel will be
dealt with in time—their punishment is yet future at Christ's second
advent. But hear this: All those who flaunt their sin in God's face may
think they're cheating justice by getting away with their crimes and
lies—and the public may even buy into their excuses and cover-ups—
but God will not be mocked. Whatever a man sows, he will reap.
God's justice will be served; you can count on it."

Cohen smiled. "Thanks for the reminder."

Douglas decided to postpone the planning session. "When you
come back we'll go over our strategy." Cohen, relieved, smiled again.

Leah walked out on the porch dressed in a cute dungaree outfit
and a baseball cap. She smiled at both of them and said succinctly,
"Time to go, Cohen."

Cohen stood up to leave and caught a glimpse of a familiar car
moving very slowly past the property line. He paused to take a hard
look at the car as his eyes opened in astonishment.

Leah turned toward his gaze. "What is it?"

"Oh, nothing, it's just that I thought I recognized someone in
that car."

Leah shrugged her shoulders, smiled and said, "Then we're off."

Cohen walked into the house to fetch his suitcase as Douglas trailed
behind. He caught up with him outside the bathroom. "I recognized
concern in your face back there," Douglas said. "Who was in the car?"

Cohen shook his head in disgust and momentarily closed his
eyes. "It was Stein."

The trans-desert trek through the Negev on the way to Israel's
famous southernmost resort community at Eilat brought opportuni-
ties for meditation. Anyone who drives from the populated central

part of Israel across the deserted plains of the Negev would think he was traveling to the end of the earth. Yet for Nathan Cohen, with his arm around his sleeping bride, the excursion through the barren wilderness brought events into focus. Now that the confrontation at the Wall was over, he needed to formulate his side of the plan to present to Douglas when they returned.

In his heart, God's Spirit testified that the reason the Urim and Thummim had indeed been found was to sound the alarm that the end-times were upon them. The confirmation of Kavidas and Stein as the antichrist and the false prophet, although concealed by them and subsequently rejected by the world, had to come from God. This being established, embattlements must be positioned. *We will amalgamate the underground group of Christians, the Kiononos, with us believing Jews into a formidable army against them. Yes!*

He thought about his dream and the hideous beast.

The Book of Revelation affirmed his dream. Conditions on earth would worsen exponentially in the days ahead. The world would follow after the beast, Satan's messiah, Kavidas, and drop to their nadir—where sexual perversion would reign as it had with the Canaanites before Joshua entered into the Promise Land. Men unwittingly having intercourse with the *Shedim* during cult orgies would produce monstrosities that would eclipse the antediluvian Nephilim. Wild beasts—probably rabid domestic animals incited by diseases brought on by bestiality—would roam and bring terror throughout the land. Demon worship would be rampant as the *Shedim*, disguised as beautiful people who flaunt gold and silver, would deceive many. Society would tolerate murder of humans, while the life of an animal would be venerated. Yet there would be no repentance. Man would show his propensity for depravity until God intervened once again.

Ahh! The 144 thousand! Yes, they will be God's servants who will assuage the onslaught of the wicked ones!

Snorkelers and windsurfers emerging from the Red Sea behind the Gateway hotel waved to the arriving Cohens as they entered the parking lot. Cohen grabbed Leah's hand and whisked her to the shoreline to witness the carnival-like environment. Off shore, amateur water skiers performed heroic feats while on the beach, sand castle builders looked on in amazement. Bikini watchers along with sun worshipers and tropical fish fanatics roamed the surf line in lazy strides as vendors meandered about peddling spicy food, cold beer, and trinkets.

"This is unbelievable!" Cohen marveled as his eyes scanned the horizon.

Leah noticed all the pleasure seekers partying on the beach and put her arm around his waist, wondering if his eyes caught the scantily clad women tourists. She turned and whispered in wonder, "Legalized hedonism!"

Cohen smiled at Leah and replied, "Let me get *you* out of here quickly!"

At midmorning, Leah munched on a bagel while Cohen enjoyed his scrambled eggs and rye toast. It was the start of a glorious day and a glorious relationship, one that God was sure to bless.

As they exchanged glances, Leah looked deeply into her husband's eyes with admiration and extended her arm across the table. He met her gaze as they connected hands momentarily. "Darling," Leah began, "I've been thinking about your dream and the outworking of it."

"Oh? In what way?"

"Well," she said with a grin on her face, "I suddenly realized that we're guaranteed to have a son."

The promise that a Cohen would be one in of the 12 tribes that make up the 144 thousand Jewish witnesses during the Tribulation period meant that Cohen was certain to have a son. The witnesses were all to be men, according to Jewish reckoning. After a moment of thought, Cohen was filled with joy and replied, "God is great, isn't He!" He pursed his lips and added, "Of course, that date is yet future, so we could have a girl before that."

Leah sighed in perfect contentment at the very thought of it.

"Mr. Cohen!" a voice from behind called. Cohen turned in reflexive alarm as a hotel messenger hurriedly approached them. "You have an urgent phone call from a David Douglas in Kefar waiting for you at the front desk."

Leah's mind seized up. She jumped up as Cohen pushed his chair back and exclaimed, "Oh, Nat, what could it be?"

Cohen's thoughts suddenly replayed his final moments at the Douglas house, and the black Mercedes came immediately into view. He shook his head and motioned with his hand to Leah in a vain attempt to disarm her paralysis. "I'm sure it's nothing; don't worry." He started to follow the messenger as Leah helplessly stood in place. "I'll be right back," he soothed. "Finish your meal." He nodded to the messenger and quickly fell in step behind him. Leah dropped her utensils and fell in step behind her husband.

Nothing could have prepared them for what happened next.

Nathan picked up the phone and answered confidently, "David, this is Cohen. What's up?" Leah grabbed his hand and squeezed it as she began praying for good news.

"Oh, my God!" he said solemnly.

Leah grimaced with anticipated pain. She could tell by his horrified look that something dreadful had happened. After 30 seconds of holding her breath she squeaked out, "What's wrong?"

He slowly and methodically lowered the phone onto its cradle and ushered Leah off to the side away from the desk clerk's hearing.

His lips twitched as he recounted the call. He tried to suppress his escalating fears, but they oozed out of his body. "Stein snatched Kathy and the kids!"

The color drained out of Leah's face.

The drive back across the Negev to Kefar was fraught with anxiety and foreboding, making the six-hour trip seem nearly unbearable. Questions embattled them about God's protecting Kathy and the children from Stein and his ability to harm innocent persons. *Lord, you promised to take care of your servants.*

A passage of Scripture came to Cohen's mind.

"Leah, remember in First Samuel when David was at Ziklag and the Amalekites raided his camp?" he asked excitedly as if suddenly given a revelation from God.

Leah's eyes pleaded for understanding. "Vaguely."

Cohen's eyes suddenly brightened as he exclaimed, "Aahhh, yes! I can see the outcome now."

He unwittingly depressed the accelerator and the speedometer went to 80 mph. Leah tapped his hand and pointed to the dashboard. He smiled and backed his foot off the gas pedal. She nodded and said, "Tell me; I could use some reassurance."

Cohen nodded in the confidence that he would encourage her. "The narrative explains that Israel's enemies, the Amalekites, attacked David's hideaway here in the Negev while they were returning from the coastal cities of the Philistines. The Amalekites burned David's campsite and took all the women and children captive. By the time he arrived, he didn't know whether they were dead or alive. His men held him responsible and talked of stoning him. He was crushed, but—and you need to hear this—the text says, 'David found strength in the Lord his God.' From there he inquired of the Lord, who told him to pursue the Amalekites. God said that David would certainly overtake them and succeed in the rescue!"

Leah looked at him in amazement. "Are you saying that you believe that will happen here, with Kathy and the kids?"

"Absolutely. My confidence is in the Lord."

Douglas was pacing back and forth on the porch when they arrived. He darted to Cohen's car waving a note in his hand. Cohen rolled down the window and said, "We got here as soon as we could."

"I'm a nervous wreck over this," Douglas prattled. "I know as a Christian I shouldn't be. Now that you're both here, things will be better." He took a deep breath, shook his head, looked at the note, and added, "You need to see this." He turned and marched back to the house as Cohen and Leah quickly fell in step behind him.

They sat down at the kitchen table where Douglas started to whimper. Leah clutched his arm to soothe his hurting heart. "The morning after the wedding," he explained in a soft monotone, "I drove into town to get some supplies, leaving Kathy with the children. A little over two hours later I returned to find this note on the front door." He opened the note and handed it to Cohen.

Cohen's eyes raced back and forth as he read the carefully worded note anonymously prepared on a word processor. *If you want to see your family again, you will agree to dismantle your campaign and leave Israel. Any attempt to engage the authorities will result in their deaths.*

The magnitude of the unfolding crisis hit Cohen like a shot between the eyes. "Ugh," he muttered as he handed the note to Leah. He nervously tapped his fingers on the table. "Do you think it's a bluff?"

Tears welled up in Douglas's eyes. "No, I do not. The other side does not bluff."

Cohen's eyes flashed at the truth. He nodded in agreement and shot a prayer to God for guidance. "We need a plan," he said, knowing full well that Douglas was unable to think clearly.

Leah nudged her husband and said, "Cohen, tell David what you told me in the car about David at Ziklag." Cohen nodded and recounted the account to Douglas as a reminder of God's providence and protection. Douglas wept uncontrollably for several moments as his hopes were renewed.

Finally he managed a smile through many sniffles. "Okay," he said with a thumbs up, "what now?"

It was not a well-thought-out plan. The diabolical Stein and Kavidas could not be trusted under any circumstances, bringing David and the Cohens to conclude that Stein would kill Kathy and the children to avoid disclosure, regardless of their response. No, they would not succumb to Stein's demands.

Emotions and fears dictated their reaction: to engage the Kiononos network of believers to assist them in a lightning raid to rescue the hostages once their location was determined. Waiting to pinpoint the source of any further communication from Stein would be imperative. The network could ferret out the hostages' whereabouts, but that would take time. The network would draw upon every investigative resource available to them outside the domain of any official agency. Once Kathy and the children were located, a select group would remove them to safety. Time was crucial. Passivity was out of the question; action was needed.

Douglas and Cohen agreed that Stein would not attempt to breach Israel's security by taking Kathy and the children out of the country. Therefore, their search most likely would be confined to the metropolitan area of Jerusalem. The waiting would be the hard part.

The plan seemed good to Douglas and Cohen, but they were not convinced it was one approved by God.

<hr />

The four custodians were in the form of men, but in her heart Kathy knew they were not men. They were not even mortals, but some kind of evil spirit locked up in men's bodies. They resembled slender humanoids, possessing gaunt faces with beady eyes, long noses, and ruddy complexions accentuated by kinky hair—void of emotions, constrained from speech, and simply looking at each other to communicate. Kathy reasoned that they were probably mutants sent from the netherworld to do Stein's dirty work. *They better not touch my kids!*

The creatures allowed their hostages freedom throughout the house, since the doors and windows were shut and secured by some alarm device that neither Kathy nor her scientific-minded son Alan could figure out. The custodians had made it clear that any attempt to escape would bring severe consequences.

Kathy walked to the kitchen window that looked down on Mamillah road and recognized her whereabouts. They were just a short distance from the old city walls near the Jaffa Gate. Mamillah road at one time had been the big commercial shopping strip of the Jewish city, but had fallen into desolation following the division of the city. People pulled up stakes and moved to the newer areas, leaving the houses with only their unwanted furniture.

Looking diagonally across from where she stood on the second level of the abandoned house, Kathy saw the Stern House where Theodor Herzl had stayed during his brief visit to Jerusalem at the turn of the century.

"Mom, Paul is beginning to lose it," Alan, the eldest son, announced as he popped his head in the doorway. "He wants to make a break for it."

Kathy looked askance at the custodian assigned to her and motioned that she was going to another room. The thing nodded its consent.

Paul, at age 13, possessed enormous courage, but little insight. He handed his mother his impromptu sketch of the layout of the house and said confidently, "I've studied the house, and we can jump to the next rooftop from your room and get out of here."

Hillary grabbed the drawings out of his hand and whispered, "You're crazy! They will not let us go! They have some weird powers that will alert them to our escape before we move an inch. Forget it!"

"Hillary's right, Mom," Alan agreed with a shake of the head. "We are no match against them." He walked several feet, turned around and added numbly, "I'm afraid an escape is out—and a rescue impossible. Nobody knows where we are."

Paul smiled at his mother as he held the sketches up in the air. "The Lord knows where we are."

In her heart Kathy was afraid, but for the sake of her testimony and her children, she determined to exhibit strength and presence of mind. "Your brother is right," she said to Alan and Hillary. "'The eyes of the Lord go to and fro throughout the land...'" she quoted. "He does know where we are and He will rescue us."

When nightfall came, Kathy battled the specter of abandonment. It came upon her as the children slept in the adjoining bedroom where their captors watched them together. Mattresses and blankets had been thrown on the floor for them, while Kathy was awarded her own room for the night.

Lord, why have You abandoned Your servants? The nagging question would not go away. *Why have You allowed this to happen?*

She remembered asking God the question *why* once before, several years ago—right after Kavidas and Stein sent an emissary to set fire to their Florida house in an attempt to silence the family. That was the last time she had asked the Lord why. *Why would God allow an attack on His servants while they all slept, an attack that nearly killed the whole family?*

Sovereignty was an imponderable attribute of God.

But then your family would not have come to Israel to minister where I want you.

"Yes, Lord, that's true," she argreed.

For My thoughts are not your thoughts, neither are your ways My ways. As the heavens are higher than the earth, so are My ways higher than your ways and My thoughts than your thoughts. "Yes, I remember, Lord," she finally admitted in a whisper when the verse came to mind. So what was the alternative? Abandon God? But to whom can I go, she reasoned with herself. *You have the words of eternal life.*

No, I cannot turn from the only One who can help me.

Douglas picked up the phone to call his Kiononos contact in Jerusalem to set the rescue plan in motion, but stopped abruptly when he realized his hand was trembling. He replaced the phone. His hand seemed to be saying what his heart was feeling. The decision to engage the network suddenly seemed too risky. The warning in the note echoed in his mind. *Any attempt to engage the authorities will result in their deaths.* "So what next?" he wondered aloud.

"We need to connect with God," Cohen answered, as the revelation that God had not been considered dawned on him.

Leah looked her husband with a rush of admiration. "I guess we're all a little out of alignment here, or somebody would have noticed earlier that we need to go before the Lord with this before we do anything foolish."

A flurry of evil thoughts suddenly blew into Douglas's mind. He envisioned Kathy being restrained by thugs while others tortured the children before her eyes. "Lord, help," he muttered to himself in an attempt to hold onto his sanity. Then flashes of his Hillary screaming as her captors hit her with clubs pulsated in his head. *Get thee behind me, Satan!* "You're right, Leah," he finally said in agreement.

They locked hands and prayed aloud to the Lord for guidance.

Knock. Knock. Knock.

They quickly opened their eyes and broke the prayer circle. "What was that?" Leah exclaimed as her heart began racing.

"Somebody's at the door," Cohen replied just above a whisper.

Douglas gestured them to silence as he stepped to the front door and peeked through the curtain. A man dressed in casual clothes stood on the stoop staring right at him. Douglas felt an icy finger touch his heart as a wave of fear swept over him. He turned to Cohen and Leah and murmured, "There's a man outside!"

Douglas gulped and squeezed his eyes shut momentarily to shoot another prayer to God. "Who is it?" he asked in a feeble tone.

"I am a friend of the Kiononos sent to help you find Kathy and the children," the voice answered.

Douglas looked back at Cohen and Leah in astonishment. He shook his head as they all realized something was radically wrong.

"But David," Leah said with a wry expression, "you didn't make the call—"

Cohen grabbed Leah and began backing away to the rear of the room. He saw Paul's baseball bat in the corner and picked it up. "David, be careful!" he warned.

"Shush!" Douglas demanded as he searched his mind for answers. Finally after a moment of frenzied thought he yelled through the door, "How did you know we needed help? Nobody called you."

"The Lord sent me to help you."

Cohen tightened his grip on the bat as Leah clutched his arm and dug her fingernails into his skin. Douglas bit his lip and shook his head as his heart pounded with anxiety and confusion. He paused, took a deep breath, and said with a wink as he unlocked the door, "Time to put our faith into action."

Time seemed to stand still as Douglas gaped at the stranger's face. A peace that surpassed all understanding radiated outwardly, overpowering him and assuring him that the man truly was sent by God. "*L'ma'an haShem* (For the sake of God)," the stranger began, "I implore you to listen to my message from the Holy One."

"David, for God's sake, let him in!" Leah begged as her eyes cast upon the stranger's face.

Cohen dropped the bat and grabbed the man's hand, pulling him into the house as Douglas closed the door behind him. "Who are you?" Douglas asked as his breath caught in his throat.

The messenger nodded at them and replied, "I am Yophiel. The Lord heard your prayer and sent me to guide and protect you." His face exuded a divine confidence when he added, "We will recover your family."

Leah burst into tears. "This is unbelievable!" she sobbed. "To think that our God cares enough about us to send this…" she paused to pat her eyes and look into his, "…this messenger. Praise the Lord."

Yophiel motioned to them to sit down as he explained, "We must act quickly to rescue your family, David, since the forces marshaled against you have been advised that you will not yield to their demands. Therefore, your family's very lives are in danger."

"But how did they know—?" Cohen gulped.

Yophiel cut him off by waving his hand in the air as if to include the entire earth. "Supernatural agents are feverishly at work to thwart the plan of God. These fallen ones overheard your conversation and prayer. They are prepared for any attempt to free Kathy and the children."

Douglas was once again reminded of the awesome power that members of the angelic realm possessed. He cautioned himself about praying aloud again, then put a hand to his forehead and slowly blinked his eyes in contrition. "What do we do now?"

"We go and get them, " Yophiel commanded with a cryptic smile.

CHAPTER

21

Jerusalem

Kathy sat huddled in the corner of her bedroom praying with Hillary as Alan and Paul listened at the door to the stranger's voice giving orders. It was the voice of authority that their captors obeyed.

It was Mortimer Stein.

"Mom," Alan whispered back toward his mother, "they're planning to kill us! I heard the stranger command them to silence us with..." he turned to Paul for confirmation, "didn't he say 'some kind of fire'?"

Paul nodded and added, "He said that Dad and Cohen called in help and that they're not giving in to the demand. They're going to show Dad that they mean business! They're going to set the house on fire—with us in it!"

Kathy motioned for her boys to join her and Hillary in the corner out of range of enemy ears. Then she willfully pushed back her anxiety and fears and mentally erected a spiritual barrier in her mind to protect her from the fiery darts of Satan, which were aimed at burning a hole in her shield of faith. Her body stiffened as she exhorted her children, "Remember what God said to Joshua, 'Have not I commanded you? Be strong and courageous. Do not be terrified: do not be discouraged, for the Lord your God will be with you wherever you go.'"

The boys sighed as they strengthened their resolve, while a tear appeared in the corner of Hillary's right eye. "I'm scared, Mommy."

"We're all scared, honey," Kathy said as her jaw tightened, "but we are not going to show them that we are." She made a fist and looked heavenward. "Don't be afraid, for those who are with us are more than those who are with them."

"Does that mean that angels will rescue us, Mommy?" Hillary asked in a feeble whisper.

Kathy smiled at her daughter's simple faith. "Yes, that's what it means."

"Come down here!" a voice screamed from the lower level.

Kathy thought she recognized the voice and her skin began to crawl. She took a deep breath as Alan and Paul embraced Hillary, who had begun to cower. Doubts of her resolve suddenly flashed into Kathy's mind as she reached for her children and walked out of the room. Then a hymn came to mind. As she descended the stairs she began singing, "He lives, He lives, Christ Jesus lives today! He walks with me and talks with me along life's narrow way. He lives, He lives, salvation to impart! You ask me how I know He lives: He lives within my heart." When the children joined in, her heart filled with triumph.

The moment she stepped into the living room she recognized Stein. She ran to him in full fury. "You monster!" she yelled in his face, then began beating his chest with her fists. "Don't you dare touch my children!"

Stein looked at her with utter disdain and pushed her away. "Hold her back!" he commanded his custodians. Without expression, one custodian grabbed Kathy and dragged her backward in front of

Stein. His gaze raked her up and down. After several moments he smiled sardonically and said as he pointed to Hillary, "Come here."

Hillary began whimpering as she slowly moved toward Stein.

Kathy's heart began pounding. Hillary's body trembled.

"Stay where you are!" Alan yelled as he jumped between Hillary and Stein to block her path.

"Lord, help!" Kathy gulped.

A custodian seized Alan and Paul so they couldn't move.

"Come here, Hillary!" Stein repeated intolerantly.

The door to the kitchen flew open. Two other fiendish-looking custodians carrying clubs stepped into the room and closed the door behind them. They both stood alert, apparently waiting for orders.

"We need closure," Stein said tersely as he gestured for the two other custodians to seize Hillary.

Hillary's face took on an angelic appearance as she quoted, " 'Whenever I am afraid, I will trust in the Lord.' "

"Stop that!" Stein yelled at her as he cupped his ears. The sound of Scripture infuriated him.

The color drained from Kathy's face at the realization that Hillary's life was being threatened. *Lord, don't let them hurt my little girl.* Physical strength returned at once as she burst forth from the restraining arms of her captor. She whirled on Stein and cried out with a lethal glare, "In the mighty name of *Jesus*, I command you to release my daughter!"

Stein cringed and began grinding his teeth in contempt at the very name of Jesus. He began to falter and looked for support as his legs began to wobble under him. The feeling of power was almost palpable in the room. After a moment of hesitation he pointed to Kathy and said through his teeth, "Gag her!" The custodians quickly obeyed.

Stein rebounded and grabbed a club from a custodian, raised it in the air over Hillary's head, and said bitterly, "This will make a statement to all who come against us!"

"NO!" Alan shrieked. "In the name of Jesus, NO!"

Stein winced and dropped the club, then motioned to his custodians to gag the two boys. He gabbled to himself for several seconds then quickly rallied and cried out as he looked to the far corner of the room, "Burn!"

Suddenly, shooting, furnace-like flames ignited in the corner, heating up the room, yet nothing was consumed. Kathy and the children struggled to move away from the spreading blaze as the room temperature soared.

"Your husband should have heeded the warning!" Stein yelled with a smirk as he picked the club up off the floor.

Hillary stiffened and braced herself for the fatal blow. "It would be better for you to be thrown into the sea with a millstone tied around your neck than for you to hurt me," she said meekly.

A crazed look came over Stein's face. "I told you not to quote Bible verses at me!"

SWOOSH! A great whirling sound came from the kitchen.

Stein motioned with his hand and said to the custodian holding Alan and Paul, "Go see what that is!" The thing walked through the doorway into the kitchen.

A screeching and a *thwack! thwack!* sound was heard.

Stein pivoted in place and rotated toward the door. "Now, what was that?!" He had no way of knowing that his two sentries were now dead.

Suddenly the door burst open! Every eye in the room shot toward the doorway.

"STAND FAST!" Yophiel commanded with eyes blazing. He pointed an outstretched arm at Stein. Spotting the flames in the corner,

Yophiel simply nodded toward them, and they were extinguished immediately. Douglas, Cohen, and Leah rushed in behind Yophiel, gaping at the scene before them. Yophiel rotated in place and growled at the custodians, "Do not move!" A queer look came over Douglas's and Cohen's faces as they suddenly realized Yophiel was no ordinary man. Alan groaned at Leah and wagged his head to signal that she should remove all their gags.

In the split-second interval between Yophiel's entering the room and his powerful command, Stein took an internal assessment and knew he was in trouble. Angelic entities instantly recognize hierarchy. He dropped the club to the floor and stood limp momentarily in shock as he awaited further instructions.

Yophiel raised his hand and in a successive motion pointed at the four custodians who began to shrink back into a corner, dreading their fate. With divine authority he yelled, "I command you vile spirts to return to the abyss from whence you came!"

Nobody in the room was prepared for their departure.

Suddenly a swirling hole appeared in the floor directly in front of the four custodians! It could not have been a demonic trick—a projection of false reality—no, this was real. Alan stood on his toes to peek into the hole, and he saw what looked like a vortex—even a kind of maelstrom—that resembled a swirling tunnel leading to a bottomless pit!

Then they heard a heavy dragging sound as if a giant slab of rock were moving off some kind of opening—perhaps an underground gateway in the earth. A hideous bellowing sound coming from some subterranean place rebounded off the walls of the house, vibrating the floor boards and shaking the ceilings. It had to be the entranceway to the place of the *Shedim*, the place called Tartaros, a singular abode of the fallen spirits who dared to mingle with mortals.

Pleading looks broke out on the creatures' faces as shudder after shudder convulsed their bodies. They placed their hands in a begging position.

"You will not receive mercy when you deserve judgment!" Yophiel declared solemnly as he looked at them with piercing eyes. "I order you to return to the place of torment!"

One by one they lined up at the precipice of the whirlpool and fell headlong into the pit. When the last one fell the floor returned to normal. Yophiel then shifted his gaze to Stein.

Few mortals have been permitted to witness apocalyptic events describing the destiny of the wicked as predicted in Scripture, for their fate is too terrible for the human mind to comprehend. The apostle John, on the Isle of Patmos, received such divine revelation. It transported him into the indeterminable future where he saw and recorded history thousands of years in advance. One of his visions depicts the final judgment of the beast and the false prophet—where they are to burn alive, yet never to be consumed, in the lake of fire where time would never end.

Immediately after Yophiel pointed to Stein he lifted his hands in a praise position. The walls, ceilings, and their surroundings unexpectedly disappeared, bringing everyone in the room to a strange celestial place, a place of divine judgment. They were being privileged to preview things to come.

Whether they were truly present or conveyed in the spirit to the heavenly location, the spectators would later discuss for years and not know for sure. But at this point in time, the room all at once became a place of virtual reality where time and dimension no longer existed.

The Douglas and Cohen families stood on a lofty precipice overlooking a huge chasm, while across the void Yophiel stood in midair with majestic wings outstretched. He had one hand on Stein's neck and the other extended, bidding the eternal fires to approach him.

From behind him came another high-ranking angelic officer dragging someone in shackles.

"Look!" Douglas shouted to Cohen. "It's Kavidas!"

Kavidas—Satan's messiah—exhausted from resisting and shouting expletives at the Almighty, hung his head like a death row prisoner being escorted to the house of execution. His pride, power, and glory had been stripped from him, leaving a hollow shell of a man who dared to defy the living God, a man who had deceived the nations with his miracles to serve his own purposes.

Together, Kavidas and Stein shook uncontrollably as the appointed time for their never-ending punishment arrived.

The immense lake of fire resembled a combination of a swirling mass and a gaseous cloud that had detached from a spiral nebula somewhere in the outer regions of the universe, beckoned by God as the infernal place of torment for all who rejected Him. It was a place where minds and souls would acknowledge the loss of salvation forever, yet without the possibility of reprieve.

The lake of fire moved closer and closer until it reached its appointed position. Then it stopped its forward movement and rotated slowly, waiting for the next command.

Leah, from her vantage point, and totally obdurate, gawked at the hand-like flames darting thousands of miles into space. Clutching her husband's arm, she whispered closely in his ear, "I can smell the sulphur." He patted her arm softly as the awesome drama continued.

For a short period, the prisoners were allowed to look at each other as episodes of their brief time on earth flashed through their minds. They remembered each other and began arguing that they too had been deceived by Satan, but with a dismissive wave of the hand,

Yophiel gave the command. They were thrown into the engulfing flames which immediately swashed their bodes with a jelly-like substance that would sear and scorch their flesh for all eternity.

The fires began to recede to a location separated from the holiness of God—but not before agonizing screams and shrieks of torture filled the chasm, echoing into the blackness of space.

As the vision faded and the room returned to some degree of normalcy, the mortals unanimously realized that Yophiel was not native to this earth. Stein, however, being of a different origin, knew immediately. Awestruck, they all simply looked to Yophiel in anticipation of his next order.

Halted by some realistic fear, Stein stood erect, casting a leering eye toward Douglas. With an associative sense excited to feverish heights, he thought unaccountably of what he had just seen—consoling himself that the judgment was still future. A wave of relief filled his heart as a smirk came over his face.

"I know your heart, Mortimer Stein," Yophiel spoke with a voice vibrating with intensity as he stared into his eyes. "It is wicked and deceitful above all things—desperately wicked—and you should be destroyed *now*. Yet, the decision has been made by the Father of lights before the laying of the foundation of the world, that you and Gregory A. Kavidas should continue in your series of shallow victories for a season. Then the conquering Prince will return. These words are sealed until the consummation."

Hillary nudged her daddy and said, "Yophiel's talking about Jesus, right?" He held her tightly and nodded.

Cohen threw up his hands and stepped forward with a strange look on his face. "You mean you're going to let him go, Yophiel? After everything he's done? Knowing that when he links up with his madman boss they'll bring the world to wrack and ruin?!"

"It is appointed," Yophiel said with finality. "Once the seven years of tribulation are upon us, evil will reign throughout the earth—assiduous titanic forces of evil that will afflict the souls of mankind until they cry out for redemption!"

" 'Blessed is He who comes in the name of the Lord,' " Douglas quoted as a reminder of the messianic greeting of Christ on His return.

"Now go your way," Yophiel commanded Stein as he pointed to the door, "and do not pursue these people of God. They are blessed with the protection of the elect."

Stein steeled himself against defeat and surveyed the faces before him, knowing full well that he would encounter them again in the future—but only with the supreme authority invested in his master. He walked to the door, turned to the spectators and said in a defiant tone, "Our measure of time is short, but our time will be measured by greatness!" With that he closed the door behind him and walked back to his life with Kavidas.

The group rushed to cluster around Yophiel. He momentarily allowed them to touch and reverently hold him. Then his clothes began to fade while his body aura radiated white light. Within seconds they were all squinting and shielding their eyes as he resumed his angelic appearance. "Remember the words of Jesus Christ, the Alpha and the Omega," he said haltingly. " 'I am coming soon. Hold on to what you have, so that no will take your crown. Him who overcomes I will make a pillar in the temple of My God.' "

Then he vanished.

Kathy ran to her husband and pointed at the empty space formerly occupied by Yophiel. "David, who was that, really?"

He scratched his head and realized with a shiver as he postulated, "I remember, from my research in the Talmud, a section in the Targum Pseudo-Jonathan that speaks about six principal angels—Yophiel being one of them—who are privileged to be within the *Paragod*, or cloudy veil of God. They reside in the throne room!"

A blanket of silence fell over the room.

The wonderful realization of God's divine presence reminded them of His future protection. "They will not go away, you know," Douglas said of Stein and Kavidas. He leaned back on a chair and let out a long sigh in exhausted triumph.

Cohen and the others nodded simultaneously as they pondered the ramifications.

"But we can overcome any obstacle through Christ, right?" Leah added gleefully.

"That's His promise," Douglas concurred. He stood up and gestured that they should leave.

"Where do we go from here?" Kathy asked her husband.

"We will have to go back to our hideout in the Judean hills near Petra and regroup until Kavidas and Stein make their next move. When they do, we will go public again. Meanwhile, we will use our location as a staging area to strengthen our Koinonos position here in Israel, while Matt Lane leads the Christians in the States to do the same."

Kathy had a follow-up question. "And when the Tribulation comes?"

Douglas pointed to Cohen and Leah. "These two are part of the progenitors of the end-time missionary force. Then we will join up with the 144 thousand Jewish evangelists. Together we will carry on our work on a much greater scale, with the help of a great multitude of Gentiles who come to believe on Christ through their witnessing efforts."

"What happens to us during the Tribulation?" Hillary asked curiously.

Douglas smiled expansively and hugged her. Then he pointed up and said with a grin, "Don't you worry about that, honey, God will take care of us!"

The Acropolis at sunset reminded Kavidas of the glory and greatness man can achieve when his imaginations are allowed to flourish and come to fruition, unrestrained by any moral boundaries or divine interference. But as the dark shadows of the remaining columns slowly marched across the ruins of the foundation, he remembered the fate of all societies who practice hedonic-narcissistic lifestyles or come up against the living God.

He determined in his spirit to suppress the thought.

Stein leaned against one of the fallen pillars and kicked a mound of dirt on the ground, then turned around to face the Aegean Sea. A warm breeze hit him in the face. "The wind is refreshing," he said wearily.

A wave of euphoria suddenly swept over Kavidas. He would rise to the occasion and not allow any negativity to intrude. He bit his lip, put his arm around Stein, and said with vigor, "Your mission to Israel was a success—Douglas and Cohen, et. al., are now out of the way! Conquest from now on will be swift! From here you will go back to America and finish your work until the Tribulation begins. Then I will manifest myself. We will bask in the splendor of glory!"

Stein's demeanor immediately brightened.

For the next hour they walked the mount while discussing the immutable plan to deceive and capture every soul that refused to name Jesus as Lord.

GLOSSARY

Atara L'yoshna	Jewish activist organization
Ateret Cohaniam	Jewish activist organization
Baruch haShem Adonai	"Bless the name of the Lord"
Beth Shean	archeological site where the Philistines hung King Saul's body after his death in battle
Biqquor Holim	name of actual hospital in Jerusalem
dahvening	Yiddish word for "praying"
Eilat	resort area in southern Israel
Haredim	Jewish radicals opposed to archeology
Haftarah	prophetic portion of Hebrew Bible
ha-kohen ha-gadhol	Hebrew for "high priest"
ha Kotel	Israeli name for the Wailing Wall
kaffiyeh	Arab headdress
kapporeth	atonement or "blood covering"
Khirbet Qumran	community of Essenes in Dead Sea region
L'ma'an haShem	Hebrew phrase for "for the sake of God"
L'Shanah Tovah	Jewish greeting that means "to a good year"

Mashallah	"What God has wrought"
Mazzal Tov or Mazal Tov	Hebrew phrase for "good luck"
Mikva'ot	baths
Mossad	Israeli Central Intelligence Unit
Paragod	the cloudy veil of God
Shedim	name for demonic group in Israeli folklore
Shin Bet	Israeli General Securities Services
Ta'amireh	ancient tribe of the Bedouin
Tanach	Hebrew Old Testament
Targum Pseudo-Jonathan	Aramaic translation of the book of the prophets in the Hebrew Bible
Wadi Murabba'at	particular name of a location in Dead Sea region
Wadi Nisnas	particular name of a location in Dead Sea region
Yod heh vav heh	Hebrew consonants for name of Jehovah (YHVH)
Zohar	Jewish book of mysticism

Additional copies of this book and other
book titles from DESTINY IMAGE are
available at your local bookstore.

For a complete list of our titles,
visit us at www.destinyimage.com
Send a request for a catalog to:

Destiny Image® Publishers, Inc.

P.O. Box 310
Shippensburg, PA 17257-0310

*"Speaking to the Purposes of God for This
Generation and for the Generations to Come"*